For Gemma and Kylie, for helping me stay sane.
Mostly.

PROLOGUE

I CAN'T MOVE.

Not even an inch.

The foul smell of rot seeping through the tiny holes in front of my face makes me gag. I've thrown up four times in—I don't know how long it's been—and but that isn't even the worst part of this nightmare.

The worst part is the terror of not knowing when he's coming back.

Night turns into day, turns into night, turns into day.

My knees, and my hips, and my shoulders scream, constricted and long dead from lack of blood flow.

I think, perhaps, that I might die.

Dying would be preferable to this.

But I don't. I keep on breathing, my mind spiraling away from me until my thoughts are unrecognizable noise.

And all I can do is kneel here.

All I can do is wait.

1

ELODIE

Thank fuck it's dark.

Nothing could be worse that arriving at a new school in broad daylight.

The Lincoln Town Car jolts as it hits a dip in the road, and a wave of panic lights me up—an immediate, unfortunate response to the last two years that I've spent living in a war zone. And no, I'm not talking about the fact that my previous home in Israel occasionally *felt* like a war zone. I'm referring to the fact that I was living under the same roof as my father, Colonel Stillwater, whose idea of a relaxing weekend was beating me black and blue during our Krav Maga training sessions.

I still flinch every time I hear someone politely clear their throat. When Daddy Dearest clears *his* throat, it usually means I'm about to endure humiliation at his hands. Or some form of embarrassment. Or both.

"Looks like they left the lights on for you, Miss Elodie," the driver says through the open privacy window. This is the first thing he's mumbled to me since he collected me at the airport, bundled me into the back of this gleaming black monstrosity, gunned the engine, and headed north for the town of Mountain Lakes, New Hampshire.

Up ahead, a building looms like a proud, ominous sentinel out of the dark, all sharp, tall spires and turrets. Looks like something out of the pages of a Victorian Penny Dreadful. I avoid peering out of the window at the stately structure for too long; I glared at the academic pamphlet Colonel Stillwater shoved at me when he unceremoniously informed me that I'd be relocating Stateside without him for long enough that the academy's imposing façade is already burned into my memory in intricate detail.

Tennis courts.

Swimming pool.

Fencing studio.

Debate lounge.

A library, commemorated by George Washington himself in 1793.

It all looked great in print. Only the height of luxury for a Stillwater, that's what my father said gruffly, as he threw my single small suitcase into the back of the cab that would whisk me away from my life in Tel Aviv. I saw straight through the building's state of the art facilities and its well-heeled, old-money veneer, though. This place isn't a regular school for regular kids. It's a jail cell dressed up as a place of learning, where army officers who can't be bothered dealing with their own kids dump them without a second thought, knowing that they'll be watched over with a military-like focus.

Wolf Hall.

Jesus.

Even the name sounds like it belongs to a fucking prison.

Mentally, I'm backing up, moving further away from the place with every passing second. By the time the car pulls up in front of the sweeping marble steps that lead to the academy's daunting front entrance, I'm back on the road behind me, three miles away, fleeing my new reality. At least that's where I would be, if I had absolutely any choice in this whatsoever.

I wasn't exactly popular back in Tel Aviv, but I had friends. Eden, Ayala and Levi won't even realize that I've been transferred from my old school for another twenty-four hours; it's already too late for them to come and rescue me from my fate. I knew I was a lost cause before the wheels on the army plane went up back in Tel Aviv.

The Town Car's engine cuts out abruptly, plummeting the car into an awkward, unfriendly silence that makes my ears ring. Eventually, I realize that the driver's waiting for me to get out. "I'll get my bags then, I suppose?"

I don't want to be here.

I sure as hell shouldn't have to lug my own bags out of the trunk of a car.

I'd never rat on the driver, that's just weak, but my father would have an aneurysm if he found out the guy he hired as my escort hadn't done his job properly once we reached our dreaded destination. As if the guy realizes this, too, he reluctantly hauls his ass out of the car and heads for the rear of the vehicle, dumping my belongings onto the small sidewalk in front of Wolf Hall.

He then has the audacity to wait for a tip, which just plain isn't happening. Who aids and abets in the destruction of someone's life, and then expects a thank you and a hundred-dollar bill for their troubles? I'm three-parts gasoline, one-part match as I snatch up my stuff and begin the hike up the steps toward Wolf Hall's formidable double oak doors. The marble is worn, bowing in the middle and smooth from the thousands of feet that have trudged up and down these steps over the years, but I'm too sour right now to enjoy the delightfully satisfying feel of them underfoot.

The driver's already gotten back in the car and is swinging out of the turning circle in front of the academy when I reach the very top step. A part of me wants to dump my bags and run after him. He isn't one of Colonel Stillwater's regular employees, he's an agency guy, so he doesn't owe my old man anything. If I offered him a couple of grand, he might be persuaded to drop me off in another state somewhere, far from my father's prying eyes. My pride won't let me beg, though. I'm a Stillwater, after all. Our pride is our most notorious trait.

My only means of escape burns off down the driveway, leaving me faced with two heavy brass knockers, one mounted onto each of the double doors in front of me. The knocker on the left: a grotesque gargoyle, clasping a patinaed ring in his downturned mouth. The knocker on the right is almost identical, except for the fact that his mouth is turned up in a leering, garish smile that sends a chill deep into my bones.

"Creepy much?" I mutter, grabbing hold of the knocker on the left. The sad gargoyle's far from pleasing to look at, but at least it doesn't look like it's about to leap down from its mounting and devour my fucking soul. A resounding boom thunders on the other side of the door when I slam the knocker against the wood, and I realize with a sense of irony that the noise is similar to that of a gavel being struck, sealing a criminal's fate.

"Wouldn't bother knocking. It's open."

Holy shit.

I nearly jump out of my fucking skin.

Spinning around, my legs nearly quit on me as I scan the darkness, searching for the owner of the voice that just startled the ever-loving shit out of me. It takes a second, but I locate the shadowy figure, perched on the rim of a white stone planter off to the right, thanks to the pop and flare of a glowing ember—looks like the cherry of a cigarette.

"Jesus, I didn't know there was anyone out here." I pat a hand against my chest, as if the action will slow my jackrabbiting heart.

"Figured," the deep voice rumbles. And it *is* a deep voice. The voice of a man who's smoked more than a few packs of cigarettes in his day. It's the kind of voice that belongs to a car thief or a back-alley gambler. The cherry of his cigarette flares again as he pulls on it, momentarily illuminating the structure of his features, and I catch a lot in the brief swell of light.

His black t-shirt is at least five sizes too big for him. He's way younger than I thought. Instead of a disgruntled, jaded professor in a motheaten blazer with patches on the elbows, this guy is young. My age, by the looks of things. He must be a student here at Wolf Hall. His dark hair hangs down into his eyes. His brows are full and drawn together into a steep frown. From my vantage point at the top of the stairs, I can only see him in profile, but his nose is straight, his jaw is strong, and he holds himself in a regal, lazy way that lets me know exactly who he is before I've even learned his name.

He's one of *those* kids.

The arrogant, cooler than cool, silver-spoon-halfway-up-his-ass kids.

It's part and parcel of being an army brat. You get lumped in with the privileged and the spoiled rotten on a daily basis. And you get to recognize the bad apples from a fucking mile away.

"I take it I need to find someone at reception?" I ask. Best to keep it short and sweet. As professional as possible.

The guy shakes his head, picking a piece of tobacco from the tip of his tongue and flicking it onto the gravel at his feet. "*I* was appointed director of the New Girl Welcoming Committee. Why else would I be sitting out here in the fucking dark?"

Ladies and gentlemen, we have ourselves a shitty attitude. Yay. Folding my arms across my chest, I descend the steps slowly, leaving my bags by the door. Arriving in front of him, I note that the stranger is at least a clear foot taller than me. Even slouching, his ass perched on the edge of the planter, legs stretched out in front of him, he's still considerably taller than me and I'm standing at my full height. "Because you smoke like a chimney and you don't wanna get busted?"

He flicks his cigarette, smirking coldly. Everything about him is cold, from the icy glint in his bright green eyes, to the way he drops his head back, assessing me like a mountain lion might weigh up a newborn deer. Clearly, he resents having to wait up and play Wolf Hall's amicable host, but hey…I didn't ask him to be my tour guide. I haven't asked anything of him at all.

"Point me in the direction of my room and I'll relieve you of your duties, then," I tell him in a clipped tone.

He laughs at this. It's not a friendly sound. I imagine scores of people have been laughed at by this boy, and every single one of them probably felt like they were being run through with a bayonet. "Relieve me of my duties?" He repeats my words back to me. "At ease, soldier. Why do I get the feeling that our parents would be best fucking friends?"

These schools aren't always full of army kids. Investment bankers, lawyers, diplomats and politicians pack their kids off to places like Wolf Hall, too. From time to time, a harried doctor or an aid worker, who thinks caring for other people's kids is more important than caring for their own. The students at these places come from a diverse range of backgrounds, but more often than not their parents *are* military.

"Look, I just got off a long-haul flight, and not the kind that had a meal service or clean bathrooms. I need a shower, and I need a bed. Can you just tell me where I need to go, and we can continue this bullshit at a later date?"

The guy tugs on his cigarette one last time, huffing down his nose. When he flicks the glowing butt off into the rose bushes ten feet away, I notice that he's wearing chipped black nail polish. Weird. His shirt's black and he definitely seems tetchy as hell, but I'm not getting an emo vibe from him. His boots are tan high-end Italian leather, and the belt around his waist looks like it cost more than my entire outfit.

"Through the doors. Stairs on the left. Fourth floor. You're in 416. Good luck with the heating," he says, getting to his feet. Without even looking back at me, he takes off, but not back inside the building. He hits the driveway, sticking his hands in his pockets as he heads away from the school.

"Hey! Where the hell are you going?" I hate that I call after him, but I need to know. I'm so intensely jealous that he's leaving that I have to clamp my tongue between my teeth to stop myself from asking if I can go with him.

"Hah! Like I board here," he tosses over his shoulder. "Oh, and don't worry, New Girl. We *don't* need to continue this bullshit later. Keep your head down, keep out of the way, and you'll have a decent chance of surviving this hell hole."

It could just be that I'm tired, and it could be that I'm hating Wolf Hall already, but that sounded distinctly like a threat.

2

ELODIE

The inside of Wolf Hall looks like someone tried to recreate Hogwarts from memory but got it really, really wrong. There are dark alcoves everywhere I turn, and none of the angles in the place are plumb. I feel like I'm walking through some sort of trippy Escher nightmare as I make my way through the austere, wood-paneled entrance way and head for the broad staircase on the left-hand side. I check hopefully for an elevator, but I already know that such a thing would be an impossible luxury in an old building like this.

The place is silent as the grave.

I've been in plenty of old houses before. They creak, and they groan, and they settle. But not Wolf Hall. It's as if the very building itself is holding its breath, peering down on me and casting judgement as it observes me reluctantly wrangling my suitcase up the first flight of stairs. The place didn't look that tall from outside, but the stairs never seem to fucking end. I'm panting and clammy by the time I hit the second set of stairs, and by the third, I'm openly sweating and laboring for breath. Through an ancient door with frosted glass panels, I find myself staring down a narrow hallway straight out of The Shining. A dim light overhead flickers ominously as I drag my bag over the dusty, threadbare runner that covers the bare floorboards, and I mentally tick off all of the ways that a person could die in a haunted-ass place like this.

I notice the brass numbers screwed into each of the doors as I pass them. Normally, there'd be colorful stickers and name plates tacked onto the wood—little personalizations that help the students make their rooms feel like home. Not here, though. There isn't a sticker, photograph, or poster in sight. Just the dark, depressing wood, and the gleaming, polished numbers.

410...

412...

414...

416...

Great.

Home sweet home.

I open up the door, glad to find it unlocked. Inside, the bedroom's bigger than I expected it to be. In the corner, a double bed has been made up with crisp grey sheets complete with military corners. Only two pillows, but I can live with that. Against the wall: a large chest of drawers underneath a grim looking painting of a gnarled old man, bent double against a howling blizzard. Such a weird choice of subject matter for a piece of art. Technically, it's good. The brushwork is so fine and precise that it could almost be a photograph. The content's miserable, however, and inspires a sense of hopelessness that feels crushing.

On the far side of the room, a large bay window overlooks what I assume are the gardens to the rear of the academy. The world's dark, all bruised purples and midnight blues, punctuated with coal black, but I can make out the shape of tall trees in the distance, still, as if no breeze, no matter how strong, could shake them.

I discard my bags at the foot of my new bed, walking to the window, wanting to get a better look at the view. It's only when I'm standing right in front of the glass that I can make out the gloomy shape of a large, complex maze in the center of the lawn between the building and the trees.

A maze? Perfect. That wasn't on the damn brochure. It has to be very old, though, because the hedges are tall, taller than any man, and so dense that there would be no way to peek through them on ground level.

I don't know why, but I shiver violently at the sight of it. I've never been a fan of mazes. At least from here, in the daylight, I'll be able to memorize the route to its center. Not that I plan on going inside the damn thing.

The showers are easy enough to find. At the end of the hall, two bathrooms face opposite each other, doors propped wide open. A large white sign hangs from the tiled wall inside both—I know, because I check—which says, 'Three-Minute Showers Enforced. Violators Assigned Latrine Duty.'

Latrine duty? Christ. It's worse than I thought.

I give the sign a hard eye-roll as I strip out of my travel clothes and shower, taking way longer than the allotted three minutes. Who the hell's going to know? And fuck it, anyway. They can't police that kind of shit with a student who hasn't even officially enrolled at the academy yet. I use the carbolic soap attached to a frayed piece of rope inside the shower, wrinkling my nose at the smell and promising myself a better wash with my own shower gel in the morning. Then, I use a scratchy, paper-thin towel to dry off before putting on my PJs and hurrying back to my room with wet hair.

I already have plans to dye my long, blonde locks dark brown again. Most fathers wouldn't want their daughters bleaching their hair at seventeen years old, but Colonel Stillwater can't stand the sight of me with my natural hair coloring. He'd never admit it in a million years, but he can't handle me with brown hair. I look too much like *her* with brown hair.

Short of forcing me to wear contacts, he can't alter the blue of my eyes. There's little he can do about the freckles that smatter the bridge of my nose, or the bone structure of my heart-shaped face.

Without dropping some serious coin on a very talented plastic surgeon, he can't alter my high cheek bones or my almond shaped eyes, all of which are gifts I received from my mother. But he could make me a blonde, and so he did. And I've hated every second of it.

Back in my room, I notice for the first time how bitterly cold it is. Compared to Tel Aviv, it's practically sub-arctic here in New Hampshire, and it doesn't seem as though the Wolf Hall administration have deemed heating a necessity for its students. After a lot of rummaging, I eventually find a cracked and yellowed Bakelite thermostat in the closet by the window, but when I crank the dial all the way to the right, nothing happens. The old fashioned and extremely ugly radiator on the wall gives a single choked cough, a bone-jarring rattle, and then falls resolutely silent.

Luckily, I'm so tired that even the cold can't keep me from sleep.

3

ELODIE

THE MORNING SMELLS like rust and burning toast.

I crack my eyes and wince at the plume of fog that gathers on my breath. Somehow, it's even colder in my room at seven a.m., which is impressive since I'm convinced it dropped down to somewhere in the twenties in the night.

If my father cared one iota about me, he would not have sprung this transition on me mid-semester. The smallest kindness he could have shown me would have been to relocate me during a break, but no. Colonel Stillwater decided that uprooting me out of the blue on a weekend was the best course of action. Far be it from me to disrupt *his* schedule; since he needed to disappear off on a training exercise at oh-four-hundred hours on a Sunday, it seemed perfectly logical to turn my shit upside down and expect me to be fine with moving country, having my world turned upside down, and starting class at a new school all within a thirty-two hour period.

This is the least of his sins. He has done much, much worse.

So here we are. Monday morning. My new life. From the strict itinerary my father shoved into my backpack, I'm supposed to be downstairs at the administration offices twenty minutes before my first period of the day, which leaves me forty minutes to get myself showered, dressed and organized. Since I showered last night, I normally wouldn't bother showering again, but I still feel gross from the journey somehow, and honestly, I think I'm going to need to soak my feet in some scalding hot water in order to defrost them anyway. It's only the middle of January; it's probably going to get colder before it gets any warmer here in New Hampshire, so I'm definitely going to have to do something about the climate control in this room.

I pull back the thin sheets, my teeth chattering uncontrollably, and I make sure to grab my own towel and my wash bag this time. In the hallway, a number of the doors to the other rooms are open, and a line of girls has formed against either wall, waiting for the bathrooms. My heart sinks. Things were miserable at home, but at least I had my own fucking bathroom. Having to share the facilities at Wolf Hall is going to take some getting used to.

I join the end of the line waiting for the bathroom on the right-hand side of the hallway, and the girls ahead of me fall quiet in unison. Eight pairs of baleful eyes look me up and down. None of the girls seem all too friendly. One of my new classmates angles away from the redhead she was locked in conversation with and turns to me, offering me half a smile.

Her brown hair is curled tightly into an enviable afro. Her skin is almost as pale as mine, though. Her doe-eyed features and deep brown eyes give her the look of a young Natalie Portman. "Hey. Four sixteen, right? You must be Elodie."

I give her a tight-lipped smile in return. "Guilty as charged." This whole new girl thing isn't actually new. I've had to do this at least four other times since I reached high school age. It's been a while, though. After three whole years back at my last school in Tel Aviv, I allowed myself to get comfortable.

Big mistake.

"I'm Carina," the girl says, holding out her hand. "Glad you made it here in one piece. Some of us waited up for you last night, but it got late and…" She shrugs.

I shake her hand, a little warmed by the idea that some of the girls here might have shown me that kindness, had the hour allowed. "All good. I totally get it."

"Curfew here's pretty strict," the redhead chips in. She's tall. Like *really* tall. Almost as tall as the miserable bastard who gave me directions to my room last night. "We have to be in our rooms by ten thirty," she says. "Although Miriam, our floor monitor, turns a blind eye sometimes if we bribe her with chocolate. It's cold as shit up here but count yourself lucky. First floor girls don't have it so easy. Their floor monitor's a fucking bitch."

"Hey!" the girl first in line for my bathroom snaps. "Watch your mouth, Pres. Some of us are friends with Sarai."

"How could I forget," Pres, the redhead fires back, pulling a face at her. "You're shoved so far up her ass, it's a miracle you haven't earned your Sphincter Patrol badge yet, Damiana."

Damiana's a cool name. Shame the girl herself doesn't seem that cool. She's three shades blonder than me and wearing a full face of makeup even before she's stepped foot inside the bathroom. Maybe all that eyeliner is tattooed on.

"Wow. Your comebacks are getting a little better, Satan Spawn. Still need work, though. Maybe you need to practice in the mirror some more."

The bathroom door opens, and a beautiful girl with a mass of black curls and cinnamon colored skin steps out, dressed in a towel. She immediately rolls her eyes. "God, not even seven-thirty and you're already sniping, Dami. Give it a rest."

Damiana growls as she shoves her way into the bathroom, nearly knocking the other girl off her feet.

"Rashida, this is Elodie," Carina says, nodding in my direction.

Hiking her towel up and pinning it under her arm, Rashida gives me a perfunctory shake of the hand, too. "We'll talk once you hit the three-month mark," she says, then hurries off down the hall, walking into room 410 and slamming the door closed behind her.

"Sorry about her," Carina says, leaning back against the wall.

"The last couple of girls who arrived mid-semester all transferred out again pretty quick. I s'pose making the effort to get to know people if you're not sure they're gonna stick around is more difficult for some of us than others."

"Transferred out?" Pres says, her eyebrows rising up her forehead. She sounds as if she disagrees with the term Carina used, but the other girl shoots her a sharp look.

"Don't," she warns. "Not yet. Jesus, let the girl settle in a little first before you go dredging up that shit, yeah?"

Uh...this has me slightly worried. "Dredging up what shit?"

"*Nothing.*" Carina says this firmly, eyeing the other girls. She's daring them to open their mouths and breathe another word, which none of them do. Apparently, they're willing to defer to Carina, because everyone standing in the hallway, Pres included, looks down at their feet.

"Okaaaay." If there's one thing I hate, aside from my father, it's secrets. There have been so many in my past, far too many things kept from me over the years, that I have a really low tolerance for this kind of shit. It's my first day, though. I just met these girls ten minutes ago. I can't go demanding one hundred percent candor from them before I've even properly learned their names. I do my best to shrug it off.

"Hey, knock on my door before you go down, okay?" Carina offers. "I'm student-teacher liaison. I can take you to the office and grab your paperwork with you. And then we can head to English together if you like? I think a lot of our classes are gonna match up."

I might be small in stature, but I'm still a big girl. I'm perfectly capable of finding my own way to the office and onto class. I learned my lesson a long time ago, though. If someone offers you an olive branch in the cutthroat waters of international schooling, you grab hold of that fucker and you don't let go.

"Sure. Thanks. That'd be cool."

* * *

The excursion to the office is uneventful, which is to say that the world doesn't end while I'm filling out my health questionnaire and grabbing all of the reading lists and mandatory textbook titles I'll need to order for my classes. Carina acts as mediator between myself and the decrepit, mostly deaf octogenarian behind the desk, shouting when the poor old girl can't hear my responses. The lenses on her glasses are so thick that they make her eyes look eight times their normal size. Despite the visual aid, she squints at me over the top of a stack of paperwork, like it might actually help her hear me better.

Once we're done, Carina snatches the map the administrator gave me out of my hands and tosses it straight into the trash, dragging me down a long, crooked hallway, lined with bunches of flowers in vases. "Won't be needing that," she sing-songs. "You have me to be your personal Wolf Hall tour guide. I can tell we're gonna get on just fine. I knew the moment I saw the fishnets."

I glance down at the fishnet tights she's referring to. I'm wearing them under my favorite pair of ripped jean shorts. The Doc Martin boots I picked out are potentially overkill, but my look wouldn't be complete without them.

I know it's cold, but my outrageous clothes were first in a long line of protests I have planned for my stay at Wolf Hall. Tragically, when I came out of my room and saw Carina's clothes, it became apparent that the students here can wear whatever the hell they feel like and get away with it. Her bright yellow bomber jacket and red jeans clash so violently, there's a risk I'll develop a migraine soon just from looking at her.

The other students' clothes are a confusion of different styles and colors, too. There are enough ripped jeans and band t-shirts kicking around to make it look like we're all about to walk through the gates of a music festival.

Quickly adding two and two together, I realize that Carina's taking me straight to class. "Shouldn't I drop my stuff off at my locker first?"

"Psshhh. We don't have lockers. If you don't wanna carry a bag around with you, you're gonna have to run up to your room between periods, and trust me, there is not enough time for that shit. Come on. You'll be fine."

The room falls silent when Carina coerces me into English. Heads whip around, conversations come to a grinding halt...and the hairs on the back of my neck stand to attention. On a battered leather couch underneath a massive picture window, the guy from last night is laid out like he downed a bunch of Special K for breakfast and the drugs have just kicked in.

He's the first thing I notice.

The second thing I notice? There aren't any desks.

Well, not in the traditional sense anyway.

A little stunned, I gape at the room as I take it all in: the armoires, the ottomans, the over-stuffed arm chairs, and the worn old writing desks dotted around the vast space. Most surprisingly, there are book stacks toward the rear of the room, wooden benches, and, low and behold, there is a monster of a fire roaring in the open fireplace.

I've never seen anything like it before in my entire life. "What... our English class is in the library?"

A chorus of snickers go up, courtesy of the other students draped over the armchairs and leaning against the writing desks. Two guys, sitting on the floor by the other large window trade a droll look, as if this whole *what-the-hell-is-going-on* bit is really old to them. I feel like I've just walked into Doctor Who's TARDIS and made the mistake of exclaiming, *'Wait a second! It's bigger on the inside than it is on the outside!'*

Carina kicks the boot of one of the guys sitting on the floor as she leads me past them toward an empty floral print couch. He lunges forward, baring his teeth and snapping them at her, but she ignores his performance. "No, the library's way bigger than this. This is Doc Fitzpatrick's den, as he likes to call it. He's basically a god around here. Gets away with murder. He's supposed to take his classes in the room they assigned him in the English block, but he says it's easier to inspire his students in a more relaxed setting."

This is relaxed alright. I've never even seen a sofa in a teacher's classroom before, let alone planted my ass on one.

"Hey, Carina? Who's that?" I jerk my chin in the direction of the guy who gave me such a warm reception last night; he's taken one of the floral print cushions from the couch he's lying on and has placed it over his face.

Carina stills, arching an eyebrow at me in a way that makes me feel like I've made yet another faux pas. "Uhhh, yeah. *That* is Wren Jacobi. He's more feral dog than human being. I...honestly..." She sighs heavily, making herself busy by pulling a large notebook out of the bag at her feet. "I'd tell you to stay away from him, but it's kind of impossible to avoid anyone in this place. Plus, Wren has a way of bullying his way into your business whether you like it or not, so..."

Wrinkling my nose, I tilt my head to one side, squinting at him. "Y'know...I'm pretty sure he's wearing the same clothes he was in last night."

This earns me a brittle laugh. "Yeah. He is."

How the hell does Carina know what he was wearing last night? Unless...she said a few of the girls waited up for me. She was obviously waiting with him; he said he'd drawn the short straw and had to stay awake until I arrived. I don't know the first thing about the guy other than he smokes, but somehow I can't imagine Wren hanging out with a bunch of girls, waiting to greet a new Wolf Hall student.

"Wren and his guys, they like to fuck with people, Elodie. And when no one's willing to play their stupid games, to live by their stupid rules, they'll fuck with each other instead. Pax bet him he couldn't bag ten girls before Christmas break. And when he failed the challenge, his friends told him he had to wear the same clothes for an entire month when we came back. So yeah. Wren's definitely wearing the same clothes he was wearing last night. He's wearing the same clothes he was wearing two weeks ago. I think they let him wash them every couple of days. But you can bet your ass he'll be wearing that same black shirt tomorrow, and the day after that, and the day after that, right up until February first. Because the only thing worse than losing a bet to a Riot House boy...is failing to settle the bill when they lose. No matter what it costs them or who gets hurt along the way."

"Riot House boy?"

"Yeah." Carina scowls. "Those three idiots have a house halfway down the mountain. They call it Riot House. Everyone does. They're allowed to live there, for some unknown fucking reason, while the rest of us have to shiver our asses off here during the winter months and cook during the summer."

"The academy has off-campus housing?"

Carina's bemused by my confusion. "No. Wren's loaded. His family owns the place. Or he does. I've never been clear on the details. All I know is that they can do whatever the hell they want down there and the rest of us have to stay up here and toe the line."

There's a bitter note in Carina's voice. She's plastered a sunny smile on her pretty face when she looks up from her bag, though. "Anyway. Pax, Dashiell and especially Wren. Watch out for them is all I'm saying, girl. You'll wind up regretting it otherwise, I can promise you that."

"Pretty speech, Carrie. Glad to see you're giving lovely little Elodie Stillwater the lay of the land."

Neither of us have noticed the guy who was sitting on the floor get up and walk over to us. He's handsome in the same dangerous way that snakes, and spiders, and wolves are beautiful to look at. His hair is shaved back to dark stubble. Tattoos peek out from beneath his long-sleeved white t-shirt. His blue eyes spark like they're brimming over with live electricity; when they home in on me, pinning me to the back of the couch, I feel like I've wrapped my hand around a live wire and I can't let go.

"Go fuck yourself, Pax," Carina hisses through her teeth; it's the first time I've heard her sound anything other than friendly, and the venom dripping from her words takes my breath away. She doesn't just dislike this guy. She fucking *hates* him.

Pax rakes his bottom lip through his teeth in the weirdest

display I've ever seen, his ice-blue eyes drilling into Carina. There's something overtly carnal about the energy rolling off him, and it makes the skin on my arms break out in goose bumps. I don't like it, but I can't seem to tear my eyes away from him. To his right, the friend Pax was sitting with groans loudly, getting to his feet.

Where Pax looks like an ex-convict with his tattoos, his shaved head, and his bizarre attitude, this guy—who can only be Dashiell—looks like a librarian. Dressed in a white button-down shirt and tight-fitting grey pants, the guy took care in getting ready before coming to class today. The thick black-rimmed glasses he's wearing give him the air of someone who likes to read—a sweeping, nonsensical generalization, but the quick intelligence in his tawny hazel eyes seems to back up this theory. Like his eyes, his hair is more than one color: light brown from one angle, but when he turns his head to look at me, it transforms to dirty blond.

"Sorry, ladies. Pax doesn't know how to behave himself around such beauty. He drank a little too much coffee this morning, too, so you'll have to understand if he's acting out a little."

Oh, wow. English accent. Smooth as silk, Dashiell's voice is immediately soothing. He holds himself with confidence and certainty, as if he's sure of his place in the world and precisely how he fits into it. It's a neat trick—the confidence thing. In a weird way, it makes him feel safe, whereas Pax feels entirely the opposite.

Carina squirms, eyes fixed on a stack of books on the other side of the room, carefully avoiding Dashiell's gaze. Her reaction to Pax was open hostility, but now she seems to have shrunk in on herself, shutting down altogether.

"Carrie? You're not going to introduce us to your new friend?" Dashiell purrs.

My new friend's stiff as a board. She looks like she's about to topple sideways off the couch, so I save her from replying. "You already know who I am. Wolf Hall isn't exactly a big place. Plus *he* just called me by my name," I say, eyes darting over to Pax. "I'm Elodie Stillwater. I transferred in from Tel Aviv. Father's an army man. Mother's dead. I'm into painting, music, and photography. I'm allergic to pineapple. I'm an only child. I'm terrified of thunderstorms, and I love flea markets. There. That enough information for you?"

I list off these random facts about myself with a smile on my face, but it's saccharine sweet and false as all hell. Pax huffs out a breath of derisive laughter, while Dashiell's response to my big speech is to turn his full attention on me, a slow, calculating smile spreading across his face. He's quick and clever, this one. You can practically see the cogs whirring in his head as he files away the data I just supplied. Why, all of a sudden, does it seem like a huge mistake that I handed over those unimportant facts about myself?

"Pleased to meet you, Elodie Stillwater. It's always nice to make a new friend. Maybe you'd like to come over to Riot House some time? We'd love to extend our hospitality to you."

At the same time, two voices speak out, one rushed and urgent, the other audibly bored.

"She can't!""Not happening, Dash."

The owner of the first voice, sitting next to me, flinches. I don't think Carina meant to blurt out her objection so loudly. She looks sheepish as she takes my hand, lacing her fingers through mine. "You know she'll get in trouble if Harcourt finds out," she says.

On the couch, with his face still buried beneath a cushion, Wren Jacobi growls. "She's not invited." The way he says it makes it sound like a decree, an order passed down from on high that is expected to be observed.

Dashiell lets out a morose sigh; he sounds honestly disappointed. "Don't worry, Stillwater. Jacobi changes his mind like he changes his socks. His current state of attire notwithstanding, of course. He's usually *very* good about changing his socks. I think that's the thing I like most about him."

"All right, class! Asses on a flat surface! Move, move, move!"

At the front of the room, a tall guy wearing a tight black dress shirt and a black pencil tie kicks out the wooden wedge that was holding the door open and boots the door closed behind him as he whirls into the room. In his mid-thirties, the guy is throwing off some heavy Clark Kent vibes. His jaw's so sharp it looks like it could cut and draw blood. Dark, wavy hair, and dark eyes, I can see why half the girls in the room melt into their seats when they realize he's arrived.

Doctor Fitzpatrick, my new English professor, is a stone-cold smoke show.

"Wren, cushion off the face, man. Sit the fuck up. You know the rules," he commands, setting down a pile of papers onto a bookshelf. There's a coffee cup in his other hand, which he drinks deeply from, the muscles in his throat working as he drains the contents of the cup in one go.

Miraculously, Wren drags the cushion from his face and heaves himself upright into a seated position. He glares daggers at Doc Fitzpatrick while he does it, but he complies.

This is unexpected. Very unexpected indeed. Wren gives off the impression that he doesn't obey anyone. I certainly wouldn't have expected him to obey an authority figure like an English professor.

Horrified, a number of things dawn on me in quick succession. It was so dark last night that I hadn't gotten a proper look at Wren. In the light that had flared off the cherry of his cigarette, I'd reluctantly acknowledged the fact that he was good looking. But in the daylight, with the weak sun flooding in through the massive picture window right behind his head, I can see so much more of him now...and I'm so desperately, absolutely beyond fucking fucked.

He's beautiful.

His black hair curls around his ears like it was painted onto his head, the artful strokes of a master's brush. It's thick and disheveled, and my fingers curl inwards of their own volition, wanting to feel the texture of it as I curl my hand into a fist.

His eyes are green, vivid and frighteningly bright. Jade—the color of fresh, new grass, and limes, and spring awakening after winter. They look borderline unreal. His mouth is unusual. His top lip is slightly fuller than the bottom, which should look odd on a guy, but Wren manages to make a sensual, feminine mouth look cruel.

I drink in the sight of him: the way his muscles shift between his shoulder blades as he braces himself on the edge of the leather couch and he pulls himself forward to lean with his forearms resting on the top of his knees. The way he smirks savagely when his quick eyes flit over the room and he catches a girl with braids looking at him. The way he steeples his fingers, all of him coming alive, like he's just been activated, when Doctor Fitzpatrick says, "Okay, fuck ups. Listen close. I read your assignments, and they were very interesting. Very raw and emotional. Very real. And some...were just plain graphic."

"What do you mean, *graphic?*" a girl sitting on an ottoman at the front asks. "The essay was on Victorian morality in English Literature."

"Yes, Damiana. Yes, it was."

Oh, great. I can only see the back of her head from where I'm sitting. I hadn't realized I was in the same class as the viper from this morning.

Doctor Fitzpatrick rocks his head from side to side, turning back to his stack of papers; he shuffles through the stapled documents on the top until he finds the one he's looking for. "This piece is titled *'The Repressed Governess'* and went four thousand words over our two-thousand-word limit. I've highlighted a number of sections that I thought were rather enlightening." He makes a show of clearing his throat, then begins reading from the assignment.

"So innocent before, now she looked terrified. The fear in her eyes made his shaft harden in his pants as he prowled forward, intent on backing her directly into his trap. Her chest rose and fell so rapidly, her large breasts were in danger of brimming over the top of her corset. Nothing could be more titillating to him than the sight of her accidentally disrobed and made vulnerable before him. The anticipation rose in him now, as it always did when he was so close to accomplishing his nefarious goals. For months he'd labored, working on the governess,

knowing her church, her faith, and her lunatic father would keep her from acting on her darkest desires. And still he hadn't given up. He'd seen the wicked fire burning in her soul, and he was determined to unleash it and set it free.

"The governess cried out when her back hit the wall. She knew she was cornered and there was no way out. No sooner had she realized her situation than she accepted it, though. Her breath quickened further, this time from excitement. There was something to be said about relinquishing control of oneself to a monster in a black top hat, and now that he was fast approaching with such a look of menace in his eyes, the governess discovered that she wasn't as afraid of her undeniable fate as she had first thought. She witnessed the threatening bulge of his staff, pressing against the front of his trousers. She saw the way he groped at himself, squeezing himself in the most lurid way, and surprised as she was, she knew that she was wet between her legs, her cunny slick with want as..."

Doctor Fitzpatrick cuts off, dropping his hands to his sides. Exasperated, he shakes his head. "Honestly, I have to say I'm impressed with the prose. Great use of the word lurid. And cunny? You must have had to look that one up, Jacobi."

All eyes turn to Wren.

Of course he wrote it. I am the most *unsurprised* person in the world. It totally tracks that this devil in a black t-shirt handed in *Victorian porn* as his English assignment. He doesn't look the slightest bit remorseful as he levels his steady gaze on the doc. "I did," he says. "The Internet's a remarkable place. All kinds of weird shit, if you know what you're looking for."

"You do realize that this piece was supposed to be on the Victorian sense of *morality*, right?" Doctor Fitzpatrick asks.

Wren shrugs. "I do. And they had none. The Victorians were just as horny, depraved and dirty as we are. They were just better at hiding it. There were just as many filthy books about fucking back then as there were books about sweet, subjugated women who lived by strict rules of propriety. They just didn't get the same kind of press."

"So, you're saying woman were painted as weak, subjugated creatures in a lot of Victorian literature?"

Wren sighs wearily, like he shouldn't have to explain any of this. "I'm not saying it. It's what happened. Austen made out like women back then were virtuous, good, wholesome creatures who never once thought about getting laid. It was all a lie, Fitz. Women have liked to get fucked since the dawn of time, just like guys. The fact that the Victorians used to guard that little tidbit like it was some huge fucking secret makes them even kinkier than us."

Doctor Fitzpatrick's eyebrows inch up. I think he's unimpressed by Wren's argument, but also grudgingly *impressed* by it, too. Tossing the paper at Wren, the doc sends the sheaf of paper fluttering down to the boy's feet. "Do it again. Forty-eight hours, Jacobi. Stick to the assignment brief or you'll find yourself doing it over for a third time. This *will* be your Groundhog Day of essays until you do it right. And no curse words. You should know by now that shock tactics won't work with me."

Wren leaves his assignment on the thin Persian rug at his feet. Most guys would be irritated by the fact that they had to rewrite an essay from the beginning, but he doesn't seem to care. He's taking the whole thing completely in stride. "Shock tactics work on everyone. I just haven't found the right *level* of shocking for you yet, Fitz. I'm nothing if not persistent. Leave it with me. I'll figure it out before the end of term."

God, this guy's a pro at concocting statements that sound like thinly disguised threats. I wonder if he speaks this way to his parents. My father would knock my head off my shoulders if I dared speak to him or any of my teachers that way. Wren might have army personnel for folks, but we must have had a very different upbringing if he knows he can get away with this shit.

Doctor Fitzpatrick smiles wide, pinching his tongue between his teeth as he turns away from Wren Jacobi, inhales deeply, and faces the rest of the class. "All right, kids. We're starting a new game today. Who wants to volunteer?" His gaze alights on me, and he comically slaps his hand to his forehead. "Ah shit. We have a newcomer in our midst. I totally forgot. Fuck, I made cookies, too. Elllloiiiise, right?" he says, wincing at me.

Eloise is a common one. I've had all sorts, though. Emily. Evelyn. Elena. Apparently, my given name isn't as common in other countries as it is in France. "Close. It's Elodie. Like Melody, but without the M." I smile when I correct him to let him know I'm not offended. He nods, wagging his finger at me. A girl sitting a bean bag three people over from me sighs deliriously when the guy spins around to face a white board on wheels and we all get to see just how tight his grey pants are across his pert ass.

"In lieu of any weird *'stand up and tell us all about yourself'* nonsense, I'm afraid you'll have to be nominated as volunteer for our game today, Elodie," he says, scrawling my name onto the surface of the whiteboard in red marker. Surprisingly, he spells it correctly first time.

"She can't be a volunteer if you nominate her," Damiana gripes, casting a sour look over her shoulder at me. "How is that fair? Some of us have been waiting our turn for months, Fitz."

"Oh, stop whining. I think we're all tired of the ceaseless droning of your voice, child."

Wow. I mean, I thought that it was wild, the way Wren spoke to Doctor Fitzpatrick, but honestly, the way he speaks to us is a little out there, too. The doc doesn't come across like a typical professor; he seems like a normal, functioning human being instead of an academic robot, trying to hustle us through the curriculum as fast as he possibly can. It's refreshing. Doesn't hurt that he calls people like Damiana out on her shit when she's being bitchy, either. I think I really like this guy.

Until he tells me to come stand in front of the class.

"Come on, Still...?"

"Water," I supply.

"Come on, Stillwater. On your feet. Front and center. You've got a job to do."

Mortified, I look at Carina, hoping for a miracle that'll mean I can remain sitting with her. Her forehead creases, an apologetic look on her face. "Sorry, dude. I should have realized he'd do this. Best to just go up there and get it over with."

Urgh. What a fucking nightmare. I get up from the sofa so slowly that it feels like I'm wading through glue. Once I'm at the front of the class, I turn around, donning a bright, cheery (fake) smile, and I face the class down. In fairness, this is a small class by anyone's standards. There are probably only fifteen students lazing around like spoiled cats in Doctor Fitzpatrick's den, which is a relief.

"What's the game?" I ask through my teeth, trying to loosen up the smile a little—it can't look real right now, it's far too tense. I hate this kind of thing. I hate moving schools, and I hate meeting new people, and I hate learning all the new rules. I hate learning all the new games, too.

Doctor Fitzpatrick beams as he perches on the edge of the windowsill near Wren's leather couch. He doesn't seem to have a desk in here, either. "Anyone care to explain the rules to Elodie, class?" This is entertaining to him. He's actually enjoying being here, teaching his students. In five different countries and in five different schools, I've never encountered another professor who enjoys his job.

A guy in the back, leaning against one of the book stacks, speaks up without raising his hand. "It's a popularity contest," he announces without looking up from the Rubik's Cube he's idly spinning in his hands. "You stand up there as directed by our venerated puppet master, and you give us a debate argument. The argument has to be related to books or the English language. If the class argues your debate topic in an entertaining way without Fitz getting bored, you score an automatic A on the next assignment he sets."

Hold up now...

What??

The doc's going to correct the guy and explain the game properly any second now. Surely. *No?* Doctor Fitzpatrick sits on the edge of the windowsill, smiling quite happily. He doesn't even object to the fact that this kid just called him 'our venerated puppet master.'

I don't quite know what I'm supposed to do. I'd love to say I don't really give a shit about my grades here at Wolf Hall, but the sad truth is that the monthly allowance my father loads onto my AMEX is directly related to my GPA. I know how it works all too well: I ace my tests and assignments, and I'll have plenty of funds to survive on here. I ding my record, or I don't perform as well as Colonel Stillwater expects me to, then I'll be left to eke out a very depressing existence on next to nothing.

I haven't explored the food situation around these parts yet, but I'm assuming there's a diner or maybe even a café. A restaurant if I'm lucky. It'd be nice to dine on edible food every once in a while, and not have to boil up water and choke down Top Ramen for breakfast, lunch and dinner, s'all I'm saying. An A right out of the gate? That'd make it *much* harder for Colonel Stillwater to garnish my allowance.

"Ookaaaay." I despise having to think of clever, interesting topics of conversation on the spot. If I'd known this was going to happen, I wouldn't have bothered going to sleep last night. I would have stayed up, scrolling for something awesome to hit these guys with in class. Regrettably, the only thing I can come up with is, "The English language is dying. Modern slang and text-speak are choking the history and the life out of an artform so rapidly that it will soon have evolved entirely. Discuss."

Doctor Fitzpatrick leaps to his feet, clapping his hands together as he bolts back toward the white board. "I love it. You miscreants are destroying my language with your text messages and your disgusting Neanderthal-esque slang. Someone say something! You can sit down, Ms. Stillwater." He nudges me with his elbow, and I dash back to the safety of the sofa, my eyes glued to the ground. Thank fuck he didn't hate the topic. Thank fuck my voice didn't crack, and I didn't stumble all over my words. Thank fuck no one laughed.

From the safety of the couch, I survey the room, waiting...no, dreading the moment when Doctor Fitzpatrick realizes no one's going to participate in my debate topic. A book snaps closed on the other side of the room. Someone coughs.

And then…

A guy with black hair, wearing a ratty sweater, sitting by the fire says, "All language is constantly evolving. To claim the English language is dead because it's changing and growing in a certain direction is like saying man became extinct when Homo Sapiens evolved from monkeys."

"Well." Doctor Fitzpatrick clicks the cap back onto his red marker. There's a huge, shit-eating grin on his face. "Anyone have anything to say to *that?*"

Damiana pipes up. "You're such a fucking moron, Andrew. Man isn't extinct because Homo Sapiens evolved. We became something new. A different species or strain of hominid. The species that we evolved *from* became extinct when we changed. What you said doesn't make any sense."

"So, you think the English language doesn't evolve?" Doctor Fitzpatrick asks her.

"Of course it does. Usually, when something evolves, it does so for the better, though. Our brains became larger and more complex because we learned how to speak and communicate using language. That was an improvement on the simpler, primitive versions of our minds. Text speak and slang isn't a positive improvement on our language. It's a lazy bastardization."

Doctor Fitzpatrick rubs his hands together. "This is getting good, guys. Anyone have anything to say to Damiana's statement?"

Wren slouches back into the leather sofa, spinning around so that his back is leaning against the arm. He kicks up his feet, lacing his fingers together and resting them on his chest. "Climb down from that high horse, Dami. You use text speak all the time. You're far from a purist."

"I do not!"

"Lol. Lmfao. Btw. NP. You text that shit to me all the time."

Ha. Why am I not surprised that Damiana and Wren are on

texting terms? They're both as vile as one another. They're probably best fucking friends.

"That's not proper text-speak," Damiana argues. "Those are just abbreviations."

Oh my god. She didn't just say that. Seriously? I hide my smile behind my notepad, trapping my laughter behind my teeth and two hundred pages of blank ruled paper.

"You look like you disagree, Elodie," Doctor Fitzpatrick says.

Oh, come *on.*

His gaze is locked onto me, his eyes dancing with amusement. I might have refrained from snickering at Damiana's comment, but I forgot about the parts of my face I didn't cover; Levi always said I smiled with my eyes more than my mouth. Swiveling around in her chair, Damiana glares at me hatefully.

"Come on, then, Stillwater. Out with it, if you think you're so fucking smart."

All high schools are the same. Even the insanely expensive private boarding school kind. Regardless of wealth, parenting styles, opportunity or diversity, there's always that one popular girl who thinks her shit don't stink. It's reassuring that I know what I can expect at Wolf Hall, but once, just *once,* it'd be nice if the whole mean girl bit wasn't a thing. From past experience, shaking my head and keeping my mouth shut in this situation will bode worse for me than speaking my mind. Just like in the natural world, display any signs of weakness and the predators will home in on it and do their best to pick you off. They're fucking relentless. Which is why I make sure my hands don't shake as I lower my notepad and look her square in the eye.

"Yes, they're abbreviations, but LOL? BTW? Acronyms. Emojis. Initials. They're all considered text-speak." I know this very well. Colonel Stillwater despises all forms of slang so violently that he swore he'd break my fingers if he ever caught me using it. And my father will break bones before he ever breaks a promise. I've never used an abbreviation in a text message in all my life.

Damiana glowers at me from under her caked-on mascara.

Some people might consider her heavy use of foundation and contouring pretty, but to me it looks like she's wearing someone else's face. "Why don't you just shut the fuck up, anyway? You've been here five minutes and you think you own the place."

Wow. What is this bitch's damage? I've barely blinked since I got here, and somehow Damiana already feels threatened by me. Powerplays are not my thing. I have zero interest in vying for her crown. All I want to do is complete my assignments, get good grades to appease Colonel Stillwater, and then get the fuck out of here the moment I've graduated. Beside me, Carina makes a disgusted sound.

"Easy, Dee. You wanna take it down a notch? Elodie's just—"

Damiana's face contorts in disgust. "And what kind of name is Elodie, anyway? She sounds like she's some sort of French whore."

"Ha! *La petite pute française*," Pax says, from his spot on the floor by the window. "You charge in euros, Stillwater? Or will a couple of greenbacks put you on *your* back? The exchange rate's murder right now."

"All right, all right. Enough," Doctor Fitzpatrick says mildly, holding up his hand. He doesn't sound shocked or even remotely bothered by what Damiana said, nor Pax's shitty comments for that matter. Everyone falls silent the second he speaks, though, obeying his lazy command. Pax still winks at me suggestively, biting the tip of his tongue. Obviously, he's scrolling through a number of lewd scenarios in his head.

"Hate to break it to you, Dee, but if you use those terms when you message Wren, you *are* using text speak," Doctor Fitzpatrick confirms. "If you—"

"Like I'd text that pervert anyway!" she cries.

Wren smirks, closing his eyes. "She does. Usually after midnight. And yes. DTF *is* considered text speak, too."

Damiana explodes from her seat, stabbing a finger at Wren, who can't see her outrage with his eyes closed. "You're a piece of shit, Wren Jacobi. I'd never fuck you in a million years. I'd sure as hell never *ask* you for it."

"Okay, okay, sit down. Wren, stop fucking talking before I boot you over to Harcourt's office. You guys know I love a lively debate, but we're getting a little off topic here. What do you think ol' Bill Shakespeare would say about all of the new words we're creating to express ourselves, guys?"

The debate continues. Every time the class somehow veers towards the topic of sex, Doctor Fitzpatrick manages to wrangle us back into order. I sit quietly, unable to take my eyes off Wren, unhappy about the way my eyes keep gravitating back to him the moment I forget to actively *not* look at him. The old adage is true: it's impossible to look away from a car crash. And I already know that Wren Jacobi isn't just a metaphorical car crash. He's a fifteen-car pile-up, and there are already people dead at the scene. I'm headed straight for him, though, and I can't steer myself away. Worst of all, I'm not wearing a seatbelt, and motherfucker's cut my brake lines.

He's brutal, and he's mean, and he's rotten down to his very core. I can't escape him, though. There's a very real danger that he'll hold his cup to my lips, and I'll drink down his poison like I'm dying and he's the cure.

All I can do now is brace myself and hope that the end will be quick.

A sharp, shrill bell drowns out Pres, the redhead I met earlier, and the students all shuffle out of the classroom, groaning and complaining loudly about the assignment that Doctor Fitzpatrick says he'll email us all later on this afternoon.

In the hallway, Carina sags with relief. "God, I'm so glad that's over."

I don't think she means the English class itself.

I think she means the close proximity to Wren and his crew.

At the foot of a steep, winding stone stairway, Carina gives me a quick hug. "This is where I leave you, I'm afraid. I need to get to Spanish. Your biology class is up there. Don't worry. Everyone should be nice."

About halfway up the stairs, my cell phone chimes in my back pocket. Excited, I scramble to pull it out and read the message that's just come through. With the crazy time differences, it feels like I've been waiting for this moment for a week. It's weird that I haven't heard a peep out of Levi and the others until now, but at least—

Oh.

Wait.

The message isn't from one of my friends back in Tel Aviv. The unknown number is American, with a 929 area code that isn't familiar to me.

The message is short and to the point.

"Be less obvious, Stillwater. Desperation's an ugly look."

4

WREN

DEAD MOTHER.

Only child.

Small, like a porcelain doll.

Pretty blonde hair.

Pouty mouth I wouldn't mind wrapped around my dick.

I don't know much about Elodie Stillwater, but I can already feel that familiar old spark of intrigue at the back of my head, an itch just begging to be scratched. In fairness, I felt the dirty, sick need long before I laid eyes on the girl. Her file had been sitting there, open and asking to be flicked through, the last time I got called into Harcourt's office. The photo clipped to the top of Elodie's paperwork had caught my eye—I've always been attracted to shiny, pretty things—and my pulse had quickened, stirring from a steady, slow thrum to a far more urgent, interested clip.

In the picture, she was wearing a white sailor's uniform—a particularly unkind school uniform, I later learned, after a bit of digging. The smile on her face was genuine. She was laughing at someone or something off camera, and her eyes were alive with energy. Innocent. That's what it was about her. She looked innocent, dressed in white, with all of that long blonde hair flowing down past her shoulders, every part of her singing with life. I'd immediately wanted to sully her.

I took the photo. Denied taking it when Harcourt asked me if I knew where it was. For two weeks prior to Elodie Stillwater's arrival, I spent a lot of time looking at that photo, jerking off to it but then refusing to let myself come, enjoying the anger that pooled in my stomach whenever I stared at Elodie's pretty face. I've loved conditioning myself ever since I was a kid. Exposing myself to some kind of stimulus and then training myself to expect a certain outcome. I love nothing more than mastering myself, both mind and body, and my first thought when I saw that girl's smiling face, was that I wanted to make myself hate her.

Why, you ask?

Why the hell not?

Just for the fun of it.

For a way to pass the time.

Mediocrity is the curse of the weak minded. I've made damn sure nothing about *me* is mediocre, half-assed, or middle of the road, and that includes my emotions. It takes a lot to make me feel alive these days, but a dark obsession? A healthy bit of intrigue, colored with a splash of hate? Yeah, that'll wake me from this dull, trite existence better than anything else.

So, yeah. I waited up for her to arrive. I *volunteered*, which should have been a pretty glaring warning to the Wolf Hall administration, since I've never volunteered for anything in my entire fucking life. I wanted to test out my theory and see if the time I spent torturing myself had had its desired effect, though, and there was only one way to do that. I had to see her face-to-face, even if it meant burning my way through my last pack of smokes while standing out in the freezing cold for two and a half hours.

When I watched her getting out of that Town Car, angrily pulling at the straps on her backpack, my body knew exactly what to do. My dick responded beautifully, roaring to life, blood surging to transform soft flesh to rigid steel. At the same time, my brain was obliterated by a need to see the girl cry, so fierce and intense that I could barely breathe around it.

Fuck her.

Hurt her.

Soothe her.

Ruin her.

I was so perfectly balanced on that invisible tight rope that it felt like Christmas fucking morning. After all, there's nothing like a little internal warfare to perk up a shitty mood. And now, after two weeks of waiting, trawling through her social media accounts and clicking through all of her photos on Facebook—who doesn't make their shit *private* these days?—I feel like I've got a solid grasp on who the newest student at Wolf Hall is.

She's a walking contradiction.

I like this about her.

I asked a friend out in Tel Aviv to do some digging on her home life, which seems to be taking a lot longer than expected, but in the meantime, I've already concocted fifteen different ways to tear Elodie into a million little pieces. I've subsequently discounted each and every one of them. This is the opportunity of a lifetime, my last chance to condition *someone else* and bend them to my will. I need to be careful how I go about it. Make her crawl for my approval right away and it'll all be over too soon. I'll tire of her and be left having to find new ways to entertain myself until graduation. Give her too much free rein, though, and she could slip out of my grasp. There's a happy medium somewhere in the middle, and now I need to work out exactly where it is. All part of the adventure.

"You broke the rules anyway," Pax says, tearing off a huge hunk of bread from his sandwich with his teeth. The man's a complete heathen. No fucking manners whatsoever. During the summer, he models for Calvin Klein, strutting up and down runways in tight grey underwear. Aside from his shaved head, he looks clean in those photos. He looks well-constructed, like a fucking G.I. Joe— American made, only the best parts and labor. His fancy agent, and his fancy friends, and the fancy fucking idiots who stare at his image and wish they were him...none of them get to see who he really is: this ruthless, simple creature that likes to break things and tear them apart with his teeth.

"By rights, she's mine," he says around his mouthful of food. "You had Damiana. Dash got Carina. I'm next up to bat."

Growling, I type even faster, spewing a thousand words a minute into the Word document, determined to get my re-write of Fitz's dumb Victorian morality assignment completed before the fun for the evening kicks off. "You know I hate sports metaphors," I snarl. "Shut the fuck up and stop whining. You're a grown ass man. If you want to go after the girl, then fucking do it. Doesn't mean my plans will change."

Do I care that Pax wants Elodie as his new mark? Sure I do. He's a good-looking guy. Calvin Klein approved. He's screwed plenty of girls here at Wolf Hall, and a million beyond the walls of our desperately boring little ecosystem, too. He's dangerously charming when the mood takes him, and I've seen plenty of intelligent women fall for his bullshit. No reason why Elodie wouldn't be the same.

To be a complete punk about it, though...I saw her first.

I've researched her. I chanted her full name inside my head—Elodie Francine Jemimah Stillwater—until it felt like a mantra, a pebble worn smooth by constant rubbing, and now she feels like she's mine. I do not share my toys well with others.

We have our rules for a reason, naturally. Riot House wouldn't exist without some kind of code or system by which its inhabitants were required to operate. There may only be three of us here, but each of our personalities are such that we'd all wind up dead if we didn't honor a line drawn in the sand from time to time.

Pax grunts, screwing up his Subway wrapper and lobbing it at the trash can on the other side of my bedroom. He shouldn't even be in here while I'm trying to work, but trying to keep Pax out of anywhere is like trying to stop water leaking from a holey bucket. You learn to give up pretty quickly. Pax is quiet for a while. This means he's thinking deeply about something. I manage to cram in three hundred words before he eventually says, "How about...a *trade?*"

I stop typing.

Turn around in my chair.

There's a worrying look on Pax's face.

I narrow my eyes at him. "Explain." From time to time, he's been known to be a little tricksy. Not as tricksy as me, but it's wise to be on guard.

He pouts, staring up at the ceiling. He's being far too nonchalant right now. He wants something big. Bigger than Elodie, which means he's about to try and pass whatever this is off as a fair exchange. "The boat," he says airily. "You have it while it's still in Corsica. Trade me the boat over spring break and I won't lay a finger on the girl."

Hah. He talks about *'The Contessa'* like it's a fucking schooner, not a forty-foot long, seven-bedroomed luxury super yacht. She's my father's pride and joy. If I let Pax stay there unsupervised during the spring break, the damn thing'll probably end up at the bottom of the Mediterranean. My father would tar and feather me, then disinherit me.

"A week," I counter.

Pax folds his arms across his chest, the casual, carefree expression he was just sporting vanishing as he settles in for negotiations. "Two weeks, man. The whole break. I'm not flying across the world for one fucking week."

"Ten days. Final offer."

"No deal. I guess you're gonna have to stand down."

He could *make* me stand down. If he wanted to, he could involve Dash, and the two of them could vote that I stay away from Elodie until the end of fucking time. House rules. We try to avoid forcing each other to do anything most of the time, it only winds up with someone getting hurt, but it wouldn't be an unprecedented move. Pax really must like the look of Elodie, which makes me want her even more.

She already *is* mine, though, and this claim he's trying to make on her is boiling my fucking blood. "Ten days, Pax. Go see your Mom in Prague afterward."

He looks horrified. "Why the hell would I do *that?*"

"All right. Fine. You get the boat. Two weeks in June. But I so much as *hear* you've been making Molotov cocktails again and I'll call in the fucking *gendarmerie.*"

If anything, this only seems to make the smile on the piece of shit's face spread even wider. God, what the fuck am I doing? This is going to be an unmitigated disaster. I can already feel it in my bones. "Stop crowing. I can hear the laughter bouncing around the inside of your thick skull from here," I grumble, spinning back around to face my desk. I won't be able to write anymore. I know I won't. I'm relieved that ownership of Elodie Stillwater has been cleared up, but there's a rank taste in my mouth that I can't shake now.

I made a copy of her file with all her personal contact information a week after I took the photo. I considered calling her before she even arrived, just so I could hear her voice and stop driving myself mad with wondering what she would sound like. I'd managed to show a little restraint, though. But I couldn't stop myself from texting after our English class. I'd wanted to rile her up. To watch her reaction from afar. Annoyingly, she'd barely reacted at all. She'd been confused at first, because she didn't know the number, I'm assuming, but then her face had gone blank.

No fear. No anger. No irritation. The only emotion I saw cross her face, from my casual lean against the wall fifteen feet away, was a brief flicker of amusement, at which point she'd tucked her phone back into her pocket and jogged up the steps towards the biology labs without a backward glance.

"Why are you so dead set on this girl, anyway?" Pax asks, making a hell of a noise as he purposefully fires the lid on a can of pringles across the room, jams his hand inside, pulls out a stack of chips and stuffs them into his mouth.

I tap out a sentence, focusing on my laptop screen. "She's nothing. She's unimportant."

"Bullshit, Jacobi. You haven't shown the slightest bit of interest in a girl since Mara and you know it."

BANG!

I think I just shattered my laptop's screen.

I shouldn't have slammed it closed so hard, but then again Pax shouldn't have just uttered that name within my earshot. He knows better than that. Closing my eyes, I inhale a shaky, uneven breath, trying to level out the rage spiking in my bloodstream. "I'm glad we ironed out a deal with *The Contessa*," I grit out through my teeth. "You gotta get the fuck out of my room, though, dude. I'm serious. I gotta get this paper done. I need to clear my head, and I can't do that with you bringing that shit up, yeah?"

I wait for Pax to argue. Arguing is second nature to him; he grew up in a house full of lawyers. For better or for worse, he chooses to keep a civil tongue in his head instead. "All right, man. No drama. I'm gonna head down to Cosgroves' and grab some beers. You want something?"

I clench my jaw so hard that it cracks when I force my mouth open to speak. "Not beer. A forty of Jack," I tell him.

"Whew. Going big on a school night. My favorite kind of Jacobi." He leaves, humming a raucous song under his breath, and I sit very still, with an image of Elodie Stillwater blazing in my mind.

Why am I so dead set on her?

Because she's innocent, and I'm not.

Because she's wholesome, and I'm not.

Because she's untainted, and I'm not.

And, most importantly of all, because she'll be *so* pretty when I make her cry.

5

ELODIE

"WE SHOULD HAVE MET YESTERDAY, Ms. Stillwater, but I've found that giving a student a day or two to settle in can be helpful. I knew Carina would do a good job of showing you around. She's a good girl. A good friend, if you're in the market for one. I apologize for putting you all the way up there on the fourth floor, but four-sixteen was our only available room. I hope you're comfortable enough. Please pass on our apologies to your father. Colonel Stillwater was very clear that he wanted you situated on the second floor, but there's nothing we can do right now. Maybe next semester—"

"Really, Principal Harcourt, it's not a problem. I don't mind being on the fourth floor." Yes, it's a pain in the ass having to hike all the way up those stairs, but apart from being in such close proximity to Damiana and the blistering cold in my room it doesn't really make much of a difference where I sleep in this godforsaken place. It's all the same to me.

Principal Harcourt nods, fidgeting in her chair. Her office is imposing, just as old and drafty as the rest of Wolf Hall, but it's light and airy and feels less oppressive than the rest of the academy. The woman herself is in her late forties, with a touch of steel grey in her long dark hair that's swept back into an uncompromising chignon. Her eyes are a little distracted, unfocused as they flit around the room, landing on everything from her academic texts, the plaques on her walls, and the wilting peace lily in the pot on her desk, but never resting on me.

"I had the pleasure of meeting your father once. Quite an intimidating man," she says breathily.

Intimidating? She really doesn't know the half of it. I fiddle with the apple I'm holding in my hands, worrying at its stalk. The inch-long woody stem snaps off in my fingers, and I let it fall to the floor. "Yes. He's very well respected." I could say so much more. I could tell her about the nights I spent twisted up and afraid beneath my bedsheets, wondering if he was going to burst through my bedroom door at any moment. She'd understand then how unimportant the location my bedroom here at Wolf Hall really is to me, so long as I'm as far away from him as is physically possible.

"Now," the principal says awkwardly, opening up the top drawer of her desk. She takes out a sheet of paper and sets it down in front of her, sliding it toward me. "I hate to have to go through this with you, but I'm afraid it's academy policy. Here at Wolf Hall, there are a number of things we do not tolerate. As you'll see from this student-faculty agreement, the use or possession of drugs is strictly prohibited. We also do not allow any sort of...*carousing*. Ahem. Contact of a sexual nature is also prohibited. No members of the opposite sex on any of our female or male floors. No inappropriate touching, or...or...well, you can read for yourself there, can't you. You can leave the academy on the weekends, but doors are locked by nine o'clock sharp. During the week, you must remain here on school grounds. From Monday through Friday, leaving Wolf Hall for any reason without prior written permission from myself or another member of the teaching staff is taken very seriously. There are other items on the list that you can review at your own leisure. I take it none of that will be an issue for you, though?"

"No, of course not." Jesus. Who does she think I'm going to be getting hot and heavy with? And I've never stepped foot in New Hampshire before; as far as I'm concerned, this place might as well be the seventh circle of hell and there's no way out for me.

"Good girl. Now, if you don't mind, I have some paperwork to catch up on. I believe you have a French class to be getting to. I'm sure you'll enjoy that, given that it was your first language."

"Actually, I never learned Fre—"

"Good, good. Off you go now. If you need anything, please let someone at the administration desk know and I'm sure they'll be happy to help you. Have a lovely day, Elodie."

I'm ushered out of Principal Harcourt's office so quickly I almost forget to collect my bag before the door is slammed loudly behind me.

I take a deep, calming breath, slinging the leather strap up and over my head. I have no idea where my French class is or which direction I'm supposed to head in, and since Carina threw out my map yesterday morning, I find I'm at a bit of a loss. Carina had to get to class, and without my guide, I—

I see the dark silhouette, hovering at the mouth of the corridor that leads to the principal's office and a cold sweat breaks out across my back.

Crap.

My scientific mind tells me that this old, crooked, rambling building isn't haunted, but the shadowy figure looks distinctly ghost-like as it moves toward me.

I could be wrong, but I'm betting none of the training my father drilled into me will be useful against non-corporeal forms. Stilling my racing heart, I step forward, swallowing down the lump in my throat, and…Wren Jacobi steps into the circle of flickering, dim yellow light cast off from a sconce on the wall.

I don't know if I should be relieved or twice as scared.

His black clothes contrast so dramatically with his pale skin that he looks like the negative of a photo, brought to life. I didn't see him again after English yesterday, so I'd tricked myself into believing that I wouldn't be seeing him today, either. Clearly a very stupid, naïve thought, because here he is, larger than life and way more threatening than any apparition. The hallway's wide but not wide enough for me to skirt around him without having to acknowledge his existence. I duck my head, tucking my chin into my chest, eager to get past him as quickly as possible...

"*Stillwater.*" My last name echoes down the hallway, ringing in my ears. His voice is cold and stiff. "They sent me to escort you to class. Come with me."

Oh. That's just...fucking wonderful.

He sounds pissed that he's been assigned this task. I move closer, dragging my heels as much as possible, trying to delay the moment that I reach him and we're standing face to face in the confined space, unable to avoid each other's gaze. It comes all too quickly, though.

God, his eyes are so green. I've never seen eyes that color before. He doesn't blink as he stares down at me, his top lip twitching like it wants to curl upward in disgust. He brushes a hand through his thick, wavy hair, blowing hard down his nose, his nostrils flaring. "Try to remember the way," he says curtly. "I'm not doing this twice."

I don't even want him to do it once.

He spins, turning around and showing his back to me, and then he takes off at a fast clip, heading for the east wing of the academy. For every one of his long strides, I have to put in three in order to keep pace with him. Tension radiates off him as he marches ahead of me, clenching and unclenching his massive hands into fists.

With the heavy, solid oak doors to all the classrooms firmly closed, concealing the students inside, a thick silence floods the hall as Wren leads the way. Cursing myself for being so damn stupid, I rip my gaze away from his ass, telling myself that I wasn't checking out the way his jeans hang a little too low, revealing the black waistband of his underwear. No, no way was I checking *that* out.

I'm hot all over and flooded with unexplained shame. If I inspected that shame up close, then I'd discover that there *is* a reason for it, and that reason has an awful lot to do with the way Wren's mouth had looked yesterday when he said the word *fuck* in Doctor Fitzpatrick's class.

A deviant shiver runs down my spine, and I shake my head to dislodge the memory. I'm quickly making new memories, though. The stubble on the back of his neck, short and black, where his hair's been cropped so close to his skin is perversely fascinating. I stare at the base of his skull, like I might be able to pierce through the skin and bone and see right into his mind, and all the while, my hands grow clammier and clammier. I nearly leap out of my skin when he angles his head down and to the left, barely showing his features in profile for a brief second as he says, "You're throwing in with Carina, then."

"Throwing in with her?"

The corner of his mouth twitches. Not a smile. Something else. "You've chosen her as a friend," he clarifies.

"Yeah, I suppose I have."

"Interesting choice."

This is the kind of leading comment that invites someone to ask questions: *what do you mean by that? Is Carina a sociopath or something? Should I stay away from her?* Unfortunately for Wren, I've spent an awful lot of time figuring people out, as well as uncovering their intentions, and he's got another thing coming if he thinks I'll give him what he wants so easily. He has something he wants to tell me about my new friend Carina? Then he's going to have to offer the information up all by himself.

I say nothing.

Wren Jacobi says nothing.

Down the hallway we go, Wren walking ahead of me, his tall frame solid, his shoulders drawn back in the same over-confident way kids who are born into money all seem to have. He takes a left, and then another left, and then a right, and before I know it, I'm completely turned around, and I have no clue where I am.

So much for remembering the way...

Wren stops abruptly, spinning around, and I almost walk

straight into his chest. Applying the brakes as quickly as possible, I pull up just in time, a mere eight inches between us. This close, I have to crane my head back, pointing my chin at the ceiling in order to look up at him. "What's she told you about Riot House?" he demands.

"What do you mean?"

"I'm sure Carina's mentioned Riot House by now. I wanna know what she's said."

Lord. He gives his orders uncompromisingly, as if it's never occurred to him that anyone might deny him the information he's seeking and tell him to go fuck himself. As far as Wren's concerned, there is no reality or parallel universe in which he isn't unquestioningly obeyed by all. Those eyes of his, the brightest jade, swirled through with flecks of amber and glorious gold, are so surprising that they almost have me blurting out the answers to questions he hasn't even asked me.

Dark chocolate.

The Beatles.

George Orwell's 1984.

My suspicious nature keeps me firmly glued to the tracks, though. It pokes at me with a question of my own: Why does he want to know what Carina said about Riot House? Was she supposed to keep her mouth shut about the place? Is Wren's home a forbidden topic of conversation, punishable by…fuck, I have no idea what kind of punishment Wren might subject a person to if they were dumb enough to displease him. I already know it wouldn't be pretty. Going back over the few words Carina uttered about Riot House, I decide it'd be harmless to just give in and tell him. Not that he deserves the explanation. "She told me that that's where you, Pax and Dashiell live. That's it."

He narrows his eyes. I don't think he believes me. "Did she tell you what we do there? Did she tell you about the rules?"

"I don't know anything about any rules. And whatever you get up to in the privacy of your own home is really fine by me, man. It's absolutely none of my business."

He blows out down his nose—a long, unhappy exhalation. I've said something wrong, apparently. "Okay, *dude*. Well, tell her that she needs to keep it that way. If we find out that she's filling people's head with shit, then—"

"Ah, there you are. Mr. Jacobi, what are you doing, loitering out here? Straight to the office and straight back to class. That's what we agreed, isn't it?" A tall, reedy woman with frizzy blonde hair and weak blue eyes stands in the hall behind Wren, holding an open textbook in her hand. Her eyes meet mine and she smiles.

A muscle tics in Wren's jaw—a sign of annoyance if ever I've seen one. "We were just coming," he says tightly. Nudging me with the toe of his brown leather boots, he urges me to go ahead of him, toward the blonde woman, who beams.

"You're my first ever French student, Elodie. I'm Madame Fournier. I can't tell you how excited I am to have someone in the class who can speak the language fluently."

"She doesn't know a lick of French," Wren mumbles, pushing his way past the woman. "Turns out our little French whore isn't so French after all."

Madame Fournier reels at Wren's statement. "Mr. Jacobi! Apologize to Ms. Stillwater immediately!"

Wren pauses alongside Madame Fournier—long enough to lean in close, bringing his face close to the French teacher's. He peers at her through his impossibly dark eyelashes, a look of quiet contempt on his face. "What's my other option? Because I'm currently maxed out on apologies."

Madame Fournier turns a brilliant shade of crimson. "*Aller en enfer,*" she spits.

Wren smiles. "Convince the old man to cut me loose and I'll head there directly. In the meantime, I'll be in the back row of your class every Tuesday until the end of fucking time." He straightens, standing at his full height—a monster wearing a black long-sleeved t-shirt and a vicious smile—and casts a bored look back at me. "Come on. There's a seat open right next to mine."

He grabs hold of me by the wrist.

Shock jitters up my arm, echoing around the chamber of my chest. It booms like a struck bell in my head, roaring in my ears louder than a raging ocean battering against a shoreline.

He has me by the wrist.

"I'm perfectly capable of walking," I say in a clear, calm voice. "I don't need to be dragged anywhere."

If he doesn't let go of me in five seconds, I'm gonna wrench myself free. I'm gonna kick him in the balls. I'm gonna break one of his goddamn fingers.

Five...

Four...

Three...

Wren releases his hold on me, smirking infuriatingly. "I don't know what got into me. I guess I'll see you in there." He goes, leaving me standing next to Madame Fournier, who flusters and chatters incessantly about manners and how *boys will be boys,* but the whole time I can see the nervous edge in her eyes. She can't hide the fact that her hands are shaking as she snaps her textbook closed and tucks it under her arm.

Inside Madame Fournier's room, massive French flags hang from the walls. By the blackboard at the head of the room, the obligatory shot of the Eiffel Tower hangs, framed, on the wall next to pictures of Edith Piaf and The Louvre. I do a quick appraisal of the desk/chair situation and quickly calculate that Madame Fournier is very low on the pecking order at Wolf Hall. Doctor Fitzpatrick gets a lofty, light, massive office with enough room for a miniature library and an open fireplace, and the French teacher gets a standard box room with only two windows, no personality and desks with lids that look like they date back to the thirties.

And...yep. *Just fucking great.*

There *is* only one open seat available, and it just so happens to be right next to the brooding, dark-haired asshole whose burning hand I can still feel cuffing my wrist. He didn't tighten his grip on me. He didn't pull me after him. He did nothing but close his fingers around my skin, but it feels like he fucking branded me with his touch, and now I'm forever doomed by his mark.

His tall, ridiculous frame is too large and unwieldy to fit behind his desk; his legs stretch out into the aisle, his body set at an angle as he leans back in his chair, his eyes sparking with curiosity, tinged with the faintest suggestion of malevolence as I walk toward him.

He doesn't breathe a word—way worse than if he was openly hostile. Slinging the straps of my backpack over the back of my chair, I grab my notebook, trying to override the churning dread in my stomach. My classmates have all been learning French for years now. I haven't even heard the language spoken since my mother died. And I could never understand it even when she was alive.

"Alright, students," Madame Fournier projects from the front of the class. "Where were we? Simone, if you could continue—"

The teacher directs a girl on the front row to continue reading or conjugating a verb or something. I can't pay attention, because I'm suddenly accosted by a pungent, overpowering odor that hits the back of my nose and my taste buds all at once.

Oh…

Oh my god. It's *disgusting*.

What the fuck *is* that?

I can actually *taste* it.

Musty, rotten, and vaguely fishy, the smell is so rank I have to fight the urge to lean over the edge of my desk and vomit.

How is no one else reacting to this stench right now? Quickly, I look around at the students sitting closest to me. None of them are paying attention to Madame Fournier. They're all tensed, looking at the floor or at their hands, or sightlessly staring at their worksheets in front of them, unusually tense. The girl sitting to my left looks like she's about to explode, her cheeks and the very tips of her ears burning a bright red.

Another wave of the fishy bouquet hits me, and…

Oh, for god's sake.

It's coming from inside my desk.

Everything falls perfectly into place. Obviously, someone's put something disgusting and fetid inside my desk to fuck with me, and I know precisely who is responsible. Of course it was him. He knew I'd be sitting here. I wouldn't be surprised if he forced whoever normally sits beside him out of their desk, so he could have the pleasure of a front row seat when I lifted up the lid of said desk and discovered whatever rotten thing he's dumped inside.

Mother...fucking...asshole.

What am I supposed to do now? Am I supposed to sit here and tolerate the reek coming from inside of my desk? Am I supposed to get angry? Cry?

I don't think Wren really cares, so long as I do something. He just wants a reaction, and preferably a violent one, if I'm reading this situation correctly.

Well, fuck him. He isn't getting shit out of me.

I lean against the lid of the desk, breathing through my mouth, listening to Madame Fournier. Scribbling away at a mile a minute, I take notes of all the exercises I need to catch up on and all of the chapters I need to read if I want to have a hope of catching up with the already advanced class.

Colonel Stillwater knows I don't speak French. My mother always wanted to teach me, she tried to speak French at home when I was little, as well as English, but my father beat her senseless for even suggesting such a thing. And now he expects me to learn the language from scratch and attain an excellent grade, otherwise there are bound to be horrific consequences. It's this thought that distracts me from the putrid smell that assaults my senses every few minutes and keeps me focused on the task at hand.

And all the while, Wren Jacobi stews.

I feel his displeasure like you might feel a hand on the back of your neck, pushing down on you, trying to force you to your knees. He's not happy that I'm avoiding his little gift. Not happy in the slightest. He wants me to open up the desk and recoil in horror. He wants me make a scene, and all I'm giving him is a serious case of hives.

The minutes tick by painfully slowly. Outwardly, I'm single minded, focused only on Madame Fournier and the complicated, confusing nonsense she writes down on the board. Internally, I am a mess. I'm so angry, I'm vibrating with rage. Every time Wren twitches or shifts in his chair, it's all I can do not to flinch away from the bastard.

I'm not afraid of him.

Maybe I should be.

I intend on taking my time and figuring out if he really is the enemy before I decide if I should treat him as a threat, though. By the time the bell rings, my gorge is rising despite breathing through my mouth. Carina promised to wait for me by the main entrance between periods, so I grab my papers, my pens, notebook and my bag and I bolt for the door without looking back. As I tear out of the door, my heart a clenched fist in the hollow of my throat, I can still feel Wren Jacobi simmering away on the back row.

IN THE DARK...

"Pretty girl. So precious. So fucking spoiled. You think you're untouchable, don't you? You think you're above punishment? You're a dirty little slut, and all dirty little sluts are punished. You've seen that for yourself. Go on. Cry some more. You know it only makes me harder."

Vile, evil, hateful words.

They slip through the little holes in the wood, making me flinch.

I can smell the alcohol on his breath.

I can hear the madness in his voice.

Through the tiny oxygen holes in front of my face, I can see what he's doing. I can see how he's touching himself.

When he comes, spraying my prison with his semen, then I can smell that, too.

6

WREN

"THERE HAVE TO BE CONSEQUENCES, man. Without consequences, how will any of them know their place?" Dashiell hits the pipe I just passed him, holding the smoke in his lungs, lips pressing together as he frowns at the naked chick gyrating on his computer screen. Other guys might save their private sex cam sessions until they had a moment alone, but Dash has no qualms about enjoying the services he pays for in front of others. Dash has very few qualms in general.

His dick is hard, which isn't out of the ordinary. He gets hard whenever he smokes pot. Some weird, fucked up wiring issue in his brain. The girl touching her pussy on the screen's purely coincidental.

Exhaling, he lets out an insubstantial puff of smoke, most of it having already absorbed into his lungs. His preppy chinos and his grey sweater make him look like he's about to head off to church. His bloodshot eyes make him look like he just arrived, fresh off the boat from hell. "I don't think Carina likes me." He points the end of the pipe at me. "I don't know if you've noticed, but whenever I enter a room, she always seems to be leaving it. If I were a suspicious guy, I'd think I might have upset her."

Hah. Sick bastard. Yeah, Dash definitely upset Carina and he knows it. These mind games he likes to play are so deeply ingrained in his very id that he sometimes forgets that he doesn't need to play them within the walls of our home, though. I grab the pipe from him, angrily packing the weed down into the bowl. When I touch the flame of the lighter to it, I pull too harshly, sending a jet of scalding hot, thick and highly potent smoke scorching down the back of my throat.

I need to cough, but I won't. I refuse to let myself. I force myself to ride out the maddening, desperate need with a sour-feeling grin plastered on my face. My eyes sting when I eventually breathe out. "Think you'd better give that one a wide berth before you decide to fuck with her again," I advise. "Carina's fiery. She'll clip your balls for you if you're not careful."

"*Aww.* You worried about my balls, Jacobi?" Dash ruffles my hair, fucking up the hap-hazard, behind-the-ear tuck I had going on. I growl half-heartedly. There are certain things Pax can get away with, like eating on my fucking bed and getting food every-where. He wouldn't live to tell the tale if he tried to fucking ruffle my hair, though. I have very specific dynamics with both of my friends, and I don't like one to bleed through into the other. That's how shit gets confusing.

"Your balls are of no concern to me, jackass. They're probably gonna rot and fall off of their own accord any day now. I'm more concerned about keeping a low profile. Last thing we need is Harcourt siccing her minions on to us again."

Dashiell throws himself back against the couch, absently grab-bing the end of his dick through his pants and giving it a squeeze. He frowns at the girl on his laptop, who's now fully fingering herself, trying to incite some sort of a reaction out of him. He scowls, irritated. Snapping the laptop closed, he slides the MacBook across the coffee table, nearly knocking over a fake potted plant he bought last week in an attempt to 'brighten up the place.'

"Fine. I'm bored of women, anyway," he announces. "You ever

fucked a guy, Jacobi?"

That's none of his damn business. However, I have no reason to hide anything from anyone. I've been calculating and careful about every single move I've made since I was nine years old. It's exhausting, having to plot and plan absolutely everything you ever do, but it also means I have very few regrets. How can I regret something if I've weighed all of the consequences and deemed them acceptable before taking action? "Tried everything at least once, Lord Lovett. No sense in leaving any stone unturned, right?"

If he asks me if I liked having a dick thrust up my ass, I'm prepared to break my 'no need to lie to the friends' rule, just this once. Or at least bend it a little. He doesn't ask that, though. He nods, the corners of his mouth pulled down in a look of surprise as he arranges himself against the couch cushions. "I might give it a shot," he says. "Might liven up the rest of the year. My mother would have a heart attack if I brought home a *boyfriend*." He laughs maniacally, his Adam's apple bobbing up and down in his throat as he closes his eyes, throwing his arm over his face. "Don't take this personally, but I can't see that fucking *you* would be any fun, Jacobi. You're too moody. You look like you bite."

I huff out a sharp bark of laughter. "You bet your fucking ass I do."

Dash raises his arm, opening one eye so he can peek at me through the crack. "You fuck angry, too, don't you? Must be terrifying to have you looming over a person, all fire and brimstone and death, knowing you're about to be destroyed from the inside out."

"I'll have you know I'm a very tender lover."

Dash nearly chokes to death on a scathing fit of laughter. "Bull*shit.* You wouldn't know tender if it leapt up and knocked your front fucking teeth out."

"*That's* exactly the kind of tender I'm talking about."

He smiles, flashing two rows of very white, very straight teeth. If Lord Lovett Snr and Lady Lovett had cared for their son even the littlest bit, they would have spared him the torture of braces when he was a kid and left his teeth a little crooked. With the set of perfect pearly whites on him now, he's completely flawless. Makes for a classically handsome profile, but it's also stripped his face of anything really interesting to look at. "Whatever you say, Dark Lord. Is that how it's gonna be with your little French girl, then? Caresses that bruise? Kisses that bleed?"

Kisses that bleed?

I nearly drop the pipe I was about to use but manage to close my hand around it just before it crashes down onto the glass coffee table. The image that phrase just brought to mind has me practically panting, my lips burning, the roof of my mouth tingling like crazy. I don't enjoy the taste of blood, but the thought of biting Elodie hard enough to break the skin…

Fuck.

"No. I'm not interested in that with her." I say it like I mean it. I sound convincing as hell. So then why does it feel like I just dumped a shit load of good MDMA down my throat, and the anticipation is building inside of me as I wait to start rolling? Makes no fucking sense.

Just like always, Dash grunts, making it clear that he knows me better and he doesn't believe me for one hot second.

"Her father's top brass. I'd be careful if *I* were *you*," he says, firing the warning I just gave him right back at me. "You know what'll happen if your father finds out you've soiled one of his colleague's precious daughters. There'll be hell to pay and then some."

Since I think through all of my actions so thoroughly, I've obviously thought about this. I've done plenty of research on Colonel Jason Andrew Stillwater, and I've gotten a decent lay of the land. Luckily for me, Elodie's father is not a well-liked man. My own father, when I briefly mentioned Colonel Stillwater during a phone call last week, called him a self-righteous, overbearing cunt. And my father likes everyone. Apart from me, that is.

"Don't worry that pretty little head of yours, Lovett. Everything's under control. I know when to say when. I'll have my fun and then I'll call it a day. Got college on the horizon, anyway. We're all better off saving our energy for when the real adventures begin next year."

"*Wren*. Be realistic," Dash chides. "You're already in it up to your neck with this girl. The way you're brooding around her is classic Jacobi obsession material. And she didn't open the desk, which I know is just driving you *insane*."

I wish he wasn't right about that. I shouldn't be so bent out of shape over the fact that Elodie didn't discover the mangled frog's legs I planted in her desk. It was a schoolboy tactic, childish as fuck, but I took one look at her the other night and I knew she'd be squeamish. If she hadn't figured it out beforehand and she'd just lifted the lid on that desk, she'd have lost her freaking mind. She robbed me of that experience, and yeah, I'm salty as fuck about it. "Don't worry. I have a plan," I say.

"Fucking hell. Sounds ominous," Dash groans. His accent always makes cursing sound way more fun. "You're not planning on breaking into her room, are you? Because the last time you did that—"

I light the weed in the pipe, sucking the thick, sweet smoke into my mouth, then blow it at Dash, who sits up, alert. He holds his hand out, gesturing for a hit of his own. The guy doesn't know how to be embarrassed. If he did, he'd do something to hide the tent his erect cock is making out the front of his pants. And I'm not talking two-man adventure racing tent. I'm talking a palatial eight-man tent with a separate fucking living area. His dick must be fucking killing him. "You can't change the subject with Mary Jane," he admonishes, taking a deep, heavy hit from the pipe. "My short-term memory's bomb proof. I remember the shit you got yourself into the last time you broke into a girl's room. And *that* room? God, you've gotta be fucking insane. If you wanna fuck the little French girl, then do it and get it out of your system, post haste. Anything else, and, well..." His eyes roll back into his head, his eyelids fluttering closed. "Anything else would be bad news for you, my friend. You know it's true."

7

ELODIE

Nᴜɴ Eʟɪᴢᴀʙᴇᴛʜ Mᴀʀʏ Wʜɪᴛʟᴏᴄᴋ was hanged for suspected witchcraft in the rectory of Wolf Hall's tiny gothic church in 1794. I learn this on Wednesday, while exploring the old tumbledown building with Carina after our last class of the day. We sift through piles of broken glass from the shattered windows, the shards worn smooth and opaque like colorful old sea glass, and Carina finds an ancient rosary. It's beautiful, the beads alternating between what looks like labradorite and solid silver, and on the end a large, delicate crucifix dangles, cast in gold. We're both too scared that it might have belonged to Elizabeth Mary Whitlock to keep it, so we bury it in the crowded graveyard at the rear of the church next to a headstone so old that the lettering carved into the stone has worn away to nothing.

On Thursday, Carina guides me to a dark, cramped crawlspace at the back of a cleaning closet at the end of our hallway and urges me inside.

At first, I'm petrified. I am not good with tight spaces. Over the past three years, I've done everything I can to master my fear, from locking myself in closets, to even tighter spaces where I can hardly move at all, learning how to breathe and to overcome my roaring terror. Against all odds, I can now endure the pressing claustrophobia, but the prospect of crawling into the dark, narrow space is still a daunting one.

Aside from my panic, I'm also suspicious. Carina, with her easy smile and her friendly, gregarious laughter, treats me like we've been friends our entire lives. I've never met a girl like her. An ugly part of me—the part that's been the subject of plenty of ridicule and abuse at the hands of other female students in the past—thinks she might be setting me up for some epic prank.

I decide to trust my gut, though, and I climb inside, ignoring the frantic thrumming of my heart, holding my breath to keep from inhaling in the dust, and I scramble forward on my belly until I'm spat out inside a huge, cavernous attic with a bank of small, dirty windows overlooking the lawn and the turning circle in front of the academy.

Carina whoops, delighted, as I explore the abandoned, cluttered attic, watching me with open glee as I scavenge through travel chests and rotten cardboard boxes, amazed by the treasures I find inside.

On Friday, the girls from the fourth floor—Pres, the redhead, Rashida, Chloe, Loren, and even Damiana all gather in Carina's room, which is at least twice the size of mine, and we all sprawl out on beanbags, pillows, and cushions, and watch *Love Actually*, which everyone's amused to learn I haven't seen before. We share popcorn. We talk about our respective countries, our childhoods, and our differing yet oh-so-similar upbringings, and everything feels both new and very much the same.

I was thrilled when I learned that I was coming back to the States. I would have been thrilled to get sent anywhere, so long as it was away from *him*. Now that I'm here and I'm actually making friends, though, it feels like I could actually be happy enough here. I'm enjoying my classes, and even Damiana seems to have defrosted a little. The only potential thorns in my side are the Riot House boys, and not a one of them has even so much as looked in my direction since Tuesday.

My room is as cold and drafty as a morgue, and the lights flicker every time I turn them on. My bed is lumpy and uncomfortable as fuck, but with Colonel Stillwater on the other side of the world, I haven't slept this well in…well, ever.

Wren aside, I'd say, as first weeks at new schools go, this one's been fairly successful.

Saturday morning arrives, and my bedroom door crashes open with an earsplitting *BANG!* I hurl myself out of bed, heart slamming in my chest, adopting an automatic fighting stance that has Carina, dressed in a bright orange jumpsuit, arching her right eyebrow at me like I'm certifiably insane. "Whoa, now, Jackie Chan. What the hell is this all about? Are you about to karate chop my neck or something?"

I take a calming breath, straightening out of my defense stance as quickly as possible, laughing nervously under my breath. "Ahh, y'know. Military father. He used to drill me harder than he drilled his men." This is not a lie. It's the truth. Just not the whole truth. She's been amazing and welcoming, but I don't know Carina well enough to be spilling that shit just yet. Maybe I'll never know her well enough.

Carina cringes, patting me on the shoulder sympathetically. "I literally thank god every day that my parents are just lazy shits and not army personnel. I'm not cut out to be duck rolling from beds and preparing to fight a split second after I wake up. You amaze me."

Uneasy, I tug at the oversized Real Madrid soccer jersey I slept in last night, wrangling it into position so that it covers the tops of my legs. Seems like Carina bought my half-truth, or at least she didn't suspect that it *was* only a half truth. Catching sight of the old digital clock on the nightstand, I groan at the time. "Oh my god, Carina. What are you trying to do to me? It's six forty-five!"

"That's what time we always get up."

"During the week! It's Saturday. Am I not entitled to a lie-in? A little R and R? It's cruel to wake a girl up before eight on the weekend."

Carrie laughs. "If you're not up and out before seven thirty on Saturdays, Harcourt makes you help serve community breakfast in the dining hall. You get stuck cleaning pots and pans until midday. And if you're not out of the building by eight on a Sunday, Mr. Clarence makes you attend his non-denominational gratitude service, and that, my friend, is a fate worse than death itself."

Ah. Damn. I guess there's still a lot to learn where the day-to-day operations at Wolf Hall are concerned. Community breakfast sounds like torture. And non-denominational gratitude service? Yeah, fuck that. "How long do I have to get ready?" I ask, already bee-lining for the closet to grab an outfit.

"Twenty-five minutes," Carina advises, checking the time on her cell phone. "Shower, makeup and hair. Let's go. One second over and we're gonna be stuck ladling porridge onto food trays like convicts on mess hall duty, and I did not wear this jumpsuit to be ironic. *Go, go, go, go, go!*"

* * *

For the past five days, my world has been Wolf Hall. The classes, the people, the building itself…it's all been so overwhelming, so much information thrown at me all at once, that my mind hasn't considered the world beyond the edge of the academy's immaculately kept lawns. Now that I'm in Carina's beaten up yet classic Firebird, speeding down the long, winding roads with the wind blowing in my hair, I suddenly feel free. Like absolutely anything might be possible.

New Hampshire is a breathtaking *feuille morte* kaleidoscope: all burnt oranges, umber, russet, crimson and carmine. The winter trees, still stubbornly grasping onto their colorful autumn foliage, whip past in a blur as Carina burns through the chicanes and hairpin corners that lead down the mountain like she was a rally driver in a past life. Soon, we arrive in the town of Mountain Lakes itself—a dozen or so quaint little shops; a high school; a football field, and not much else—and I'm pleasantly surprised to discover that the town *is* actually bordered by two beautiful, vast and shining lakes.

Carina pulls up outside a diner called Screamin' Beans and slams the parking brake on the car before the vehicle's even stopped moving. I haven't driven much since I passed my driver's test in Israel, so I can hardly judge, but Carina's a little hair-raising behind the wheel. "Come on," she commands. "These guys have the best breakfast, but they stop serving super early so the Wolf Hall kids don't bother them."

"Aren't we Wolf Hall kids?" I call after her, as she bounds toward the diner entrance.

"We don't count! Come on!"

Carina picks out her own table—a corner booth next to a vintage juke box—and makes herself at home. I sit opposite her, wondering exactly how many coffees she had before she kicked down my bedroom door this morning. It's unholy that anyone should have this much energy at such a horrendous hour, even if the sun *is* shining.

"Well, well, well. Look who it is. Miss Carina Mendoza, in the flesh. Thought you'd gone and died up on that mountain, girl. Where you been? All our lemon cake went bad last weekend. We don't make it for anybody but you." The waitress who comes to serve us smiles broadly at my friend, leaning casually against the side of the booth. She slaps her notepad on top of Carina's head, studying me suspiciously out of the corner of her eye. "And who, pray tell, is *this*?"

"Jazzy, this is Elodie. Elodie, this is Jazzy. She's worked at Screamin' Beans for the past twenty-five years."

"*Twenty*, girl! *Twenty* years! Don't go makin' me older than I already am!" She pretends to sulk, stuffing her notepad back into the front pocket of her apron. "I take it you don't want no lemon cake today. No coffee neither."

"Oh my god, Jazzy, you know five years wouldn't make a differ-ence," Carina says, catching hold of her by the hand. "You're gonna look eighteen until the day you die. Pleeeeeeaaasssee don't take away the coffee."

Jazzy laughs, rolling her eyes. "Okay, okay. I'd hate to have to see a poor, undernourished, impoverished child such as yourself having to beg for some caffeine," she says, laying it on thick. "I'll be right back. You want coffee too, child?" she asks me.

"Hot tea, please. If you've got it. And a little cold milk on the side?"

I don't think my out-of-the-ordinary order does me any favors in Jazzy's eyes. Straight black drip coffee, she can get on board with, but hot tea with milk? She probably thinks that's a posh Wolf Hall kid type of order. She jots down my request all the same and hurries off in the direction of the kitchen.

"Most of the other kids drive over to Franconia in search of a Starbucks. They don't realize the coffee here is so good," Carina says.

"And you haven't been going around, sharing your secret?"

"Hell no!" She smirks, waggling her eyebrows. "This is my cloak and dagger spot. I only bring the best, most trustworthy people here."

"Glad to know I made the cut."

She's about to hit me with a come-back, her eyes dancing and sharp, but then the mirth radiating from her abruptly vanishes. She sees something over my shoulder and everything about her changes. The bell above the diner door jangles, announcing a new customer, and Carina shrinks down into her seat, all of her enthusiasm vaporizing in a puff of smoke. "Yeah, well. I'm usually very good at gauging who should be allowed into the Screamin' Beans club, but sometimes even *I* make an error in judgement."

Behind me, a male voice with a thick English accent asks for a table for three, and my insides tangle themselves into a knot at warp speed. Impressive how quickly I go from relaxed and at ease to frozen and uncomfortable. Carina and I must be quite the sight, sliding down into our seats.

"We can get our breakfast to go?" I suggest. "Drive until we find somewhere nice, or we could eat by the lake?" It's shitty to have to leave just because Dashiell's showed up, more than likely with Pax and Wren in tow, but we're not at Wolf Hall now. I don't want the weekend ruined by their bullshit.

Carina shakes her head. "He's seen us. It'll look weak if we bail now. We should just chill and make the most of it. I'm sorry, I didn't mean to react that way, it's just...Dashiell knows exactly how to get under my skin."

She might not want to talk about it, but my curiosity's getting the better of me. I have to ask her. I have to know. "I take it something happened between you guys? Something...*romantic*?"

"Hah!" She shakes her head, looking up at the ceiling. "Romantic? Yeah. I guess you could call it that. He was charming, and polite. A real gentleman. Treated me with respect. Took me out to dinner. Wined and dined me. Made me feel so special that I thought I was the only girl he'd ever been interested in. And that fucking *accent*. He got me good, Elle. I swear, I've always prided myself on being smarter than the dumb girl who gets duped by a handsome guy with a few cheesy pickup lines. I should have seen it coming. I should have seen *him* coming a mile off, but he totally blindsided me.

"I was saving myself. Hadn't even let a guy graze my fucking kneecap with an index finger before. I was a virgin. And I'm talking *virgin*. No experience whatsoever. And then, low and behold, Lord Dashiell Lovett the fourth comes along with his family fucking title, and his airs and graces, and he looked deep into my eyes and told me that he loved me, and I just..." She throws up her hands in disgust. Her knuckles bang the table, clipping the wood when she drops them. "I just spread my damn legs for him like it was nothing. Two days later, he asked me to meet him in the observatory after dinner. So I went along, excited about getting to see him, getting to kiss him, getting to tell him that I'd fallen head over heel in love with him...and I walk in to find Amalie Gibbons on her knees with his dick aaaaaallllll the way down her throat."

A tear streaks down her cheek, and my heart squeezes tightly, aching for her. Reaching across the table, I hold her hand, shaking my head. I don't even know what to say...

"And you know the worst part?" she says, laughing shakily, batting away the rogue tears. "The worst part was that he didn't even care. He wasn't embarrassed. Didn't scramble to push her off him, or pull his pants up, or come after me. He saw me, standing there in the doorway, saw the hurt and the pain in my eyes...and he fucking *laughed*. He said—" She clears her throat, frowning deeply. "He said, 'Looks like I might have made a scheduling error. Can you come back in an hour? I should be ready to go again by then.'"

"Wow. What an unbelievable prick." So, so, SO shitty. Who does something like that? *Any guy with money, a title, an accent, and a name like fucking* Dashiell? a voice in the back of my head offers. It seems so obvious after the fact, but I get it. Carina *is* a smart girl, but guys like Dashiell are master manipulators when they want to be. They're exceptionally talented and very well practiced at getting what they want. It can feel so *real* at the time...

I can't count how many guys I've come across like Dashiell Lovett. The only reason I never fell for their bullshit and gave them precisely what they wanted was because my father would have murdered me ten times over and then some. He only let me hang out with Levi because he knew he was gay. It never ceased to amaze me that my father could hate so many people to such brilliant and astonishing degrees, for all kinds of stupid, pointless reasons, but he never had a problem with me having a gay friend.

"I wish I'd been here then," I tell her. "I'd have kicked his ass for you, no question."

"There's still time," she jokes, smiling lopsidedly through a fresh round of tears. "You're a good friend. Maybe if you *had* been here, you might have been able to talk some sense into me and stop me from making such a fool of myself."

"Don't do that. You didn't make a fool of yourself, okay. You trusted someone who lied to you and broke your heart. That reflects poorly on him, not you. At some point karma's gonna come along and render him infertile as punishment."

"Jesus. I really hope not."

Goddamnit, what the hell is it with these boys, sneaking up on people? I should have been paying attention to Dashiell's precise whereabouts, especially since we're talking about him, but I dropped the damn ball. Dressed like he's off to watch a polo match, the smug motherfucker leans up against the counter, popping a toothpick into his mouth as he glances from me to Carina. His gaze settles on her, full of contradicting emotions. For a second, I think he looks remorseful, but then I see the cruel delight flickering in his blue eyes, and I want to leap up out of my seat and kick the fucker right in the kneecap.

"Can you kindly fuck off," I hiss. "This is a private conversation. You're not welcome at this table."

Dashiell looks to his left and then to his right, his eyebrows hiking up to his hairline. "Sorry, *mon amour.* I'm over here at the counter, minding my business. What fault is it of mine if you're talking loud enough to wake a dead man and give him a hard on? I heard something about Amalie Gibbons on her knees with some-one's dick in her mouth and I lost all sense of propriety. And then..." He laughs, holding up a finger, "...and then, I remembered that *I* had Amalie Gibbons on her knees and *my* dick was in her mouth, and things just got really messy. Because that was a really fun time, girls. A *really* fun time. I am sad you don't want to play with me anymore, though, Carrie. I guess I should have said I was sorry or something. Better late than never, though, right?"

Ho-ly shit. The stones on this prick.

Jazzy arrives with our drinks at the worst possible moment. She hums under her breath, swaying from side to side as she sets Carina's coffee down in front of her and then arranges my tea paraphernalia for me. Her smile disappears when she sees that Carina's been crying and her cheeks are still wet. "What in god's name..." She looks at me like I'm responsible for her friend's distress, but then she sees Dashiell loitering by the counter and her expression darkens. "Oh no. No, no, no. I don't know who you are or what your name is, boy, but you better be outta my sight in two seconds flat or you are gonna wish you had never been born."

Dashiell nearly purrs. "Ma'am, I am a nihilist. I don't really care if I live or I die. Mustering up the amount of energy it would require to wish I'd never been born is very unlikely on my part. I commend the rousing speech, though. Can I get a wet cappuccino when you have a second?"

Jazzy just stares at him. "Boy, you musta got knocked on the head when you was a child. You ain't getting no wet nothin'.' Now get the fuck outta here before I call the cops on your ass."

I admire Jazzy's tenacity. She's a waitress in a small-town diner, probably scraping by on minimum wage. She knows Dashiell's a Wolf Hall student. She must know that, with one call from Dashiell to his father, Screamin' Beans will have been bought out and shut down before she can even aim a kick in the spoiled bastard's pants. Still, she speaks her mind; she won't let herself be cowed by him. A brave woman, indeed.

Dashiell grins. It's unsettling, that grin. It makes me want to duck for cover. "You remind me of my grandmother. I didn't like her very much. She was a very outspoken woman." He runs his tongue over his teeth, shoving away from the counter. "I'll honor your request and make myself scarce. My friends might order a to-go for me, though. I'd appreciate it if you kept the saliva to a minimum. There's a love." He stalks off without acknowledging Carina again.

"That smug little piece of shit. I'm betting he never had his hide tanned for him. I oughta do him a favor and put him over my knee. Wallop the shit out of him on account'a that smart ass mouth of his."

"I wouldn't, Jazz," Carina says morosely. "He'd only enjoy it."

An hour later, after we've picked over our meals and emptied our coffee cups, neither of us really in the mood to hang out anymore, Carina drives me back to the academy. She stops in the middle of the road a couple of miles before the long, winding driveway that leads to Wolf Hall. She sits in the middle of the road with the car engine idling, staring straight ahead out of the windscreen.

"Carina? What is it?"

She blinks, as if coming back into her body. "On the right. Through the trees. Look hard enough, and you'll see it."

"See what?" I squint over my right shoulder, peering through the thick tree foliage.

"The house," she says. "Riot House. That's where they live. The three of them, together—their little fortress against the world."

It takes some effort and a re-angling of my head, but there...yes, I see the outline of the building now. A three-story affair—wood, concrete, glass—so expertly blended within the camouflage of the forest that it'd be impossible to pick out if you didn't already know it was there.

"If you ever find yourself stranded and alone on this road, do *not* go knocking on that door for help, Elodie," Carina mutters. "Whatever you do, no matter the circumstances, do *not* step foot inside Riot House. For better or for worse, you won't come out the same."

I didn't even see Wren back at the diner, but I'd felt his presence sure enough. As Carina throws the car into gear and slams her foot on the gas, I experience that same prickling sensation again. It feels as though Wren Jacobi is watching me. And Carina can speed away from Riot House as fast as she likes.

I won't be able to escape that place...

...or *him*.

8

WREN

BACK AT THE DINER, leaning against the table in our booth, I'd pressed the flat, dull blade of the butter knife into the fleshy pad of my thumb, staring at the back of her head, wondering what the hell was going on inside her skull.

I've *never* cared what a girl's thinking or feeling before, but I can't stop myself from trying to piece together the enigma that is Elodie Stillwater. Does she miss her old life? Her old friends? Does she miss the sun, and the heat, and the ocean, and the sand? Would she kill to be back there in Israel with her father and the life she was accustomed to?

I've become a parody of myself as I walk the old, familiar pathways to my classes at Wolf Hall, trying to maintain an exterior of practiced boredom and complete disinterest, when in truth, I am anything but disinterested. I am anything but bored. For the first time in a very, *very* long time, my ears are pricked, my mind's engaged, and every part of my being is turned toward a girl I do not know in the slightest.

I want to know everything there is to know about her, and I want to possess that knowledge, to own it, just as I want to own her. I'm determined to make her my creature. My pet. The challenge of such an inconceivable task makes my dick harder than fucking tungsten.

"All right. Settle down. Eyes on me, friends. I need to know each and every one of you is listening. That includes you, Jacobi. Come on. Shades off. Why the hell are you wearing shades indoors anyway?"

Fitz is wearing his corduroy blazer today. Baby shit green. He only wears that blazer when he's been reading *Byron* or *Rilke* and fancies himself one of the romantics. Poor bastard. He hasn't been tortured enough in this life to make a good poet. With exaggerated care, I slide my Wayfarers down the bridge of my nose, eyes drilling into him as he dumps his record bag down at his feet. I don't have to explain myself to him. I'm sure as hell not gonna tell him that I wore sunglasses to this English class so I could watch a certain delicately beautiful student sitting on the other side of the room, undisturbed. "You know me, Fitz," I rumble. "You *always* have my undivided attention."

He pulls a face. "Yeah. Right." No come back. He mustn't have had a coffee yet. Even as I'm thinking this, our illustrious leader flips back the front of his record bag and pulls out a Thermos, popping the little white cap from the top of it and unscrewing the seal, flooding the room with the bitter, fragrant smell of arabica. "It's that time of year again, guys. Storm season. We've had a number of new students since the start of last winter, so this infor-mation's important. Even if you were a student here last winter, I'd still appreciate a few seconds of your time to go over this. Think of it as a refresher."

On the other side of the room, sitting on a yellow, worn sofa beneath a cliché and utterly classless print of Gustav's Klimt's 'The Kiss,' Carina nudges Elodie with her elbow and whispers some-thing into her ear. In my mind, it's me leaning into her, bringing my nose to her hair, close enough to catch the scent of her and store it to memory. I've imagined what the silken, smooth texture of her skin looks like up close, too. I've pored over her image on electronic screens and studied it committed in ink, but I haven't held her down and inspected her features in person yet. I want to. More than anything, I want her underneath me, straining against me, as I figure out the way she frowns. I want to see what her fear looks like. Most importantly, I want to see the lie on her. The one all girls try to tell, when their panic catalyzes with their desire and they try to comprehend their own traitorous nature.

"In case you haven't bothered to check the weather report over the past twenty-four hours, the entire state's about to face down a major storm front," Fitz says. "These storms can get pretty hairy. Lightning strikes. Flash flooding. Luckily for us, we're on the top of a mountain, so we aren't in any danger of getting washed away. Wolf Hall's basically bomb proof. It was built to withstand crazy weather. The wind can get pretty treacherous up here, though. Once the storm hits, there'll be strict rules in place. No venturing off academy grounds. No leaving the building in general. If things start to look really sketchy, there have been occasions when Principal Harcourt deems it fit to move everyone into the basement, just in case. In the unlikely event that we need to evacuate the site, every student needs to be aware of the protocols set in place..."

Fitz rambles on about the buses that will come to take us down the mountain if a state of emergency is declared. He goes over the emergency exit points, first aid points, blah blah fucking blah. I turn off, bored to my back fucking teeth. I've heard it all a thousand times before. Elodie hasn't, though. She's transfixed, hanging on Fitz's every word, taking mental notes in case disaster comes looking for us here at Wolf Hall. A strange, unfamiliar part of me wants to reassure her and let her know that there's nothing to worry about. The rest of me, the part I'm intimately acquainted with, relishes the sight of her, all timorous and concerned.

I like her clothes. Her *'smile if you're dead inside'* t-shirt's just as cliché as the Klimt painting, but it tells me something about the way she sees herself. Her distressed jeans are so tight, they look like they've been painted onto her thighs. My palms ache with the idea of what her skin, muscle and bone might feel like through the worn, soft denim. The scruffy Chuck Taylors look so lived in that I can tell she's put hundreds of miles on them. I prefer the Doc Martins she usually wears, but I enjoy the way the Chucks make her feet look small and petite. My little Elodie has the feet of a fucking geisha.

"That said, these warnings sound scary, but there really is nothing to worry about. This will be my tenth year teaching at Wolf Hall. A few fallen trees are the worst I've ever seen. Go about your day as normal. Do your work, make sure you follow the rules, and everything will be business as usual."

Fitz's statement doesn't make Elodie feel better. Our eyes lock from across the room, and the panic in her gaze makes my pulse soar. She frowns, creases forming across her forehead, and I realize that I'm staring without the convenience of my Ray Bans to disguise my interest.

Look away, Jacobi.

Look away.

I should, but I don't. I'm trapped by the pressure of her eyes on me. A slow, cunning smile begs to be unleashed across my face, and I relent, giving it free rein. Elodie jumps, startled, like I just dumped a bucket of ice-cold water over her head. She looks away first, and the satisfaction that courses slow like tar through my veins feels like victory.

"Miss Stillwater, are you okay? There's no need to look so worried," Fitz says. "I promise, it's gonna be fine. If you're worried about anything, come and find me. I'm nearly always here in my room. Aside from sharing the brilliance of Lord Byron with you—"

Oh, Fitz. I can read you like a fucking book.

"—it's also my job to keep you guys safe."

Damiana shoves her hand in the air. "Can all of us rely on you to be our knight in shining armor, Doctor Fitzpatrick? Or does your heroic valor only extend as far as Elodie?"

Fitz's disgusted look is dirtier than the sock Pax uses to jerk off into. "I'm here for all of my students, Dami. You're well aware of that. No need for ugliness."

Damiana snorts. "I couldn't be ugly if I tried, Doc. And you're the one showing favoritism to the new girl because she's got that doe-eyed innocent thing down and she's rocking a great pair of tits. I'd say *that* was ugly, if you asked me."

"I didn't. No one did. Thank you, as always, though, for your valuable input, Damiana. If *anyone* feels unsafe over the next forty-eight hours, please know that my door is open to everyone and anyone, regardless of their—"

Dashiell won't look at a girl unless she's got double Ds. Pax... god knows what the fuck Pax likes. He's never demonstrated any sort of pattern where the women that he selects are concerned. He's far more interested in their personalities. That sounds like bullshit, but it's true. There are certain flaws and weaknesses Pax looks for in a girl, usually heavily revolving around their daddy issues. Me? I like my girls to have smaller breasts. Anything more than a handful is a waste. I didn't need Dami's shady comment to draw attention to Elodie's chest—I've spent plenty of time thinking about it before—but since she's brought the matter up, I treat myself to a cursory glance at Elodie's tits.

Her shirt is two sizes too big, swamping her frame, but there's a suggestion of breasts there. And the suggestion of breasts is always far more exciting to me than, say, Damiana's obvious, in-your-face cleavage. That shit's grotesque.

Fitz rambles on, talking about safety and using common sense. I spend a lazy thirty seconds picturing how pretty Elodie's lips would look, parted and wet, if I slipped my hand up underneath that tent of a t-shirt, yanked down the cup of her bra and viciously rolled her nipple between my fingers.

When I snap out of my deviant reverie, Kylie Sharp is reading aloud from a bound book, but no one's paying attention. Damiana snaps her gum. Dashiell's eyes are fixed on Carina. Pax is openly asleep, head lolling on his shoulders, his arms folded across his chest, legs crossed at the ankles. Fitz's gaze is on his shoes, and—whoa, whoa, whoa... *Hold the fuck up.* Covertly, Fitz looks up, glancing at Elodie out of the corner of his eye. I wait for him to look away, but he lingers on her, just that little bit too long. The muscle in his jaw tics. That's when he finally looks away.

What the fuck was that, Fitz? I do not fucking think so, homie.

As if my thoughts were piped directly into his mind, Fitz's head snaps up, his eyes meeting mine, where they waver for a beat. He knows exactly what I've seen, and the motherfucker doesn't seem to be worried. He knows me, so he should also know that I don't take well to other guys eyeing my property. Possession, regardless of the fact that the other party is *unaware* they're someone else's property, is nine tenths of the law. And I've always been willing to defend what's mine.

Fitz has the audacity to smile at me.

Smile.

That piece of fucking shit.

Overhead, a deep, threatening rumble of thunder growls over the top of Kylie's dark words.

"I had a dream, which was not all a dream.
The bright sun was extinguish'd, and the stars
Did wander darkling in the eternal space,
Rayless, and pathless, and the icy earth
Swung blind and blackening in the moonless air..."

The thunder crashes again—a portent of what's to come, an ill omen, sending an anticipatory shiver racing down my spine. When I turn away from the delusional English teacher, Elodie Stillwater is staring at *me.*

Over the next thirty minutes, I catch her watching me again and again, peering at me from under dark eyelashes, and every time it happens, my resolve strengthens. There's a connection here. A bizarre, uncomfortable link that makes me sweat every time I think about severing it. I wonder if she feels panicked, and distressed, and turned on whenever she hears *my* voice.

She's the first out of the door when the bell goes. She ducks her head, throws her bag over her shoulder, clutching a turquoise file to her chest, and she whirls out of the room before Carina's even on her feet.

I haven't been paying attention to Carina. I haven't even spared her a sidelong glance. She is Dashiell's self-imposed punishment, not mine. It looks like her skin is crawling and she's about to throw up as she navigates a pathway through Fitz's worn, haphazard furniture, slowly crossing the room toward me.

Fucking wonderful.

I know what's coming next.

Carina, Carina. Sweet little Carrie. The mother hen of the fourth floor. Fuck knows when Harcourt designated her protector over all new female students, but she must take her role very seriously if she's willing to come here and face *me* down.

She clears her throat, announcing her presence. I'm looking down at my cell, feigning ignorance, but of course I know perfectly well that she's there. "*Carina.*"

"You could have the decency to put the phone down for a second." Her voice is colder than the glacial tone my ex-step-mother used to affect whenever she addressed my father. Smiling wickedly, I give her what she wants: I raise my head, looking her right in the eye. It's been my experience that plenty of people want to get my attention. When they have it, they very quickly want to give it back. Carina's no exception. She flinches under the weight of my gaze. She's stronger than most, though. She doesn't look away.

"I've got one word for you, Jacobi. *Don't.*"

Oh, ho, ho. This is gonna be entertaining. "*Don't* be so devastatingly handsome? *Don't* be smarter than every single man in this place? *Don't* make my heart flutter in my chest every time you look at me?"

Carina clenches her jaw, nostrils flaring. "You're many things, Wren, but slick isn't one of them. You know exactly what I'm talking about. I've seen you looking at her. Just *don't.*" She spins on the balls of her feet and hurries toward the exit, making her escape before I can toy with her some more. Carrie never was any fun. I have no idea what Dashiell sees in her.

"That looked like a cutting exchange."

The classroom's empty now, bar myself and Fitz. Dashiell and Pax might be my boys, but neither one of them can stand Fitz. They have their reasons; they won't linger in his classroom a second longer than is required to maintain their grades.

Casting a menacing scowl in the teacher's direction, I get to my feet. "I'm pretty pissed at you, old man."

Fitz leans against the writing desk next to him, resting his hip against the wood. With his arms folded across his chest and a wry smirk on his face, he looks like he's the one who's pissed at me. "We've been through this," he says, letting out a weighty sigh. "You've made your intentions perfectly clear. I've told you I think it's a bad idea. After what happened with Mara, you've—"

I grab his face with one hand, digging my fingers into his cheeks. The stubble on his chin bites into my hand, bringing back memories I'd rather forget. "I'd appreciate it if you didn't bring her up again, y'know. This situation's nothing like what happened with Mara. You, more than anyone, should know that. Right?"

My blood turns to ice as Fitz's eyes roll back into his skull; he looks like he's caught in that confounding middle ground between fury and ecstasy. "Right. Yeah. I—you're right."

"Elodie's mine. I've already cleared it with the boys. And I don't need to clear *shit* with you. You won't go near her."

Nodding, Fitz reaches up and takes hold of me by the wrist, slowly pulling my hand away from his face. "I won't go near her." He swallows hard.

I leave his room just as the first bout of rain begins to lash at the windows.

9

ELODIE

+972 3 556 3409: I can't believe you're gone. Everyone at Mary's is devastated. We're all in shock. We'll never forget you, Elle. You'll always be missed. I love you – Levi x

I smile down at the WhatsApp message from my friend, relieved that he's finally reached out. Dad replaced my phone with a device from a US cell provider when he packed me off to the airport, and I lost all of my numbers. And annoyingly, Levi's one of those *'technology is evil and I will have no part in social media'* guys, so I've had to wait for him to make the first move. The tone of his message is super weird, though.

ME: Wow. No need to go making out like I died, dude. It's not like I moved to Mars. We can figure out a way to hang in the holidays if your mom doesn't whisk you off to Switzerland or something. How's everything going? Has Professor Marshall checked himself into rehab yet?

Our old science tutor was forever nipping into the back of his room to sneak a hit from his hip flask. There were rumors he was using the chemicals on hand in his lab to concoct his own—

My phone buzzes, it's loud ringtone echoing off the walls as I climb the endless stairs up toward my room. I cringe, silencing it, checking to see if there are any members of faculty in sight. Phones are prohibited in common areas. Luckily, I'm already on the second floor and the only people in close proximity to me are other students.

"Hey, dude! I wasn't expecting you to call right away. I'm almost back at my room. Give me a second to—"

"*Elodie?*"

There's something about Levi's tone that stops me in my tracks. He sounds...I'm not sure what he sounds like. Something isn't right, though. "Lee? What's up? Is everything okay? What's happened?"

"You're *alive?*" he whispers. I've been friends with Levi for two years now. Not a long time in most people's books, but we've crammed a lot into those seven hundred and thirty odd days. I know him inside and out, and he knows me, too. Every dark, dumb, stupid, embarrassing little secret I've ever had. From Sweden, he's fairly representative of his people. Stoic, serious, ever calm and deeply grounded, he doesn't really let anything affect him. He keeps his emotions close to his chest. Those words, though...his voice was choked with tears when he said them. My friend is fucking *crying*.

"What are you talking about, *I'm alive?* Of course I'm alive. I'm in New Hampshire."

Levi sniffs, making a strangled sound. "I'm—I'm sorry, I just need a..." He stops talking. Draws in a deep breath. He sounds like he's trying to compose himself. And then he says, "Your father told the dean you were in an accident, Elodie. The entire school's been in mourning all week."

I've reached the fourth floor landing now. Thankfully I've left the stairs behind or I'd probably fall face-first down them. I slap my hand out against the wall, steadying myself as my vision dims around the edges. "Sorry, *what* did you say?"

Levi coughs. I can picture him in his bedroom back at Mary Magdalene's, in his pajamas, perched on the edge of his bed, his wonderfully brown eyes vacant as he tries to process this news.

I'm alive.

I'm speaking to him on the phone, back from the fucking dead.

The whole thing is too confusing to comprehend. "I'm really struggling here, Lee. Sounds like you are, too. Can you explain what you meant when you said my father told the dean I was dead, though? 'Cause my brain's melting out of my ears right now."

"He came to the school on Monday. Showed up with a full military guard. We thought there was some sort of threat to the school at first. Then Ayala saw him with the dean. She said he talked to him for a second in the hall, that Dean Rogers looked shocked and tried to put his hand on Colonel Stillwater's shoulder, but he backed away, spoke for another brief second, and then marched off, got back into his car and disappeared. Next thing we know, we're being pulled into our home rooms and we're being told that you were in a plane crash over the weekend. They said you didn't make it."

"*What?*" What the *fuck* is he talking about? Why the hell would my father tell such a vicious, flagrant lie? It makes no sense. "He didn't do that. He couldn't. I mean…" I mean, I can *totally* imagine him doing it. On his nicest day, he's a vile monster who doesn't give a flying fuck about anyone else but himself and his own precious career. Why would he have said *that*, though? He could have told the staff at Mary Magdalene's I was being relocated. It happens all the time—students coming and going from these kinds of schools.

"I'm sorry, I know this is crazy. I'm fine, though, Lee. Really, I promise, I'm totally fine. Never been better, in fact. I know you probably have a thousand questions, but I have to go. I need to call my father and find out what the fuck is going on before I have a nervous breakdown."

"Uhhh...okay," Lee says, laughing shakily. "All good. Call me back, though, yeah? If you don't, I'm gonna think I dreamed this up and you're still dead."

"Don't worry. I'm one hundred percent gonna call you back. You have my word."

I hang up, reeling from the brief conversation. Over the years, my father's done a shit load of cold, hurtful things to me. He's done the most heinous things imaginable. He's never told people that I'm fucking dead, though. *Dead*. What the fuck is wrong with him? I'm numb all over and dizzy as I hit the call button on the only number my new phone came equipped with when Colonel Stillwater gave it to me: the number to his personal aide.

The phone rings eight times. Nine times. Ten. I think it's about to go to voicemail, when Officer Emmanuel finally picks up. "Colonel Stillwater's office. How can I assist you?"

"Carl, it's Elodie." Carl's only been with my father for six months, but that's three months longer than any of his other military aides have lasted. Usually, the lucky ones are reassigned pretty quickly. The guys who had no strings to pull or favors to call in had to somehow make it through month after month of my father's explosive, borderline abusive behavior before he finally lost his temper with them and had them demoted to cleaning out latrines.

"Elodie? Great to hear from you. How are things Stateside? Are you enjoying being back home?" I like Carl, and I think Carl likes me. He was always appropriately apologetic whenever he had to pass on a hostile message from my father. It kinda felt like we were co-conspirators who empathized with one another, because we each knew what the other person had to deal with on a daily basis.

"I just got off the phone with one of my friends from Mary Magdalene's, Carl."

"Oh. Oh, man..." The chipper pitch in his voice takes a nose-dive. "Well. I can imagine you're pretty pissed right now," he says.

"I'm *confused* right now. I have a sneaking suspicion that I'll be angry soon, though." A group of girls pass me in the hallway, concerned looks on their faces. I realize what I must look like, hugging the wall, white as a sheet, tension pinching my features into a pained expression; I give them a tight smile to let them know everything's fine, even though it's not. "Why the hell did he do that, Carl? Why did my friend just call me in tears, devastated because he thought I was *dead*?"

"Urgh. I—I don't think you're gonna like the explanation."

"Spit it out, Carl!"

"Your father had me look into your old school's tuition rules. It turned out that the only way to get a partial refund for the semester you were already halfway through was if you were...was if you had died. So..."

Oh. My. God. Un-fucking-believable. "So, he told them I'd died. In order to get a partial refund for the remainder of the semester. What does that come to? Four thousand dollars?"

Carl gives up the exact amount reluctantly. "Not quite. Uh... two thousand, eight hundred."

"He has millions in the bank. MILLIONS!"

"I know..."

"He let my friends believe I'd died for the sake of two grand and change?"

"I did try and explain to him how it might make you feel. I suggested we tell you what was happening so you could let your friends know you were okay, but he—"

"But he didn't give a shit about hurting me, or hurting my friends, and he told you to keep your mouth shut, right?"

"Something like that."

"Jesus Christ."

"Sorry, Elodie. I should have sent you a heads-up."

With elastic, wobbly legs, I walk down the hall, toward the door to room 416. I need to get into my room and sit down before I fall down. "It's okay. It's not your fault. None of this is your fault. My father shouldn't be such an unbelievable bastard."

Carl titters nervously. He wasn't the one to call my father an unbelievable bastard, but these lines are generally recorded. If the top brass finds out he was even present to hear trash talk against my father, he could wind up in some serious shit.

"Want me to let him know you called? I could try and persuade him to reach out and explain his actions for himself?"

I'm at my door. I twist the handle, pushing it open. "God, no! No, that really won't be necessary. I already know the details, what good would talking to him—" I grind to a halt, halfway through the door, my ears suddenly filled with a high-pitched ringing. "—do?"

The room...holy fuck, my room has been *destroyed.*

My clothes are everywhere. My books, the few I brought with me from Tel Aviv, are scattered all over the floor, pages torn out of them in clumps, strewn all over the hardwood floorboards. Every single drawer has been ripped out of every single piece of furniture, the contents upended and thrown around in disarray. My photographs are in shreds. My laptop lays on its side beneath the window, its screen shattered and flickering, a spasm of color interrupting the static every few seconds. And there are feathers. Feathers everywhere. They've settled in a thick layer over everything like powdery, delicate snow, covering the Persian rug, and my shoes, and the comforter that's been ripped from the bed.

Both of my pillows are in shreds. With my mouth hanging open, I walk toward the bed, too many thoughts bumping into one another for any of this to make sense. The sheets have been ripped back from the mattress, and the mattress itself...a giant bowie knife protrudes from the center of the pillowtop mattress, it's rugged, carved handle glinting threateningly as I duck down to get a better look at it.

Whoever did this didn't just stab the bed once. Numerous three-inch long rents in the material, as well as longer, jagged tears where the foam and the springs inside the mattress have been exposed.

"...perhaps handled in a more...empathetic way. I can't really say any more than that, of course, but..."

Shit. Carl's still talking on the other end of the phone.

"Uh, sorry, Carl. Something...I've gotta go. I've gotta go into class now. Thanks for explaining things to me. I'd be really grateful if you didn't tell my dad I called."

"Of course. Anything for you, Miss. E."

"Thanks." I kill the call, dropping the cell phone to the ground. What...the fuck...happened in here? Who...who would do this? And why?

"Holy shit!"

Carina's standing in the doorway. She gapes at the chaos in horror, her eyes roving over my broken and ruined possessions. I see the china bird my mother gave me on my tenth birthday, smashed into tiny fragments and ground into the low pile of the rug, and a pained cry slips out of my mouth.

"What the fuck happened in here?" Carina whispers, stepping over an empty drawer. She comes and wraps her arms around me. It's here, stiff as a block of wood and unable to breathe properly, that I realize there are fierce, hot tears streaking down my cheeks.

"I don't know." It comes out as a moan. A cry. A desolate and mournful sound that shocks the hell out of me. It's not my clothes, or my books, or the bed that's done it. It's the bird. My mother's bird. She's dead, and she's gone, and there will never be another gift from her. The bird was all I had and now it's gone, too.

"Fuck. Come on. Come with me." Carina guides me out of my room and down the hall, past Presley and some of the other girls who came to watch the movie with us on Friday; I make an effort to avoid making eye contact with any of them. I can't face their open pity. I don't want to even acknowledge that this is happening right now.

Carina leaves me in her room and tells me to keep the door closed. She disappears for a long time, and I do nothing but stare into space, thinking about the bird...

The pink nail polish on Mom's fingernails when she gave it to me.

The little chip on its tiny orange beak that I used to rub my fingertip over whenever I cradled it to my chest.

The white of his chest, that faded to the blue of his back, that deepened to the dark, midnight blue at the tips of his wings.

The song Mom used to sing when she would hold it high in the air, pretending he was in flight and swooping around my head.

An eternity passes. Principal Harcourt comes to see me. Tells me they've already gotten another mattress out of storage for me —*"Very lucky, actually. It's brand new, still in the plastic!"* —and they've tidied up most of the mess. She informs me that it's safe to go back to my room now, which feels laughable and absolutely stupid because of course it's not fucking safe, someone *knifed my bed to death*, but I follow after her, my legs mechanically doing their job as I re-enter room 416.

Carina hugs me, an anxious smile on her face. My clothes have all been folded and returned to their rightful places in the closet and the chest of drawers. The furniture is reassembled and back where it belongs. The bed's been made up, sheets on the mattress to disguise its newness, and there are two fresh pillows plumped up like fluffy sheep, leaning against the headboard. Everything appears normal, if a little emptier now.

"There was no point keeping the books," Carina says softly. "We wrote down the titles, though. Principal Harcourt says she's going to get replacements for you."

My eyes sweep over the surfaces of the furniture, searching. "And the little china bird?"

"I'm afraid Gustav vacuumed up some of the pieces before he realized there was something on the rug," Principal Harcourt says from the doorway. Her voice is clipped and harsh, and she clearly doesn't want to be dealing with this anymore. She has better things to be doing at eight p.m. on a dark and stormy night, and none of them include pacifying a troubled teen about a broken ornament. "If you know where it came from, we'll happily get you another bird as well, Elodie. We'll have a new laptop for you soon hopefully. Just make a list of anything you need, and we'll make sure it's taken care of."

She turns around and walks off down the hall, her heels clipping angrily against the hardwood as she goes, leaving me and Carina alone in my bedroom, which now smells of chemicals, and plastic, and brand-new mattresses.

"Want me to stay with you?" Carina tucks a strand of hair back behind my ear. "I don't mind. We can watch something on my laptop. Polish off some chocolate? I have a stash in my room."

Wearily, I shake my head. "If it's alright with you, I'd kinda like to be alone. I just…this is all a lot to wrap my head around."

Carina looks unsure, but she accepts my decision with a sorry smile and gives me one last hug. "All right. I'm just at the other end of the hall if you need me, okay? Shoot me a text if you change your mind."

The moment she's gone, a fissure of lightning rips open the sky outside my bedroom window, bleaching the gardens and the trees outside the academy bone white, throwing tall, menacing shadows across the lawns. Darkness descends a moment later, shrouding everything in black, the rain continuing to hammer against the glass, but in that brief moment of illumination, I see something: a figure cloaked in shadow, standing at the mouth of the hedges that lead to the maze.

10

ELODIE

No one said a word about the knife sticking out of my bed.

Strikes me as a little odd, that fact.

I'd have thought it would have been the first thing Principal Harcourt wanted to discuss with me. Surely, she should have wanted to reassure me that I was safe, and that no one would be allowed to harm me here at Wolf Hall Academy. She seemed far more concerned with replacing my damaged property instead of getting to the bottom of the matter, though.

And no one, *no one*, had any ideas or suggestions as to who might have done this to my room, or what they were hoping to achieve by trashing my stuff.

The military-style training that passed as my childhood wasn't just physical, though. It was mental, too. I was taught how to read and assess a situation on sight from a very young age. I know how to read a room and take it apart, piece by piece, without touching a single thing. Colonel Stillwater trained me how to draw educated conclusions about a person's intent from their actions, and I've already drawn a number of educated conclusions about the break in, based on what I observed during the first five seconds after I walked into my room.

Whoever tore my room apart wasn't trying to threaten me.

Or at least that wasn't their main purpose, anyway.

The pages ripped out of the books? That was a pointed exercise, as were the drawers that were pulled off their runners and dumped upside down onto the floor. Whoever broke into my room was looking for something. Something concealed inside the jacket of another book or taped to the bottom of a drawer. And the pillows and bed? Same thing. They were searching for something that I don't think they found.

It's possible that the knife in the bed wasn't a threat. It's possible that whoever tossed my room got disturbed at some point, either by me or someone else, and they fled, leaving the blade buried up to the hilt by accident.

I have no reason to believe it was Wren who did this, but every cell in my body is screaming that it *was* him. The way he was staring at me during our English class...it looked like he was plotting terrible, evil things, and for some sick reason I couldn't force myself to stop looking at him. That hour, trapped inside Doctor Fitzpatrick's room, was an embarrassment. I should have had a little more self-control. I should have been able to block Wren out. I've never had an issue ignoring a guy with an attitude problem before, but this guy. *This guy.* He's different.

I suspect he's way more than I can handle. And invading my room? Breaking every personal possession I own? Destroying the only thing I really, truly hold dear? That's so cold and calculating that I'm actually worried I might not be able to manage the attentions of a guy like Wren Jacobi all by myself.

I'm too agitated to sleep, so I pace back and forth by the window, turning things over in my head. What the hell does he want from me, for fuck's sake? And what the hell did he want in this room? I know so little about Wren that guessing the answers to these questions is near impossible.

So, what do I do about him? What do I do about this troubling fascination I feel coiled like a snake around my insides every time I think his cursed name? How the fuck do I make it through these final months at Wolf Hall without falling foul of some terrible, dark act? Because it feels like something terrible and dark is about to happen. Just like the storm clouds amassed in the sky above Wolf Hall, this sense of foreboding presses down on me from above, filling me with dread.

From the way Carina reacts any time Wren, Dashiell or Pax are close by, my worries seem justified. Dashiell treated her horribly and broke her heart, but something in my gut tells me there's more to that story than she's letting on. I think she's keeping secrets, and I don't begrudge her them. We've only been friends for a little over a week. I can't expect her to trust me and take me into her confidence, when neither of us have figured each other out yet.

She warned me not to go near the boys or their precious Riot House, but shit. If there's something I need to know, something specific that could prevent me from getting seriously, actually hurt, then that *would* be useful information.

The best thing I can do is stay the hell away from Wren and his friends. Avoid contact with them at all costs. And get a fucking lock on my bedroom door, even though they're forbidden according to the Wolf Hall rule book. Fire Ordinances, or health and safety, or something like that. I dare anyone to challenge me over a little protection for myself and my belongings, now that this has happened, though.

By midnight, the storm outside has gotten so bad that the wind howls through the gaps in the windows, and the rain slamming down on top of the eaves above my window sounds like my father's old unit are practicing their drills right on top of me. It's so dark outside that I can barely make out the boughs of the huge live oaks that loom over the maze, tossing and groaning under the elemental assault.

I've lived in all kinds of different places, climates and landscapes. For a time, my mother insisted I stay with her for a year in Chicago when I was a child, but aside from that all of my other homes have been in warm climates. Deserts and beaches, for the most part due to my father's dislike of the cold. That he sent me to live in such a bitterly cold spot now really speaks to the fact that he plans on *never* visiting me here. Which is totally fine by me.

But this kind of weather feels unnatural to me. I've never experienced anything remotely like it. I've hated thunderstorms since I was a child, but my fear is amplified a thousand-fold tonight, given what took place in my room.

Urgh.

The clock on my cellphone reads 2.15 am when the storm reaches its climax. Somewhere, a shutter door bangs loudly, crashing every few seconds in the gale-force winds. I try to sleep, but with the normally silent building moaning and sighing so deafeningly, there's absolutely no way I can pass out. Agitated beyond measure, I get out of bed, throwing back the covers, shivering against the cold that seeps through the thin material of my pajamas. I stand in front of the window, baring my teeth at the sheet rain that obscures the view on the other side of the glass, willing it to fucking stop...

...which is when I see the light.

Not a streetlight, or a bedroom light: a flash of light, in the form of a narrow pillar of brilliant white, shooting straight up into the air from the very center of the maze.

I blink and it's gone.

Probably imagined it, Stillwater. No one's out there tonight, after two in the morning, in the pouring rain and cold. There's just no fucking way. No one in their right minds—

The pillar of light blazes through the darkness again, this time spearing straight up and then lowering so that it's shining directly at my window. I'm blinded as the intense beam hits me in the face. I step back, shielding my eyes, but the beam of light has already shifted, swinging from left to right through the maze.

"What the hell?" I squint out of the window, trying to see where it's coming from, but with the rain and the impenetrably thick

cloud cover tonight, it's impossible to see much more than dim outlines of the world beyond my room.

"Whatever this is, it's none of my business." I say it out loud, meaning it with every fiber of my being. If someone's dumb enough to brave this madness, then it must be for a good reason. It's probably one of the professors, dealing with some kind of weather damage, battening down the hatches.

Get your ass back in bed, Elodie. Draw the damn curtains and go the fuck to sleep. Now.

Sometimes I don't obey my own commands. I do dumb shit even though I tell myself to do the exact opposite. I never disobey myself when I use my father's angry bark as the voice of reason in my head, though. I pull the curtains closed and get back under the covers, determined to get at least a couple of hours sleep before Carina comes knocking on my door tomorrow morning.

I can do this. I can switch off my brain and relinquish myself to sleep. I close my eyes.

The storm outside rages on, and I breathe into my diaphragm, pushing out my belly, filling myself up with oxygen. Breathing like this is a great calming tactic during a panic attack—I still get those from time to time—but it also has the added benefit of making me sleepy. If I do this for a couple of minutes, the tension in my body will ebb away and I'll pass out before I'm even aware that I'm about to drift off. There's something hypnotic about the pull and draw of so much air filling and rushing out of my body. It's rare that this trick doesn't work.

I clear my mind...

Breathe in...

Exhale...

Pause.

Breathe in...

Exhale...

Pause.

I repeat the motion, rinse and repeat, over and over again, but my mind just will not quiet. Goddamnit. I open my eyes, sighing out a weighty groan. And there, on the far side of my room, projected over the wooden door, is an imperfect rectangle of light.

Fuck. I mustn't have pulled the curtains closed properly. Growling, I sit up, about to swing my legs over the side of the bed again, when the light flicks off and disappears.

Huh.

Okaaaay.

It's returned before I can settle back into my pillows.

It flicks on and off in rapid succession, like a faulty strip light. It looks random at first, but when I stare at it a little longer, I realize that the strobing light isn't random. It isn't random in the slightest.

It's Morse fucking code.

The same short burst of Morse code, repeating itself over and over again. I wait for the cycle to pause for a second, indicating the end of the message, and when it starts up again, I do my best to keep up with the flashes.

Dot dash dash dot. That's a P.

I miss the next part. Whoever's standing in the pissing rain, sending covert messages to another student in this building, is signaling too fast for me to keep up.

I wait, biding my time until the message begins again.

P, and then dot, dash, dash. That's a W. The last letter, dash, dot, dash, dot, is a C.

PWC?

Anyone with half a brain cell and a father in the military knows what PWC stands for: *Proceed With Caution.*

Hmm. Some kind of lover's tryst? An invitation? A warning? It's warm in my bed, as well as considerably dryer in here than outside. On any other night, I'd be so curious about the message and what it meant that I wouldn't be able to stop myself; I'd *have* to sneak out and see what kind of salacious meetings were taking place inside the maze, but tonight my own self-preservation instincts tell me that I'm much safer right where I am, protected from flying debris, gale force winds, icy rain, and hypothermia.

About to try my breathing technique again, my eyelids flutter... and the light starts flashing again, with a whole new message:

A...R...E

Y...O...U

A

C...O...W...A...R...D

S...T...I...L...L...W...A...T...E...R

?

The light goes out, and this time it stays out.

What the *hell*? I launch myself out of bed. The rain's so bad, even worse than before, rolling across the window in sheets, that there's no way I can see the maze anymore. All I see is the gauntlet thrown down, the challenge of someone waiting out there in the dark. *For me.*

"Nooooo," I groan. "You have *got* to be kidding me."

* * *

Thanks to Colonel Stillwater's rush evacuation from Tel Aviv, I didn't have time to go shopping for new clothes before I was bundled onto that personnel carrier. I have no coat with me. Not one that would provide any sort of protection against the gale that's blowing outside. As I step out of the front door, I tighten my light, too-thin bomber jacket around me, thankful that at least my feet should stay dry inside my Doc Martins. The rain hits me square in the face, ice cold and shocking, forcing a string of curse words out of my mouth as I duck my head, forging forward, out into the maelstrom.

The wind rips my hood down and whips my hair up around my head. I don't have to worry about it flying around my face for too long, though. By the time I've reached the corner of the building, it's soaking wet and plastered to my skull.

"This is fucking insanity," I hiss, jogging along the perimeter of the school, doing my best to keep my footing as I skid in the bog of mud that was once the border of the rose garden. Each second feels like a minute. The distance from the wall outside Doctor Fitzpatrick's room to the entrance of the maze stretches out, increasing with every step I take instead of growing shorter, and I question whether I've lost my goddamn mind.

This is not a good idea.

This is a horrible idea.

No one knows where I've gone. I decoded a fucking Morse code message in the middle of the night, cast onto my bedroom wall, and like a stubborn idiot I decided to prove I wasn't a coward rather than stay where it was safe and warm. Who fucking *does* that?

Dumb girls in horror movies, my father's voice informs me. *The stupid ones who wind up dead, with their body parts strewn across the lawn.*

"Didn't ask for your opinion, thanks, *Dad,*" I growl, gritting my teeth as a freezing cold gust of wind pelts droplets of rainwater into my face.

At the mouth of the maze, I consider turning back. For a long second, I give myself the opportunity to turn around. To return to the relative protection of my room. Then I remember that knife sticking out of my bed, and I scoff at that idea. My room *isn't* safe. And I'm already drenched to the bone. My calves are covered in mud. And someone's waiting for me in this maze, likely the person responsible for wrecking my belongings, and I want to face them. I want to face *Wren*, because I already know it was him who sent the message.

If I face him, I can nip this whole thing in the bud. I'll be tackling the situation head on, and isn't that what my father taught me? *Never run from the enemy, Elodie. Never show them your back. Any sign of weakness will be your ultimate downfall. The most remarkable generals in history always met force with force.*

Still. I'm aware how ill-advised this is. I should have left a note, requesting that something pithy and deprecating be engraved on my headstone: *She lived recklessly and died the same way. God grant her the wisdom to make better choices in the afterlife.*

Something about the view of the maze from my bedroom window gave me the creeps. I didn't like looking out at it, but I did force myself to map out a vague route to its center. Left, left, right. Straight, left, right, right, then the hairpin, then, left, then one last right. My teeth chatter, clashing together violently as I try and follow the directions I have committed to memory. The walls of the hedges are high, though, sinister and imposing; it feels like there are arms reaching out at me from within them, hands grabbing for me, pulling at my clothes, trying to yank me into the sharp, dense walls of the labyrinth. It's just rogue branches and twigs, catching on my jacket and the thin knee-length cotton of my pajama bottoms, but I can't shake the awful panic rising in me that I won't make it out of this godforsaken obstacle course alive.

Soon, I've gotten so turned around that I have no idea which way I'm supposed to be heading. I can feel my father's disappointment radiating all the way from the Middle East. He wouldn't have gotten lost in this nightmare place. He'd have bulldozed his way through the fucking walls, armed and ready to face whatever danger awaited him at its heart.

I'm not too worried about having lost my way. I know if I just keep turning in the same direction, over and over again, I'll eventually reach its center point. So that's what I do, turning to the left at every intersection or fork in the path, the soles of my boots crunching on the gravel, and I work on calming my nerves.

Panic will kill you quicker than anything else.
Panic will kill you quicker than anything else.
Panic will kill you quicker than anything else.

That's what my old surfing instructor used to tell me, back when we lived in South Africa. I repeat it over and over like a mantra, driving the words into my brain, making them feel true. I just need to stay calm.

"Fuck!" A rumble of thunder crashes directly overhead, and I nearly jump straight out of my Docs. The force of it vibrates inside my body, resounding in the hollow of my chest. Lightning rips across the sky—giant forks of brilliant, piercing light that shoots from left to right. I try not to picture what it would feel like if one of those fearsome fingers of light were to strike down and make contact, using my seventeen-year-old dumb ass as a conduit to the ground. It's enough to know that it would really fucking hurt.

I keep on walking, head bent, shoulder constantly into the wind, which doesn't seem right since I change direction every few seconds, but it appears the wind is just as trapped inside this maddening network of pathways as I am. It skirls and eddies around, around, around, and no matter how quickly I hurry, I can't get ahead of it.

Just when I'm about to give up and look for a place to shelter, another hand reaches out and grabs hold of me, fingers closing tightly around my upper arm.

I scream.

Jesus, do I scream.

I hate that I react so dramatically, but in the moment, it feels so fucking real that I believe it. I *know* with a terrifying certainty that some unknown specter has emerged from the eye of the storm, taken me by the arm, and is about to drag me down into the darkest pits of hell. I'm not cut out for hell. I'm more of a cotton candy and endless backrubs kind of girl. An eternity of damnation does not sound go—

"Jesus, Stillwater, quit screaming. You'll wake the fucking dead."

Startled, I close my mouth, my teeth making a sharp *crack* as they snap together. Not an unknown specter, it turns out. I'm familiar with this demon, with his raven black hair and his shock-ingly green eyes. Even in the rain and the darkness, Wren Jacobi's eyes look too, too vivid. He smirks, his hair arranged in artful, wet curls that flick up around his ears, rivulets of water coursing down his handsome face, and I almost let out another blood curdling scream.

My maternal grandmother told me stories about the devil sometimes. She told me that he was the most beautiful of all the angels. That God gave him a countenance that made women sigh and curdled men's hearts with jealousy. The last time I saw her, at the tender age of eight years old, she warned me, "Elodie, child. Be extra careful of the handsome ones. They'll trick you with their beauty, but it's all a façade. Their eyes may peer into your soul, and their mouths may leave you breathless, but beneath their pleasing exterior lies a wickedness bestowed by Saint Nick himself. All good-looking men have been tapped on the shoulder by evil."

I assumed it was just the ravings of a mad old woman, but looking at Wren now, standing in the rain like he's out for a stroll on a balmy summer's day, I'm beginning to think she might have been right.

"What the fuck are you *doing?*" I rip myself free of his grasp. "You think this is some sort of game? People die from exposure in this kind of weather."

He laughs—a soft huff of amusement down his nose, like I've just said something fucking funny. "Prone to hyperbole, Stillwater? You've been outside for five whole minutes. I doubt you'll catch hypothermia from a bit of wind and rain. Unless you have a weak constitution?"

Weak constitution. I'll give him weak fucking constitution. I'm gonna tear him a new one.

Wren's dark eyebrow arches, the right corner of his mouth lifting up as he makes a show of slowly offering his hand out to me, palm up. "I know the way," he says darkly.

I glare at his extended hand like it's covered in a deadly bacterium. "To where?"

"To warmth. Shelter. Unless you'd rather spend another thirty minutes out here, spinning your wheels in the mud before you figure this thing out. Up to you. Woman's prerogative and all that. It's all the same to me." He tips his head to one side, both eyebrows rising now, and my Judas of a heart stumbles over itself. Damn, I want to punch him in his smug fucking throat more than I've wanted anything in my entire life.

"I don't need your hand. I can follow you just fine," I snap.

Another burst of thunder crashes, deafeningly loud right over our heads. Wren's thrown into stark relief, shadows stretched out across his face, bleached black and white by the staggering display of lightning that chases on its heels. The moment is so surreal that I'm struck by the absurdity of my situation. Wren drops his hand. "Keep your eyes open, then! You'll need to actually look where you're going!" He shouts to make himself heard over the din. I watch the muscles in the column of his throat work, wondering if he'll chase after me if I run from him.

No. *He* won't run.

I'll run, and I'll stagger, and I'll trip, and I'll stumble, and Wren will calmly walk after me, untouched by the elements. He'll capture me, and he'll expend zero energy doing it, because that's just who he fucking is.

He turns around, his black shirt clinging to his back like a second skin, and he walks off, turning left into the maze.

I'm left with no choice but to follow.

* * *

In five sharp turns through entrances I don't even see until the very last second, Wren has us at the maze's center. Amongst a riot of rose bushes, whose late blooms have been smashed and obliterated by the driving rain, their peach-red petals strewn all over the ground, a squat gazebo stands on a raised platform beneath the massive boughs of one of the giant live oaks that stands guard over the maze.

I can't see the structure from my bedroom window. From that vantage point, all I can see are the high hedge walls and not much else. Here it stands, though—a small, solid structure crafted out of wood and glass, small and utterly charming, painted white and blue. Inside, a warm orange glow promises light and protection from the cold.

Wren climbs the steps that lead up to the enclosed gazebo's entrance, pausing in front of the door, his pale hand resting on the weathered brass knob. "This place is off limits," he says. "We're not supposed to be out here."

"No *shit*." I gesture up at the sky. "We aren't supposed to be outside in general."

He laughs that laugh again, breathy and entertained, as though everything about me is quaint and silly to him. "I assume you're okay with breaking a few rules, Stillwater. If you'd rather toe the line, I can take you back to the academy. I'd just need a moment to grab my things."

He can't hear me growling under my breath. I trust that he can read my annoyance from the scowl on my face, though. "Open the door, Jacobi. I'm turning blue, for fuck's sake."

He seems pleased. It's hard to tell with him, though. He could also look like he wants to murder me. I can't really make up my mind. Twisting the knob, he shoves the door open, standing back and sweeping his arm in front of him, gesturing for me to go inside.

I eye him suspiciously as I sidle past him into the gazebo.

Grateful that I'm no longer being lashed at by rain, I lean against the wall, sighing with relief. The interior of the gazebo is surprising to say the least. I was expecting a couple of peeling wooden benches and some empty soda cans rolling around on the bare concrete, but I'm dead wrong. The décor—because the place actually *has* a décor—is stunning. Polished parquet flooring around the edges of the room gives way to a plush, thick cream carpet. A sofa and two overstuffed armchairs have been arranged in front of an unlit open fireplace on the far side of the room. Around the curved wall opposite the door, a low three-shelved bookcase bows under the weight of countless thick, heavy tomes with leather spines and gilded edges. Potted plants sit on every flat surface: vines, and ferns, and rubber figs, all jostling for space and light at the windows, which are patinaed with grime on the outside but clean from within.

"What is this?" I whisper. This isn't just some forgotten place. This is someone's hideaway. A secret, well-loved sanctuary.

Wren kicks off his muddy boots, discarding them by the door. He isn't wearing any socks, which makes me shiver for no good reason. The sight of his bare feet, as he pads across the thick rug toward the fireplace, makes me so unexpectedly uncomfortable that I don't even have the decency to look away. He bends at the waist, grabbing a piece of chopped wood from a wicker basket next to the fire, and he looks down at it, turning it over in his hands. "It's supposed to be for the faculty. We commandeered it when we first came here, though. Fitz is the only one who knows we come here, and he turns a blind eye."

Nothing about this place feels like it belongs to Wren. It's too... too grown up and simple, and too...I don't even know how to explain it. I've never considered what Wren's personal space might look like. Not even for a second. *Knowing* he has a bedroom some-where is very different to being able to *imagine* what it would look like. It'd make more sense if he crawled out of a coffin in the ground at night. Or if he materialized out of a cloud of black smoke.

He tosses the piece of wood into the grate in the fire, his mouth twitching; he wants to don that ruinous smirk of his, I know he does. For reasons known only to him, he decides to restrain it this time. "No need to look so uncomfortable, Stillwater. Take off the jacket. There's a blanket on the back of the couch. You can wrap yourself in that while it dries."

I remain motionless, hugging the wall. "Why am I here, Wren?" I ask in a cold voice.

He grabs more wood, crouching down to arrange the pieces to his satisfaction, before he tears pages off an old newspaper at his feet, balling up the sheets and poking them into the gaps at the base of his unlit pyre. He doesn't say a word.

"Wren. I'm serious. The message. What was the point in sending it? *Why the fuck am I here?*"

"When I was a kid, my father used to send me messages in Morse code. He used to drum his fingers against the table at breakfast. Tap his pen on, well, anything… It was our secret thing. My step-mother used to hate it."

"Thanks for the heartwarming story. Now answer the question." It has to be three in the morning by now. I may be young, but I still require a lot of sleep. I like sleep, and Wren's depriving me of my rest for no apparent reason.

He looks back at me over his shoulder, his lips parted, a strange look in his eyes. The brief moment of eye contact we share makes me want to hide behind the fucking bookcase. Turning away, he strikes a long match and holds the flickering flame against the paper until each one of the scrunched-up balls is alight. "Your father taught you Morse code, too, right?"

"Yes." I don't want to relinquish this or any other piece of information about myself, but it's a simple enough question. I have no reason to withhold the truth.

"It wasn't a game for him, was it? It was a punishment."

A shockwave of panic detonates in my chest. It ripples out, sending adrenalin chasing through my veins, spreading through me like that lightning that fired across the sky before. He can't know anything about my father. He can't know shit about my past, or about me. Anything he *thinks* he knows is wrong, so why do I feel like he's just cracked me open and rifled through all of my ugly secrets? It makes me feel suddenly dirty. "My father's irrelevant," I say tightly.

"Our fathers shape us," Wren says, standing up to his full height. Behind him, the fire he built roars to life, like the infernos of hell just leapt at his command and obeyed his summons. "I've read a lot about your old man. What else did he teach you? Muay Thai?"

"No."

"Oh right. Israel. He probably taught you Krav Maga."

I do *not* like that he's able to deduce so much about me. It's unfair that he's armed with information that I don't know about him in kind. There are things…things that he can't know. Things that have been buried so well and so deep that even he couldn't have dug them up. "I don't see how any of this is important," I say.

He pouts. "Do you still practice? I know a little Krav Maga myself. We could spar."

"*No.*"

"No, you don't practice anymore, or no, you don't want to spar with me?"

"No, I don't practice here. Why would I when I don't have to? And can we stop talking about my father, please? That stuff's private."

Wren shrugs off my cold tone. "Your wish is my command."

Quiet and as leonine as a panther, he crosses the small room, coming to a stop in front of me. Flicks of his hair hang down into his face, creating a dripping curtain that shields his eyes. I still feel the intensity of them, though, burning into my skin. He licks his lips, his hand reaching up, making me flinch.

He pauses, an inch away from my face. He has pianist's hands, with long, dexterous fingers. I'm riveted by the sight of them. By the thought of what he might do with them if left unchecked. His nails are still covered in that same chipped black nail polish I noticed on my first night at Wolf Hall. "You're a flighty little thing," he rumbles. I resent the way his voice makes my skin break out in goosebumps.

"Forgive me for being cautious, but I don't know anything about you. We're not friends," I volley back at him. "I'm not accustomed to people thinking they can touch me uninvited."

He drops his hand back to his side, a slow smile spreading across his damnable face. "I'll be sure to wait until I'm invited, then. You have a rose petal in your hair. I was just gonna get it out for you."

I automatically check my hair, finding the petal and disentangling it. Wren sucks his bottom lip into his mouth, his eyes full of an emotion I can't rightly decipher. It's a dangerous look. Sharp. The type of look that could cut if administered correctly.

Retreating a couple of steps, he shrugs, grabbing hold of the hem of his black long-sleeved shirt.

"If you want to stand there in your soaking wet clothes, that's your call, Stillwater. I'm not one to suffer discomfort willingly, though."

Before I know what he's doing, he's pulled the sodden material of his shirt over his head and turned around, walking back to the fire, where he hangs the item of clothing from the rough-cut mantlepiece for it to dry. I'm left staring at his back—a naked expanse of muscle and flawless skin that makes my throat pulse and throb. That shirt, the same shirt he's been wearing day in and day out since that very first night when I met him outside Wolf Hall, has been hiding a multitude of sins: strong arms, a broad, strong back, and a chest that would make Michelangelo weep. His body's nothing short of divine.

He faces me and just stands there, letting me shamelessly take him in. I should have some self-respect and look away. I can't, though. I've never seen anything like him before, carved and sculpted, magnificent in his perfection. I refrain from counting his abs. It's enough that they're there, and they're defined. From the crown of his head to the low-slung waistband of his jeans, Wren is the stuff of sweet, heavenly dreams, and twisted, terrifying nightmares.

His eyes burn, feverish and fierce, as he uses them to pierce me to the core and gut me with a practiced ease. How many girls has he brought here and pulled this shit on? How many students at Wolf Hall has he dragged out here in the middle of the night and stupefied by stripping down to his bare and glorious skin? His list of casualties must be too long to comprehend.

"I thought you weren't supposed to take off the shirt," I mutter, finally looking away.

"Oh, I could have taken it off all I wanted," he muses. "I just wasn't allowed to wear anything else. It's past midnight now, though. February first. I'm released from my punishment."

"You'll be wearing bright red tomorrow, then."

He laughs quietly. "I'm not a very colorful person. Black suits my demeanor best."

"Hah. Yeah, I can see that. Black like your heart? Like your soul?"

"Ouch." He slaps a hand to his chest. "I'm hit. Let the record show, I'm officially *hurt*." He sinks down onto the couch, kicking out his long legs in front of him. With the light from the fire casting a warm glow across the solid expanse of his stomach and his chest, as well as across his face, he cuts a frustratingly handsome figure.

"I can find something to put on," he says. "If I'm making you uncomfortable."

This is all so pointless and irresponsible that I'm furious at myself all of a sudden. He's playing me, and I'm letting him, allowing him to manipulate me and pull at my strings. He knows what he looks like. He also knows how his looks must affect members of the opposite sex. By clinging to the wall and choking on all my words, I'm feeding his need for attention. "You know what makes me uncomfortable?" I snap, stalking across the room. "Coming back to my room to find a bowie knife sticking out of my mattress and my belongings in pieces. That makes me really fucking uncomfortable indeed."

From the couch, Wren looks up at me with a subtle, convincing frown pinching his brows together. "Bowie knife?"

"Don't give me that shit, Jacobi. You know exactly what I'm talking about. You trashed my room and slashed up my mattress. If you were trying to put the fear of god in me, then it didn't work, okay? So just...stay away from my room."

The frown deepens. "Your room was trashed." He's deadpan, the words flat, devoid of emotion. He repeats the words as a statement, not a question. "I didn't have anything to do with that. Not my style. Breaking and entering is pretty...*pedestrian*."

"Cut the shit. I know it was you. Who else would bother?"

He smirks. "Why would *I* bother?"

"You were looking for something in there. And you wanted to

scare me." I proceed with my accusation, trying not to second guess myself now that I am looking into his clear green eyes and I can find no hint of a lie within them. He's an excellent actor, I'll give him that.

"The best butchers don't scare the animals before they take them to the slaughter, Elodie. The fear taints the meat."

"What the fuck is *that* supposed to mean?"

Wren sighs, looking into the fire. "Why would I try and scare you, Little E? What would I have to gain from petrifying you half to death?"

I've asked myself this already. There are plenty of reasons why he'd want to intimidate me, and I've considered them all. Now that *he's* posed the question, all of the reasons I came up with seem ridiculous. He doesn't need to frighten women into his bed; they probably fall over themselves in their rush to go there willingly.

There *is* no good explanation why Wren would have messed up my room.

"Don't fret, Little E. Again, I assure you, I didn't enter your room without your permission," he says, toying with the seam on the back of one of the couch cushions.

Do I believe him? Hell no. It's pointless going back and forth with him, though. "Whatever. It'd be great if you finally spit it out and tell me what I'm doing here. I'd love to get back to bed, and—"

"I'll answer your question but not until you come and sit down," he interrupts. "With you standing over me in that giant fucking coat, this is starting to feel like an interrogation."

I want to go. The weather hasn't improved in the last five minutes, though. The chances of me finding my way back out of the maze are slim at this point. It won't do me any good to get lost out there again, and I don't think Wren's going to help me back to Wolf Hall unless I humor him.

Swift jab to the throat.

Knee to the balls.

Elbow to the solar plexus.

I have a few self-defense maneuvers already prepped and ready to go in my head, as I skirt around the small coffee table and reluctantly sit myself down in the armchair. At least here I'm close to the fire; the warmth radiating from the flames feels amazing.

Satisfied, Wren runs a hand back through his hair, sweeping the wet curls out of his face. "I wanted you to come here because you're smart," he says. "You're observant, which means you'll have noticed *me* noticing *you*. You must know that I'm interested in you."

I narrow my eyes. "Why do I get the feeling that being the subject of your interest is bad for a girl's health?"

The boy with the black hair and the vivid eyes looks bemused. "Maybe I've been bad in the past. I'm sure Carina's told you plenty about that."

"She's told me some. Mostly about your failed plan to fuck half of Wolf Hall before Christmas. A bet, right? Between you and your Riot House buddies? Or are you gonna tell me that she made that up?"

Wren's hand stills, a tassel from one of the cushions trapped between his long fingers. He looks at me—*into me?*—unmoving and unblinking. "There was a bet," he confirms. "I was supposed to sleep with ten girls between Halloween and Christmas, and I didn't. That's how I got stuck wearing the same shit for a month."

Huh. I'm surprised he actually admitted it. "What happened?" I ask. "The girls start talking and comparing notes? You failed at the last hurdle after putting nine extra notches on your belt?" The comment sounded cool and indifferent inside my head. Out of my mouth, it sounds sour and silly.

"Let's not fuck around with any of that." Wren leans forward, resting his forearms on his thighs. "Petty quips will get us nowhere fast. Does it bother you that I haven't been saving myself for marriage or something?"

Heat rises in my cheeks. "Why would it bother me? Your sex life has nothing to do with me. It's none of my business."

"And yet, from the judgmental tone in your voice, it sounds like it bothers you very much."

"Really. I don't care. If the girls you sleep with are consenting, then—"

"I'm not a *rapist*, Elodie. I've never done anything without a girl's consent. Usually, I only ever indulge a girl with my affections if she's on her knees, begging for it."

"Oh, and I'm sure you just love that, don't you? The begging. Must do wonders for your over-inflated ego."

"Begging leaves no room for misunderstanding." He rests his chin in the palm of his hand, propping up his head as he looks at me intently. "I don't like uncertainty. I like things to be very black and white. Clear cut. What about you?"

"Yes, I like when things are clear cut. Which is why I'll let you know here and now that I will never lower myself to my knees for you. You're a monster, who loves to treat women like shit—"

"You don't know how I treat women. You don't know anything about me, remember?"

This motherfucker. He has an answer for everything. "Appearances would indicate that you chew women up and spit them out like they're a disposable commodity. I'm sure you were furious that you lost that bet, weren't you? It must have stung that you weren't able to convince ten poor girls to dive into bed with you."

My heart's pounding in my chest, but Wren just sits there with his chin in his hand, the light from the fire still playing across the elegant, masculine frame of his body, completely impassive as he watches me rant. He seems pensive as he says, "You've figured it all out, haven't you? You wanna know the truth? The truth is that I didn't have to try and win that bet. The moment Pax told Damiana about it, it was all over the academy by the end of the day. And then I had girls tripping over themselves to fuck me. I could have tripled my quota twenty-four hours in. Not even *I* have that kind of stamina."

"Oh wow. Big man. So, you won the bet after all. You just accepted the punishment for the sheer hell of it?"

"No. I didn't screw any of those girls. They wanted to throw their hats into the ring for the hell of it. To say they danced toe-to-

toe with one of the Riot House boys. My dick doesn't get hard for that kind of shit. A girl's gotta earn me, not think she's doing me a favor."

"Whoa. Careful. That ego's bordering on ridiculous now."

"It's not ego. It's just a fact."

"So, you're a good little boy after all. A saintly virgin. Is that what you brought me here to tell me?" Preposterous. If he legitimately tries to convince me that he has morals and has never slept with a student at Wolf Hall, then I'll know him for exactly who he is: a bold-faced liar.

Wren wiggles his toes in front of the fire, baring his teeth in a wolfish smile. "I'm about the furthest thing you'll find from a virgin here," he says. "I was deflowered a *long* time ago."

That choice of word—deflower—is laughable. It implies that Wren was once innocent, before he was plucked and sullied at someone else's hand. Wren was never innocent. He came out of the womb corrupt and depraved, I'm certain of it.

"And no. I can already see it on your face. You know the truth. I'm the furthest thing from good you'll find here, too. Don't you want to know what I lost by not playing along with Dashiell and Pax's bet?"

"No. I don't really care. It's so predictable, this whole thing. Bored rich boys placing bets to stave off boredom, not caring how their stupid bullshit affects the people around them. Don't you care about anyone else here? Don't you feel bad about hurting people?"

Wren weighs his response quickly. He barely has to think about the answer at all. "I care about Pax. I care about Dashiell. But not in a traditional way that most guys in high school care about each other. They're not my bros. They're not my homies. They're oxygen. Daylight. Warmth. Familiarity. Shelter. Home. Safety. The other people wandering around the halls of this godforsaken shit hole? Do I care about them? No, Stillwater. I don't. I don't give a fuck about a single one of them, and I'm not afraid to admit it."

I'm cold in spite of the fire. It's as though there's a block of ice sitting in the pit of my stomach and it will not melt. I'm weary down to my bones. I should never have left my bedroom. I'm a fool for coming all the way down here in the blowing wind and rain to sit here and listen to this. He *did* trash my room. He's not ashamed of who he is in the slightest. Fool that I am, I guess that I was hoping I'd discover a few redeeming qualities that Wren's been hiding from the world, but there's nothing to redeem here. Wren's a barren wasteland, and I have no intention of wandering that wasteland, knowing I won't find anything to nourish me there.

Urgh. It's really gonna suck walking back out into that storm. I get to my feet, already shivering at the prospect of the driving, icy rain slapping me in the face. "I'm going back to my room. This is a waste of time. I—"

"For some reason, I care about *you*, though," he says, clenching his jaw. He's not looking at me now; his eyes are fixed on the rug in front of the fire. From the expression on his face, I can see that this admission has cost him something. He doesn't *like* whatever it is he's feeling right now. "I'm cursed with this bewildering fascination over you, and it's really becoming...*inconvenient*, Stillwater."

I roll my eyes, fighting back a dramatic sigh. "What is this? What's the point? This is just another bet, isn't it? You're looking to redeem yourself after your last embarrassing failure and you figured I'd make an interesting new target in one of your wagers. Well, I'm not your plaything, Wren Jacobi. I was not put on this earth for your amusement. I'll be cold and dead in the ground before I let you use my heart as a punching bag. So, you can just forget it. Forget *me*."

Panic sizzles under my skin as Wren slowly gets up from the couch. His eyes are alive with electricity, that bottom lip of his trapped between his teeth again. My big speech hasn't had its desired affect by all accounts. He prowls forward, his muscles shifting beautifully under his skin, and I nearly trip over my own damn feet in my hurry to back away from him. He looks like he's going to fucking *eat* me. "My brain doesn't work like that, I'm afraid. I don't just *forget*. If I want something, I can't just move on and pretend like it doesn't exist."

I inch away from him, and my chest tightens when the backs of my legs hit the armchair I was sitting on a moment ago. I'm going to have to climb over the fucking furniture if I want to get away from him, which is not going to look graceful or dignified. I'll willingly do it, though, if it means I escape him.

Wren has other ideas. He takes one last step, so close to me now that I can feel his warm breath skating over my cheek, can see the flecks of amber and gold surrounding the black well of his dilated pupil. I can't move. I can't breathe. If I even blink, I suspect that he'll pounce and tear me apart. He takes hold of a lock of my damp, tangled hair, winding it thoughtfully around his fingers. "You're not a bet, Elodie. I've had to bargain with them for you. I've had to break my own rules in order to claim you, and it's cost me greatly."

Over the top of my paralyzing panic, a hot, furious anger begins to rise. Who the hell does he think he is? So fucking entitled. So fucking arrogant. "You can't bargain over a person. I don't belong to any of you. I won't be haggled over like a piece of meat." My pulse is hammering at thirty different points all over my body: in my temples, in my ears, in the tips of my fingers. In my lips...

Wren stares down at my mouth. He's stopped breathing, wound tight, coiled like a hunter, ready to attack at any moment. I —Jesus Christ, I've got to get out of here, before—

Wren tugs on my hair, leaning in even closer, his eyelids half closed as he angles his head to one side, assessing my features. I rock back on my heels. A weightless, terrible moment passes, where I register how unbalanced I am and I realize I'm about to fall. Then I'm sitting down heavily in the chair behind me, the air huffing out of my lungs as Wren continues to press forward. He places one hand on the arm of the chair, the other against the back of it, right above my head. I'm trapped in a cage made by his body, and all I can smell is *him*—a dark, heady, beautiful scent that teases the back of my nose. It reminds me of night blooming flowers, and cold winter walks with my mother, and the ocean, and my Uncle Remy's carpentry workshop.

Holy shit. The next time I smell this scent, it won't remind me of any of those things. Powerful enough to overwrite my memories, the next time I smell this scent, it will remind me of this moment, trapped in this chair, the way my heartrate is soaring and I feel like I'm about to die a most delicious death. "Get away from me, Wren," I whisper.

He smiles sadly. "Wish I could, Stillwater. But it ain't on the cards."

I'm poised and ready to react. He's about to fucking kiss me. I'm not afraid of it. I'm shaking all over and I can't fucking think straight, but I am *not* afraid. "Back up, Wren."

His lips are parted, his pupils close to swallowing up his irises. My palms burn, my fingers itching. I don't trust myself to move right now. A part of me wants to slap the intense, doped, lust-filled look right off his stupidly handsome face. A part of me wants to fist a handful of his hair and pull him to me, so that his full lips collide with mine.

I want the kiss. I want him to suffer for this invasion of my personal space. I'm at war with myself, and I honestly don't know how I'm going to react if he makes a move.

"Your heart's racing, Stillwater," he whispers. "I can see your pulse in the base of your throat. *You want me.*"

"I want you to leave me alone. I want you to stay away from my room."

"*Elodie.*"

My voice is uneven and full of nerves. "I *know* you're lying."

Slowly, as if he's got all the time in the world, Wren shakes his head. A droplet of water falls from the riot of curls that are hanging down into his face, and it lands right on my mouth. "I haven't lied to you. I never will. I'll give you all my dark, ugly truths, even though they'll frighten you, Little E. I won't hold back. You..." He dips his head, and I freeze beneath him. The air between us buzzes, brimming with a tension so sharp that it bites at my skin. Millimeter by millimeter he leans closer and flicks out the tip of his tongue, licking the water droplet from my lips. I close my eyes, my lungs seizing.

Fuck.

Fuck, fuck, fuck.

"You *are* going to be mine, Elodie Stillwater. Of all my sins and misdeeds, making you fall in love with me will be the very worst of them all."

11

WREN

FOUR DAYS LATER

I walked her back to the house.

Against my better judgement. Against every impulse roaring through my body, I walked her back to the house and I didn't lay a finger on her. Thus far, the only part of my body that has been in contact with Elodie is my tongue, and that blissful moment when I dared to lick her delectable little mouth has sustained me through some highly frustrating, very long nights.

She hasn't looked at me since. I've passed her in the hall. I've watched her in class. I've sat in the same room as her, buffeted by her tangible rage, and every second of it has been heaven. She hasn't left Carina's side. I know she's making sure that we aren't alone together, and this little game we're playing has driven me to the point of insanity. I could have pulled her into a closet by now. I could have dragged her into the locker rooms, or cornered her in the cafeteria, or stalked her right into the girl's bathrooms, but I've come to the glorious realization that this thing between us—this intoxicating anticipation that keeps me awake when I throw myself into bed at three in the morning—is so much more entertaining than trying to quicken the situation along.

She *will* come to me. She won't be able to resist. It's only a matter of time. And I have plenty of things to keep my mind occupied while I wait for her curiosity to get the better of her.

DAMIANA: Wen R U gonna give it up? U know we make sense. We're cut from the same cloth. Why would U wanna settle for some prissy little prude wen U already know how good I taste?

Damiana tasted like desperation. It coated my tongue and left an oily residue in my mouth that three days' worth of Listerine couldn't budge. I thought about sterilizing my junk in bleach after I was dumb enough to fuck her, but I figured my dick had already suffered enough and settled with a scalding hot shower instead. A master craftsman should take better care of his tools.

I did complete a full profit and loss assessment the night I allowed Dami into the house and I screwed her over Pax's poker table. At the time her neediness was something I deemed manageable, but that was after a bottle of vodka and two Percocet. It was also before I knew Elodie Stillwater even existed. And now I find the consequences of my little tryst with Wolf Hall's resident viper were not worth the twenty-one minutes of bare flesh and porn star approved moaning that she offered in exchange for a ride on my cock.

ME: Let it go. Some mistakes aren't destined to be repeated.

DAMIANA: MISTAKE? U weren't calling it that when I swallowed ur cum, motherfucker.

I jam my phone into my back pocket, growling out loud. Crazy bitch isn't worth another megabyte of my data. I shouldn't have replied in the first place, but I figured there was a chance she'd walk away and let this thing go gracefully. Girls like Damiana never know when to give up, though. They persist and they persist until they've thoroughly embarrassed themselves, and even then they won't fucking drop it.

The land surrounding the house is a bog. It rained all week, an incessant downpour that only paused long enough for Dashiell to talk me into a race up Mount Castor (which I won). This morning's the first day that any of us have woken up to blue skies, and the pale, almost white dawn has made me unreasonably irritated. I liked the dense, angry cloud cover and the charged, threatening energy that's been hanging over Wolf Hall. It exacerbated the roiling tension that's been building between me and Elodie. It felt like that moment right before you come, when you hold your breath and you feel that pleasure mounting, and you're riding this wave that will crest over you any second. This morning's sunny, fresh beginning feels like that wave failed to crash, leaving me left unsatisfied and wanting.

Using sex metaphors is a mistake. I just have to think the word and my mind goes overboard, painting graphic images of Elodie, naked and spread out for me. I haven't let myself imagine what it would feel like to fuck her. I *can't* imagine it. In my daydreams, I get as far as hovering over her with my dick in my hand, rubbing the tip against her pretty, pink little pussy, and my mind just fucking blanks.

She isn't a virgin. She's been fucked before, I can tell, but that doesn't matter to the cock-blocking bastard inside my head, who keeps telling me that she's pure and my cock has no business being anywhere near her cunt.

Pax whistles through his teeth as he pulls up through the black, sucking mud in front of the house at the wheel of his Charger; he's chewing on a tooth pick that he shuttles from one side of his mouth to the other, left to right, left to right, left to right. "You're gonna owe me a car wash, you know that, right? This baby was clean when I pulled out of the garage and now look at her. She's fucking filthy."

"If you took as much care in your presentation as you do in that car, people wouldn't mistake you for a vagrant all the time," Dashiell says in a sunny voice.

"Fuck you, *Lord Lovett*." When anyone else calls Dashiell by his full title, it's typically said with a certain amount of gravity and respect. When Pax uses our friend's full title, it sounds like he's chewing on wasps. Dashiell's impervious to Pax's foul moods, though. He gracefully slides himself into the front seat next to Pax, folding his body like a fucking dancer as he crams himself into the car.

All of us are painfully aware of the fact that none of us should get along. Pax is the spikiest, angriest, poutiest guy I've ever met. The chip on his shoulder is glaringly obvious and kind of sad, really. Dashiell's spoiled rotten and so hopped up on Valium and Xanax that his world is fluffy and so mellow through his medicated rose-tinted lenses that he barely exists in the same plane of reality as us at all.

And me. I'm the recluse. The pressure cooker. The guy who hardly speaks, who's skin begins to itch if he has to say more than three sentences in public, in fact. Who hates almost everyone, and finds the *idea* of having friends hanging around utterly repugnant.

Pax and Dashiell somehow worked their way under my skin, though, until it felt normal that they were just there all the time, bickering and sniping at each other, roughhousing and calling on me to mediate their dumb, affectionate arguments; now it would be weird if they weren't around, taking up space and irritating the shit out of me.

Pax cackles like a deranged hyena as he peels out of the driveway and heads in the direction of the academy. Any other day and the three of us would have run the two miles to Wolf Hall and wouldn't have broken a sweat, but it's Friday. We'll be burning down the mountain the moment the final bell of the day rings, and we won't be coming back until the early hours of Monday morning.

"How many people are gonna be at this thing anyway?" Pax grumbles.

"Five hundred and change. The crème de la crème of East Coast society. My father hasn't set foot on American soil for three years, so even the most pampered, blue-blooded snobs, from the old money to the nouveau riche will be crawling out from under their rocks to pay tribute to the old man."

Inwardly, I groan. Five hundred people, all crammed into the same ballroom, waiting for their turn to bow and scrape at the feet of a man most of them have never even fucking met. Sounds like pure fucking torture. Add in the fact that it's a black-tie event and I'm looking forward to tonight's charity dinner about as much as a root canal, sans anesthetic.

"You're quiet back there," Dashiell accuses, looking over his shoulder at me where I'm sprawled out across the back seat of the Charger. "Goddamnit, Jacobi. Are you physically incapable of sitting up straight?" He curves one of his dirty blond eyebrows into a question mark. "I don't think I've ever seen you utilize a chair correctly. You know you're supposed to bend in the middle and sit at a ninety-degree angle, yes? Your posture's atrocious."

"My posture is directly correlated to my level of interest in my surroundings."

"*Ouch.*" Pax fakes a sniffle of hurt. "Sorry if we're boring you, Your Highness."

Dashiell angles the rearview mirror to face him, using it to check his tie in the mirror. Ties are not mandatory at Wolf Hall; Dash wears it of his own volition, which is just fucking sick in my book. "He's bent out of shape about the new girl," he says, his eyes meeting mine in the mirror. "He's taking his time with this one."

"I'm not taking my time. I'm laying the groundwork. There's a difference."

Dash ignores me. "How long did it take him to sully Erica Judge when she first showed up?" he asks Pax.

"Two hours, thirty-eight minutes. From setting eyes on her for the first time, deciding he wanted her, getting past the small talk, actually fucking her in the art room, and her parents turning around and coming back to get her. *Two hours and thirty-eight fucking minutes!*" Pax crows. "Living fucking legend. Pretty little Elodie's been here for two whole weeks now, an' he's barely even looked at her. Waste of fresh meat, if you ask me. If you've changed your mind about our deal, man, we can trade back, y'know. Corsica's one of my favorite places in the world, but that girl looks like she's got one of those perfect, tiny, neat little porn star pussies. I'd love to crack that oyster open and go hunting for the pearl." He holds up two fingers, flicking his tongue between them, making a grotesque slurping noise, and the back of my neck prickles. I kick the back of his headrest hard enough to make his skull bounce off the calfskin leather.

"Hey! What the fuck, man!" Pax glares at me over his shoulder. "If you're having trouble getting your dick hard, I got plenty of meds that'll help you get the job done. Pull *that* shit again, though, and you can get out and fucking walk."

"Fine," I hiss.

"Fine, you want some dick pills?"

"Fine, pull over. I'll get out and fucking walk."

"Don't be a little bitch, Jacobi. We're five hundred feet away from the entrance."

"Stop the car, or I'll do more than kick a headrest," I purr, in a flat, calm, perfectly amicable voice.

"Jesus Christ," Dash groans. "Let him out before he blows like fucking Etna. There's no need to get so grouchy, y'know," he tells me, spinning around in his chair. "You like something about this girl. For some weird reason, you've decided she's the Morticia to your Gomez. There's no need to let your temporary insanity cause contention between the three of us, though, is there."

The Charger's tires kick up hunks of gravel as Pax purposefully slams on the breaks. I open up the door and climb out into the cold.

Dashiell offers me a winning smile. "Take a minute to think about what really matters on your pilgrimage to school, won't you, fella? See you in three whole minutes."

The Charger jumps its brakes, surging down the driveway towards the academy's imposing building, and a thick cloud of exhaust fumes envelops me for a second, obscuring the dismal view up ahead.

I wish it would fucking rain again.

I wish the day, along with Dashiell's father's vexing charity dinner, was already over.

I wish my smug fucking friends weren't right.

My attention's inexplicably snagged on Elodie, and her appeal seems to grow on a daily goddamn basis. Under any other circumstances, I *would* have charmed the back teeth off of the girl and screwed the living shit out of her already, but this isn't about sex. It isn't *not* about sex, I s'pose. But it's more about the quiet confidence the girl puts out. It's about her upbringing, and the things she's experienced, and the way she sees the world. I want to know what's going on inside her head.

I want what any guy in my position would want: *her complete and unconditional surrender.*

Pax and Dashiell wait for me on the worn marble steps that lead up to the entrance of the academy. They're almost exactly the same height, and their builds are pretty similar, too. That's where their similarities come to a grinding halt. Without me, the two men standing side by side in front of those lacquered black doors would probably despise each other with a burning intensity usually reserved for members of opposing religions.

"That little time-out fix your salty mood, princess?" Pax asks. His eyes are still full of fury over the headrest incident. He won't forgive me until I apologize, and even then he might not absolve me of my heinous crime; that car is his pride and joy.

I couldn't give a fuck. Today, I'm surrendering myself to my saturnine funk. It can fucking have me. Pax is gonna have to wait 'til tomorrow if he wants any sign of remorse out of me.

Fridays are weird at Wolf Hall. None of our classes align, the three of us separated and banished to different wings of the school in a way that definitely seems planned. Harcourt made sure none of us Riot House boys were close enough to scheme up any disruptive plans for the weekend around any of the other students, which is usually annoying. I'm glad that I won't have to see either of them again until the end of the day, though.

I just need…

I don't know *what* the fuck I need….

"I'll be ready to leave at six," I say, slapping a hand on each of the boys' shoulders as I pass them. "See you back at the house."

I yank open the heavy doors and walk inside the school, leaving them behind. Pax can't let me go without having the final word, though. "You're acting like she's the pot of gold, waiting for you at the end of the rainbow, man. But you're embarrassing yourself, Jacobi. She's just a girl. *She's just a fucking girl!*"

IN THE DARK...

I stop drinking.

He shoves the thin straw through the hole, goading me, trying to coax me into taking a sip, but I've made up my mind.

"Stubborn, stupid little bitch. Drink, damn it. DRINK THE FUCKING WATER!"

The human body can survive for weeks without food so long as it has water.

But if I don't drink...

...then maybe it won't take as long to fade away.

12

ELODIE

Being resurrected from the dead has its benefits.

Most important of which: my friends have started messaging me again.

I jog down the stairs, head buried in my phone, trying to read Ayala's most recent text without getting busted by a member of staff. I'm smirking, cheeks aching, totally entranced by the look of abject sorrow on Peter Horovitz's face—the guy even wore a *suit* to my memorial at Mary Magdalene's—which is why I don't see the dark black smudge fast approaching down the hall on my left.

Oh my god. Peter, Peter, Peter. That's what you get for not asking me to the winter formal, isn—WOAH! The impact drives the wind right out of my lungs. I lunge, fingers grasping at thin air as I fall sideways, trying to close my hand around my cell phone. It's too late, though. The device spins end over end, moving too slowly as it plummets, plummets, plummets…and hits the polished marble floor in the entranceway with a heart-rending *crack!*

My hip likely made the same unnerving sound when I hit the floor, but I don't care about my damn hip. My phone. Jesus, if my phone's broken, I am totally *fucked.*

"Impressive, Little E," a cool voice says above me. From my

sprawling vantage point on the ground, I look up and find Wren standing over me. He isn't smiling. Not even his smug ass, arrogant, *I'm gonna make you fall in love with me* smile. Nope. Today, his face looks like it was carved from granite. Very *angry* granite. His eyes are so glacial and distant that a physical chill runs down my spine. "Pink and white polka dots. Didn't have you pegged as a cotton brief kind of girl," he says, arching an eyebrow as his gaze travels down my body...

"Oh my god!" *My skirt.* Embarrassment claws at me as I rip the tartan material of my skirt down, covering my ass, which was, until a second ago, on display for all the world to see. Of course. Of course I picked out my ugliest underwear this morning, and of course I walked straight into Wren and flashed him my dowdy granny panties.

Just fucking...great. Seriously. Just great.

Wren's top lip curls upward; he looks disgusted as he steps over me. I get a close-up of the tread of his boots, three inches away from my nose, before I close my eyes, eaten alive by shame. "Looks like your phone's just been decommissioned," Wren grunts. "Too bad. Nearest repair place isn't for fifty miles. Should've looked where you were going."

I bite the inside of my cheek until I taste blood. Propping myself up on my elbow, at last registering the dull ache in my side, I reach out for my iPhone and go to grab it before it can sustain any more damage, but Wren's foot sweeps out, kicking the device across the floor. It comes to a stop at the base of a plinth, on which the copper bust of a balding Victorian-looking gentleman angrily sneers down at me.

"God, Jacobi. Way to go. Didn't think it was possible for you to be even more of an asshole, but you just keep on leveling up." Carina arrives, dressed in a yellow and blue Wolf Hall tracksuit, her hair tied back in tight, neat braids. She grabs the phone first, presumably so Wren can't stomp on the damn thing and grind the screen to dust under the heel of his boot. She comes for me next, giving me a hand and pulling me to my feet.

Fuuuuck. My phone is *toast*. The screen isn't just cracked. It's dark and the back light's completely out. This is just typical. The moment I finally get back in touch with Levi and Ayala, boom! With my laptop still out of commission and it taking an excessive amount of time to be replaced by Harcourt, my only means of communication with the outside world just died a death right before my eyes.

"Shit," Carina whispers, looking down at the defunct glass and metal; it's nothing more than a paperweight now. "God, I don't think that thing's salvageable."

"It's gonna have to be. My father won't let me put a new phone on my credit card. No way. He just gave me this one. He—"

Stupid fucking girl.

Careless...

Reckless...

Thoughtless...

I flinch away from each word, bracing for a fist that doesn't come. When I look up, Wren's cold veneer's cracked a little, and I glimpse something else—something that looks like...*concern?* Hah. Yeah. Now I'm imagining things. I must have hit my head.

"I'd drive you to get it fixed tomorrow, Elle, but I promised I'd help organize a party in town. I can take you next weekend, though?"

"*Elle?* Doesn't suit you," Wren sneers.

"Mind your own business, Jacobi. Go on. Fuck off before I go tell Harcourt what you did."

His coal-black eyebrows shoot up. "What *I* did? She ploughed into me. I was minding my own business, on my way to class."

"*Just go,*" Carina snarls.

I want to look down at my phone. I instruct my nerves and muscles to obey, but they pointedly disregard the command. Instead, I stare at Wren as he shrugs, his gaze searing into my skin like a brand as he backs away down the corridor. Carina waits until he's out of ear shot before she says anything else.

"Arrogant *prick,*" she seethes. "I fucking hate that guy. I'd rather contract herpes than have to spend another minute at this school with him roaming around the halls like he owns the fucking place."

I snort out half-hearted laughter, slapping the busted phone into the palm of my hand and cringing mournfully when tiny fragments of glass rain down onto the floor at my feet. "Herpes? Wow. You really *must* hate him."

Carina scowls. She takes me by the sleeve of my sweater and pulls me toward our science class, just as the bell announces our tardiness. "Like you wouldn't believe, Stillwater. Like you wouldn't fucking believe."

* * *

"Um…hey. Um…"

I glance up from my vegetable pesto pasta, surly and hostile. I must *look* hostile, too, the way I'm brandishing my fork like it's a murder weapon and I'm about to sink it into the neck of an unsuspecting passerby. The pale guy with the grey eyes standing on the other side of the table quails when our eyes meet. He seems to grow even paler as the seconds tick by with neither of us saying anything. Poor guy. If I weren't in such a monster of a bad mood, I might feel sorry for him on account of his awkwardness. My mood being what it is, however, I have no pity for him. He's done this to himself. I'm putting out some blisteringly negative energy, and he made the decision to come over here and bother me. If he gets second degree burns from my withering stare, then that's on him.

"My—my name's—it's Tom. Tom Petrov. That's my name. And I just—" He puffs out his cheeks, blinking rapidly, shaking his head. I notice that he's got a split lip. Looks fresh. Resetting himself, he steps forward and holds out his hand. "I'm Tom. Nice uh…to finally meet you. I just came over to introduce myself and to offer my services."

I release him from my tractor beam stare, spearing a piece of undercooked carrot onto my fork, ripping it from the tines with my front teeth. Tom jumps when I bite down and the carrot crunches loudly. "I'm having a bad day, Tom. I'm probably not gonna be into the services you're so kindly offering."

"Oh, really?" He fiddles, picking at his fingernails. "'Cause I heard Carina saying you broke your phone and you were gonna have to wait until next week to get it fixed, and I—well, I fix phones in my spare time, so..."

My fork clatters down onto my lunch tray. "You fix phones," I say. "*You* fix phones?"

Tom nods. "Screens mostly. Sometimes I need to pull data, though. It can be tricky to get absolutely everything off a device. Did—did you drop it in water?"

"No. No, it just hit the floor pretty hard. It won't even turn on."

Tom nods. "Is it brand new?" he asks. "If it's brand new and I replace the screen, it'll void the warranty."

"New to me. Not brand new." Dad makes out like he's giving me one of his fucking kidneys every time he replaces my cell phone, but I know from the little scuffs and nicks that they've always had at least one owner before me. Usually his military aide. He's never been one to shell out money on something he can get for free.

"Then it's probably outside of its warranty, anyway. You got nothing to lose, having me take a look at it."

The dining hall's emptier than usual. People have been cooped up inside all week because of the rain; now that it's finally stopped, they're braving the cold and taking their food outside. I love the quiet, and I'm thrilled that I'm not being stared at by thirty people I don't know the first thing about, but the thing I like about eating in the dining hall? The thing I like the best? Wren and his cronies are too good to eat in here with the common folk. Not once have I seen any of them disgrace this communal area with their presence, which means I'm safe here. I don't have to worry about snide quips, or dirty looks, or a face so fucking pretty and evil that it makes me want to weep.

Wren would probably get a kick out of my inner conflict. It doesn't take a rocket scientist to know that he'd be rubbing his psychotic hands together if only he knew how many traitorous thoughts I have about him every single fucking day.

But...

Jesus, I've just spent a solid twenty seconds thinking about Wren when there's someone standing in front of me, waiting for me to hold up my end of a conversation. What the fuck is wrong with me?

Back to the matter at hand.

Giving my full attention to Tom, I size him up. "What happened to your lip, Tom?"

His eyes round out. "Huh?"

I point my fork at him again. "Your bottom lip. It's split wide open."

He touches his fingers to his mouth like he was unaware of the injury. "Oh! Oh, I was lying in bed this morning, looking at Instagram, and I dropped my phone. It hit me in the mouth. Stupid right? You ever done that before? Hurts like a bitch."

I clear my throat, giving him another once over. "Why are you being nice to me? We've never spoken before."

He shifts from one foot to the other, clearing his throat. "Well, I'd hate to crush any ideas you might have had about my philanthropic spirit, but, well, I get *paid* for this kind of work. I'm here on a scholarship, so..."

Oh, come on. I am *such* an asshole. It's easy to forget that not every single student at these schools is rolling in paper. Some schools do have scholarship students. Some students at places like Wolf Hall even have jobs and need to work the weekends to help support themselves. I feel like a grade-A asshole for completely disremembering people whose fathers haven't squirreled away millions and are required to pick up the slack.

I sit up straight, pushing my food away. "How much?"

"A hundred if it's just the screen. Including parts. If it's one of the newer phones, I should have what I need here on campus. If not, I'll have to order the stuff online, which usually takes about a week to arrive."

"It's last year's model."

"So, yeah. I should have you covered."

"And if the phone's fucked and you need to pull the data?"

"That's an extra thirty. It's not super hard. I could show you how to do it if you wanted to save money, but most people have me do it to save themselves some time."

The data on my phone is minimal. No photos. No huge text strings that I'm sentimental over. It was clean when Colonel Stillwater gave it to me, so I'm not really concerned about that. Going radio silent, after my friends have only just discovered I'm not dead, though? I'm fairly concerned about *that*. "How quick could you get it back to me?"

Tom jerks. He looks surprised that I might actually be considering hiring him. "Uh, oh, well usually three days or so, but since you're new I figure I could try and put a rush on it."

"Okay."

"Okay?"

"Yeah. I can't get to Albany this weekend. I'd prefer not to have to wait until next weekend to get this taken care of, so...sure. Take it." I dig around in my bag until I locate the busted phone, and then I hold it out to Tom across the table. He swallows, relief dominating his features. Damn, the poor bastard must be really hard up for cash.

He puts the phone in his pocket, backing away from the table. "Okay. Okay. Well, uh, thanks. If I can get it back to you any quicker, I'll let you know."

13

WREN

BREATHING. Blinking. Swallowing.

Some skills are innate. We're born with them. Without them, we'd die the moment we come screaming into the world, vulnerable and covered in viscera. I feel like *I* was spat out of my mother's womb capable of tying a half-Windsor knot. It feels like a skill I came equipped with at birth. Because when you're born into a family like mine and you're landed with the kind of father *I* was landed with, such talents are required if you hope to survive.

I twist the black silk around on itself, tucking it up through the loop, feeding the length of material through the gap between the front of the knot, fiddling with it until it sits perfectly at the base of my throat. Who needs a fucking mirror for this shit?

"They're gonna think you're the waitstaff again," Dashiell states, holding the door to the ballroom open for me.

"They always do."

"A white shirt. That's all you'd need to differentiate yourself. White's *totally* acceptable, Wren. A white button-down wouldn't put a dent in the whole bad guy façade you've got going on in the slightest."

I follow him into the politely seething crowd, flattening down my collar with a smooth flick of my wrist. "I'm fine with what I'm wearing." Actually, I'm far from fine. This is only the second set of clothes I've been able to wear since my punishment ended, and some ripped jeans and my favorite, ratty sweater would be much more preferable. This monkey suit is a fucking torture device.

Dashiell's suit is classically cut and perfectly tailored. Pax's suit is a Tom Ford, and retails for twenty grand. Both of them look so content in their luxuriously fitted finery that I hate them a little for it; I'm happy as a pig in shit during the most awkward, miserable, wretched situations, but being restrained by a suit is something I've never handled well. If my father could see me now, he'd laugh his fucking ass off.

"Don't suppose any of the women at this thing are fair game," Pax observes. Though it's more of a sly enquiry than a true observation. There's just enough of a lilt at the end of his statement to suggest that he's open to Dashiell correcting his assumption.

Wise to his tricks, Dashiell snags a glass of champagne from a passing waiter holding a silver tray aloft in the air, his expression all business. "Pax, if you so much as look at a single one of the women in this room tonight, I will personally castrate you and feed your testicles to my father's hunting dogs."

Pax adopts a grumpy air as he, too, grabs himself a glass of champagne. "People don't have hunting dogs in America, Lovett."

Dashiell clinks his flute against the one in Pax's hand, *cheers*ing him. "Yes, they do. But either way, I'll happily fly back to Blighty with your balls in a mason jar, buddy." From the outside, Dash doesn't look like the kind of guy who'd deign to get his hands dirty. There's a soft, well-heeled vibe to him that has people betting against him in a fight. Looks can be, and *are*, very deceptive, though. Dashiell's as fierce as they come. Irrespective of his breeding and his education, he's not afraid to throw a fist or two. I've seen him shove his finger up a dude's nose and rip his nostril wide open in a brawl before. Guy really does not give a shit.

Pax grumbles unintelligibly under his breath as he drains his drink in one. He doesn't doubt Dash's threat. He will steer clear of the women at tonight's event, but that doesn't mean he has to be happy about it.

"And don't drink too much, either," Dash says, surveying the room. He looks cool and collected, but he's on edge, I can tell. He looks like he's casually taking in the chandeliers, and the antique furniture, and the handsome people, dressed in all their regalia, but Lord Dashiell Lovett the fourth is looking for his father. It could be said that Dash is always looking for his father. For his approval, that is.

"Remind me again why we agreed to come to this travesty?" Pax growls. His eyes are steel-grey tonight, the color of the angry North Sea.

"Because you both owe me," Dash answers brightly. "And because I asked you to. And because you're good friends who would never fuck over their mate."

Urgh. Doing things I don't want to do in order to make someone else happy is not in my nature. "I need to send a text. I'll be right back," I mutter.

"Don't wander too far, Jacobi. I need you back here in ten."

Smiling thinly, I sketch a mock bow. "Back in five."

Outside, the night air is brittle in my lungs. The chatter from inside still rings in my ears as I become accustomed to the deafening silence. The manor house is on a hundred acres, which might not be a lot of land in the grand scheme of things —even Wolf Hall sits on three times that—but it's as though the dense woodland stretches on forever into the dark, and it feels like we're the only living things for a thousand miles. Right on cue, an owl screeches in the distance, and the sound is eerie and piercing, as if the creature's indignant that I forgot about him.

Grim as an undertaker, I pull out my phone and power it on, waiting for the screen to light up. I could fidget and tap at the display to hurry the process along, but that'd be ridiculous. Technology can't be expedited by willful human impatience. So I stare at the phone instead, grinding my teeth together as I wait for the illuminated Apple logo to blink out and the home screen to appear.

There.

Finally.

Working quickly to avoid the inundation of texts and notifications that begin to pour in, I open up a blank message and tap out a quick message.

+1 (819) 3328 6582
Did you get it?

Niceties aren't required here. Even if they were, the recipient of this text wouldn't be getting any. I place the phone down on the flat railing that skirts the balcony, and I turn back to face the building, blankly observing the people through the windows, wondering what they could all possibly be so happy about.

The woman in the gold, sparkling dress has so much credit card debt, she's about to lose her house.

The guy with three fingers of whiskey in his cut glass tumbler, even though it's only seven thirty and we haven't even sat down to our four-course dinner yet, has just been diagnosed with prostate cancer.

At the back, near the bar, the couple fawning over each other and making a show of their affection as they talk to an elderly gentleman wearing a smoking jacket have just filed for divorce.

The dude by the piano fantasizes about touching his wife's twelve-year-old daughter from her previous marriage.

The bartender, smiling so professionally, so politely, as he makes cocktail after cocktail with flare, has been considering suicide for months.

Vrrrrrn vrrrrnnnnnn. Vrrrrrn vrrrrnnnnnn.

I glare at the lying, deceptive degenerates, despising everything that they are and everything they stand for. I could be wrong about the people I've just picked apart—it was all blind conjecture at best—but I know this set. They're expert fabricators and masters of their craft. The shiny veneers they present to the world are wafer thin and disintegrate like wet paper when inspected up close.

Revolted, I turn back to my phone.

Incoming Message:
+1 (819) 3328 6582
Yes.

ME: Operational?

+1 (819) 3328 6582
Yes. What should I do with it?

ME: Leave it where we discussed.

"Well, well, well. What's this? Do my eyes deceive me? Wren Jacobi, alive and in the flesh."

Oh, for fuck's sake.

Exhaling sharply down my nose, I turn the phone off and pocket it before I turn around. The girl emerging from the doorway isn't really a girl anymore. She's all woman, with her exaggerated curves and the seductive sway to her hips as she walks toward me. Her jet-black hair's long and wavy, fixed in place like some sort of forties Hollywood starlet. The crimson color of her lipstick suits her perfectly. She looks like a pale, porcelain-skinned vampire, who's just had her mouth clamped around someone's jugular and spilled her main course.

In every way, she's perfect. In every way, I hate her.

Detestable creature.

"Mercy. If I'd have known you were gonna be here, I'd have torched the building to the ground and fled to Europe."

"Charming, as always," she purrs, sauntering to the balustrade. There's a fifteen-foot stretch of open space to my right, but of course the bitch comes and stands as close to me as humanly possible. The subtle scent of her perfume makes my stomach roll. "I saw your illiterate friend inside. The one who looks like a murderer. I spent all of three seconds trying to calculate where you'd be before I came up with the answer."

"Yeah. You know me so well, Mercy. Excuse me. I have to get back inside."

She doesn't listen, or else chooses not to hear me, talking over me as I step away. "Can't I bum a smoke?"

Halting, I roll my eyes up at the clear night sky, resenting the moment I ever agreed to come to this fucking party. Under normal circumstances, I'd pin her up against the side of the building by her throat and tell her to go fuck herself, but the consequences would be disastrous. Mercy's the queen of theater, a lauded actress whose ability to cry on cue has already landed her three reasonably large speaking parts on Broadway. I lay a finger on her here, at Lord Lovett's Charity Benefit *for Battered Women*, and she'll undertake the role of a lifetime. After a flood of tears and some smeared mascara, I'll be carted off in fucking handcuffs.

No, thanks.

Grudgingly, I offer her the pack of smokes I had in my pocket, resigning myself to the fact that I'm gonna be out here with her until she's finished with me.

She places the cigarette against her lips, smiling knowingly as she snaps the catch on the small silver lighter she always carries around with her, lighting up. A thick fog of smoke spills down her nose, curling off into the chilly February air.

"You weren't in the city at Christmas. I drove all the way to the Upper East Side only to find out you were off galivanting without me in the Czech Republic."

I give her an icy grin. "Yeah, well. It's the only place that I'm safe from you. I know how much you loathe Prague. Sorry you had a wasted journey. Driving yourself has always made you feel poor, hasn't it?"

A vicious light sparks in her green eyes. "We could have gone somewhere together, y'know. The fireworks over Sydney Harbor on New Years' Eve were epic. You said you wanted to go there last year."

Hah. Last year. Many things have changed in the past 12 months. "I'm sure you had a great time without me, Merce. You're milking that cigarette for all its worth. Get it finished so I can go."

Her smile morphs into a mirthless slash across her face. "No need to be so belligerent all the time, Wren. Is it so bad that I might wanna spend a couple of minutes with you? Am I really *that* awful? All that frowning and pouting's gonna prematurely age you. And then what?"

"And then I'll be hideous, and people will see me for who I truly am," I spit, sarcasm dripping from each word as I storm toward the door. I thought I could handle being out here with her, but I was wrong. She asked if she's really all that bad? Hell fucking yes, she is. She shouldn't even fucking be here. There's no way Dash's father sent her an invite, which means...

No.

You've got to be kidding me.

I'm going to fucking kill him.

"You can't just keep storming off," Mercy calls after me. "I always know where you are, Wren. *Always.* We'll be spending plenty of time together soon enough."

I almost hesitate. I almost ask what the fuck that was supposed to mean, but I refuse to give her the satisfaction. Knowing Mercy as well as I do, she's fully explained her intentions with that carefully delivered, off-the-cuff remark: she's coming back to Wolf Hall.

I find Dashiell talking to a balding man by the overloaded buffet table. Manners dictate that I should wait until he's finished his conversation, but I'm too steaming mad to observe social etiquette. "Mercy? You invited *Mercy?*"

Dashiell stops talking, his mouth hanging open. He closes it, then opens it again, groping for something to say.

"Excuse me. I see my wife beckoning me," the old bald guy says, making a sharp exit.

Dash looks like he'd do the same if he could. "Look, I just think that this thing with this new girl...You're not seeing things straight, Jacobi, and you seem to reset whenever Mercy's around, so I thought—"

"So you thought, *I know what I'll do. I'll drag the poisonous cunt who ruined Wren's life across state lines. She's bound to make everything better.*"

"Goddamn it. You're whispering. I don't like when you whisper. Means you're about to start smashing things. Can we—can we please just talk about this later? Avoid her if you have to, but maybe the four of us can sit down after—"

"Intentionally allowing that girl within a two-hundred-mile radius of any of us is folly and you know it. I am not *sitting down* with her."

As if magnetically drawn from the other side of the room by the promise of an argument, Pax appears with a napkin full of grilled shrimp in his hand. He looks devilish. "Guess who I just ran into."

"I've already seen her," I snarl.

Pax tosses a shrimp into his mouth, tail and all. "Mercy got hot, dude. And I'm talking *hot.*"

This must be payback for kicking his headrest this morning. "Be very, very careful," I hiss.

"What? It's just an observation. No need to get so bent out of shape."

Amused, he chews with his mouth open, watching me intently. I think he's waiting for me to throw a fist at him. Between his blatant attempt to rile me and Dash's utterly thoughtless attempt to smooth over troubled waters, I want to break both their goddamn necks. "Fuck this. I'm outta here."

"You can't leave. We came in one car," Dash says smugly. Obviously, he thought about that; he knew I wasn't going to be able to jump in my own vehicle and bail if Pax brought the Charger. Dash's trouble is that he isn't an immediate problem solver, though. I pat my phone, fury sizzling underneath my skin. "Don't worry. *I'll Uber.*"

"For god's sake, Jacobi! Don't be so melodramatic. Stay! Have a drink. Enjoy yourself!" Why he even bothers is a mystery. Dash knows that once my mind's made up, it's made up. He calls after me as I barge my way through the crowd, toward the exit.

"Come on, Jacobi! I thought twins were supposed to get on better than this!"

14

ELODIE

"Come on, girl. You know you want to."

I don't want to. I *really* don't, but Carina has a pleading look on her face that's making it hard to say no to her. "I'm sorry, I'm just so tired. And a party? I won't know anyone apart from you."

"You'll know me," Pres sings, as she flies past my door, her hands full of a hot pink dress that will, one hundred percent, clash horribly with her auburn hair.

"See." Carina crosses her arms, acting like she's already won this battle. "And Rashida's gonna be there."

"Rashida's barely said more than three words to me since I got here." I burrow deeper into my covers, pulling my duvet up underneath my chin. "It's so nice and warm in here. And anyway, I'm already in my pajamas."

"Don't lie, Stillwater. You're fully dressed under there, aren't you?"

"Urgh. Having to spend hours at a party, mocked and ridiculed by Riot House boys, does not sound like a good time, okay?"

"Hah! They don't attend parties in town. They're too pretentious and stuck up their own asses to mingle with Mountain Lakes kids. And anyway, I heard Pax telling Damiana that all three of them were heading to Boston for the weekend. Dash's father's hosting some kind of charity thing. So you can forget about using them as an excuse right now."

I scowl, sticking out my bottom lip. "Look. I'm horrible in large social gatherings. I don't know how to talk to people. I'll only embarrass you, and then you won't wanna be friends anymore."

"Garbage. We're cooped up here all week long and you wanna stay here all weekend, too? Sorry. Can't allow it. Come on. Let's blow this pop stand."

I am not gonna be able to get out of this, I can tell. She is right, though. It doesn't make sense to cloister myself up in my room all weekend, when we're forbidden from leaving during the week. Seems like some form of barbaric self-inflicted punishment that I'm not entirely sure I deserve.

"Who's throwing this party again?"

She jumps up and down, clapping her hands together. "Yay!"

"Carina, nooooo, I didn't agree to anything. You gotta tell me who's throwing the party!"

She shrugs her denim jacket off one shoulder, posing dramatically, grinning like a fiend. "Does it even matter? There'll be booze. There'll be boys. There'll be music. Come on, Elle. Throw on your shortest skirt and let's GO!"

* * *

The mansion—a sleek masterpiece perched on a cliff edge overlooking the town's largest lake—is big enough to house an entire football team. And the guy who's throwing this party, Oscar, is the son of an ex NFL player, so that kind of makes sense.

It takes the entire drive down the mountain to figure out who knows Oscar and if we've actually even been invited to this thing, by which time I've stopped caring and I'm ready for a beer.

The party's in full swing when we walk through the front door —people dancing and whooping along to the loud, hectic bassline that's pumping through the professional speakers; shots being thrown back; not one but *two* beer pong games underway; and so many people I recognize that I immediately relax. Half of Wolf Hall is here. I might not be on first name terms with most of these guys, but I recognize them, and if they're allowed to be here, then I'm sure I am too.

"We need a bathroom pitstop," Carina declares, dragging me through the swell of dancing bodies. I apologize to people as I bump into them, but I'm met with friendly faces. No one seems to mind a little jostling. When Carina tracks down a restroom, she pulls me inside and slams the door, spinning around excitedly and leaning against it, laying her palms flat against the wood. "So. I might not have mentioned this. But there's a guy."

I hoist myself up to sit on the marble counter by the sink, pulling up my pantyhose, careful not to catch my fingernails on the sparkly, thin material. "Of course there's a guy," I agree. "Who is he? What's his name? Does he go to the academy?"

"He's a freshman at the University of Albany. His name's Andre, and he's beautiful. He's friends with Oscar's older brother, and he promised he was gonna be here tonight."

"And we like this Andre guy?"

Carina nods enthusiastically. "We like him a lot. He's smart. Kind. Funny. Asks permission before he kisses me, which is actually kind of weird, but it's better than the alternative. And he looks like a young Andy Samberg, so there's also that."

"*Andy Samberg?*"

"I have a very unique sense of taste, my friend. Haven't you already figured that out from the clothes?"

In fairness, she's wearing a pair of purple corduroy dungarees with four leaf clover patches sewn all over them. The t-shirt she's wearing beneath the overalls has a deranged-looking cat printed across the front of it.

"Okay. I get it, I get it," I say, laughing. "But the only other guy I've known you to be interested in is…well, *you know who*, and he looks like a classic Greek statue. There's nothing quirky or weird about *him* at all. He's like...vanilla ice cream. But the most expensive, most decadent, luxurious vanilla ice cream money can buy."

Carina snorts, regarding herself in the mirror. She runs the tap, wetting her fingers and smoothing down her hair, which she's wearing *au naturel* tonight: big, and beautiful, and bouncy. "That's the thing, though, isn't it? Everyone likes vanilla ice cream. You could be into pistachio, or licorice, or...I don't know," she laughs, "fucking *wasabi* flavored ice cream, but when a to-die-for vanilla ice cream comes along, you're still gonna want to give it a try. Because vanilla ice cream looks so good, and it tastes so good, and you think you know what you're getting. But *then* you realize that the milk's actually turned and you've been poisoned, and..." She runs out of steam, shaking her head. "I don't know. Vanilla ice cream turned out to be disgusting."

"What kind of ice cream do you think Andre is?" I ask, watching her as she applies some lip balm.

"Easy. He's a cilantro-lime ice cream sandwich." She grins, biting down on her tongue playfully. "A little off-beat. A little kooky. A little strange. But all of his weird parts somehow all work together. I like that about him."

It's nice that she's this excited about a guy. I thought after her tears at the diner last weekend that it'd be a long time before she found anyone she might like to swoon over. And yet here she is, swooning away.

"What kind of ice cream do you think *Wren* is?" she asks, fluttering her eyelashes at me.

"That's a messed-up question to ask. Why would I be thinking about what kind of ice cream that boy is?"

"I don't know. You tell me..." She sounds airy and unaffected, but I'm looking right at her face in the mirror. I can see the cautious expression she's trying to stave off. "You look at him a lot. He looks at you a lot. I figured, what with all the negative tension floating around in the air, that something might be going on..."

"Wren Jacobi is *not* ice cream. He's a lump of stale cheese smothered in rat poison, and I have absolutely no interest in sampling him."

Carina laughs good-naturedly, clicking the lid onto her lip balm and dropping it back into her purse. "All right. I'll believe you, girl. But just so you know...millions wouldn't."

* * *

Oscar looks like a linebacker. He's six foot three and almost as wide, and when he moves, everyone at the party moves with him, gravitating toward him like they're trapped in his orbit. You can hear him laugh—a rich, warm, booming sound—over the driving beat of the music, which he changes every minute or so, unable to commit to one song without having to switch it over to something else.

I'm introduced to him on four separate occasions, and he doesn't remember me once—an impoliteness that's tempered by how happy he is when he learns my name all over again and hugs me like he means it.

In between my run-ins with Oscar, Carina feeds me beer after beer like the party's about to run out of booze any second. I'm no stranger to alcohol. I've tried every drink known to man, but admittedly it's been a while; I'm buzzed by beer number three, and drunk by the time I hit the bottom of cup number five.

At around eleven, Carina turns bright pink and points out a guy across the living room that really does look like a young Andy Samberg. He beams at her the moment he sees her, and then that's it. My friend has eyes for no one but Andre. I don't begrudge her the time spent with her new cilantro-lime ice cream sandwich; when you find your yum, you gotta enjoy every second of it while you can.

And anyways. I have Presley to keep me company.

"People tend to overlook the one with the skinhead," she says, rocking beside me on her chair. She's drunk, but still making sense. I think. Maybe we've hit that perfect equilibrium where she's so drunk that she's not making sense, and I'm so drunk that her mumbled words and fuzzy statements actually sound like real words.

"People think he's stupid because he's a model, but I had to work with him on a science po—prop—*project* last year, and he was really smart. Really, really, really smart."

I pass her the beer we're sharing. "Really, really, really smart?"

"Yes!" she says, snickering. "Really, really, really...really, really..." She forgets what she was going to say. "Anyway, his name is Pax. That means peace in Latin. Did you know that?"

"I *did* know that."

"Oooh, look at you. Clever little Elodie. I like *your* name. What does Elodie mean?"

I hiccup loudly, trying to focus on Presley's pretty, freckled face, but there are currently three of her swaying about all over the place and I'm not sure which version of her I'm supposed to be addressing. "It means 'foreign riches,'" I tell the middle Presley. "In French. It was my mom's middle name."

"It's rrrreally pretty," Pres slurs. "Really, really, really, rea..." She realizes what she's doing and bursts out laughing. "God, at least you weren't named after a fat man in a wig who...who fucking died sitting on the toilet, while sim...ul...ta...neous...ly—" She struggles with this one, "—eating a hamburger and taking a giant shit."

"I don't think that was ever proven," I splutter, trying not to laugh. How am I supposed to keep a straight face when she's coming up with this stuff?

"God, I'm really fucked up," she says, wobbling as she tries to get to her feet. "I think I need a speed walk around the grounds to wake up. You ever seen those speed walkers? They look fucking ridiculous, don't they? Hey! Oh, hey! Tom! Look, Elle, it's Tom from the academy. He hasn't seen us. Come on, let's go scare the shit out of him."

"Pres, I think I'd rather just stay...here..." It's too late, though. She has me by the wrist and she's dragging me up onto my feet.

Before I know it, we're on the other side of Oscar's living room, and we're standing behind Tom, who's telling a very animated story to some of his friends. "And then he was, like, leaning his forearm against my throat, looking at me like he was gonna fucking kill me, and I couldn't fucking breathe, and I was like, "All right! All right! I'll fucking do it. Just get the fuck off of me, man!'"

"The guy's unhinged," a tall guy with glasses says. "I heard he stabbed one of the teachers during spring break last year."

"Don't be stupid," the only girl in Tom's little group says. The ends of her bright blonde hair have been dyed purple. She rolls her eyes. "If one of the teachers got stabbed, don't you think we'd know about it? And why the hell would they let him continue attending the academy if he hurt one of the faculty. You should really run this shit through a filter before you let it spew outta your mouth, Clay. You know the rule. We fact check *everything* before we announce it as gospel."

"Relax, Jem. Jesus. He's just telling us what he heard," a short guy breaking apart a brownie with his fingers says. He tips back his head and drops some of the gooey chocolate cake into his mouth.

"Urgh! None of you are listening to me!" Tom holds his hands up, exasperated. "Jacobi threatened to fucking *kill* me. And if I don't get that girl's phone back by the end of tomorrow, she's gonna know something's up. She'll probably report me to Harcourt. I'll get expelled, and my grandfather will kill me, and I end up dead in either scenario, so I'd really like some fucking *help*, please, 'cause I'm kinda freaking out right now, and—"

The kid eating the brownie swallows. "Hey, Tom?"

"What, Elliot? *WHAT?*"

"What's this girl look like? The one with the phone?"

"I don't know. She's hot. Short. Petite. Blonde hair. She has nice eyes. What the fuck does that matter?"

Elliot grins humorlessly. "'Cause I'm pretty sure she's standing behind you. And she looks pissed, man."

Tom whips around like he's just been poked up the ass with a cattle prod. "Oh, shit. Elodie! Uh...yeah, it's Elodie. How you doing? Are you, um—" He rubs frantically at the back of his neck. "Are you enjoying the party?"

I was enjoying the party.

Now, I am not.

Now, I'm the embodiment of rage.

I'm a blistering sun, about to go supernova.

I'm eighteen different kinds of angry.

I'm mentally listing off all of the ways I could kill Tom and make it so that the authorities never find his skinny ass.

"*Explain,*" I growl.

"Uh, uh, well, I don't know what you heard or anything, but—"

"You know what? Don't bother with the explanation. Just tell me what he wants with my phone and I might not break your miserable neck."

Tom's pupils dilate—a panic response. Some guys might not believe a girl so small and so *blonde* as me could ever be violent. Tom believes me, though. He sees the murder in my eyes, and he knows, drunk though I am, that I will skin him alive. "He, I mean, I don't know. I guess...I have no clue why he wanted it. He told me to fix it as quickly as I could and then take it over to his place. He told me to leave it on the desk in his room, and then get the fuck out of there. That's it. That's all I know." He grabs the white napkin Elliot was holding his brownie in and waves it in the air. "I'm sorry, okay. Look! I surrender! I'm not good at this kind of stuff, all right? I'm used to people like you and like...like *him* ignoring me. I don't exist to you people, and I wanna go back to being invisible, because this really *sucks.*"

It's taken me a beat to notice the split lip again. I see it now, though, because he's been talking so animatedly that he's reopened the wound, and a snake of bright red blood's running down his chin. Wren did that to him. Beside me, Presley coughs uncomfortably. "Maybe we should go find Carina. I don't wanna get tangled up in Riot House shit. This sounds like a you and her kind of thing."

I advance on Tom, pitying him and hating him in equal parts. He goes very, very pale. "What does that mean? People like me?"

"You know," he says softly. "Popular kids. Members of the social elite. You…you're like them."

The fury that's been spinning around like a ball of white, searing heat in my chest detonates, shattering my mind apart for a moment. Jem awkwardly sidles her way out of the group, slinking away, her eyes glued to the floorboards. Elliot and Clay look too stunned to move. "I'm not like them," I hiss. "I'm nothing like them. How can you say that? You don't know me at all."

Tom lowers the napkin as if resigned now to his fate. He knows he's said the wrong thing. I'm a microsecond away from throwing myself on him, when Carina arrives in a swirl of purple fabric and braids. "Hey! What's up, guys? Jem just said a fight was about to break out in here."

I can't bring myself to look at her. "Tell her what you did, Tom."

He blinks. "It isn't like I had a choice," he moans.

Carina's friendly tone evaporates. "Tom Petrov. *Tell me what you've done.*"

15

ELODIE

"For the record, this is a horrible idea. You know that, right?"

I grunt, tucking my chin into the collar of my jacket. It's freezing in Carina's car. Her mood's frosty, too. She's pissed that she's had to leave her Samberg lookalike unattended back at Oscar's, but this *was* her choice. "I told you to stay," I grumble. "I could have ordered an Uber."

"Uber drivers won't take us up the mountain," she grouses. "Too many entitled Wolf Hall kids have thrown up in the back of their Priuses. We're blacklisted, down to a man."

"Well, *that's* bullshit."

"So, no, you couldn't have ordered an Uber. I'm the only way you were getting back up this hill, and I'm telling you, categorically, that this is fucking *insanity*."

"You said it yourself, Carrie. Those arrogant motherfuckers are in Boston tonight. They won't be back until tomorrow at the earliest. So what does it matter? They'll never even know we were there."

"Of course they'll know! Wren will know as soon as he sees that your phone's not in his room. And then what?"

"Right. And then what? He can't exactly report it as a theft, can he? He obtained my property via means of assault for unknown, nefarious purposes. The last thing he's gonna do is tell anyone that I went into their precious house to take back what is rightfully mine."

"Christ," Carina mutters through clenched teeth. "You have no idea what you're getting yourself into, girl. No idea what you're getting *me* into. You're still drunk. Why don't we wait until morning, have a think, and see if we can't come up with a better pla—"

"I'm stone cold sober now and you know it. Look, I totally get it. If I were you, I wouldn't want any part of this either. Why don't you just drop me off in front of the house and go back to the party. I can walk the rest of the way from there."

"Two miles, Elle? In the middle of the night? In the cold and the dark? Along windy, narrow roads? You'll get smoked by a car. They won't even see you until it's too late. What kind of friend would that make me, huh?"

I have nothing to say to that. What *can* I say? Hiking my way back to Wolf Hall sounds like a shit time. There's no sugarcoating it. And she would be a crappy friend if she left me on the side of a mountain road. I'm grateful that she's in possession of a fully functioning conscience. That said, I don't want to put her in a compromising position, though.

We sit in silence, watching the twin beams from the headlights pierce through the dark like swords of light, illuminating fifteen feet of blacktop in front of us. After a while, Carina says, "Fucking piece of shit. I knew he was creepy, but I didn't know he was *this* creepy. He was probably gonna load up that phone with spyware apps. He'd have been listening to your calls and reading all of your texts. He would have been able to access your camera whenever he wanted…God, I didn't even think about that until now."

"Mmm." I've thought about it. I have experience with cloned phones and all manner of different spyware. It's all been loaded onto my phone before. What Carina doesn't know is that my phone is already brimming over with ghost apps and dummy screens, all designed to trick me into thinking I'm not being watched. My father would have made sure of it. "We'll get in, get the phone, and then we won't have to worry about any of that," I mumble.

"You should call the cops, Elle. I'm serious. This is some shady shit."

"Let's just see what we're dealing with first." I'm fobbing her off. I'm sure she knows that. But getting the police involved now would be bad. For starters, Wolf Hall will report the incident to my father, and there's no way in hell I'll risk him jumping on a plane to come and find out what's going on in person. I'd rather be dragged over hot coals than have to face him.

My pulse jumps all over the place when Carina kills the headlights and turns into the driveway that leads through the forest to Riot House. I can tell by the way she grips onto the steering wheel that she's anxious. About getting caught breaking into the place or being here in general, I can't tell, but I'm beginning to feel really bad for putting her through this.

In the pressing darkness, all I see are trees. And then we turn a sharp corner, and the house appears out of nowhere, the three-story structure so large and imposing that it's a miracle it isn't more obvious from the road. It's difficult to tell how old the place is. Perhaps it would be easier to assess when the place was built during the daytime, when there's a little more light to work with. Right now, the floor-to-ceiling glass windows on the second floor makes it look modern, but the exterior makes it appear very old indeed.

"Just looking at the place makes me wanna throw up," Carina murmurs. "Doesn't it look like it was conjured right out of your nightmares?"

I look at the house, shrouded in shadows, each window cast into darkness, and…the place looks desolate. "No," I tell Carina. "I don't have nightmares."

She blows out a long breath through her pursed lips. "I envy you. That must be nice." She twists the key in the ignition, killing the engine. "Then what are you afraid of? Monsters? Ghouls? Flesh-eating beasts?"

"No," I tell her, staring up at the house with a steely resolve. "I'm afraid of real life. The people who are supposed to care for you the most."

* * *

Carina doesn't ask how I know how to pick a lock. She urges me to hurry up and get it done, peering over her shoulder into the forest as if she's expecting Dashiell to emerge from the night with a hatchet in his hand, ready to dismember both of us into tiny pieces. He doesn't come, though, and I have the door to Riot House open in record time.

I enter, preparing myself for the avalanche of empty beer cans and festering takeout containers, but the place is neat as a pin. Scratch that. It's actually *beautiful.*

Carina turns on the flashlight feature on her phone, dispersing the dark, and I marvel at the grand entranceway I find myself in. A huge, magnificent staircase stands before me, splitting off to the left and to the right, leading to the eastern and western wings of the house. On the first floor, huge paintings hang on the walls— mostly cool, sleek contemporary art that doesn't seem to be *of* anything in particular, but as I gaze at them I'm hit with the unsettling certainty that they're all depictions of raging storms, brought to life in swirling blacks, and blues, white and greys. They feel angry. "Wren's," Carina murmurs. "He might be the biggest shithead to walk the Earth, but the bastard *can* paint."

I reel in my surprise, storing that information away for later.

The house has a unique, dizzying smell to it. Far from the sweaty socks and unwashed teenaged boy odor I was expecting, the air's colored with notes of bergamot, black pepper and rosewood.

There are knick-knacks and small keepsakes everywhere I look, placed with thought and care on the exorbitantly expensive-looking sideboards, tables and the bookcase that runs along the back wall, by a door that leads off into the unknown.

I gasp when I look up. "Holy *shit.*"

"Yeah," Carina agrees, matching my stance as she cranes her head back, staring up through the winding staircases that wrap around what can only be described as the inner courtyard of the house. From where we stand, you can see all the way up to the top floor of the house, and beyond that, in the roof high over our heads, a vast skylight gives access to a view of the night sky that takes my breath away. Scores of brilliant pinpricks of light, burning away in the heavens, form the roof that Wren Jacobi sleeps under, and it's one of the most beautiful things I've ever seen.

"Come on." Carina takes me by the arm, pulling me toward the stairs. "No time to admire the architecture. We need to grab the phone and get back to the academy. I have an awful feeling about this."

"Where's his room? Tell me and I'll go find it myself."

Carina shakes her head. "We'll go together. It's easier to get lost in here than you'd think."

I squeeze her hand, giving her a reassuring smile. "I'll be fine. Stay here and keep watch. If you see lights headed up the road, shout and we'll get the fuck out of here. One of us needs to be on guard."

Uncertainty shines in her eyes, but there's relief in them, too. She's glad of the excuse to stay downstairs, within sprinting distance of the exit. "All right. Go, and be quick about it. The top floor. When you get to the top of the stairs, turn right on the landing. Wren's room is the door right in front of you. There's a black feather nailed into the door frame. I haven't been in there. I can't tell you where his desk is, but—"

"Don't worry, shh, it's okay. It's a desk. It's not like I'm looking for a hidden trapdoor or anything. Give me one minute and we'll be out of here."

Shaking ever so slightly, Carina nods. Jesus, she looks like she's on the verge of tears. I don't know what she's so terrified of here, but her emotions are proving to be contagious. My heart thumps aggressively in my chest as I jog up the first flight of steps, where I take the next flight on the right. My lungs are burning like crazy by the time I hit the third floor, and by the time I reach the fourth all I can hear is my blood charging behind my eardrums.

Gulping down breath after breath, I don't waste a second. I head straight for the door on the right, curiosity eating at me like nobody's business when I see the lush black feather my friend told me would be nailed into the wood. It's right where Carina said it would be.

Now.

Will his door be locked?

A part of me thinks, yes, absolutely, Wren's a private creature and he likely guards his personal space fiercely.

But then, he's also arrogant. Would Pax or Dash dare enter his inner sanctum without his permission? Highly improbable. And in what kind of world would Wren ever imagine an outsider having the gall to break into his home and then breach the privacy of his *bedroom*? Certainly not this world—the one in which everybody he comes into contact with, students and teachers alike, are afraid of him.

When I place my hand on the brass doorknob, a quiver of strange energy ripples up my back. How many times has Wren placed his hand here, on this same polished, cool brass? A thousand times. More. Hundreds of thousands of times. He touches this door knob more frequently than he touches almost any other thing in this house, and that knowledge makes a bolt of color creep into my cheeks; it feels like he and I are here together, the palms of our hands resting on top of the same buffed metal, like he and I are holding hands, and—

Dear god, Elodie. What the fuck is wrong *with you?*

I wrench the doorknob around, not really wondering if it will be locked anymore, knowing that it won't be…

And it isn't.

Next thing I know, I'm standing in Wren Jacobi's bedroom.

If I were brave enough, I'd turn on a light and get a proper look at the place, but I'm more jittery than I thought I'd be. There's enough moonlight flooding in through the two huge north facing bay windows that I can see well enough, anyway, and I don't want to risk alerting any passersby on the road that there's someone inside the house.

The room is massive, at least twice the size of my quarters on the fourth floor of the academy. A monster of a king-sized bed dominates the space, with a carved, solid wood headboard behind the mountain of pillows that is stunning in its intricacy. With all the colors in the room muted and muddied by the encroaching dark, the sheets could be grey, but they could also be blue. Something inside me twists sharply when I see the military corners Wren must have folded this morning, the moment he got out of that titanic fucker of a bed.

The walls are covered in shelves, which are stacked high with books. There are so many books, old and new, tatty and worn, glossy and unopened, that they're jammed into the spaces, lying flat on their sides, and wedged into tiny gaps wherever they'll fit.

What else do we have? Let's see…

No photographs in frames hung proudly on the walls. No pictures at all. A patinaed mirror in an antique gilt frame is propped up against a chest of drawers to the left of the bed. Aside from that, there's no real decoration to the room.

Hmm. No television.

Stacks of paper sit forgotten on top of the shag rug, before the open maw of a recently used wood burning fireplace. Balled-up scraps of paper sit in the corners, discarded on the floor and forgotten about. In some form or another, there's paper everywhere: old ticket stubs tucked under the lip of the paneling by the window; a pile of old posters, dogeared at the edges, rolled into tubes and held together by elastic bands, lean drunkenly up against the closet door; stacks of letters collecting dust on top of an old-fashioned writing desk.

I look up, and my breath stoppers up in the base of my throat. Well, fuck me. This place is full of wonders, especially when you take a beat to check out the view above your head. The ceiling is no ordinary ceiling. It's pure metal. My grandmother used to have a tin ceiling in her parlor that was stamped and embossed back in the 1890s, but this is nothing like that.

It's copper, burnished, beaten and shining even in the half-light —a vast expanse of polished copper that rises in the center, forming a focal point that draws the eye.

It's staggering and beautiful and completely impractical, and I can't picture Wren commissioning something like this. Nor can I imagine him squabbling with the other boys to make sure he bagged this room before either of them could.

It must look incredible when one of the floor lamps has been switched on. When Wren gets into bed each night, he gets to stare up at the light playing across the striations and the grain of the beautiful metal, and he probably doesn't appreciate it. Its magnificence is probably lost on a miserable fucker like him.

Something about the room feels nautical, like the captain's quarters of an old galleon ship. There's no reason for me to feel that way—there are no nautical trinkets, or themed decorations. It just does. There's a haphazard disorder to the place, combined with the ruthless organization of other aspects within the room, that gives the impression that this bedroom is occupied by a most eccentric mind.

"Elle! Hurry up, for fuck's sake! I'm sweating down here!" Carina's voice floats up to me from downstairs, crystal clear and loud enough to startle the crap out of me.

She's right, Stillwater. You didn't come here to gawp at the guy's interior design skills. Get moving!

I obey the voice of condemnation whispering into my ear, hurrying across the room toward the desk. Up until now, I've been roiling in doubt. I've believed (hoped? God, I'm pathetic) that Tom was lying for some reason, and that my phone wouldn't be here. That hope is ground to dust when I see the familiar gold case sitting on top of an open book, right there in the center of Wren's desk.

I flip the phone over, and low and behold the screen has been completely repaired. Tom must have worked so quick; I can't believe I'd trusted him when he said it was going to take three full days to get this back to me. Asshole.

I hold my finger over the home button and the screen lights up, listing all of the calls and the texts that I've missed from Eden, Ayala and Levi. Tempted though I am, I resist the urge to unlock the phone. There's no time for that.

"Elodie! I'm not kidding! Let's *go!*"

I drop the phone into the pocket of my jacket, already plotting and scheming all of the ways I am going to hurt Wren Jacobi for this infraction, when my eyes catch on a phrase on the page of the open book that glues my feet to the bare floorboards.

...here, I opened wide the door;—darkness there, and nothing more...

I know that line.

I know it from somewhere, but I just can't think where...

A soft creak disturbs the hush, the sudden, weighty silence of a presence at my back. My skin prickles, each small hair on my arms and down the back of my neck bristling under the force of another consciousness entering the room.

Ohhhhh fuck.

"*Deep into that darkness peering, long I stood there wondering, fearing, doubting, dreaming...*" a hushed voice murmurs. A voice of silk and honey and the rough edge of a blunt blade. It stabs into me with a tender sweetness that fills me with fear. "*Dreaming dreams no mortals ever dared to dream before. But the silence was unbroken, and the stillness gave no token...and the only word there spoken was the whispered word, "Lenore?""*

Slowly, I straighten, taking a step back from the desk.

"Poe," the voice states behind me. "A little over done these days, given his recent hipster rise to fame, but I've been a fan of 'The Raven' for a long time."

With all the care in the world, I turn around, and there,

standing at the foot of his bed, is Wren. After only seeing him in his tatty black tee and his jeans for so long, I'm staggered by the sight of him in a suit and tie. The cut of the blazer is exquisite. The pants are perfectly tailored, too. He looks nothing short of incredible, but it isn't his clothes that have stolen my ability to form words. It's just...it's *him*. His jet hair, and the way it curls around the tops of his ears. The purse of his full lips, and the casual, amused upward tilt of his mouth. The faintest hint of stubble at his jaw, and the sharp, assessing eyes that bore into me like lasers from the other side of the room.

Oh, how I hate that I love to look at this boy.

He slips his hands into the pockets of his suit pants like he hasn't got a care in the world. "Got a favorite, Stillwater?" he purrs.

"*What?*" My voice cracks on the word.

"Poet." Wren smiles softly, then looks around the room, as if he's suddenly remembered he came in here looking for something but can't recall for the life of him what it was. He goes to the bookcase, running his fingers along the spines. "Good poets bleed their pain out in their words. They capture the desolation and the hopelessness of life and transcribe it to paper in a way that makes you feel like your throat's just been cut. It's visceral. All troubled souls have a favorite poet."

What the fuck is happening right now? Why the hell is he going on about poets and not quizzing me over the fact that he's just busted me in his room? I have to get out of here. Immediately. "Who says I'm a troubled soul?"

Wren glances at me out of the corner of his eye. "Like recognizes like, Elodie. You and I...we share many commonalities."

"No, we do *not*." I deny it with a little more passion than intended. "We're nothing alike. I'd never hurt someone until they agreed to steal someone's phone for me."

Wren taps his finger along the shelf as he walks from one end slowly to the other. His eyes glint with amusement, a small flash of his teeth visible as he parts his lips. "I'm sure there are plenty of things you'd lower yourself to if you wanted something bad enough."

"You're sick, Jacobi. Where...oh my god, *where the hell's Carina?*" I didn't hear her panicking downstairs. She didn't shout that someone was coming. She's been silent since she last called for me. "You'd better not have fucking hurt her, Wren," I snap, hurtling toward the door.

He doesn't try to stop me. Laughing softly, he pulls a book from the shelf, running his hand over the cover with a gentle reverence. "I didn't touch her. Don't panic. I might use force on misbehaving nerds from time to time...but I don't hurt girls." He runs his tongue over his teeth, his eyes fixed on the book in his hands— from my position by the door, his face is lit by the moonlight pouring in through the windows, highlighting the obsidian coloring of his long eyelashes against the stark paleness of his skin. "She's still downstairs, waiting by the front door. I came around the back."

I stare him down, looking for the lie.

Wren shrugs. "Stick your head over the bannister and take a look. You'll find her right where you left her, hearty and hale, doing a really shit job of keeping lookout."

I won't take him at his word. I back out of the room, my body awash with adrenalin, railing against the voice in my head that's screaming at me to run. When I lean over the handrail and look down to the first floor, I see Carina hopping nervously from one foot to the other, standing by the open front door, scanning the night for the guy who's already snuck his way into the house.

"You can tell her to go back to the academy if you like," Wren mutters. He's leafing through the pages of his book now, his eyes roving quickly over the pages. How can he just stand there so nonchalantly? How can he not show the slightest signs of remorse for what he's done? He's taken my private property, planned on doing god knows what with it, and now he's just standing there, calm as you like, suggesting that I send my friend away and stay here with him? The guy is out of his fucking mind.

"Why the hell would I do *that*?" I hiss. "You could skin me alive and wear my fucking head as a hat if she leaves me here with you."

"Ha!" Wren throws his head back and laughs, just once, snapping the book closed in his hands. The tendons and muscles in his throat work as he swallows.

"Elodie! Was that you?" Carina calls out. "Did you hear that?"

I lock eyes with Wren, waiting for him to tell me to keep my mouth shut, but he just shrugs again. He doesn't care if she knows he's here, clearly. His wordless confidence is driving me up the fucking wall. "She'll call the cops, y'know. If you do anything weird," I warn him.

"I should think so," he agrees.

"And you don't care?"

"No. I have nothing to worry about. I'm not gonna do anything to you, Elodie." That smile spreads, taking up more real estate on his treacherously handsome face. It'd be so satisfying to slap that smug arrogance right off him. I imagine what it'd feel like to do it and my right palm tingles beautifully.

"Elodie! What the hell!" Carina yells.

"I'm coming!" I volley back to her over the handrail. "Just a second!"

Wren holds out the book to me, curving a villainous eyebrow at me in an open challenge. He's daring me to come close enough to take it from him. "A Study in Scarlett. Sir Arthur Conan Doyle. It's not poetry, of course, but I think you'd like it," he says.

"I didn't come here to talk books. I came here to get my phone back. Why the hell did you want it in the first place. What were you going to do?"

He frowns, giving this question some real thought. "Would any explanation be sufficient?" he muses. "If I tell you my reasoning and give you the truth, will it make what I did okay?"

"Absolutely not."

"Then if it's all the same to you, I think I'll save my breath."

I'm gonna kill him. I am going to fucking murder him until he's dead three times over. "What is *wrong* with you! Just tell me what you were gonna do!"

Huffing, —*He's* frustrated? *He* is? —he steps toward me, holding the book loosely in his hands. I go rigid, frozen still in place as he draws closer. It isn't until he's standing a foot away from me that I realize how close I've let him come, and that he could probably stave my skull in with that book if he wanted to. "I should have run," I whisper. Out loud? God, I said it out fucking loud. Never mind Wren: what the hell is wrong with *me?*

"Yeah, you probably should have," he says. "But everything's okay. I'm not a psychopath. Do you have any idea how beautiful you are when you're panicked?" he asks. "You get these spots of color in your cheeks and your eyes come alive. I'm glad you didn't run." He tacks his last statement on at the end, like he's only just realized this himself. "It means you're not scared of me. I knew that, but it's nice to be proven right. As for your phone, I'd say it was pretty obvious, wouldn't you? I wanted to strip all of your father's malware from it so I could message you, safe in the knowledge that I wasn't being spied on by one of the most belligerent men in the United States military."

"Hah! Lord, you are fucking with me, right? You seriously expect me to believe that?"

"I don't expect you to believe anything."

"Then why are you trying to paint yourself as a good guy?"

"I'm not. Would I have gone through your photos? Looked at your texts? Gone through your call list?" He laughs bitterly. "Sure. I'm not a good guy, Elodie. I've been informed by numerous trustworthy sources that I'm utterly reprehensible. But do you wanna know my one glorious and shining redeeming feature?"

"Not really."

"I *never* lie." He declares this with a gravity and sincerity that rings true. An absolute. A check I could take straight to the bank. And I believe him. "I never lie, so when I tell you something, Little E, you can believe it's true."

This superior, self-righteous ass. I hate him. "All right. Let's try this again, then. Try telling me that you didn't destroy all of my stuff after you broke into my room. Let's see how that pans out for you, because—"

"I didn't." He looks me dead in the eye when he speaks, his shoulders square and back, his chin held scornfully high. And the same honesty I heard in his last statement lives in these two small words, too. "I *could* have broken into your room. I had no reason to."

My throat's on fire. Out of nowhere, my eyes are stinging like crazy. "My mother's bird was smashed to pieces, Wren. So...maybe you didn't break into my room yourself. Maybe that's how you're getting away with this vague half-lie, but you could have had someone else do it. Whoever came into my room broke the only thing I had left of my mom, okay? It was the only thing that was precious to me. It broke my heart, seeing it shattered to bits. And I will *never* forgive you for that."

My voice is thick with unshed tears. I've been putting off thoughts of Mom's bird ever since Harcourt told me it had been vacuumed up, but now the emotion crashes down on me. It feels as though I'm trying to breathe around a brace of broken ribs. Wren's shoulders drop. He lowers his chin, looking down at his hands. His expression's hard and unreadable. "I'm sorry you lost something so precious. I know what that feels like. But I didn't have anything to do with it. I swear on my own blackened heart."

"Elodie! Oh my god, Elle! I think he's in the house! Move, move, move!" A thunder of footsteps crashes up the stairs. Carina arrives on the top landing, gripping hold of the handrail. She bends over, panting, and looks up at me with wide eyes. "I heard a voice. I can't see anything, but I think he's in th—OH MY GOD! FUCK!" She rockets a foot off the ground, her eyes bugging out of her head when she looks to the right and sees Wren standing right there.

"Hi, Carrie," he says smoothly. "Yeah, I'm in the house."

Carina draws herself up to her full height, doing a stand-up job of marshaling her surprise. "You should be ashamed of yourself," she says, flattening down the front of her purple dungarees. "I tell you to stay away from her, and then you go out and steal her phone? You're fucked in the head."

Wren folds his arms across his chest, leaning against the wall beside his bedroom door. "Jesus. Stop. I've had enough screeching for one night, thanks. The drive back from Boston was miserable. I had to hike all the way back here from town because the Uber driver wouldn't come up the mountain. And then I arrive home to find two petty thieves in here, sneaking around in the dark."

Carina grabs me by the hand. "Did you get what you came for?" she asks me.

"Yeah, I got it."

"Then let's get out of here."

"Elodie, wait." Wren shoves away from the wall. "Here. Take the book. I want you to have it." He holds out the maroon leather-bound book with the gilded edges, offering it to me.

"Don't," Carina warns. "Remember Persephone? She accepted those pomegranate seeds from Hades and doomed herself to the fucking underworld."

Wren grins wickedly at Carina. "I appreciate the comparison, but you're being a little dramatic. It's nothing but a book. There's nothing magical about it. Or...rather, it's magical in the same way that *all* books are magical. But it'll hardly bind her to hell."

"Elodie..." Carina tugs on my arm, trying to pull me away.

Only a stupid, foolish girl with no common sense or care for her own well-being would take a gift offered by Wren Jacobi. I know this. So why do I reach out and take the book from him? And why can't I break eye contact with him as Carina drags me away down the stairs?

16

ELODIE

A WEEK PASSES. And then another. I go to class. I read the book Wren gave me under my sheets at night, armed with a flashlight, like someone might burst in and catch me doing something perverted. When I finish it, I read it all over again. I hang out with Carina and Pres.

The residents of Riot House don't even spare a look in my general direction, which is to say that Pax and Dash continue their lives like I don't exist, and Wren studiously ignores me whenever he gets the opportunity. A seat miraculously opens up on the front row of my French class. Doctor Fitzpatrick doesn't call on me for any more embarrassing tasks in English. Wren sprawls out on the couch with his usual, practiced level of boredom, but he also keeps his snarky comments to himself.

If I didn't know any better, I'd suspect that he was on his best behavior.

This all changes on a Thursday afternoon, however, when a tall, willowy girl with luxuriously thick, long black hair saunters into Doctor Fitzpatrick's den, and Pax curses so loudly and so unexpectedly that Angelica, the timid girl who always wears her hair in braids, snaps her plastic ruler in two.

"What the *fuck*?" Carina groans next to me. "This has *got* to be some kind of sick joke."

"Greetings, Fitz." The girl with the black hair preens, doing a little curtsey for the Doctor, whose jaw is on the floor.

"Mercy? To what do we owe the pleasure?" His mouth says pleasure, but his eyes say *Dear God, no.* "I had no idea you were swinging by for a visit. I assume that's why you've come all this way? To see how your brother's faring?"

She slaps him lightly on the top of his arm in the flirtiest display I've ever seen. "No, silly. I re-enrolled! Switzerland was beautiful, but the cold got the better of me. New Hampshire's tropical by comparison, this time of year."

Staring at this old/new student, I get the feeling that everyone in the room is leaning away from her. Including me, and I don't even know why. "Uh...what's going on?" I mutter out of the side of my mouth.

"That's Mercy," Carina says, rolling her eyes. "She was a student here until last June. She decided to go study in Europe because America was too *'gauche.'* No one was sad to see her go. Least of all Wren."

"Wren? Why? Was he...were they...?"

"Eww, no!" Carina kicks me right on the ankle bone, and it hurts like a fucker. "Check yourself. She's his sister."

His sister? *Seriously.* What fresh hell is this? No one's ever mentioned another Jacobi. Another creature who shares the same diabolical genes as Wren.

"They're twins," Carina continues.

Oh, ho, ho, this just gets better.

"Wren's eight hours older than Mercy. Their parents were gonna call her Helena but they changed their minds when Mrs. Jacobi kept screaming *Mercy! Mercy!* during the delivery. Their mom got so sick after giving birth to them that she went away for six months to recuperate afterwards and their father hired a nurse maid to care for them. Mrs. Jacobi died when they were three. Apparently, she never regained her strength after the pregnancy and she just faded away until there was nothing of her left. She was a pretty awful mom by all accounts."

I've had questions about Wren for a long time. I know so little about him, but there was no way I was asking Carina. Especially not after the fucker tried to tamper with my phone. She would have strung me up and gutted me like a fish for being so stupid. But I feel like I should have known *this*, somehow. I should have known that there was another piece of him out there in the world.

Mercy turns and beams at the class, and I lean back into the couch, startled by the striking resemblance she shares with her brother. Her features are more refined and delicate, but they have the same shape face. The same chin. The same eyes, though the green of Mercy's eyes is nowhere near as vivid as Wren's. She sees her brother and waves. In his usual spot on the leather couch, Wren stares straight through her as though she isn't even there.

"Yeah. Like I was saying. Wren and Mercy used to be close. But not anymore," Carina whispers.

"Well, I guess you should find yourself a seat then, Ms. Jacobi," Doctor Fitzpatrick says with a tight smile.

Mercy waltzes over to the leather couch and sits herself down on the end of it, at her brother's feet. She swats at his boots, trying to get him to give her space, and a look of disgust forms on Wren's face. He gets up, silent as the grave, and heads for the exit. For the first time in two weeks, he looks at me properly as he walks right out of the door.

"Wren! Wren, these classes are not optional!" Doctor Fitz-patrick yells after him. He's wasting his breath, though.

Wren's already gone.

* * *

The next evening, when I return to my room after dinner, I open the door and something rushes upward in the air, swirling in front of my face. I shriek, lashing out to defend myself in a rather shameful display of panic. I assume it's a bat, but I realize my mistake when the fat, lush feather softly floats down to the ground.

It's black. Deeply black. But when I pick it up and hold it up for closer inspection, an oily, metallic, blue-green catches the light and shines through. It's beautiful, its vane on either side of the thick, woody spine perfect in every way.

A feather is a miraculous thing. So commonplace and every day, we barely even notice them poking out of our pillows, or caught on a gentle breeze, or bobbing along the surface of a lazy river, caught in the eddies and rushing vortexes as it's swept downstream. But a feather is a feat of engineering. And this feather, the one that must have been slipped beneath my bedroom door, is a beautiful one to be sure.

It's also a message. Some guys would slide a note under a girl's door. Even lazier guys would just send a text and have done with it. The guy who flicked this feather under my door is a fan of more subtle forms of communication. It started with the Morse code during the storm but even that must be too obvious for him now.

What is this feather saying? Beyond, *Remember me? I exist,* I have absolutely no idea. All I know is that Wren was on the fourth floor of the girl's wing and he was standing right outside my door.

"Hey, are you almost ready?" Carina stands in the hallway behind me. She's got a cheeky grin on her face, because things have been heating up between her and her Andy Samberg lookalike and we're due to meet him in front of The Vista theatre in an hour to catch an evening movie—some sci-fi flick about robots taking over the world. I slowly hide the feather behind my back.

"Uh, y'know what? I think I'm getting a migraine. I'm not sure sitting in front of a brightly lit screen is the best thing for me right now."

She pouts. "Oh no!" Her eyes are bright, though. She invited me to see the film before Andre asked her out on a date, so she asked me embarrassedly if it would be okay if he came along. I told her I didn't mind if she went with him alone, but she'd railed against that suggestion, wouldn't even consider it, and I didn't want to be an asshole and flat-out refuse to go. This is a convenient out—no one in their right mind wants to wind up as a third wheel in a movie theater—and Carina looks secretly pleased. In her shoes, I'm sure I would be, too.

"You're sure you're not just saying that to give me some alone time with the boy?" she asks.

The boy. She says it affectionately, with a giddy glimmer in her eyes; she's attempting to hide her excitement about this date, but that really isn't working out for her.

"Yes, I'm sure. When I get a migraine, I need to curl up in bed and sleep. It's the only way to get through it. I'll probably throw up everywhere if I come. You should swing by my room when you get back, though. Tell me how it all went."

Carina bites her bottom lip, grinning like an imp. "But what if I don't come back?"

"Carina! You're gonna sleep with him?"

She shrieks like a five-year-old, ducking out of my reach as I try to slap her arm. "I don't know. Maybe? I filled out the absence sheet just in case. Does that make me a slut?"

"No! Not at all. If you think he's a good guy, and he's treating you right, and you think you're ready, then why the hell not?"

My friend smiles from ear to ear, though a little calmer now. "Yeah. I mean, he's really sweet. I have to instigate every piece of contact between us 'cause he's trying to be a gentleman. Honestly, I kinda want him to just throw me up against a wall and fuck me already."

"Carina!"

She laughs. Her expression changes when she sees what I'm holding in my ha—

Ahh, *shit*.

I've forgotten all about the feather. I've been absently twirling it around in my fingers, pressing the blunt end of the hollow shaft into the pad of my thumb while I've been talking to her.

"That's pretty," Carina says, taking it from me. She holds it up to the light. "Wow, that really is beautiful. Where did you get it?"

"Oh, it was out on the lawn. I found it on the grass." It's amazing how easily I lie to her. I don't like doing it, but I'd be a fool to tell her the truth. She'd freak the fuck out if she knew Wren had been up here. She'd cancel her date and spend the rest of the night trying to talk me into reporting Wren for sneaking up onto the girls' floor. This incursion is the least of his many sins, but Carina will seize it with both hands if she thinks it'll be enough to get him expelled from the academy.

"I've never seen a feather like that before. It's perfect," she says, offering it back to me.

I take it from her. "Yeah, it is."

"You should keep it. Do something pretty with it. I know how to make it into a hair clip. I can show you if you like?"

"That'd be cool."

She claps, pulling in a deep breath. "Okay. I'm gonna get out of here. Wish me luck! I might have stories to tell when I get back."

I wait for her to disappear down the hallway and turn the corner before I take out my cellphone and begin to type out a message.

ME: It's beautiful, but I'm not keeping it.

Three dots appear, almost immediately.

WREN: Liar.

ME: You've got to stop.

WREN: Why say something you don't mean?

ME: What the hell are you talking about?

WREN: You tell me I have to stop. But you don't want me to stop. That's the last thing you want.

Goddamnit, this asshole makes me want to scream.

ME: You don't know that. You have no clue what's going on inside my head.

WREN: I know it's Friday night, and you aren't going anywhere.

ME: Yes, I am. I'm going out with Carina.

WREN: Strange. I just saw her burn down the road in that shitty Firebird of hers. And you weren't sitting in the passenger seat.

ME: Stalker!

WREN: I notice things, Little E. Sue me. You stayed at the academy because you want to see me.

ME: You think so fucking highly of yourself, don't you?

WREN: Raw honesty looks a lot like arrogance to the untrained eye.

ME: God, just stop!

WREN: Meet me.

ME: NO.

WREN: Give me one hour. If you don't come, I'll have to come to you. Then you'll see just how much of a stalker I really am.

ME: YOU'RE INSANE! You wouldn't dare come to my room.

My blood's almost at boiling point. I can't believe this mother-fucker. He's unconscionable.

WREN: I might. I might not. Safer for you to come to me, though.

ME: You really think I'm stepping foot back into that house? Where the three of you could do god only knows what to me?

The little dots don't fire up right away this time. It takes a full minute before they reappear, and I stand by the window in my room, staring out at the gradual dusk that's creeping toward the academy, questioning my own sanity. Why do I want him to reply so badly? How can I be this stupid?

WREN: Pax and Dashiell would never lay a finger on you. They know they'd never walk again. But whatever. If you don't want to come here, I'll come there. Meet me in the attic. 8pm.

The *attic*? He knows about that place? God, is nowhere at Wolf Hall safe from this guy?

ME: NO, WREN.

He doesn't reply.

ME: I'm not gonna meet you, Jacobi. I do NOT have a death wish.

My phone sits in the palm of my hand, silent, until the screen fades to black.

17

ELODIE

"I TOLD him I didn't love him, but he just won't let it drop. I don't know what to do. He follows me around like a lost puppy that I just kicked. If I didn't feel so guilty about hurting him, I'd probably be mad at the fucker. He's even got Levi petitioning on his behalf now. Stop laughing, Elodie, it's not funny!"

Jesus, I've missed the sound of Ayala's heavily accented, beautiful voice. Her parents are both from Dubai, but she grew up in Spain. She spoke just as much Spanish as she did Arabic when she was in kindergarten, and by the time she was eight she could speak French and German, too.

"Poor David," I groan. "He's been obsessed with you for so long. He must have thought he'd won the lottery when you agreed to go on a date with him. And then you crush him like an ant beneath the heel of your Manolo Blahniks. It's just...it's *so* sad, Ayala," I tease. "Maybe you should give him a chance."

"Lord, don't you start. You guys are *my* friends. You're supposed to be on *my* side."

Lying on my bed, I stare up at the ceiling, trying not to think about the space above my head. The attic isn't directly above my room. I haven't been able to pinpoint the precise spot that it sits

RIOT HOUSE | 175

over; from my many educated guesses over the past eighty minutes, I've decided that it's probably over the stairwell that leads up to the fourth floor and the entry way on the first floor, but I can't be one hundred percent sure. Regardless of where the attic actually is geographically, architecturally, whatever, it feels like it's right over my head, and Wren is up there already, sitting there in the dark, waiting for me like the eternally patient predator that he is.

"I am on your side," I tell my friend. "He's just so sweet."

"And when was the last time you went all weak at the knees for a *sweet* boy?" Ayala counters. "I know you, Elodie. Where guys are concerned, you and I are carbon copies of each other. We might think we want someone kind and caring to dote on us, but the moment that becomes a reality, we run for the hills. We're both as fucked as each other. We like our boys bad and belligerent, or there's just no spark."

My cheeks grow very, very hot. "I don't fall for bad boys, Al. I just don't. Why would *I* wanna punish myself like that?"

Ayala's boisterous laughter pours out of my headphones. "You're kidding, right? You do remember Michael? The guy you lost your virginity to? He treated you like a goddess, and you broke up with him because he, and I quote, *'didn't stand up for himself when you had a fight.'*

"That's normal," I argue. "Who doesn't defend themselves if their girlfriend's being crazy?"

"So you were being crazy, then?"

"Yes! I was crazy all the time, and Michael just sat there and took it. Which meant he was even crazier than me! I'm not gonna date a psychopath like that!" I'm aware of how crazy I'm sounding *right now,* but I'm sticking to my guns on this one. Just because I wanted a guy with a backbone doesn't mean I have a thing for bad boys. Ayala's *so* wrong.

"All right," she laughs. "Well, I'm gonna have to go anyway. It's four thirty in the morning, and I need to go drink a gallon of water so I don't end up with a hangover in the morning. We miss you so much, y'know. I can't tell you how glad I am you're not dead."

"Thanks. I'm glad you're not dead, too."

"You know what I mean. Your dad's such an asshole, Elodie. Seriously. If it wouldn't earn me a whole heap of really shitty karma, I'd wish something really bad on the guy. Like two broken legs. Or that he'd be involved in some horrific accident while on a training exercise and his dick and balls gets blown off by an I.E.D."

"I'd prefer not to talk about my father's junk. But yeah, a couple of broken legs would be nice. I'll wish it on him for the both of us and take double the bad karma if that helps?"

"It does. Night, girl. Please come back and visit us soon."

"You come here and visit me!" No way Colonel Stillwater's going to allow me to fly back to Israel for a vacation any time soon. If I could figure out a way to head back there without him knowing, that would be one thing, but my father would know the instant I left Mountain Lakes. He'd fucking kill me.

"Okay, okay," Ayala says—I can hear her broad, infectious smile in the tone of her voice. "Call me, Elodie."

"I will."

The line goes dead. I just lie there for a minute, staring up at the ceiling, feeling the pressure of the headphones in my ears, not willing to take them out and admit the call is over just yet. It went dark a long time ago. The tiny lamp by my bed casts a fuzzy orange halo on the ceiling, warped and stretched by the pitch of the ceiling's uneven surface.

I will not *check the time.*

I will not *check the time.*

I won't fucking do it.

A door slams a few rooms over, and a gaggle of high-pitched female voices ricochet off the corridor walls as a handful of my fellow classmates head off out together somewhere. I close my eyes, fidgeting on the mattress, which still feels too new and too hard and not broken in yet.

Take a look.

What'll it hurt?

Knowing the time isn't going to knock the planet off its axis, dumbass.

Just open your eyes, for fuck's sake!

I relent, even though I don't want to. The clock in the top righthand corner of my cell phone's display reads seven forty-nine in the evening. Eleven minutes to eight. Wren's probably walking up the driveway to the academy even as I'm lying here, moping around like some sort of friendless, hopeless, moronic loser. I get up, pretending to myself that I need to stretch, which is so pointless and stupid that I give myself a firm telling off in my father's voice. I know perfectly well that I've gotten up to look out of the window and trying to convince myself otherwise is pure folly.

Frustration sweeps over me when I realize I can't see the driveway from the vantage point my window offers. Only the maze, and the sprawling expanse of lawn is visible from the east wing of the house, which means I won't be able to see if Wren's on his way here or not.

He won't come. He's testing you. He wants to know if you'll jump when he commands. You are not *going up into that attic, Elodie Stillwater.*

I don't know why I'm repeating this to myself. I already know I'm not going up into the attic. I do have a *little* self-respect.

The clock on my phone updates: seven fifty-three p.m.

If I had my laptop, I could be watching re-runs of The Office right now. I could be doing some of my homework. I could spend five hours spiraling down a YouTube hole, watching videos about rescue dogs finding their furrever homes, and Adam Driver, and Timothée Chalamet, and fifteen hundred movie trailers promoting films I'm never likely to watch.

Hurling myself back onto my bed, I close my eyes, stacking my hands on top of my stomach. "God, this is so fucking stupid," I mutter.

Vrrrn Vrrrrrrrnn. Vrrrn Vrrrrrrrnn.

I'm so startled by the powerful vibration that buzzes my ribcage that I nearly fling my phone out of my hands. My ears are full of the sound of rushing blood as I check to see who the message is from.

WREN: Don't disappoint me.

And that's all it takes. Suddenly, I'm livid. Just who the fuck does he think he is? Don't disappoint *him*? He's not my father. In actual fact, he's no one to me. I owe him nothing. I definitely don't have to worry about making him fucking happy. He can kiss my fucking ass.

Launching myself off the bed, I grab my hoody off the back of the door, jamming my arms angrily into the sleeves as I fly out of my room and down the hall, toward the cleaning closet by the bathrooms. I'm muttering under my breath like a crazy person when I reach the closet door, not caring if anyone hears the very colorful and highly offensive curse words that tumble out of my mouth.

The inside of the closet reeks of bleach and must. I breathe through my mouth as I flip over a steel mop bucket, standing on its dented base so I can reach the lip of the crawl space that leads to the attic. Curse my short ass; without Carina here to give me a boost, it takes three failed attempts before I manage to jump high enough to pull myself up using my upper body strength. I graze my knuckles and scrape my back in my haste to drag myself through the crawl space, telling myself that my hurry is all about my simmering rage and not my claustrophobia.

Finally, I reach the other side, huffing and puffing and spitting wads of dust out of my mouth, still cursing like a sailor. I slide from the crawl space without a lick of grace, landing with a hollow thud on the ancient, splintered floorboards of the attic.

"Wow. It's like watching a fully grown, fully clothed person emerge from a birthing canal." The voice, emanating coolly from the other side of the attic, doesn't sound all that impressed by the miracle of birth. Rather, he sounds quite put out by it. I sit up, slapping the sleeves of my hoody, whipping up a cloud of dust that makes me cough.

"*Fuck...you...Jacobi...*" It's all I can manage around the hacking and spluttering. A glass of water appears directly in front of my face. A glass. A real one. Cut crystal, with a pretty flower design etched into its surface. Where the fuck did he get this kind of a *glass* up here? Stunned, I look up, prepared to tell him that I'm not drinking out of a receptacle that's been packed away in a travel chest for the past three decades, but then I see the thick pile of very new, very luxurious looking blankets on the floor, and the basket, and the wine, and the *hundreds* of candles that have been placed on top of every available surface, their flames flickering and waving as they work industriously to drive back the dark, and the words turn to ash on my tongue.

"What the fuck is—" I finally look up at Wren, my tongue suddenly seems too big for my mouth. Holy hell, he looks incredible. His hair's perfectly messy, tumbling into his face. Black shirt, with actual buttons down the front, the top button of which is unfastened. His sleeves have been cuffed to his elbows, exposing muscled forearms. His jeans are faded and frayed at the heel, and the denim smells distinctly of laundry detergent. I know, because he's standing so close to me that his knee is right in front of my face. Not that I'm smelling his freaking *knee*. That would be weird.

Wren smirks down at me, and an unbearable ache swells in my chest, all the way up to the base of my throat. I can't fucking *breathe* around it. "What the fuck is *this?*" he asks, finishing my sentence for me. "This is what a Friday night attic date looks like. No need to look so horrified. I didn't bring any weapons with me."

"I wish *I* had," I growl. "You're delusional. You know that, right? This is *not* a date."

Wren spins around, holding the glass to his lips and draining the water inside. I force my eyes to the ground, mortified by the fact that I don't *want* to look away. He walks back to the cozy set-up he's arranged, sinking heavily to the floor. He faces me, lounging back onto the blankets, toying with the glass in one hand. "What would you call it, then?" he asks. "Maybe...a war council? You wanna go to war with me, Little E?"

"I just want you to leave me alone. Is that so much to ask?"

Wren huffs down his nose, his gaze wandering around our cluttered, curious surroundings. "You don't really want that, though, do you." He states it—a raw, undeniable fact. "You daydream about my mouth on yours all the time. I can *see* it playing out in your head. It's quite the show. You imagine what it would be like, trapped in a dark room with me, my hot breath in your ear, my sweat on your tongue, my dick rubbing up against your cunt, and you can barely sit still. And when you really lose yourself, you let your mind off its leash and you fantasize about what it would be like to have me actually *inside* you. You sit so very still, beautiful Elodie. So, so still. You don't move a muscle, not even a twitch. You stare straight ahead, you don't even dare to breathe, but I see your white knuckles and your pulse hammering away in the hollow of your throat. The way your eyelids shutter. The red shame that colors your cheeks when you're done with me in your head." He picks up the bottle of wine next to him and rips out the cork, holding the mouth of it to his lips. "It's the most distracting, arousing, incensing thing I've ever seen. And I've seen some shit, let me tell you." He drinks, just as deeply as when he just polished off the water a second ago. This time I force myself to make eye contact as he swallows once, twice, three times.

When he sets the bottle down, I get to my feet and slowly walk toward him. "You know what?" I whisper.

"What?" he whispers back.

"I wish I could pick up that bottle and smash it over your fucking head, Jacobi."

"What's stopping you?" He fires back the taunt so quickly, he must have known I was picturing that, too.

"Because I'm not insane. I don't just go around assaulting people because I feel like it. I'm not a slave to my compulsions."

"Shame." Wren lets his head fall back; he looks up at me with a lazy, self-assuredness that makes me so angry I want to cry. "If you were, we'd have dispensed with this bullshit and fucked already."

I curl my lip up at him. "Is that all you care about? Fucking me? If I gave in and let you have me, would you finally grow bored and move on to your next victim?"

"No." He says it without surprise or condemnation. "I won't ever be done with you. Just as you'll never offer yourself up to me just to get me to leave you alone, sweet girl."

"Don't call me that. I'm not sweet."

He laughs. "That's the part I like the best. When was your last tetanus shot?"

"*What?*"

He points the bottle of wine at me. At my feet, specifically. "You forgot your shoes, Stillwater. I did my best, but it's far from clean up here. You're also bleeding from your hand."

I look down, shocked to see my own bare feet against the floorboards. How the hell did I neglect to put shoes and socks on? Kicking and scrabbling my way through the crawlspace alone could have cut me to ribbons. Damnit, what the hell was I thinking?

That you wanted to kill the conceited asshole lying on the blankets in front of you, that's what.

Urgh. I was in such a rush to get up here and tear him a new one that I wasn't thinking at all. My knuckles buzz with pain as I clench my hand into a fist, inspecting the damage I did there. It's not as bad as it could be—the gash isn't that deep, but it definitely *is* bleeding. I pull my hoody sleeve down over the injury, covering it up with the cuff. "It'll be fine," I clip out. "It'll stop in a minute."

Wren's sharp gaze flays me down to the bone. "Sit down, Elodie."

"I will not. I only came up here to ask you who the fuck you think you are."

"And once I tell you who I *think* I am, you're gonna wriggle back into that crawlspace and disappear back downstairs?"

"Yes. Exactly."

"Exactly. Okay. Well I think I'm the only guy in this godforsaken hellhole who you've looked twice at. I think I'm the guy you can't stop thinking about. I also think I'm the only guy who's ever made your heart race out of your chest. Am I wrong?"

I narrow my eyes to slits. "*Yes.*"

Using the wine bottle again, Wren points at me rudely. "You are completely incapable of telling the truth, aren't you? That's pretty sad."

"I am telling you the truth."

"Okay. Then deny all I've said. Tell me I'm wrong. You don't imagine me. You're not plagued by me day and night, the way I'm plagued by you. See, I have no problem with the truth. I made friends with it a long time ago. A lie only makes a fool of the liar. The truth always comes out. I am besieged by you, and it fucking *sucks*. You're in my head when I wake up. You're in my head when I wander around this wretched place, and you're still there, tormenting the ever-loving shit out of me when I close my eyes at night. So, do it. Lie to me some more, Little E. Please feel free. But you'll excuse me if I choose to get wasted while I settle in for the show."

I wasn't expecting this confession out of him. I've always thought him too proud and too arrogant to ever admit that he has a weakness out loud. It's impossible to comprehend that *I* am that weakness.

Wren takes another drink, then spreads his arms wide, as if encouraging me to get on with it. He's so fucking sure of himself. He's so certain that he knows me. Knows precisely what I'm going to say. I don't plan on living up to his expectations. "Fine. You're right. I'm rotten and eaten up on the inside because of you. Is that what you want to hear? I let something spoiled and bad into my head, and now I can't rid myself of it, and it's festering away, driving me madder and madder by the day. Congratu-fuck-ing-lations. I'm going against every ounce of common sense I own every damn day, and I'm making decisions I *know* are fucking stupid, and I can't do anything about it! How fucked up is that!"

If I were back in Tel Aviv, this wouldn't be a problem. None of it. Colonel Stillwater's foreboding presence would have nipped this bullshit in the bud the day I arrived here. I wouldn't have been weak enough to let my head run away with these thoughts, and Wren...well, let's face it, Wren would probably be dead by now. My father would have cottoned on to what he was doing and the guy would have mysteriously wound up in pieces, scattered along the embankment of a fucking highway in black garbage bags.

He drums his fingers against the side of the wine bottle, shifting so that he's lying on the welter of blankets now instead of sitting. His shirt's risen up, exposing a few inches of bare stomach, and my chest pinches tightly. I'm the worst kind of addict. I know precisely how bad he is for me, and yet I can't stop myself from craving more. I had my first taste of him in the gazebo during the storm, the memory of his naked torso's been driving me to distraction ever since, and now I want that shirt he's wearing gone. I want it fucking gone, and I hate myself for it. Where's all of the self-control my father taught me? And the common sense?

Like a sated cat, basking in a patch of sunlight, Wren closes his eyes, resting one hand on his solar plexus. "Was that so painful?" he murmurs. "Sit down, E. You have questions for me."

"I don't. I—" For fuck's sake. Why *is* it so hard to be straight with him? I have a million questions, and I'm dying to know the answers to all of them but sitting on that blanket is inviting a kind of trouble into my life that I don't need. "Whatever questions I have are irrelevant. The answers aren't going to change anything," I tell him. I'm beginning to feel a little hopeless now. This situation's miserable; I'd give anything to get myself out of it, but the bitter irony of it all is that I'd also do anything to have him.

He's the bad guy. The monster that crawls out of the shadows to hurt and maim those around him. Nothing good can come of him. But fighting this attraction I feel for him seems so futile and pointless that my will no longer feels like my own. I'm his prisoner, and Wren Jacobi is not a benevolent jailer. He'll keep me under his lock and key until he's bored of me, and I get the impression that his obsessions are for life.

"What harm can it do?" he murmurs. "You speak. I speak back. It's a conversation, Elodie. It won't fucking kill you."

My heart is a sharp-edged lump of rock. It refuses to beat as I step onto the blanket, the thick woven material soft on the soles of my feet, and I lower myself down into a seated position. Wren smiles to himself and my temper spikes. "I don't know why you're grinning. You haven't *won* anything. Don't go marking your score card yet, Jacobi."

Instead of squashing his smile, my annoyance only encourages it to grow in size. "I'm not keeping track of points. And the only thing I'm interested in winning—"

"God, don't even say it," I interject. "Do not. It'll only make me hate you more."

He opens his eyes, watching me askance, his lips slightly parted. Both his eyebrows shoot up, and I know he's going to finish his ridiculous sentence. "—*is your trust.*"

"When I was six, I stayed up every night, waiting for Peter Pan to fly through my window. I waited every night for him to come take me away. I wanted fairy wings, and a beautiful dress, and I wanted to escape with him to Neverland. Guess what? It didn't happen. I grew up and I realized it was dumb to wish for things that were impossible. You should probably do the same." My tone is so thick with sarcasm that it feels oily and uncomfortable coming out of my mouth. I've never spoken to anyone like this before. Honestly, I don't like how it makes me feel.

Wren rolls onto his side, his brows crimping together. He props his head up with his hand. "Have you stopped to question why you harbor this kind of negativity toward me, Stillwater? I mean, really asked yourself why?"

"I know why. You're an arrogant fuck boy with no conscience who terrorizes the people of this academy without a second thought."

"And you have proof of this?" he asks evenly. "You've seen it with your own two eyes?"

"Are you serious? You're being *serious* right now?"

He nods.

"Well. Let's see. You dumped a load of rotten meat in my desk. It smelled like rotten meat, anyway. And you threatened Tom when he didn't want to manipulate me into giving him my phone. And you broke into my room—"

"You know I didn't do that."

"I know you *did*," I argue.

He shrugs a shoulder, laughing bitterly under his breath. "What else do you know?"

"I know that—I know that you—you're—" Ahhh, fuck.

"You know that Carina doesn't like me. She's been your primary source of information about me, right? And she's so wounded over Dashiell slighting her that she'd hate me and Pax along with Lord Lovett no matter what. What else?"

"Just because I haven't experienced you being a dick firsthand doesn't mean that it's not true."

"So, I put a couple of frog's legs in your desk. I'll admit, that wasn't very nice. I apologize for it. And I'm sorry I threatened Tom. I'm not very good with people sometimes."

"No shit. That has to be the understatement of the century."

He pins me beneath a very serious, very green stare. "Are you done?"

I bite the tip of my tongue, glaring back at him.

"I'm sorry that I'm imperfect. I'm fully aware of my flaws. But I'll work on a few of them if it'll make you happy."

"Hah! Like my happiness means anything to you."

Sitting up slowly, Wren turns so that we're facing one another, his expression frighteningly intense. "I care very deeply about your happiness. More than I should. I care about being *personally* responsible for your happiness, and that—" he shakes his head, "—is a confounding realization, believe me."

He looks so astonished by this turn of events that I actually believe him. "Must be weird, caring about someone else when you've only ever cared about yourself before."

Wren flashes his teeth—a quick grimace that looks pained. "There you go, making assumptions again. How about this? You suspend judgment against me for three nights. You come up here and you meet with me, and we talk. You actually listen. And then…*then* you can decide if I'm the Anti-Christ. At which point, I swear on my family honor that I'll leave you alone if that's what you want."

"Three nights? If it'll take you three whole nights to convince me that you're not a horrible person, then I'm not sure I sho—"

"Just quit being so spiky and agree already," he groans. "Tonight, tomorrow night, and Sunday night. That's it. Three nights. I'll be on my very best behavior."

"And I'll see that you're not some evil monster and I'll fall in love with you?"

"Maybe," he agrees. "Or maybe you'll see that I *am* a monster. And maybe you'll fall in love with me anyway."

IN THE DARK…

I kick and scream.

I learned a long time ago that kicking and screaming doesn't help, but I have no choice.

I am a deranged, trapped animal, howling for freedom.

A freedom that will never come.

"Please! Please, I promise…I won't tell anyone. I won't breathe a word, I swear. I promise, I promise, I promise. I won't tell a soul what you've done. PLEASE! LET ME OUT!"

18

WREN

SHE AGREES to my proposal like the prospect of spending the next three nights with me will be so traumatic that she'll need a decade of therapy afterwards. And perhaps she will. If that turns out to be the case, then I know a great guy in Albany whose rates are reason-able, and I'll happily pass on his information. But until that comes to pass, I'm going to make the most of the hours I get to spend with her. She sits Indian style on the blanket, using the material to cover her bare feet—they must be freezing—staring at me like she's facing down the most daunting experience of her existence.

"Ask me your questions, then," I tell her, flopping down onto my back again, affecting an air of carelessness that I don't feel. I'm far from careless, actually. This is a risky move on my part. I'll be brutally honest with her, so that I can say I gave her the truth, the whole truth, and nothing but the truth, but it *is* dangerous. She could decide that I revolt her and she really doesn't want anything to do with me. If that happens, I'll have to honor the deal I've made with her, and I'll have to leave her in peace. Only, I know how badly that'll affect me. It'll destroy me from the inside out, and I won't be able to do shit about it. A promise is a promise, and I

"Where are you from?" she asks, her voice as dull and flat as can be. She's trying her best to show me how tiresome she's finding this entire thing, and she's doing a really fucking good job of it.

"I was born in England. Surrey, to be exact. My mother was English. My father's American, though. New York. The Jacobis have lived in New York since the city was established. We were money guys in the beginning. Bankers and investors. My grandfather joined the military, though, and then my father after him. Career army guys, both of them. I'm a blistering disappointment to both of them."

"Because you aren't going to join up?"

"Oh, no. I could enlist and I'd still be the biggest let-down either of them has ever suffered. See, I'm not traditional Jacobi stock. I'm *disobedient.*" I laugh as I say the word, hearing the identical ire in both my father and my grandfather's voices at the same time. "I've always poked at the fences designed to control me and keep me in line. Tested their boundaries. It seemed imprudent not to."

"If your father's anything like mine, then I'm sure that didn't go down well."

Ruefully, I shake my head. "Not particularly, no. Are you telling me you railed against the almighty Colonel Stillwater?"

"No," she answers stiffly. "I decided at a young age that I didn't like pain."

A knot forms in my stomach, tightening until it reaches the point where it'll take days to unravel. "He hurt you?"

"Oh, come on, don't sound so surprised," she says bitterly. "Don't tell me yours didn't hurt *you.* That's all they know how to do, men like our fathers. We just made different choices, didn't we? I didn't fight back. You did."

I can't tell if she sounds so angry right now because of the topic of conversation, or if it's because I'm forcing her to stay here and do this with me. The why isn't really important, though. I don't like the harshness of her voice. Makes me think that she's suffering. "No," I answer. "I don't like pain, either, Little E, but I couldn't let him use it to control me. You should never give anyone that kind of power over you. No matter how much it hurts."

She makes a strangled, unhappy sound. "You haven't met my father. You have *no* idea how badly he can make something hurt."

I don't like the sound of that. Not one little bit. The beast inside me snarls, a low, threatening growl rumbling out from between jagged, sharp teeth. It rages against the idea that a grown man would hurt his own daughter. It demands to know what happened in crystal clear detail, so it can formulate an appropriate punishment for this heinous crime. On the outside, I marshal my face into a blank mask, struggling to maintain an air of calm.

"You'll be eighteen soon," I say. "Then you'll be legally free of him."

"It's not that simple and you know it. My father's not the kind of man to let me go, just because I became an adult. He'll still be controlling every aspect of my life when I'm thirty for fuck's sake." She doesn't sound upset, just resigned, which is even worse than if she were sad. Arguing with her will get me nowhere at this stage in our fragile proceedings, so I abandon the topic altogether. Our shitty fathers aren't going anywhere, which is, in fact, the problem.

"What else do you wanna know?" I ask.

"Where have you gone to school?"

"Always here. Always at Wolf Hall."

She seems surprised by this. Her eyes have been sparking with annoyance since she tumbled out of that crawlspace like a legless newborn deer, but her irritation falters as she looks at me now. "For real? You've *never* gone to another high school? Most parents shunt their kids from pillar to post until they don't even know where they're from anymore."

Goddamnit, she's too fucking beautiful. It's like staring at the fucking sun—I look at her for anything more than a second and my retinas threaten to explode. Neither Pax nor Dashiell would say she's the prettiest girl enrolled at Wolf Hall, but to me, Elodie Stillwater's the most enchanting thing I've ever fucking seen. The defiant pout of her mouth. The always slightly messy, in-need-of-a-brush unruliness of her hair. The bright, wide-eyed stare that catches you off guard. Her hands are so fucking small, it makes me want to weep.

She's tiny. Her waist, and her slim shoulders, and her feet, for fuck's sake. It's like she was crafted in miniature, the details of her hand-painted in with unwavering attention to detail. She looks as though she needs wrapping up in tissue paper, to keep her safe like a precious treasure. But isn't that just the kicker? Because everything about Elodie is a deception. She's small, yes, but she can defend herself. She's made out of tempered steel, not wafer-thin glass, and she sure as hell doesn't need keeping safe. Underestimating her would be a regrettable mistake. One a guy wouldn't walk away from uninjured.

"My father thought routine was more important for me than having him around. My mother died when I was three, and my new stepmother was highly allergic to small children, so it all worked out quite well for everyone concerned. They packed me off to boarding school when I was four. They've bought three new houses over the past thirteen years. I've always stayed in a guest room whenever I've been so graciously invited to stay for the holidays."

"They never gave you a bedroom?" Despite herself, little Elodie actually looks interested in what I'm saying. And then she goes and says something that counters any concern she might have been displaying. "That's fucking cold. I guess that explains where *you* get it from."

I grin tightly. I mean, she's not wrong. But still. "I have no reason to be warm to anyone outside of Riot House. Why would I wander around this place, beaming like a lobotomized monkey when half of these idiots don't have two brain cells to rub together?"

"My case in point." Elodie reaches out, her hand darting forward; she takes the bottle of wine from me, her eyes growing round when I laugh. "What? You expect *me* to sit through all of this sober now? No thanks." She pours a large amount of the Malbec into one of the glasses I brought up here, shoving the bottle into my chest when she returns it.

Feisty.

"It's a cycle of misery, Wren," she tells me. "You cling to your social outcast status like it's a shield that'll protect you from the realities of this life, but the truth is that it's isolating you more and more from everyone around you. It's not a smart defense mechanism. And, moreover, I can see straight through it. That's how all of this started for you—you wanted to build up a wall around yourself so high that no one would ever be able to breach it. Now, your heart's so frozen and iced over that it's got fucking freezer burn."

"My heart is *not* top sirloin."

"Whatever. It's fucked is all I'm saying, and you telling me you're capable of caring about anything is frankly so unbelievable that this seems like a massive waste of both my time and yours."

"I'd hate to waste your time, Little E." God, how can I want to kiss her so fucking badly while she's telling me that I'm a lost cause? It's nothing so predictable as the fact that most girls normally trip over themselves to be in my presence and she decidedly does not. There's an element of that, yes, but this need...fuck me, it's so much *more* than that. She's weighed me and found me wanting. I've never given a shit about what other people think of me before, but this girl's low opinion of me matters more than I can bear. Her defiance, and her strength, and her self-assuredness are addicting. She knows exactly who she is and what she stands for, and I want to breathe her like she's life its very self.

"Don't look at me like that," she says, turning her head away. The candlelight glows against her hair, creating a golden halo around her head.

"How am I looking at you?" This is sheer insolence on my part. I know precisely how I'm looking at her, and I'm not planning on dialing it down one iota. I want to devour her. Claim her. Bind her to me any way that I can. And if she can read that in the burning fire in my eyes, then so fucking be it. I'm not ashamed of how I'm feeling, and I sure as fuck won't be hiding it from her, either.

"Just...*behave*," she warns. "You promised."

"Alright, fine. Have it your way. Ask me another question." I wait with bated breath, tension building between my shoulder blades as I anticipate what she's going to say next. It's thrilling, this exchange, to know that the things she's asking me here and now represent moments in the past when she sat alone in her thoughts and *wondered* things about me.

Elodie takes three deep mouthfuls from her glass of wine. "Okay. Why did Dashiell treat Carina so badly? Was it some kind of bet between you guys?"

"Dashiell likes to break his toys when they become too important to him."

She wrinkles her nose in disgust. "So, what? He did something to humiliate her and cause her pain because he liked her too much? *That's* the excuse you're arming him with?"

"I'm not arming him with shit. And it's not an excuse. I'm giving you the facts. Dash reacts badly to situations where he finds his power diminished in any way. And liking Carina made him weak. He saw that weakness as a perceived threat, and so he rooted it out with his bare hands and crushed it before it could hurt him."

The attic falls silent, the dusty old space breathing around us as Elodie studies my face. Her eyes rove over my brow, down the line of my nose. Her clear blue eyes hover over my mouth for a split second before they snap up to meet my own gaze. She looks like she's stewing on something, words piling up in a traffic jam on the tip of her tongue.

"I know what you wanna know," I whisper.

"Oh? Then please go ahead. Enlighten me with an answer, if you're suddenly so all-powerful and all-knowing."

My breath catches in my throat—the strangest, most alien sensation. Something I haven't experienced in a very long time. "You want to know if that's how *my* mind works. You want to know if that's what I'll do to you, if you let me in. But you can't allow yourself to ask me that, because asking is admission that you're thinking about it. Letting me in. And that terrifies you."

"Jesus, Wren, I'm—"

No. I won't let her dispute it. It's so fucking obvious. I'm sick of biding my time, waiting for her to relinquish herself to me. In one quick, predatory lunge, I rise up onto my knees, lean across the blanket, and I cup her face in both of my hands. I don't kiss her. Not yet. It's almost impossible, but I hold myself back. "My toys have never been important to me, Little E," I whisper. "I don't throw them away because I'm afraid of what they'll do to me, or because I'm bored of them. I discard them because they never live up to my expectations. But you..." Her eyelids shutter. "You're not a toy. I have no expectations of you. How can I when you're constantly surprising me and throwing me off my fucking guard. If you let me—"

Panic flares in her eyes. She's staring at my mouth again, complete terror radiating off her in waves. "Wren—"

"*If you let me,*" I repeat. "I'll surprise you too. Just you wait and see."

She closes her eyes, a single tear streaking down her cheek. Out of nowhere, it's as though she's coming apart in my hands. "Please. Please. Please," she whispers.

Numbed all the way down to my bones, I let go of her, a bitter, acrid taste spreading across my tongue. I wasn't trying to scare her. I wasn't trying to break her. I—for fuck's sake—I lean away, ready to do something monumental that I haven't done in years —*apologize*—when she shakes her head and hurls herself forward, throwing herself at my chest. "*Please,*" she repeats. This time it sounds like she's begging me to *do* something rather than to get the hell away from her. The desperation on her face makes my blood roar inside my head, clouding my vision and making my pulse soar.

"All right. Okay. I've got you." She's in my arms, then. I crush her to me so hard that even I can't breathe. My lips meet hers, and the kiss is nothing like it was supposed to be. Yeah, I've planned this. With the same meticulous attention to detail I put into all of my actions. I was supposed to tease her, my mouth hovering over hers, my tongue skating over her swollen lower lip, my hands in her hair, making her breath come quick until she was frantic and couldn't stand for there to be any space between us a second more. There's no patience to this kiss, though. No teasing to be had by me or by her. Only need, and want, and a form of panic that kindles in us both and spreads like wildfire. How easily this could all end in disaster. How quickly I could lose myself, and how effortlessly I could break her.

I feel it in her, as she must feel it in me.

We're both so afraid of the ending before we've even truly arrived at the beginning, but there's nothing either of us can do to stop this thing now. It's gained too much fucking steam, and neither of us know where the brakes are.

Elodie's heart is racing; I can feel her pulse slamming up against my chest, and she's so alive and vital and fucking *real* that I can't actually believe that this is happening. She kisses me back, her hands reaching up and winding into my hair, and my blood turns to nitroglycerin in my veins. One small spark is all it will take and I'll go up like a motherfucking H-bomb. She pulls back, nothing more than a split second to suck in a desperate breath, and my world splinters apart.

I was supposed to be puppeting this charade. There was an order in which this was all supposed to go, and *at no point* was I supposed to lose my goddamn mind.

When was the last time I felt something like this?

When have I *ever* felt something like this?

Elodie makes a soft, whimpering sound as she brings her lips back up to meet mine, her fingers grasping tightly onto a thick tangle of my hair, and everything stills and blurs.

She tastes like sunlight and honey.

She smells like the last time I can remember being fucking happy.

In my arms, her small frame feels like the most important, valuable thing I've ever held.

Ripping my mouth away, I duck down, kissing the column of her throat, burying myself in the crook of her neck, and she begins to shake so violently that I have to press my forehead against her cheek in order to stop myself from going further.

"Wren. Wren. Oh my god..." She pants my name, breathless, still arching her back and pressing herself up against me in a way that makes it very hard to think straight. "What the fuck are we doing? What *is* this?" she moans.

"I don't know. I thought I did, but..." I shake my head, placing my hands so carefully on her hips that I can barely feel the material of her jeans against my palms. I pull back, putting some space between us.

We stare at each other, neither of us shifting an inch as we try to figure out what the fuck just happened.

Something prodigious.

Some sort of shift in both of us that makes no good goddamn sense.

One moment.

How can so much change in one blink of an eye?

Elodie swallows. "I, uh...I think I have to go." Frantically, she gets to her feet, full of energy and electricity as she spins around in a circle, holding her hair out of the way as she scans the surrounding area for... for...

"Where the hell are my shoes?!"

"You didn't bring any," I remind her calmly. I don't feel calm, though. I feel...untethered. Like I'm adrift, and nothing makes sense anymore.

"Fuck!" Elodie spins around one more time, still looking for her shoes that aren't there, and then she spins on me, glowering like a she-demon. "You shouldn't have done that," she hisses.

"I didn't do anything. You're the one who kissed *me*."

"All right, whatever. No sense in assigning blame. This is still your fault!"

"Hah! I thought there was no sense in assigning blame."

"How can you just sit there like that?" she cries. "How can you not...I don't know! *React!*"

She's being patently ridiculous, but I know better than to tell her so to her face. I don't think I could summon the words, anyhow. Elodie growls like a feral cat, hurling herself toward the crawl space that'll take her back to the girl's wing on the fourth floor. I watch her disappearing into the darkness, knowing I should tell her about the tiny *doorway* on the other side of the attic that leads out onto the boys' wing, but my throat's too jammed up to manage it. I sit there on the blanket, very still, staring down at the half-drunk glass of wine Elodie left behind, reeling. An hour passes, and then another, and the candles blink out one by one.

I'm cold and sore by the time I eventually get up and leave.

The walk back to Riot House is a perplexing one to say the least.

I needed to fuck with her. It's been the only thought that's consumed me for weeks.

I wanted to wreck her, but back in the attic, kneeling alone in the dark, I saw everything so much clearer than before. I came to a stark and horrifying realization that's turned my entire existence on its head.

I will not be the one to wreck Elodie.

She'll be the one to wreck *me*.

This knowledge is cemented well and truly in place when I get back to my room and see the manila envelope there, waiting for me on the end of my bed. I come apart at the seams when I read the police report inside it, a fury like no other pinning me between sharp, steel teeth.

19

ELODIE

"Where the hell did *you* sleep last night?"

"*What?*" I open my eyes and all I see is sky—a gunmetal, angry, petulant sky, laden with clouds that promise rain. Carina appears a second later, her upside-down face materializing right above mine. Her hair's tugged back into a fluffy ponytail. Her entire face is a grimace. Instantly, I suspect that she found out what happened last night and she's come to cart me off to the mad house. "What do you mean?"

"I came by your room at six-thirty and you weren't there," she says. "Your bed didn't look like it had even been slept in."

This is one of the many things people without military parents will never understand. "I got up early to run. And if I get up, I have to make my bed immediately," I explain. "It's physically impossible for me *not* to make it."

Carina makes a revolted sound, stepping over me and sitting down beside me. "Sounds like you were living under a dictatorship before you moved back to the States," she says. If only she fucking knew. "Running sounds horrible, too. Did you nearly kill yourself? Is that why you're star-fished out here on the lawn all by yourself in the wet grass?"

I can't tell her that I ran myself until it really *did* feel like I would die, and then I collapsed here, unable to move, because I was too lost in the memory of trying to climb Wren fucking Jacobi like a tree. So instead I nod, groaning very loudly and very miserably.

"Damn, dude. Physical exercise is *bad*. I highly recommend you avoid it in future," Carina advises.

"I'm used to working out hard every day, actually. It's the only thing that makes me feel human." I grab a handful of the grass I'm lying on and tear it out at the root, sprinkling the loose blades through my fingers, letting them fall to the ground.

"Clearly it didn't work this time," Carina observes. "No need to go taking it out on the grass. What's up?"

"No, no, no, I'm totally fine!" I say it too quickly with far too much enthusiasm. Carina looks at me like I've got a screw loose.

"Okay. Well I'm gonna pretend like you're not acting super fucking weird and I'm gonna wait for you to ask me how last night went."

"Last night?"

"With Andre! Damn, Elle, I told you I might not come home last night and now here I am at eight in the morning, wearing the same clothes as last night with mascara smudged all over my face and you can't put two and two together? Spit it out right now. Tell me what's up with you. Did you have another run-in with Wren?"

My cheeks burst into flame. I shake my head so vehemently that I can feel my brain rattling around inside my skull. "No! Who said anything about Wren? Why would you think that? I haven't seen him since he waltzed out of Fitz's class yesterday. Two fifteen? I think it was around two fifteen in the afternoon."

Carina frowns deeply. "Okaaaay. That was oddly specific."

"How *did* everything go with Andre?" I ask, diverting the conversation into safer waters. "Did you enjoy the movie?"

"Fuck the movie. I saw the opening credits and that was it. Ask me what happened. I've got no idea. As soon as the lights were out and people started acting, we were all over each other. It was so intense. Like *so* intense. Have you ever kissed someone, and everything just faded? Reality just slipped away? Have you ever felt like you were melting into someone so viscerally, both physically and mentally, that you don't even know who you are anymore or what planet you're fucking on?"

Wren's hands cupping my face.

Wren's mouth, fierce and demanding on mine.

Wren's hot breath, skating over my neck.

His teeth nipping at my skin.

His arms, pinning me to his chest.

The attic, pitching and swimming, fracturing into a million disjointed pieces...

I shake my head, blinking in a daze. "No. No, never. Can't say that I have."

"Sounds fucking dumb, but it was magical. Like, *real* magic. Once the movie was over, I walked with him back to his place, and, well...let's just say I didn't get any sleep. I'm exhausted, and my body feels like it's been stretched in every direction. I can't lay my legs flat on the floor without my hips creaking like a squeaky door. I'm telling you. That man knows exactly where a woman's G-spot is. I didn't have to provide a detailed road map or anything."

"I'm assuming Dash needed some direction?" I say, closing my eyes. The sun's far from out, but the sky's really goddamn bright. I wouldn't be so blinded by it if I sat up, but I'm still wallowing in too much self-pity to muster up the kind of motivation I'll need to drag my carcass into an upright position.

"No," Carina says bitterly. "He knew perfectly well, too. But we're not talking about him. We're never talking about him again. As far as we're concerned, that boy is dead, and no one went to his funeral."

I try not to smile. "Your wish is my command."

Carina dives into a full explanation of what happened with Andre. She paints a vivid picture of his house, which he shares with three other guys from college, and how clean and tidy his bedroom was. She told me about his shelves, bristling with football trophies and academic awards—"*See! Not all jocks are dumb!*"—and then she tells me in intimate detail how Andre made her come three separate times before coming himself, which apparently makes him a gentleman of the highest order.

And the whole time, I lie in the grass, my sweat gone dry and itchy on my skin, and I try not to think about my illicit rendezvous in the attic. Thoughts of Wren plague me. He's an affliction I can't escape, no matter how hard I try. The look in his burning green eyes, when he pulled away and ended our kiss, was...fuck, it *felt* honest. He didn't seem like he was putting on a show. He appeared to be as flustered and stunned as I was, which just doesn't seem possible. My gut tells me otherwise, though.

"Elodie? Are you listening? And why are you holding your fingers to your mouth like that?"

Shit. My fingertips suddenly feel singed. I lower my hand, guilt gouging dagger-sharp claws into me. I wasn't listening. I was replaying the kiss, remembering Wren's mouth crushing down on mine, and the way everything that was important to me before that moment became so irrelevant and small.

"You need to get out of this damn place," Carina informs me. "We should go to the arcade tonight."

"I can't." The words are out of my mouth before I can trap them behind my teeth. "I have something...uh, something I need to do." I cursed myself out for my own stupidity for at least an hour before I fell into a fitful, restless sleep last night. I promised myself I wasn't going to go back to the attic tonight, but I fear I may have been lying to myself again; it's becoming a troubling habit. I want to go back. Against every instinct I possess, I want to go back and hold up my end of the bargain I made with Wren. I know that, if I don't, he's never going to let me live it down. Heat pools like a boiling pit of lava in my stomach. The prospect of another kiss... Damn it all to hell, what the fuck is *wrong* with me?

Carina says, "That's very cryptic. And here I was, thinking I was your Wolf Hall bestie. Have you been making friends behind my back, Stillwater?"

"Haha! No, of course not."

"All right." She seems neither happy nor convinced. I know she's only playing around though. "So long as you're not planning on replacing me with Damiana then I guess I'll be okay with you keeping your mysterious secrets."

"Nope. Nothing mysterious. Nothing secret. Just got a group video chat with some of the guys back in Tel Aviv, that's all." Lie, lie, lie. It's all I'm good for. I'm the worst, most deceitful cretin to ever live. "I also have to get some work done or I'm gonna have to cram all of my assignments into tomorrow, and I don't feel like frittering away my Sunday like that."

"This weekend's workload is unusually punishing," Carina agrees. "You feel like hitting the library for a couple of hours this afternoon, then? We can combine research notes for English."

Relieved that she's not going to press a hang-out later on tonight, I relax into my shame, attempting to ignore it. "Sure. Okay, that sounds great."

* * *

Given my obsession with books, it's surprising how little time I've spent in the academy's library. I inspected the place briefly when Carina gave me the nickel tour of the school, but I've only been back once to get my library card since then. Cool afternoon light floods in through the vast banks of windows that form one side of the massive space. Carina leads the way through the loaded book stacks, her hips sashaying as she weaves a route through row after row of reading desks, complete with Emeralites and piles of scrap paper, toward the desks that have been arranged right next to the glass, giving a view out over a steep hill that leads down to a large, immaculately groomed playing field with goal posts at either end.

"Wouldn't have pegged Wolf Hall as a football kinda school," I mutter, dumping my bag down onto the desk and unzipping it, rooting around inside for my notebook.

"It isn't." Carina shrugs. "The football field, the basketball courts and the tennis courts are all for show. They're to encourage parents who care about sports to enroll their kids here. Wolf Hall only cares about academics, though."

It's true, I haven't attended a single P.E. class since I got here. Now that I've realized this, it does seem weird. "Surely they have to do some form of physical exercise here?"

Carina scowls. "Yeah. Well. Just wait until spring properly sets in. We're *cross country runners* here at the academy. Ms. Braithwaite says it builds stamina, fortitude and mental discipline."

Cross country running. Hmm. "Sounds like a riot," I grumble.

"What the hell are you talking about, *masochist?* You voluntarily went on a six-mile run this morning. You'll be just fine."

I will. I know I will. Colonel Stillwater ran me, screaming in my ear like I was one of his shit-kicking grunts, until I could easily clear fifteen miles. But still. There's a difference running because you want to, to clear your head and escape your demons, and running because you have no other option. And running as part of a pack of people, all jostling and vying for the best possible time? Sounds like bullshit to me.

"That's at least a month away, anyway. We have plenty of time to train for it if you're interested. In the meantime, let's get this assignment out of the way and ace this motherfucker. My mom promised I could go to Spain for spring break this year if I maintained my grades, and there's this amazing tango festival in Granada I wouldn't mind checking out. Hey! You should come! Oh my god, traveling through Europe together for a couple of weeks would be so much fun!" Carina's enthusiasm's contagious. I find myself nodding along with her, getting swept away in the excitement, but there's no way I'll actually be able to go with her. My father would never allow it. He'll either expect me to stay put at the academy or come back to Tel Aviv, and I am so torn between the two options. I miss my friends and desperately want to see them, but staying with *him* in that house? For two whole weeks? I honestly don't know if I would make it through to the other side.

We study, flipping through pages of textbooks and reference

documents, sitting in companionable silence while we work, and the calm of the library sinks into my bones. The place is serene and full of light. I love being able to look out of the window and see the trees stretching on forever into the distance.

At around midday, my phone buzzes in my pocket. It's on silent, but the vibration's still noisy enough to get Carina's attention. Her dark eyes flick up to meet mine, her brow arching into a question mark. "You gonna check that?" she whispers.

I take the phone out, tight-lipped, dreading what I'll find. And sure enough, there's Wren's name blazing across the screen, sending my pulse rocketing skyward. "I'll read it later," I say, turning the phone over in my hand.

"Don't be stupid. We're miles away from the front desk. They can't see you over here. Read your message. We aren't prison inmates on lockdown."

It'd be weird if I refused. I think it would be, anyway. I can't remember how to not act suspicious now, and I'm questioning every little thing I want to say or do. I flip the device over in my hand, opening the screen with my passcode and the text messages open up automatically. Wren's message sits there at the top in bold, ready and waiting for me to read it. My hand trembles as I tap his name, my eyes quickly skipping over the brief message that opens up for me.

WREN: Where are you?

Three words. Gee. I mean, I don't know what I was expecting but three short, clipped words that somehow manage to convey the bastard's extreme arrogance—well that's underwhelming to say the least. Where am I? Like he has a right to know my location at all times? Uhhh, I don't think so, buddy.

ME: None of your damn business.

"You okay, girl?" Carina asks, around the end of the pencil that she's chewing. "You look like you're about to hurl a chair through one of these windows."

She's too perceptive for her own good. Or I'm just really terrible at hiding my emotions. I should probably work on that. I cut her a sorry smile, sighing heavily. "Yeah. Just my dad. He's… difficult to please. We don't really see eye-to-eye on much." The things I've just told her are one hundred percent true. Describing Colonel Stillwater as 'difficult to please' has to be the understatement of the century. And we don't see eye-to-eye on anything whatsoever. I still lied to Carina by pretending it was my father who just messaged me, though. Wren Jacobi's turning me into a liar, and I don't fucking like it.

WREN: Are you at the academy or off-campus?

ME: I repeat: None of your damn business.

WREN: You might as well tell me. I'll find you either way.

I send him the thumb emoji—the most passive aggressive of all the emojis.

ME: Good luck with that.

I stick my phone back into my pocket, resisting the urge to growl. Tapping the end of her pencil against the pages of the open book in front of her, Carina studies me sympathetically. "I'm lucky I get on with my folks. Seems as though every other student in this place has fucking sociopaths for parents. What's your dad's damage?"

"I'm sorry?"

"Yeah, y'know. Why's he such a prick to you? Why does he treat you like dirt all the time?"

Because I remind him of my dead mother. Because I've seen what he's capable of, and I know his self-righteous, holier-than-thou attitude is all an act. Because I could turn his world upside down with one tiny phone call.

"Because he's my father. That's just what he does," I say softly.

She seems to stew on this for a beat. After a moment, she shoves away from the desk and gets to her feet. "You like chicken?"

"Everyone likes chicken."

"Okay. I'm gonna run over to the cafeteria and get us some food. I'll sneak it back in and we can eat here. They won't even notice."

I have no idea how vigilant the librarians are here, Carina knows better than I do, so I take her word for it. I offer to come with her, but she tells me to stay put and save our spot for us. I get back to work, hunting for references and information that will be useful in our essays, but as the minutes tick by, I grow more and more restless. I can't concentrate. Trying to focus on any one thing is almost impo—

"The Assyrian came down like the wolf on the fold,
And his cohorts were gleaming in the purple and gold..."

The hairs on the back of my neck stand up, adrenalin singing through my body, bringing my focus to a very sudden, sharp point.

"And the sheen of their spears was like stars on the sea,
When the blue wave rolls nightly on deep Galilee."

I slowly close my eyes. "Don't you have anything better to do with your time than quote grim poetry at me," I ask, valiantly maintaining my cool, as the phantom owner of that voice comes to stand behind me. I can *feel* him there, his presence like a raging inferno at my back.

"I wouldn't call it grim." I nearly jump out of my skin when something touches me. My hair, specifically. I see his hand out of the corner of my eye, as he coils a length of my hair around his index finger, his nail still marked with the tiniest chip of black nail polish, rubbing the pad of his thumb lightly over the blonde strands.

Fighting for an even breath, I remain very, very still. I lick my lips, my mouth too, too dry, and then I speak.

"For the Angel of Death spread his wings on the blast,
And breathed in the face of the foe as he passed;
And the eyes of the sleepers waxed deadly and chill,
And their hearts but once heaved, and forever grew still..."

Wren lets the loop of hair he wound around his finger fall loose. He moves silently, walking around the desk so that he's no longer hovering behind me but standing, brazen as you like, as if he doesn't care who sees us together, right freaking beside me. "So, you do have a favorite after all," he muses, looking down at me with curiosity kindling in his eyes.

I try not to look at him, but not looking at him is like not picking at a scab, or not poking a wobbly tooth with your tongue. Impossible. "Not really. I had to memorize that poem for a class last semester. I guess I haven't scrubbed it from my memory just yet. Byron's poems were too flowery for me. I don't like how they rhymed so obviously most of the time."

Wren catches his bottom lip between his teeth, his eyes glowing in an amused way I've never seen before. He skirts the table and sits down opposite me, leaning across the polished wood. *"You like poetry."* That's all he says, but it looks as though this revelation is the most amazing thing that's ever happened to him.

"That seat's taken, y'know," I reply bleakly. "Carina's gonna be back any second. If she sees you sitting here, talking to me—"

"The whole world will implode and burn to ash, and the seas will dry, and meteors will strike the Earth, obliterating all life as we know it."

"—she'll piece this together, whatever this is. And—"

He looks confused. *"Whatever this is?"*

"Oh. I forgot. *Piece of Shit Playbook, rule number three.* This is the part where you pretend like nothing happened between us last night, right?"

Wren smothers a dark grin by resting his chin in his hand, covering his mouth. His hair looks extra wild and unkempt today, which only makes me want to run my fingers through it even more than normal. He's wearing a thin black sweater with a tiny hole in one of the cuffs. I can't stop staring at that little hole, as I wait for him to confirm my suspicion: that he truly is a mother-fucking asshole.

"Is this the part where you judge me again and make assumptions about what I'm gonna do?" he fires back.

God, I'm too tired for these kinds of games. I barely slept last night, and after jogging so far this morning, grinding myself into the ground before dawn even broke properly, I'm running on fumes. Rolling my eyes heavenward, I sag back into my hard-backed chair. "Is there something I can help you with, Wren?"

My disloyal, double-crossing heart jackhammers away beneath my ribs as he stops smiling, pinning me with that rude green gaze. Normal people don't look at others the way Wren looks at me. It's as though he's searching for something in my face and he won't blink or turn away until he's found it. It's extremely uncomfortable to be studied this way. "You can start by telling me what you meant by, '*whatever this is.*'"

"Fuck. I don't know! I didn't mean anything by it. It was an off-the-cuff comment, okay? Don't worry, I'm not expecting you to declare me your girlfriend now."

He tips his head back and laughs. In the library, where silence is golden, he tips his beautiful fucking head back and he *laughs*. A stern *sshhhhhh*! echoes across the room, and a horrible heat creeps up my neck. It was bad enough before, when only a few of the other students working at the desks had noticed Wren's arrival. Now everyone in the place knows that he's here, and that I just said something that he found patently ridiculous.

"You might not have figured it out, but *I* know exactly what this is, Elodie," Wren says, his laughter dying on his lips. "If you ever scrape up the courage and want to find out, all you need to do is ask. You know I'll be unfalteringly honest."

"Oh yeah. I can always rely on your unfaltering honesty." I wonder what the punishment would be for slapping another student. If we were in the art rooms, or Fitz's den, or the food hall, I might do it and find out, but not here. I wouldn't *dare* risk my library card.

A ruinous smirk tugs at Wren's mouth. That wicked curve to his lips is absolutely torturous. When I see it, all I can think of is the heat of his mouth as he kissed me on that blanket. The smell of fresh pine and salt air and half-forgotten beaches in his hair as he dipped down to press that cruel mouth to my neck…

"Is this the part where you tell me how excited you are to meet up tonight?" he asks.

I ignore the question. "Are you seriously going to risk Carina coming back here and seeing us together?"

He looks at me like I'm speaking in tongues and nothing I'm jabbering about makes any sense. "I'm sorry, Little E. I don't know what I did to encourage this belief that I give a flying fuck what Carina Mendoza thinks about anything but let me clear this up. I don't care if Carina comes back and finds me sitting in this chair. I don't care if she knows that I want you. I don't care if she knows that I had my tongue down your throat last night and you made my dick harder than it's been in two fucking years."

Wow.

I look down at my hands, my cheeks burning like crazy.

"Oh, *Elodie*," Wren whispers breathlessly. "You don't like hearing that? That you made my dick hard? Or...do you like hearing it too much?"

"For god's sake, can you not say stuff like that in public, please?" I despise myself for blushing. From the way he's staring at me, his lips parted, eyes wide, he's fascinated by my reaction to his outrageous statement. It would have been so much better for me if I'd kept my cool and not reacted at all. For some reason, it matters to me that he doesn't think I'm some stuttering, stupid, inexperienced schoolgirl. It shouldn't, but fuck, it really does.

Wren slides his hand across the table, palm facing upwards, his fingers curled up toward the ceiling, his eyes fierce and intense. "You do know how crazy you drive me, don't you, Little E? You know that my body isn't my own anymore. I fucking *crave* you. And I really don't give a fuck *who* knows it."

He looks down at his hand, resting between us on top of the lacquered table's surface. Clearly, this is some sort of test. He's waiting for me to reach out and take his hand. I have no idea what his end goal is here, but it feels like a trap and if I put my hand in his I'll be endangering myself. I follow his gaze, staring at the lines of his palm, tracing them with my eyes, wishing very badly that I could reach out and trace them with the tips of my fingers, to feel the heat and the roughness of his skin...

"I *know* what you're thinking," he whispers.

Numb. I am so fucking numb. I can't feel anything bar my own churning fear. It's impossible not to feel that. "You do?"

Wren's voice is as soft as silk, as hushed as snow falling in winter. "Yes. And I swear you're wrong. This isn't some bet between me and the other guys. I've pinned no wager on whether you care if I live or die. I'm not trying to make you feel something for me that you shouldn't, purely for my own entertainment..."

"But that's what you wanted, right? When I first got here, you decided you were gonna target me as your next plaything. You wanted to hurt me, and you were going to smile while you did it. I saw it in your eyes."

"And what do you see now?" I barely hear the words, they're so quiet.

Fuck. Please *do not look up at him, Elodie. Do not fucking do it.*

My breath stoppers up in my throat; it must have been stuck there for a while, because my lungs are beginning to burn. I can't help myself. I do it. I look up at him, dead in the eye, and it's as though I've been shot in the chest, a cold, creeping sensation spreading outward from my solar plexus. His eyes are clear. I see no deception in them. I see plenty of pride, and a whole heap of ego, but I also see the faintest, weakest glimmer of hope.

I can't bear the pressure building between us a second longer; I look away, out of the window. Wren closes his hand into a fist, withdrawing it back across the table.

"Is this the part where you leave now?" I ask morosely.

"Yeah. This is the part where I leave." He stands, running both his hands back through his hair—a gesture of pure frustration. "I came to tell you that I left something by your door for you, Little E. I thought about going inside and putting it by your bed, but we both know how you feel about people breaking into your room, right?"

He goes before I can say another word.

Goddamnit.

An invisible hand closes around my throat, choking the life out of me as I sit there, waiting for Carina to come back with our lunch. After a while she shows up with a couple of sandwiches, two apples, and a giant bag of Doritos balanced in her arms. I let her chatter away, and I chew and swallow the food she so kindly brought back for me, but I'm not really here. I'm just waiting for an opportunity to bolt. That opportunity arrives when Carina's phone begins to buzz and she holds up her cell, grinning like an idiot, and tells me that Andre's calling.

I make my excuses and I leave her to go talk to her boyfriend.

On the fourth floor, outside room four sixteen, I find a small turquoise box with a pale green ribbon tied around it, sitting there, waiting for me. With shaking hands, I collect it from the floor and hurry inside, my insides twisting themselves into knots.

He left me a gift?

I place the box down on the bed, glaring at it with my hands on my hips.

He should *not* have brought me a gift.

It takes all of my courage to gingerly untie the ribbon and lift up the lid.

"Oh my god!" I cover my mouth with my hands, trying not to cry out. My eyes sting as I take a step forward, bending over to get a closer look at the tiny little object nestled in amongst a bed of lilac tissue paper inside: the white of his chest, that fades to the blue of his back, that deepens to the dark, midnight blue at the tips of his wings...

It's the bird, my mother's bird, the one that was shattered into a million pieces...and he's somehow been pieced back together.

20

WREN

A PARADIGM SHIFT.

That's what philosophers would call a change like this.

Because I haven't simply changed my mind about something. I've had a change of heart. Ponder that for a second. A man's heart is his footlocker, where he keeps the key pieces of his identity. Where his very purpose and the traits that make up his character reside. His hopes, his dreams, and his nightmares. And Elodie Still-water has come along, taken a knife to my chest, and removed my heart. She's switched it out for another one entirely, and now I don't know where the fuck any of my shit is. I don't know who I am, or what I'm supposed to be doing, and quite honestly the whole thing is a fucking mess.

More than anything, I want it to be *over*.

I get the feeling this isn't gonna be over for a very long time, though, if ever, and now I find myself in a position where I feel obliged to do something very rash.

That manila goddamn envelope. I tried to forget what I'd read, but the words are still there, burning brighter than the sun, whenever I close my eyes. It's put me in the foulest fucking mood.

I cut through the rose garden, grinding my teeth so hard that they'll probably be little more than dust by the time I reach the gazebo. The maze is both prison and sanctuary as I wind my way through the memorized pathway to its center, biting out curse words colorful enough to make steam blow out of my father's ears. Pax and Dash are already waiting for me when I arrive at the small building hidden beneath the oak trees. Sprawled out on the steps that lead up to the front door, Pax takes one look at me and starts howling like a wolf. "Dear god, Jacobi, you look even saltier than usual. I take it your little meeting with the French whore didn't go according to plan."

With murder in my eyes, I turn and glower at Dash, who's leaning effortlessly against the wall, plucking the petals from an unopened rose bud. "What?" he asks, feigning innocence. "I had to tell him something. He wanted to know why you bailed on our Albany College plans last night. He'd been looking forward to that sorority party all month."

"You could have gone without me," I snarl. "I wasn't stopping you."

Dash pulls a pouty face. "I know, man, but, for some ungodly reason we both like having you around and it really wouldn't have been the same if you weren't there to ruin everybody's fun. In the meantime, you're bailing on us for the second time in twenty-four hours to go and see the same girl. We're beginning to feel like you might be struggling a little with your priorities. Need I remind you that we've had your back for the past four years. We've lived together and gotten into a whole heap of shit together." He holds his hands up. "We've done so many drugs in so many countries that I have stamps in my passport I don't even recognize. I could have sworn I'd never been to Brazil. Anyway, the point is, we're gonna need you to rein this thing in a little. Just for a while, yeah?"

"Yeah. We need regular, normal, wicked Wren back this weekend."

I narrow my eyes, already sensing that something bad's on the horizon. "Why? What's happening this weekend?"

Pax scrambles up, dusting off his jeans. He jumps down the

steps, boots thudding when they hit the dirt, and he throws his arm around my shoulder. "It..." He pauses for dramatic effect, "is your *birthday*, you sneaky fuck! You really think we'd forget? We're having a last-minute *Jacobi turns eighteen!* party, and there's nothing you can say or do to stop it."

Christ. I really had hoped they'd have forgotten about that. Chances are they would have—they're not very good at remembering important dates at the best of times—but then Mercy showed up. And my sister isn't one to let anyone forget *her* birthday. Unfortunately for me, we happen to share the same one. "We're not having a party."

"Yes, we fucking are." Pax nods like he's just parachuted a bunch of speed.

"We're not having a party," I repeat.

Dash crosses his arms in front of his chest. "Yeah, mate. We are."

"We're not. I need your help with something this weekend and it can't wait. I've already bought the tickets."

The boys look intrigued. "What tickets?" Pax asks suspiciously.

"Plane tickets. We need to leave the country for a couple of days. And you can't tell anyone where you're going, or we'll all be fucked."

Now I've got their attention. Really got it. They love a covert trip more than anything else in the world. Including Riot House parties. "How long are we gonna be gone for?" Dashiell queries, pretending to scrutinize a loose thread hanging from the cuff of his shirt.

"Three days. We leave tonight."

"Wow. Well, someone's feeling presumptuous, aren't they? What if we don't wanna go on this little jolly of yours? What if we don't wanna miss two days of school?"

"Then I'd have wasted thirty thousand dollars. And you'd be the most confusing person in the world, because who *doesn't* want to miss two days of school?"

"We haven't filled out the paperwork with Harcourt," Pax points out, taking a smoke out of a dogeared pack and lighting it.

"I took the liberty of completing it on your behalf this morning."

"Asshole," Dash groans. "You've thought of everything, haven't you?"

"Come on, Lovett. Wouldn't want to ruin *my birthday* now, would you?"

"That's a low fucking blow."

"At least it sounds like we're flying first class," Pax mumbles.

I grin. "Nothing but the best for my boys."

"God, don't you just hate it when he does that? It's fucking terrifying when you smile." Dash's shoulders sag in resignation, though. He's coming with me on my little sojourn. And if Dash is in, then so is Pax. The guy in question rubs a hand over his shaved head. "Fine. We'll go where you command, no questions asked. But we *are* having a party when we get back, Wren. I get the feeling you're gonna owe us one after this. And there had better be fucking strippers."

* * *

Cosgrove's is a squat, ugly building on the outskirts of Mountain Lakes—a bar, managed by a short, balding guy called Patterson, who has the misfortune of looking like Danny De Vito. The guy's in his late fifties, has a penchant for polishing a glass at least three times before putting it back on a shelf, and does not like me in the slightest. Primarily because I'm underage and shouldn't be drinking in his bar. But also, because I'm his boss.

He complains murderously under his breath when he sees me walk through the door into the empty establishment, his beady, almost black eyes boring a hole into the countertop as he studiously ignores me. "We've been over this," I say, sitting myself down on a stool in front of him. "Pretending I don't exist won't make me go away. It'll make me mad. *Madder*," I say, correcting myself. "And I'm sure neither of us wanna be dealing with that today."

"Shouldn't you go lurk out the back?" Patterson grumbles. "Sheriff King likes to come in here drinking on a Saturday afternoon."

"No, he doesn't."

"He might. Wouldn't wanna risk getting this place shut down now, would you?"

I laugh, theatrically pointing out the sea of empty seats that surround me. "Hell, Pat. Wouldn't want to jeopardize the roaring trade we've been doing of late? It'll make zero difference to me if this place closes its doors to the public. It didn't make money before I bought it, and it hasn't made a dime since either. You should be grateful I keep you gainfully employed on the off chance that I might wanna get out of the house."

Patterson's mouth twists to one side. He opens up the register and begins to count the money inside it, shuffling through rumpled bills and the same coins I'm sure have been sitting inside it since the dawn of fucking time. "I need more money for the float," he says.

I squint at him, laying my hands flat on the bar; the wood's splintered, the varnish worn off years ago. I should do something about the general state of disrepair in here, but Cosgrove's is a dive bar. The cracks in the walls and the fact that you run the gambit of getting a splinter whenever you order a drink, well, that's all just part of the charm of the place. "You do get how a float works, right? It's there to make change for paying customers, not for you to dip into every time you wanna buy a pack of smokes."

Patterson just glares at me. Mountain Lakes isn't a thriving town. Used to be a logging town before the surrounding forests were designated national park land. Now, the only real industry here is the pulp mill three miles beyond the town limits. And Wolf Hall, of course. The people who don't work at the mill, or tend the gardens, cook in the kitchens, or clean the hallways at the academy, work odd jobs or in the stores along the main street to get by.

It'd be fucking easy to replace Patterson. I could have someone else here, grateful for the job, inside half a fucking hour and the grumpy old bastard knows it. Like I said, though. The tumbledown, broken, worn patina of the place was a selling point when I decided to buy the bar, and Patterson's curmudgeonly snark was a part of that, too.

"Forty bucks should do it," he says flatly.

I pull a hundred dollar bill out of my wallet and flick it across the bar at him. "I want a shot of whiskey in front of me in the next thirty seconds, asshole. And I swear to god, if you try and pour that lighter fluid from the rail for me again, I will end your sorry existence."

He pockets the hundred instead of putting it into the till, which I say nothing about because, at this stage in the proceedings, I find his open belligerence entertaining more than anything. He steps up onto the wooden box he keeps behind the counter and takes down the bottle of Johnny Blue from the highest shelf Cosgrove's has. Instead of pouring me a fifty mil pour in a shot glass, Patterson flips over a rocks glass and free-pours four fingers of the burnt golden liquid into it, smiling sarcastically. And yes, the man has perfected the art of the sarcastic smile. He's one of only a few people I've ever seen accomplish the task.

I lift the glass to my mouth, eyeing the one hundred and twenty dollars' worth of whiskey he just so artlessly dumped into it, and I smile my most savage smile. "You really are a fucker aren't you, Pat?" The whiskey leaves a trail of fire all the way down my esophagus, but it's a smooth burn. One that glows rather than bites. I manfully swallow down the rest of the whiskey, polishing the lot off in two mouthfuls, and then slam the glass down on the woodwork.

"Having a hard time up there on the mountain?" the bartender asks, without the faintest hint of sincerity in his voice. "They run out of fois gras? Has the champagne stopped flowing out of the faucets?"

"Fuck you, man."

"I can imagine how difficult it must get for you poor kids up there, having to brush your own teeth and wipe your own asses. Must be pure torture. They really oughta hire some extra serfs to cater to our little princeling's more *intimate* needs."

"If you don't quit with the vitriol, I'll lock you in the beer cellar again."

That shuts him up. 'Cause he knows I'll do it. I've done it before. I think Patterson enjoys our verbal (and occasionally physical) sparring almost as much as I do. He doesn't like it when I kick his rotund ass down the stairs that lead into the basement and I lock him down there for the afternoon, though. He flashes teeth. "Where are those friends of yours? The English toff and the addict."

"Hah! What makes you think Pax is an addict?"

"He looks like that guy out of that movie with the Scottish junkies."

"I don't think you can accuse someone of being a drug addict because they have a shaved head and they bear a passing resemblance to a young Ewan McGregor."

He grunts, clearly of a different mind. "You want more?" He thrusts the Johnny Walker at me.

"It's the middle of the afternoon, man. Despite what you might think of me, I'm not a degenerate." Laughable. The lie is just so fucking laughable that even *I* grin like a piece of shit when Patterson holds his belly and roars. The things he's seen me do. The states he's seen me in. Jesus. "I have a question for you, Pat," I say, leaning forward so that the edge of the bar digs into my ribs. "You're a married man, aren't you?"

If Pat had any eyebrows, they'd be up around his receding hairline right now. "Yeaahhhh?"

"That big lady with the mustache? The one who cleans the toilets? She's your actual *wife*?"

His eyes, already so set back into his face, practically disappear as he glowers at me. "Are you looking for a smack boy?"

"No, no! No offense meant."

"Oh, well, in that case, none taken!" There he goes with that sarcasm again. He's a fucking pro.

"I just mean…how long have you been married to the lovely Mrs. Patterson," I ask, changing tack.

"Seventeen years."

"Shit. How…how the hell did you *do* it?"

"Do what?"

"How did you convince her that you weren't an evil, heartless piece of shit in the first place?"

Patterson rocks back and forth on the balls of his feet, chuckling merrily to himself. This time, he doesn't seem to be mocking me with his laughter; he seems genuinely amused. "Oh, lord, Wren. God, you crack me up sometimes."

"I'm being serious."

"So am I. Oh god." Gathering himself, he plants his meaty hands on the other side of the bar, bracing himself like he's preparing to lay some serious wisdom on me. "The key to convincing a woman that you're not an evil, heartless piece of shit, Wren, *is to not be an evil, heartless piece of shit.*"

Well, I can see that I walked myself right into that one. Even so, a lick of fury rises up my back, tingling between my shoulder blades. It's in my nature to want to punish the guy for such insolence, but now there's this nagging voice in the back of my head, asking how I would be acting if Elodie were here, and I don't even know what to do with myself anymore. "Duly noted," I say tightly through my teeth.

"I never thought I'd see the day!" Patterson caws. "You pompous Wolf Hall asses come in here, reeking of privilege. You play at participating in society like normal folk, but you're so like those fancy, expensive cars you all drive—too low to the ground, no room for more than one person inside. The moment you hit a bump in the road, or you're asked to think about carrying even the slightest burden, you're bottoming out and struggling to carry anything at all."

"Your metaphor's falling apart, Pat."

"Doesn't matter. Look, heaven help whoever this girl is if *you're* interested in her, but this shit is simple. Don't be selfish. Don't be a dick. Put her needs before your own. Jesus, what the fuck am I..." He shakes his head. "*Why am I even bothering?*"

I leave Cosgrove's feeling even more confused than when I went in. It all seems straightforward, and I know that Patterson's speaking the truth. In order to get Elodie to trust me, I need to make a few changes. But for the life of me, I can't figure out how the fuck I'm going to alter my very genetic cod—

whhaaAAAAT THE FUCK?

I stop dead on the sidewalk, the wind whipping at me, tugging on my clothes, but I barely notice the cold. I can't be seeing clearly. There's just no fucking way...

Across the other side of the street, in a deserted parking lot on the other side of high chain link fence, two people stand at arm's distance, talking animatedly. The tall guy on the left gesticulates, using his hands to make his point. The girl—much shorter, dressed like she's about to clock on for her shift at a strip joint, a sheet of black hair hanging down her back—laughs, shoving him playfully in the chest.

I'm crossing the street before I even know what I'm doing. There's no entrance to the parking lot from this side of the road, it must be on the other side of the lot, but that doesn't stop me. In one jump, I'm halfway up the fence. A second after that, I'm vaulting over the top of it, jumping down, landing on the ground with a bone jarring rattle that makes it through my ankles, knees, hips, back, and ends with my teeth crashing together so hard that I nearly bite off my fucking tongue.

They see me.

But only when it's too late.

My fist launches into Fitz's jaw, connecting with an almighty, satisfying *crack*. He goes down like a sack of shit.

"*What the fuck!*" My sister's shrill scream is loud and high-pitched. I grab her by the arm and pull her out of the way. "Get the fuck off me, Wren. Christ, what's wrong with you, you fucking psycho!"

On the ground, Fitz presses his fingers to his mouth, laughing like a maniac when they come away red. His blood coats his teeth and runs down his chin. "Nice to see you, too, Jacobi."

"Are you invincible, Doc?" I snarl, grabbing him by the front of his t-shirt. "Have you discovered the secret to eternal life?"

He arches a sardonic eyebrow. Not a flicker of fear in his eyes. Not a scrap of concern on him. He glances down at my mouth, his eyes lingering on my lips, and I just *know* he's getting fucking hard right now. "No," he says.

"Are you indestructible? Are your bones unbreakable? Do your wounds close immediately and stop you from bleeding out?"

"No, Wren. As well you know, they do not." He enunciates every single word, purring like a cat.

Alive with rage, I shove him, hard enough that the back of his head bounces off the concrete. *"Then stop doing shit that's gonna wind up getting you killed, motherfucker."*

"What the hell are you *thinking*?" Mercy's in front of me, now, her hands on my chest, pushing me, pushing, pushing, pushing, forcing me to take a small step away from the English teacher. "We're in fucking public, Wren. Are you insane? You can't fucking hit a member of faculty in front of people."

As menacing as can be, I dip down so I can shove my face in hers. *"I'll hit him anywhere I like.* Go and get in the car, Mercy."

"I'm not getting in any car with y—"

"GET IN THE FUCKING CAR!" I'm vibrating, overflowing, spilling over—pure and blinding rage. It takes chunks out of my insides with every ragged breath I suck down. Mercy's expression voids out, turning blank. She blinks, then turns around and begins to walk across the parking lot, towards the red Volkswagen Beetle our father bought for her last year.

"I don't see the harm in talking to a student if I see them out in the wild," Fitz says airily, propping himself up on one hand. "What am I supposed to do? Ignore you guys?"

Oh, ho, ho. My god, *this* motherfucker right *here*. Slowly, I crouch down in front of him, resting my forearms on top of my thighs, observing him with utter contempt. "You don't look at anything that belongs to me. You don't touch anything that belongs to me. Outside of your remit as a teacher, you don't *speak* to anybody that's connected with me. Do you understand?"

With eyes full of heat, Fitz sucks on his bottom lip, both nostrils flaring. "It doesn't have to be like this, y'know. Things could be like they were before."

Fuck, he just doesn't listen. I close my eyes, shaking my head, unable to believe the gall of the bastard. "Just keep your word, Wes. Or life's gonna become really unpleasant for you, yeah?"

I get into Mercy's stupid, girly red Beetle, slamming my fist into the dashboard so hard that the plastic cracks. "Wren! You asshole! What the fuck are you doing?" Mercy hits me, landing a blow to my upper arm. She's always been far more interested in being skinny than fit, so she doesn't pack much power. Won't even bruise. "Just because you've already broken all of your stuff, doesn't make it okay to break mine," she pouts.

I feel like I've just run a marathon. I can't catch my breath. "Grow up, Mercy."

"You don't think he's gonna report you to Harcourt now?" she hisses, her eyes flashing daggers at me. "You think he's just gonna keep his mouth shut if you knock him on his ass *in the middle of town?* You *humiliated* him."

Yeah. I fucking humiliated him. But there won't be any recourse for my actions in this parking lot and Mercy knows it. I know it, and Wesley Fitzpatrick knows it most of all.

He isn't gonna say shit.

His problem has always been that he *wants* me to hurt him. To humiliate him.

Almost as badly as he wants me to fuck him.

When we get back to the school, I pull over at the side of the road by Riot House and I get out of the car. Mercy switches places with me.

"You're fucking insane!" She yells, as she burns off up the hill toward the academy. If she expects this to be some sort of revelation to me, then she's shit outta luck. What I'm about to do is proof enough that she's right. I take out my phone and I type out a quick message before heading inside to throw some clothes into a bag.

ME: Going away for three days. Catch you when I get back.

21

ELODIE

THERE ARE CRACKS EVERYWHERE, of course. And a few spots where the color of his wings is gone, replaced by smooth, white ceramic, where a chip or a shard of his original veneer was lost. But the bird my mother gave me is mostly whole again, and of all the people in the world, Wren Jacobi put him back together for me.

For me.

I have questions. Namely: where did he find all of the pieces? How did he retrieve them? Harcourt said they were vacuumed up and disposed of. Did he tear open the vacuum cleaner to get them out? And how the hell did he piece the figurine back together? It would have taken hours. Days. I can't even comprehend how much time it must have taken. How much patience such an undertaking would have required. Far more patience than I credited Wren with possessing, that's for sure.

It doesn't take long for an uncomfortable suspicion to take root in my mind, like a weed pushing its way up through the cracks in a pavement. Wren didn't put the bird back together. He just couldn't have. In no reality would he have taken the time to do something that required that much effort. Which means that he forced, bribed or threatened someone else and made them do it. And then he dropped his little turquoise box off at my door, smug as fuck, pretending like he's some kind of hero for returning something so precious to me. I go from grateful and amazed to jaded and disappointed in three seconds flat. It's the only explanation that makes any sense.

At six in the evening, I get a message from Wren, saying that he's going away for three days. His short, *'catch you when I get back,'* makes me so unreasonably angry that I lock myself in my room and I don't come out until Sunday afternoon. What happened to the attic? Three days getting to know him my ass. I've expected this kind of behavior from him since the word go, so then why does it still sting?

I skip dinner, telling Carina I'm not hungry when she asks if I want to join her in the food hall, and I brood in my room, pacing up and down, wearing a trench in the floorboards as I whip back and forth like a lion in a cage, all the while staring at the bird like it's a hand grenade, about to go off on my mattress.

How can he do something like this and then just bail? It makes no sense.

Monday and Tuesday scrape by, and every little thing gets on my nerves: the line in the cafeteria; Damiana's snarky, relentless comments in English; the fact that there's no creamer left for my coffee; my assignments, which have piled up to the point that I have to stay up all night on Tuesday to complete them. Carina notices my shitty mood and comments on it, but I tell her I'm PMSing, and she seems to take it all in stride. Inside, I'm boiling away like a pot left on the heat. It shouldn't bother me that he just left without explaining himself. I shouldn't care at all that I find out it was Mercy's birthday over the weekend, which means it was Wren's birthday, and he went off with his friends to celebrate. But it affects me. All of it does. God, what kind of fragile, pathetic kind of loser have I become?

When Wren doesn't show up for class on Wednesday, I've become so irritated by the whole thing that I decide I need to do something about the situation. For the sake of my own sanity, if not for poor Carina's.

Underneath all of the frustration and anger lies the sickening worry that I hurt Wren when I didn't take his hand in the library. He could be pissed that I didn't immediately drop to my knees in gratitude when he told me that he cared about me. I'm sure that's what he was expecting me to do. If he's salty because of some perceived rejection on my part, then maybe that'll be it. He'll leave me alone and I won't have to deal with his attentions anymore.

This thought should make me happy. I've been frustrated by him for weeks, and with him backing off I'll be able to settle into life at Wolf Hall properly now, without fear of further complications.

But.

Urgh, why is there always a fucking but? Why can't I just do a celebratory dance and move the fuck on like any sane person would do?

I sit in the dark in my room, stewing. I scarf down half a bar of chocolate, but the sugar tastes sour and the candy curdles in my stomach, making me nauseous. I do whatever I can to take my mind off of the fact that Wren still hasn't messaged me, frittering away an hour playing Animal Crossing on my Nintendo Switch, then chatting with Levi on WhatsApp, but I still can't shake the disagreeable funk that has me in its grasps.

The clock on my cell phone finally clicks over to ten p.m. and I tell myself I should go to bed, but... fuck, what the hell is *wrong* with me? Why can't I just forget about this entire thing? This is for the best!

I should text him.

I should ask him what the fuck he's playing at, sending me the most confusing mixed messages. I mean, what is he hoping to accomplish here? I've wound myself up so tightly that I feel like I'm going to snap by the time I grab my Doc Martins from the bottom of the closet, jamming them angrily onto my feet.

A text message isn't good enough.

I need an explanation from him, face to face. I need to know if he did force someone else to fix the bird for me. And, loath as I am to admit it, I want to know if I actually hurt him by rebuffing him in the library.

You're such a fool, Elodie. He's not worth your energy. Seriously, take your shoes off, get into bed, lose yourself in a good book and forget about Wren Jacobi. He's a manipulative creep and nothing more.

Instead, I pick up the book he loaned me—Sir Arthur Conan Doyle's, *A Study In Scarlett*—and I jam it into my bag.

You're better than this. Better than him. You don't damn well need him.

The pep talk's a good one. I repeat it in my head as I try to tip-toe down the hallway. It's on a playback, cycling over and over again as I sneak my way down the stairs. I hear it again and again as I slip out of the academy and I begin to run down the long driveway, headed down the mountain.

* * *

I didn't have a car in Tel Aviv. I didn't need one. A vehicle would be really handy here in New Hampshire, though, especially since I live in the middle of bumfuck nowhere. Carina offered to lend me the Firebird and said I could use it whenever I wanted, but I couldn't ask her for the keys tonight. She'd have wanted to know where I was going, and no way could I have told her the truth: *"Oh, y'know, just thought I'd pop down to Riot House. After hours. Alone. To discuss my non-starter, bizarre relationship/rivalry with the boy that you've warned me until you're blue in the face to stay away from."*

Yeah, that wasn't going to happen.

So here I am, jogging down the hill, jumping out of my skin at every sound I hear, just waiting for something nasty with sharp teeth to come lurching out of the forest. I haven't seen a single car since I snuck out of the academy, and with no streetlights anywhere on the windy, hairpin road, I only have the small flash-light on my cell phone to ward off the darkness.

I knew this was a horrible idea before I left Wolf Hall, but it's only hitting home now just *how* horrible an idea it was. If anything happens to me, I'd better just die and get it over with. If I don't, Carina's gonna murder me, and I'd rather get eaten by a bear or buried in a shallow grave by the Riot House boys than have to see the look of disappointment in her eyes when *she* puts me down.

Eventually, I reach the narrow dirt track that branches off from the main road, leading to Wren's home, and panic closes around my heart like a fist. I can't see any lights. There are no lights coming from inside the house? There's no one home. Which means I've come all this way in the dark for nothing, and Wren... Wren's still not back from his party weekend with the boys, and he's out there somewhere, having a great time, having completely forgotten my existence.

Juuuust fucking great.

Oh.

Wow.

The realization hits me like a bucket of ice-cold water's just been dumped over my head: this is not the kind of person I want to be—some stupid girl wandering off on her own in the dark, all bent out of shape because of some boy who can't seem to make up his mind about her. I have more common sense than that. More self-respect. Clenching my hands into fists, I stare off into the night, my decision made. I'm going back to the academy. I'm not falling prey to this kind of insanity.

Before I can start the long walk back to Wolf Hall, a light suddenly comes on up ahead, casting a yellow glow out into the darkness. Riot House rises up out of the ink-black forest, appearing out of nowhere, and my frantic heartrate slows. So, they are home after all. A part of me is relieved by that knowledge, but the rest of me is frustrated that I'd even let myself ca—

A steel bar wraps around my neck, cutting off my air supply. "Scream and you're fucking dead," a vicious growl warns.

What the...what the *fuck?*

For a second, I am fear personified. My mind just...blanks. I can't breathe, can't move, can't think...

The impossibly strong band around my throat tightens. "Little sneak," the voice hisses. "Tiptoeing around in the dark, spying on people. Very bad, *petite pute française*. Very bad indeed."

The blockade that slammed up inside of me shatters, falling apart. That phrase: little French whore. That's what Pax called me when I walked into my very first class at the academy. I have no doubt that it's him standing behind me, trapping me in a choke hold, and with that knowledge my fear evaporates. He's not a monster. He's not some supernatural creature, prowling out of the woods, looking for his next meal. He's just a guy with an attitude problem, and I've been trained how to deal with *those*.

I slam my elbow back and up into his ribs. He's so much taller than me that he's had to bend himself over to grab me, which means I can get a lot of momentum behind the blow. Pax huffs out a surprised breath, winded, and I use the opportunity to my advantage. Twisting, spinning in his arms, I jam my knuckles into his throat, slamming them into his Adam's apple, and his hold on me disappears.

"Fucking...*bitch!*" he roars. "Come here. Get your ass here *right fucking now!*"

He blinks, shocked, when I obey him without a second thought. *Sure, I'll come to you, motherfucker. I'll be* right *with you.* He exposes his teeth, anger burning brightly in his eyes, and makes a grab for me. I have him by the wrist, though. I yank his arm around, slamming my palm against his elbow, forcing the joint to bend the wrong way, and Pax reacts the same way all the big boys do when they're about to get their arm broken: he drops to his knees, crying out in pain.

From there, it's easy enough. I release his arm, but I'm not done with him just yet. The sole of my Doc Martin lands between his shoulders when I kick out, putting all my strength behind the blow. He topples forward into the leaf litter, cursing furiously, and then I'm on his back, anticipating what he'll do next, already waiting for him to try and twist around underneath me. My fist's raised, wound back as far as it can go, ready to break his fucking nose and end his pretty boy modeling career for good, when—

"I don't think that'll be necessary," a polite voice informs me. A hand closes around my wrist, tight enough that I can't wrench it free. Pax jackknifes, bucking me off his back, and I fly sideways onto the ground. Dash stands over me, his face a blank mask, his expression utterly unreadable. With only the dim light from the house spilling over his features, he looks like a statue of a man. An inanimate carving left out for the elements to claim.

"Crazy...little...fucker..." Pax pants, whirling around to face me. He's about to lunge down and grab hold of me again, when a third figure materializes out of the shadows. Like a pale wraith, Wren stands over me with his hands hidden in his pockets, dark hair obscuring half his face. His crooked smile looks more than a little wolfish.

"Well, boys. Better break out the good china," he rumbles. "Looks like we have ourselves an unexpected house guest."

22

ELODIE

THE COFFEE'S bitter and warm and sends a shiver of pleasure running down my spine. Dash sits on the very edge of the leather sofa, watching me drink from the cup with a level of fascination that makes it seem like he just woke from a three-thousand-year coma and he has no idea what coffee is. Or mugs. Or sofas. Or girls who know Krav Maga.

"That really was quite impressive," he says, resting his chin in his hand.

"No, it was fucking *dumb*," Pax snaps, massaging his throat. "She knew I was fucking around. She cranked that shit up to eleven for no reason." He's sitting on the floor, leaning up against the wall by the open fire, glaring balefully at me while he tends to his 'bruised' windpipe. I barely fucking touched him.

Wren hasn't said much. He stands by the doorway that leads through to the kitchen, his shoulders tensed, as he watches his two friends. His jade eyes have skimmed over me once or twice, but his main focus has been on Dash and Pax, as if he's waiting for something to happen. He's wearing a black hoody and some loose sweatpants, and boy does he make them look sinful. The son of a bitch could make a garbage bag look good, though. I look away from him, only to catch Dash frowning deeply at me.

"What brings you over, love? We adore receiving people, but the place is kind of a bombsite. It's past midnight and we just got back from a very long trip. We were about to start some party planning."

The house is spotless. The thick cream rug that Pax's annoying ass is sprawled out on looks recently vacuumed. The glass coffee table doesn't have a single fingerprint on it. The beaten brass panel above the fireplace is so polished, it's as reflective as a mirror. The moody paintings on the walls—black, blue, white, slashes of emotion on canvas—are much more breathtaking now that I'm seeing them properly lit, and don't have a fleck of dust gathering on their frames. The magazines and books on top of the sideboard are so perfectly aligned that not a rogue corner or dogeared edge pokes out from their stacks. The place looks like a fucking hotel lobby.

Wren coughs into his balled-up fist, apparently trying to muffle his snort of laughter. The corner of his eyes are crinkled, betraying his amusement, though. I never thought it possible for him to smile, but it actually happens pretty frequently. You just have to be paying attention in order to catch it—

I catch something else, as he holds that hand in front of his face: his knuckles are bruised. One of them is split open, red and raw. They weren't like that the other night in the attic, nor in the library, either. I would have noticed. He's hit something since I saw him on Saturday, and by the looks of things, he hit that something hard. As if he can feel my gaze on him, Wren unclenches his fist, stretching his fingers out, and lazily shoves his hand back into the pocket of his sweatpants, looking down at his feet.

"Sorry for interrupting your party planning," I say in a droll tone. "I just...came to return a book I borrowed from Wren."

I pull A Study in Scarlett out of my bag, holding it sheepishly in the air, as if showing them the book will inexplicably make my excuse less lame.

Wren looks up at me from under dark, banked brows, giving me all of his attention at last. He looks pained, though. His mouth twitches, slanting up at the side. "Ahh. Sherlock Holmes. Yeah. I wondered where that had gotten to."

"God, you're pathetic," Pax laughs. He rips the sock off his right foot, balls it up and hurls it at Wren's face. "A girl skipped down the hill in the dark, by herself, and you're standing over there, all, *'Ohhh, Sherlock Holmes. My favorite book of all time?* Credit us with a little common sense. She came here to get some *dick*, Jacobi."

Dash laughs down his nose but manages to cut it off pretty quickly. He studiously stares up at the ceiling, looking anywhere and everywhere but at me. The only person who actually does look at me is Wren. He must see the bright red stains on both my cheeks. My embarrassment can probably be seen from outer space. Ducking my head, I crack my neck, letting out a steady, even breath. What does it matter if that's what they think? Who fucking cares anyway? They're a pair of jackals, these two. Equally detestable, for a variety of reasons. I won't be cowed by their stupid, inane comments or their adolescent tittering.

Slowly, I get to my feet, still holding the coffee mug and the book in my hands. "Whatever. I'm gonna go up to your room, Wren. I'll give you a beat to figure out those party planning duties. No rush."

The three of them just stare at me as I waltz across the open plan living room area and I begin to climb the stairs. My heart slams like a jackhammer, my pulse roaring, but I don't falter. I hold the mug steady in my hands. I put one foot in front of the other, cool and even, a picture of calm. Until I reach the second-floor landing and they can no longer see me, that is. My hand shakes so violently that the coffee in the mug sloshes over the side, splattering to the polished floorboards. Thankfully the liquid misses the plush grey carpet runner, but I've still made one hell of a mess.

"Fuck, fuck, fuck!" Quickly shrugging out of my zip-up hoody, I drop it to the ground, stepping on it and using my foot to mop up the coffee, shaking all over now. What the fuck did I just do? In front of Dashiell and Pax. *And* Wren. What the fuck? I'm gonna go up to your room? *I'm gonna go up to your room???* Oh my god. I barely know the guy. Sweet Baby Jesus, why couldn't I have just sent him a shitty text message for ghosting me and stayed in my fucking room?

Lord knows how I make it up the second flight of stairs or the third, but I do. My legs are unsteady, barely holding me up as I open the door to Wren's room and go inside, hurriedly closing it behind me. Well this could not have gone any worse. I should have made a plan. I mean, even if they hadn't found me stalking about outside the house like a fucking psychopath, what was I gonna do? Just walk up to the front door and just fucking *knock*? Like that would have been a *sane* thing to do?

I toss the book on the bed, and then I discard the half-empty mug of coffee on a shelf by the door, no longer needing the prop to make myself look normal, definitely not needing the caffeine—I'm already jittery enough, thank you very much—and I turn around, leaning back against the wall, closing my eyes for a second.

Breathe, Elodie.

Just breathe.

In and out, in and out.

Everything's okay. This is a totally *salvageable situation.*

It isn't, though. And breathing makes things worse. The bedroom smells so acutely of Wren—all salt sea air, and fresh wood shavings, and the faintest hint of citrus—that my slowing heart rate ratchets up all over again, the pounding, pounding, pounding threatening to blow out my ear drums.

Calm down, Elodie.

Calm down.

Name five things you can see. Come on. Five things you can see. You can do this. Just calm the fuck down.

I lock onto the first thing I lay eyes on: a tattered notebook, sitting on top of Wren's bed. Even from the door, I can see the scribbles of black ink all over the lined paper. It looks like some kind of journal...

The second thing I see: a canvas, set up on an easel in the corner of the room, right by the floor to ceiling windows. There's a sheet on the floor underneath the easel, splattered with paint. A pot full of brushes sits on Wren's desk not far away, their bristled ends sticking out of the glass jar, their wooden handles flecked with even more paint. On the canvas itself...I walk over to it, my heart finally calming a little as I take in what I'm seeing.

Black, and moody, midnight blue, and grey and white. I remember thinking to myself, when I broke into Riot House with Carina, that the paintings downstairs all looked like raging, angry storms. They had no point of focus or subject, but I could feel the unrest radiating off of them even in the dark. This painting is a far cry from those pieces of art hanging on the walls on the first floor floor. There most definitely is a subject to this painting...and that subject is *me*.

Broad, flat, sweeping brushstrokes make up the lines of my torso and my shoulders, but the details of my neck and my face are finer and more delicate. Half of the painting looks like it was done quickly, angrily, with resentful slashes, while the other half appears as though great care and effort was taken to carefully stroke in each minute detail.

I'm not smiling in the painting. I'm sitting on a couch, the floral print of the fabric smeared and blurred out of focus behind me. The jumble and confusion of shapes and patterns directly behind my head tells me where I am—sitting beneath the print of Gustav Klimt's 'The Kiss' that hangs in Doctor Fitzpatrick's den. I'm looking off to one side, the line of my jaw hard like I'm clenching it, and there's a detached, aggressive light in my eyes that makes *me* look hard, too. Fierce.

"I liked you best when you were angry. In the beginning," Wren says. He stands in the doorway with his arms loosely folded across his chest, watching me with another of his unreadable, unfathomable expressions on his face. "I don't know anymore, though. Now, I like seeing you smile, but it's hard to paint you like that."

"Why?" The word comes out as a whisper. A single, rush of air past my lips.

"Because you've never smiled at *me*, Little E. I could steal those moments where you looked angry, when you weren't looking, because they were familiar. I'd already earned the anger and the hate you wore. But when you laugh with Carina, or you smile at someone you don't even fucking know as they pass you in a hallway..." He shakes his head. "I don't own those moments. They don't belong to me. I sure as shit have no right to take them and make them my own."

"I didn't even know you painted," I whisper.

He arches a dark eyebrow, canting his head to one side. "Didn't you?"

"Urgh, yes. I did. I don't even know why I said that. I just..."

"You don't know what to do. You don't know how to feel. You're scared of the truth and what it could mean. Down is up, and up is down..."

He makes it sound so confusing. It's as though he's reading my mind. "Yes. All of that," I agree.

He enters the room, approaching with slow steps that seem designed to give me time to react and escape. I remain rooted to the spot, not daring to breathe as he gets closer and closer. He stops, close enough that his arm brushes up against mine as he comes to stand in front of the painting, his sharp green eyes assessing his work with a cold detachment. "I don't like painting people," he says quietly. "No matter how well I capture their likeness, I always end up projecting my own emotions onto them. They always end up angry and ready for a fight." He touches his fingertips to the deep furrow he painted in between my eyebrows, rubbing them as if he might be able to ease the tension he created on my face.

"You shouldn't have come here, y'know," he says tightly. "This isn't exactly a safe place for someone like you."

"Someone like me? God, I'm not some weak, pathetic, defenseless girlchild who can't look after herself. I think Pax's esophagus

238 | CALLIE HART

will attest to that. And this is your home, anyway. What the fuck do you get up to here? Am I supposed to be worried for my safety?"

"*Yes!*" He sounds so exasperated. Looks it, too. Dragging his hands back through his hair, he wheels away from the painting, stepping toward his bed. "I can't spell this out for you, Elodie. It's too…it's fucking complicated, and I should never have pursued you the way I have been doing, but I'm a prick, all right? I'm not known for doing what's best for other people."

Biting down hard, clenching every muscle in my body, I gather up what little courage I have, and I ask the question I came here to ask. "You disappeared, Wren. You vanished for three whole days without any word of explanation. Are you gonna tell me where you've been?"

He shakes his head so slowly, looking down at his hands. "No. I don't think that would be a very good idea."

Wow. He's really not going to tell me? "Were you—were you hooking up with girls. Is that why you won't say?"

A small smile tugs at the corner of his mouth. "Would you be jealous if I had?"

It kills me that I let myself ask that. It kills me that he looks so damn pleased with himself now. I just revealed a soft, vulnerable part of myself; I bared my neck, exposing myself to him, and now he has all he needs to rip out my throat. "Just answer the question, Wren."

Still glowing with satisfaction, he sucks on his bottom lip, shaking his head again. "No, Little E. There were no other girls."

Relief should be the very last thing I feel, but it surges up inside me nontheless. "Okay. So, what? You're just done with me now? Because normally guys don't make you promise to spend time with them and then just disappear into thin air."

He goes still. Doesn't look up. Not really. Just turns his head slightly toward me, his eyes half-closed, turmoil written on the lines of his face. "That's what you wanted, right? What you've wanted this entire time. For me to leave you alone?"

Yes. It *is* all I've wanted. I've waded through thigh-deep frustration and anger in my attempts to distance myself from him. But now that we're here, he's giving me this out... I'm pretending like this is some new revelation, striking me out of the blue, but that isn't the truth. I've wanted him since the moment I set eyes on him, smoking that cigarette outside the academy, waiting for me in the half-drawn shadows. Even with his shitty attitude, and his sharp tongue, and his suspect history, I've wanted him. And that kiss we shared on Friday night made me unravel in a way that thrilled and terrified me.

"Who did you pay to find the bird?" I demand.

"What?"

"The bird. My mother's bird. You left it for me outside my room. Who did you pay to sift through a filthy vacuum cleaner and collect all of the pieces?"

Wren's head jerks back; his brows hike up his forehead, crimping together. "Who did I *pay*?"

"Yes."

"I didn't *pay* anyone. And the pieces were a lot more difficult to come across than that. The janitor had emptied the vacuum into the dumpster by the kitchen. It was empty otherwise, but it was still an unpleasant task."

Do I believe what he's telling me? He not only didn't force someone into doing his dirty work, but that he did that really, disgusting, unbelievably gross dirty work *for me*? I'm having trouble conjuring the image of him vaulting over the side of a dumpster so he can pick through grime and muck in order to do something kind for another human being. I get as far as seeing him there, beside the dumpster, but the rest of the image won't materialize. In my head, he lights up a smoke, leans against the dumpster, curling his lip up in an arrogant, smug way as he tells me to go fuck myself.

"You were gonna ream me out for bullying someone into putting it back together for you. I'm right, aren't I? That's why you came here?" Wren asks. He sits down on the edge of his bed, waiting for me to answer. I don't know that I can, though. Now that I'm here, and he's acting weird and vulnerable, I'm at a complete loss.

"Yes," I confess reluctantly. "I was. I figured you'd had a friendly conversation with Tom or one of his friends and suggested they do you a little favor or wind up with a black eye."

Something doleful and unhappy plays out across his face. He studies his hands, picking absently at a chip of black nail polish. "I might have done that. Another time. But not for something I planned on giving to *you*, Little E. You seemed cut up over losing the thing, and...I don't know," he says, "I wanted to make it right. *I* wanted to make it right. Not coerce someone else into doing it for me. So, yeah. After the night of the storm, I went and found the janitor. He pointed me in the right direction, and I spent a couple of hours every night sticking my fucking fingers together with Gorilla Glue, trying to make it whole again. I had to use clay to fill in the parts where pieces were missing. And that was it. I fixed it. I gave it back to you. No need to make a big deal out of it."

I've never seen him look more uncomfortable than this. He looks like he's simultaneously being bitten by thousands of fire ants and having bamboo spikes shoved underneath his fingernails.

"I don't understand you. How can you look so wound up and miserable over the fact that someone found out you did something nice for them?"

"Because I'm *not* nice," he grinds out. "I don't *do* nice things. I don't know how to...*be* nice."

This is not the Wren Jacobi I know. That Wren is confident and so sure of who he is. This Wren is tense, it feels like he's going to blow any moment now. I sit down next to him without considering the consequences—how his close proximity might affect my breathing, or how the heat from his leg resting against mine might make my head spin like a top. "You didn't answer the question," he says.

Indecision has me by the tongue. I did avoid answering the question he posed to me, yes, but I don't know how the fuck I'm supposed to reply. Carina would tell me to run like the wind, get away from this as quickly as possible and thank my lucky stars that I escaped unscathed. But, then again, Wren was right. I haven't seen him do anything unforgiveable since I arrived at Wolf Hall. I have no reason to think he'd do anything to hurt me.

"You asked me to trust you," I whisper, afraid of the words even as I'm saying them. "And I've been scared to. I know that wanting to be with you, in whatever capacity, is probably the stupidest thing I can possibly do, Wren. But I do. I do want you, and...the answer's no. I don't want you to be done with me. I feel like there could be..."

"*More*," Wren supplies. "A lot more. Between us."

"Yes."

The points where my body is making contact with his—my knee, my thigh, my hip, my shoulder—all feel like they're pressed up against a vat of boiling water, and that vat has been growing gradually hotter and hotter as I've been sitting here, so slowly that I haven't noticed that it's too, too hot until the contact is suddenly scalding me. I want to pull away, but Wren angles his head, looking sideways at me, and I'm staked to the spot, unable to move a muscle. "I can't promise I'm not gonna hurt you, Little E. But I can promise that, if I do, it won't be on purpose. I can also promise that I'll do everything in my power *not* to." He swallows thickly, his throat bobbing. "Do you think that might be enough?"

The air's so laden with tension that it feels syrupy as it trickles down into my lungs. His muscles lock up, his shoulders rising a fraction as he waits for my answer. Aware of how idiotic this whole thing is, I slowly nod my head.

Wren's eyes come alive. "Thank fuck for that." Twisting, he grabs me, holding my face in his hands, and his mouth is on mine before I can even react. Heat roars up from the very soles of my feet, flooding my body until it's burning at the very crown of my head, and nothing, *nothing* feels stable anymore. The bed tilts, the floor shifts, my mind capsizes, and I'm moving, scrambling to get closer, climbing into his lap like some wild animal, trying to wrap myself around him.

This is no slow burn. We've already done our little dance, our back and forth with each other over the past few weeks more than enough foreplay for either of us. His tongue drives past my lips, tangling with my own, tasting me, licking me, exploring my mouth with a frantic urgency that has me panting and whimpering like a needy fucking dog. Wren's hands move to the small of my back, pulling me to him, and I arch into him, crushing myself up against his chest, wanting so badly to be even closer. Wren lets out a groan, breathing heavily into my mouth, and hearing it, hearing *him* coming undone, ignites fireworks in my head.

This is happening.

This is *really* happening?

"Elodie," he pants. I wind my fingers into his hair, relishing the thickness of it, gulping down breath after breath as I try to master this crazy, out of control feeling that's whipping around in my chest like a hurricane. "Elodie," he repeats. He pulls back a fraction, tugging on a handful of my hair hard enough that I have to tilt my head back to look up at him. "This is the part where I'm supposed to tell you that we should stop if you're not... if you... if you don't..."

"*Shut up and fuck me, Wren.*"

His eyes flash a green so vivid and intense that they steal the oxygen right out of my lungs. "As you wish." In one swift, powerful move, he flips me over and throws me down onto the bed, grinning like a demon as he kneels over me, eyes roaming the length and breadth of my body without a lick of shame. "For every filthy thought you've had about me, Stillwater, I've bested you ten times over. You've no idea how many times I've wrapped my hand around my cock and made myself come to you here in this bed. How many times I've almost bitten through my own fucking tongue, aching for you as I've shot my load all over my own stomach. I've always been a depraved and dirty thing, Elodie Stillwater, but the idea of *you* has corrupted me to the point of insanity."

*Oh...my...fucking...*god.

The thought of it. The very idea of him lying here in this bed, touching himself, stroking his dick, closing his eyes and painting himself pictures of *me* as his pleasure mounts...

It's just too fucking much. Want burns between my legs, so urgent and demanding that I have to press my thighs together to prevent my hips from bucking of their own accord. Wren takes me in; he can see how glazed over and hungry my eyes are, and it only seems to urge him on.

"I've painted you on canvas, Little E, but it hasn't been enough. All I've wanted to do..." He takes hold of the bottom of my shirt, fisting the hem of the thin material. "All I've been *desperate* to do..." He rents the material in two, tearing it from my body, exposing my stomach and my chest. *"Is paint your entire body with my come."*

He isn't shy. He reaches out and palms my breasts through my black, lacy bra, growling through his teeth in an animalistic, possessive way that has my back arching off the bed. He bows himself over me, huffing down his nose, kissing and licking at the skin of my neck, and down, down, down, until he's hovering right over my chest. How many times have I stared at that cruel, beautiful mouth of his and worried about how much damage it was capable of inflicting? It was too dangerous to imagine how much pleasure he could deliver with it. And now, here I am, spread out for him on his bed, finding out firsthand just how capable he is...

He rubs his jaw against my breasts, then clamps down over the thin, sheer material, pinching my nipple between his teeth, and—

"Fuck! Wren!"

Pain lights me up, brilliant and blinding, and a wicked smile spreads like sin across his face. With painstaking slowness, he slides his hand up my body, starting at my hip, moving over my stomach, my ribs, my shoulder, briefly taking hold of me by the neck, though not closing his fingers tight, and then continuing upward, until his palm is pressing down, featherlight, over my mouth.

"Believe me, Little E. You do *not* want them to hear this."

He's talking about Pax and Dash, of course. His asshole room-mates are probably lurking out there in the hallway, slapping each other and acting like dicks, straining to hear what's going on in here. Wren's expression is all warning. "I can fuck you, Elodie. I can take your breath away. I'll make you come around my dick so fucking hard, you won't be able to walk straight for a week. But you can*not* make a sound. Do you understand? If they hear..."

He doesn't complete the sentence, but I can see that he's being serious. Gravely so.

Dipping down, he kisses me roughly, his tongue and his teeth and his raw desire crowding in on me, making me dizzy. "Can you do that?" he asks, nipping at my bottom lip with his teeth. "Can you be quiet for me? Can you do what I tell you, when I tell you, without screaming the house down?"

I nod. I'll gag *myself* if I have to, so long as he keeps on kissing me, and his eyes continue to feast on me like I'm the most delectable thing he's ever seen. His hands are calloused and deli-ciously rough as he runs them down my body. I shiver, completely at his mercy as he hooks his fingers into the waistband of my jeans and tugs at them suggestively.

"Lift your ass," he commands. I do it without so much as flinch-ing, planting my feet on the bed and hiking my hips up off the mattress. Wren unfastens my pants with quick, deft fingers, ripping the zipper down, then grabbing hold of the material and yanking it over my hips, tearing the denim from my legs. His eyes burn into me, devouring my bare flesh as he slides off the end of the bed and takes off his hoody. He does it in that lazy way that guys do, one hand reaching behind him, grabbing the material and tugging it over his head in a smooth move. His t-shirt goes with the hoody, both items of clothing dropping to the floor at his feet.

Then he's standing there in nothing but his sweats, his thumbs dipping down below his waistband, smirking ruinously at me. There's a dare in his eyes—something insolent and brazen that tells me he's going to be naked if he pulls down those sweats.

"Wanna go back downstairs and drink more coffee?" he asks.

He's giving me an out. A chance to back away from this situation before it goes any further.

"I appreciate the offer," I say breathlessly, "but I'm gonna explode if you don't get back over here in the next three seconds and take care of me."

Wren smiles, but it's a humorless expression. He must feel it. This electricity between us must be eating him alive, the way it's eating away at me. He takes down his sweats, and as I expected, his cock springs free from the thick material, standing proud as he steps out of the pants. A moment passes, where I dig my finger-nails into my palms, so close to breaking the skin, and Wren stands absolutely still, allowing me to see him.

He's hard as hell. And really fucking big. I expected nothing less; Wren gives off mad big dick vibes twenty-four hours a day, seven days a week. I just wasn't expecting him to be *this* big. The heavy head of his cock bobs, and I feel like I'm sinking into the bed beneath me, disappearing into it, being swallowed up by the comforter and all the confusion of pillows.

Wren takes one step forward, palming himself in his hand. "Sure about that coffee?" He gives me an open-mouthed grin that almost makes my eyes roll back inside my head. Jesus wept, he's fucking beautiful. I snuck a peek at him back at the gazebo, the night of the storm, but I didn't let myself drink him in the way I've given myself permission to do now. His abs are ridiculously cut, his pecs standing proud from his muscled chest. And the defined vee that leads the eye down, down, between his legs, guiding me right to his erect dick...I can't fucking look away. So, I look down instead. His balls are big—suspended, heavy and swollen between his thighs. Wren notices where I'm looking and moves his hand down, cupping himself, shuddering slightly when I let out a breathy whimper that's embarrassing as hell.

"*Is* this what you came here for, Little E? Did you know this was going to happen? Were you thinking about my dick the entire way down the mountain?"

I swallow, trying to make sense of what's happening inside me right now. I've never been so conflicted before. There are too many thoughts and needs and wants, all quarreling with one another, screaming over the top of one another, begging to be heard. My emotions are like one of Wren's stormy paintings—a swirling mass of color and light and darkness, all mixed together, blurring and surreal.

Is this even really happening? Am I even really fucking here? Is this a feverish, delicious nightmare that I'm going to wake from, panting and covered in sweat?

"No," I whisper. "I didn't let myself think...this." I didn't. Such a thought would have been far too dangerous. If I'd let myself for one minute think that this might happen, I'd have been running back up the hill like the very devil himself was at my back.

Smart girls don't tangle with the devil.

Girls who have a good head on their shoulders steer clear of this kind of trouble.

I used to know exactly who I was—someone who'd make the right call when faced with temptation. I'm only realizing now that I've never truly been tempted before. It was easy to walk away from parties, and booze, and cute boys when I was back in Tel Aviv. My father made it easy. The promise of a hot and heavy make out session with a guy I liked couldn't compare to the never-ending world of shit I'd be in if my father found out. But Wren... fuck, I've never wanted anything as much as I want Wren. And no matter how stupid it is, I'd risk everything to have him.

He grabs his dick, too, groping squeezing himself with both hands now, his eyes hazy and unfocused as he approaches the bed. "Since you've made it perfectly clear that you're disinclined to beg, I'm gonna need you to tell me what you want out of this situation."

My heart trips and topples over the edge of a forty-foot cliff, taking my stomach with it. "Probably more than you have to give," I admit in a timid voice.

He seems intrigued by that. "You're not talking about my body. You're talking about something else."

I'm frayed, coming apart at the seams. I'm aching and burning for him so fucking badly that I don't even know what I want anymore.

"You don't know what you're asking for," he says, the words dark and full of gravel, promising pain untold. "There's only so much of me a person can take before it starts to hurt, Little E. And no, I am not talking about my dick." He smirks ruthlessly. "My heart's a grenade. It's safer where it is, locked in its cage. You take it outta there and you're essentially pulling the pin."

"What happens then?" I'm shaking all over.

Wren's reached the bottom of the bed. He lets go of his straining erection and places his hands on my ankles, curling his fingers around them tightly. "I don't know. No one's ever tried."

He drags me toward him by my feet and claims me as his prize.

23

WREN

CHRISTMAS MORNING.

Wren Jacobi, a tender six-year-old boy, sat down next to his twin sister and waited eagerly to open his presents. At seven, eight, nine, and ten, he did the same, heart beating out of his chest, unable to contain the excitement at what delights he might find inside the stacks of colorfully wrapped and ribboned gifts that awaited him.

All of those Christmases combined don't even come close to the excitement I feel now, as I pull Elodie down the mattress toward me. I'm no longer a naïve little boy, filled with juvenile anticipation over a box of Legos. No, now I'm far more interested in taking things *apart* than putting them together, and Elodie promises to be the most precious gift of all.

The part of me that took that photo of her from Harcourt's desk—the very same part of me that relished the prospect of breaking her heart and making her cry—rears its ugly head, making all sorts of vile commands. My dick strains harder, and my blood roars through my veins, an unstoppable, deadly tidal wave... but I close a fist around that dark shadow, banishing it from my mind. Wren from three weeks ago would have already figured out what cruel, cold thing he was going to say to Elodie once he'd had his fill of her tonight, but now I'm left scrambling, turned around and unsure what the fuck I'm going to do once this is over.

I won't shatter her, though. I'll make her fall to pieces in my arms, and I'll watch her splinter apart as she comes. After that, who knows what the fuck comes next. Anyone's guess is as good as mine.

Her eyelashes flutter like butterfly's wings as she looks up at me, her winter-blue eyes full of desire and panic. Her tongue darts out wetting her bottom lip, and I beat back a snarl at the sight of it. "Answer me, E. What do you want? How far do you want this to go?"

Mrs. Hopkins, our hapless statistics teacher, drew the short straw the day the students of Wolf Hall had to be given the whole *consent* talk. She'd be proud as hell of me right now. *'Boys, I know you're all far too young to be thinking about sex yet* (hah de fucking hah) *but you must always make sure that your lady friend consents to your advances. If you don't hear a clear yes from her, then always better to assume that, uh, it's a no.'* Her pride would be misplaced, though. I'm not asking for Elodie's consent. She already gave it, the moment she announced she was coming up to my fucking room in front of Pax and Dash. No, I want to know just how filthy my precious Little E is gonna let me be.

She wriggles, her chest rising and falling rapidly, her toes curling against the flat of my stomach. God, I want to bite her. I want to fucking consume her. I want to take all of that beautiful blonde hair and wrap it around my fist as I drive her mouth down as deep as she can go onto my cock. Her eyes shutter, like she has a window into my depraved, debauched mind, and what she sees through it is making her unravel. "You know what I want," she says.

Ahhh, poor Little E needs to loosen up that tongue of hers. I have a few tricks up my sleeve that should grease those gears. One step at a time, though. Still holding both her ankles, I spread her legs apart, holding her feet on either side of my thighs. The taut cord inside me—what passes for my patience—pulls even tighter, threatening to snap, when I see the damp patch of silk in between her legs. Her pussy's already wet enough to have soaked through her panties. *"Oh, E."*

She squirms, two twin patches of color burning high on her cheek bones, trying to close her legs at the knee, but I jerk roughly on her ankles, slowly shaking my head. "Don't. You didn't fucking come here to hide yourself from me. You know you didn't. Don't you want me to taste your cunt?" I'm straight forward. To the point. Her cheeks flame even redder, and that twisted, wicked part of me crows.

"Yes," she says quietly. "I do."

"Good. You want me to fuck you with my fingers?"

"Yes."

"You want me to fuck you with this?" I ask, grabbing hold of my cock.

She shudders, goosebumps forming underneath my palms, covering her legs and the flat, toned stomach she's been hiding under those massive, stupid fucking t-shirts she wears. I watch, fascinated beyond belief, as she nods her head. *"Yes."*

"You want me to come inside you? You want to feel my dick getting harder as I get closer and closer?"

"Yes." Now that she's admitted that she wants my cock, the word comes out a little easier; poor girl probably thinks that's the hardest thing I'm gonna make her admit to. I haven't even gotten started.

"Take your bra off," I command. "Panties, too. Put them on the nightstand."

She hesitates for a second, pulling in a deep breath through her nose.

"Now, Elodie."

Fire and brimstone simmer in her eyes, a little of that defiant spirit finally breaking through her nerves. There's a message for me on her face, plain as day, as she sits up, reaching behind her back to unfasten her bra: *Careful, Jacobi. Talk to me like that again and I'll bite your fucking dick off.*

I'd probably let her, too, if it meant she'd slipped it inside that pretty mouth first.

She never takes her eyes off me as she shrugs her bra straps from her shoulders and the material drops, leaving her chest bare. She's fucking perfect, just like I knew she would be. Not big, and not small, her tits are the perfect fucking size. Her skin is like fresh poured cream, completely flawless. Her nipples are the softest shade of pink, so pale and pretty that I can't stop myself from groaning. My mouth's already watering at the prospect of sucking on those nipples. My hands are aching, begging to be full of her. Elodie smiles as she shimmies her panties over her hips, pushing them down her thighs.

The cord inside me snaps.

I grab the black, sheer material, ripping it from her body with one hand, baring my teeth in an approximation of a smile as I offer them back to her. "On the nightstand," I repeat. "Then on your back for me, Little E. I want to get a proper look at you."

She places her bra and her panties on the small table beside the bed, just as I've told her to, and then she carries out the second part of my command, lying down on the bed. Her hands rest by her sides, but her fingers spasm and twitch, letting me know that she's desperate to cover herself with them.

Mercilessly slow, I climb up onto the bed and crawl up the mattress, shoving her legs open again so that I'm kneeling between them. She closes her eyes for a second, knowing what's coming.

"Open," I order. "All the way. I want to see all of you. Your clit. Your pussy. Your asshole. Wider, Elodie." I growl when she only inches her legs apart a fraction. "*Wider.*"

Her legs tremble as she gives me what I want. I bite the inside of my cheek, staring down at her, losing my fucking mind as I scan every minute detail of her most secret, most sacred parts. Her clit's swollen and glistening, wet like a pearl. Her flesh is slick, flushed darker around her opening, but a pale, pale pink like her nipples everywhere else. I've never really cared about anal before, but my need to inspect Elodie's asshole is tantamount to fucking criminal. She's so good, so pure, that witnessing the most taboo part of her angelic body makes my dick so hard that it feels like I'll come if she so much as fucking breathes in my direction.

I don't fuck around.

I don't hold back.

I reach out and I touch her like I already own her, like she's *always* been mine. Her wet heat coats my fingertips, covering them in her desire, and I cannot fucking look away. She goes stiff, so rigid that her fingers drive into the sheets, forming fists around the material. When I look up at her, her eyes are clenched shut.

"Breathe," I tell her. "Unless you're into auto-erotic asphyxiation. In which case, carry on."

She inhales, her ribs showing through her skin, her tits heaving, nipples peaked—the most devastatingly beautiful thing I've ever seen—and when she breathes out, I push my fingers inside her. Inside her pussy *and* her ass.

Her eyes fly open. "Holy *fuck*," she hisses. God knows how she does it, but she locks her legs up even tighter. The pressure around my fingers, up to the second knuckle inside of her, reaches intense levels as she fights to accommodate the alien sensation. God, this is just too fucking good...

"I knew you'd been fucked before," I snarl. "But you've been holding out on me, Little E. You're *ass* is virgin, isn't it?"

She blows out a long, steady, calming breath, nodding her head against the pillows. "Ahh...yes," she whispers.

"Are you going to let me fuck you there?" I rumble.

She pants, breathing in sharp, shallow gasps. "Yes," she says. "I —I—oh my god..."

Too pleased to think straight, I take my hand away, and she melts right into the mattress. I am going to have a lot of fun with this girl. If my suspicions are right, she'll be the most fun I've ever had. Before she can open her eyes, I drop down onto my stomach, my cock complaining bitterly at the lack of attention, and I sink myself down between her legs, burying myself in her pussy.

"Fuck! Oh—oh gggo—*WREN!*"

Using my front teeth, I nip savagely at the inside of her thigh. "*No.*" I chide her like she's a misbehaving child. "What did I tell you? Pax and Dash can't hear this." I can't tell her how miserable my housemates will make her life if they know about this. They'll taunt and ridicule her in front of everyone at the academy, and I won't fucking have that.

She looks down the length of her body, nodding frantically. "Okay. Okay."

Once I trust that she's got a handle on herself, her bottom lip firmly trapped between her teeth...I get to work.

Eating pussy well is not just a skill. It's a God-given talent that I've been reliably informed not all men are blessed with. *I* can have a girl screaming and shaking with nothing more than the very tip of my tongue in less than a minute, though. I can have her denouncing her god and claiming me as her new religion in the time it takes most men to figure out where the clitoris is. Eating a girl's cunt is intimate as shit, though. I rarely like a girl enough to bother with it at all, but tonight's different.

If I could spend the rest of my life with my face buried in Elodie Stillwater's sweet, perfect pussy, I would die a happy death. She fists my hair, her thighs squeezing around my head, and I take my fucking time with her. Her frantic, staccato breathing brings her to the edge of hyperventilating while I lick, and lave, and suck, driving my tongue inside her and fucking her with it. Three separate times, she bucks against my mouth, pleading and whispering for me to let her come before I give in and shove her over the edge of her climax, sucking the sweetness of her into my mouth, allowing her to coat my tongue as she comes.

She's fucking magnificent. She's incredible. She's *mesmerizing* as she writhes beneath me, shivering out her pleasure, and I feel something jarring grind to a halt in my brain. Like a clock that's been *tick, tick, ticking* for the past three years, has suddenly just...*stopped*.

The silence is deafening.

Sitting back onto my heels, I lick her from my lips, savoring the taste. The restraint I've been showing up until now has finally run out. "On your stomach," I tell her. Elodie peers up at me through hooded eyes, her lips swollen and red. The post orgasm glow she's radiating makes me want to fucking weep. She's *so* fucking beautiful.

Until I see the flicker of hurt on her face. She gets up onto her knees, turns around, then lowers herself onto her front. "Face down, ass up, right?" she says in a harsh voice.

I grab her hips and pull them back toward me, so that she has to go up onto her knees. So that I can see all of her perfect cunt, and her perfect, tight little asshole, as I settle myself behind her. I take my cock in my hands, relief already washing through with the knowledge that I'll be up to the hilt inside her in a moment. I rub the tip of it up and down between her legs, smearing her come all over her flesh, making her quake.

"Has anyone ever told you how lovely you are, Little E? Has anyone ever worshipped you the way you were built to be worshipped?"

She shakes her head, jumping when I lightly trace my fingers over the center of her. *Oh, E. I'll show you what it is to be worshipped. I'll show you just how good it can feel to be deified by a guy like me.* She's trembling, rocking her hips back, rubbing herself on me by the time I decide to stop teasing her and I sink myself into her pussy.

"Jesus...fucking...Christ!" There's no resistance, but she's so fucking tight, it wouldn't take much to convince me that she *is* a virgin. Her shoulders stiffen, a cry working free from her lips, and we both go very still for a long moment, coming to terms with what's just happened. I'm inside her. I'm fucking inside her, and she feels so, so good.

"Wren—" she pants, her fingers grasping for the sheet again. And everything changes in the space between heartbeats.

What the fuck am I doing?

What the fuck am I doing to her?

Something nasty and uncomfortable creeps up the back of my neck—a strange and unfamiliar sensation that makes me pull away, gritting my teeth together so hard I hear one of them crack. My dick bobs, glossy with both our lust now, begging for me to thrust it back inside her…but I can't. Not like this.

Elodie looks back at me, and there are two small, vertical lines between her eyebrows, worry in her eyes. "What—did I do something—"

"God, no," I growl. In one swift move, I lunge for her, wrapping my arm around her waist and lifting her off the mattress. It's the work of a second to slide myself to the edge of the bed, spin her around and plant her on my lap so that she's facing me. She doesn't resist as I grab her legs, guiding them around my waist.

Her face is three inches away from mine as I roll my hips back and up, guiding myself up so that I'm spearing her on my cock. Her head tips back, her eyes losing their focus, and she goes stiff in my arms again, hissing out a startled, "Shit! Oh my g—holy *shit*, Wren."

I share her sentiments. It felt frighteningly good being inside her from behind, but now that we're face to face and she's clinging onto me like I'm the only thing keeping her afloat in a sea of madness, it feels… I don't even know how to describe it.

Holding my breath, not wanting to move too quickly, I place one hand in the center of her back, pulling her closer to me, and I cup her neck, guiding her head back up so I can bring my mouth down on hers…

She huffs, her tongue sweet and tentative as she sweeps it past my lips into my mouth. I'm usually the one to claim a girl's mouth, but shit…I hold very still while she kisses me, tasting and exploring me with a curiosity and a determined need of her own that makes my heart thump like a drum in my chest.

She rocks, grinding her hips against me, sliding up the length of my dick, and fucking fireworks light up the inside of my skull.

Fireworks.

Goddamn, bona fide *fireworks.*

It's like the fucking fourth of July inside my head as I lean into her and I finally let myself kiss her back. Her breath skates across my face, her tits smashed up against my chest, and I lose all hope of controlling myself. It feels too good. It feels too strange. It feels new, and weird, and so intense, this bizarre connection that I'm feeling, that I don't even know what to do with my hands. So, I give in. I stop trying to rein myself in, and I let it all happen.

We move as one, grinding against each other, mindlessly devouring each other's mouths, and I don't even know if she's keeping quiet anymore. I don't know if I'm keeping quiet. The only thing that matters is the feeling of her wrapped around me. Her mouth on my mouth. Her breath and my breath. My hands on her skin, and hers on mine, her nails raking across my back, the desperate, wordless pleading in her eyes as she arches away from me, her head falling back, and she shudders as she comes.

I'm managing to keep my shit on lockdown fairly well, pushing back the rising feeling that I'm gonna come, but the moment I see her surrendering to her orgasm, her nipples peaked and tight, her eyes rolling back into her head, I have no fucking choice in the matter.

I come with her, clenching my teeth and pressing my forehead against her collar bone, my ears fucking ringing, my head spinning like I'm trapped in a tailspin and I can't even tell the difference between the ground and the spinning sky.

It ends. After a long, dizzying moment, trying to figure which way is fucking up, it ends. Elodie falls limp against me, her forehead beaded with a damp coat of sweat, her hair mussed and all over the place, and something foreign squeezes painfully in my chest.

This beautiful girl with the freckle on her chin, hair the color of sunlight, and a heart as fierce as a lion's—she carefully lifts her hand and strokes my hair back out of my face, searching my features with a stunned look in her eyes. "That was—" she says, obviously struggling to find the right word.

"Intense?" I can't move. If I do, this strange spell we're trapped in will break and we'll have to disentangle ourselves. I don't want that. Not yet.

Her eyes shine brightly as she nods. "Yes. Intense. Why did you —" She trails off again, her fingers trailing down over my chest. She watches her own hand, golden and beautiful against my paler skin, as if she's as stunned as I am that she's actually touching me like this. "Why'd you move me?" she asks.

I laugh softly, arching an eyebrow at her. "Why? Wasn't this position to your liking?"

She laughs, too, ducking to hide behind her hair. "No. It was perfectly satisfactory," she says.

I jerk back, feigning surprise. "*Satisfactory?*"

She squeals when I bury my face into the crook of her neck and I bite her, reminding her that I still have teeth. Her question's forgotten, which is a relief.

I promised back in the gazebo that I'd always give her my truths. I just don't know how to tell her this, though. That I wanted to face her when I was inside her. That I wanted to kiss her. That I wanted to hold her. That I wanted to *see* her.

I don't even know how to admit it to myself.

24

ELODIE

A SECRET IS a terrible and wonderful thing. It's a flickering candle flame in your chest, warming you from the inside. It can have you grinning into the crook of your elbow, face hidden in your shirt, while you wish away the hours until 'later' arrives, when you get to see the object of your infatuation again. But a secret can also make you feel *soooo* shit.

"I'm so glad you transferred. Honestly, I was so miserable before you showed up. Senior year at Wolf Hall was going to be so fucking horrible thanks to Dash. But even those Riot House pieces of shit can't ruin the last few months here now. My grandmama always said a good friend can fix anything. God, your hair is beautiful," Carina says, her fingers quickly working over my head. Sitting on the floor in between her legs, I stay still as she works her magic, taming my unruly hair into a complicated braid. "Have you ever thought about dyeing it back to your natural color?" she asks.

She's no idea that I feel incredibly guilty over what she just said to me. I'm not a good friend. I'm an *awful* friend. I can't fix anything. I've gotten myself mixed up with a guy Carina hates, who's best friends with the guy who broke her fucking heart, and I can't see myself getting out of the situation any time soon. Selfishly...god, I can't even believe that I'm letting myself think this...I don't *want* to extricate myself from the situation, even though I know how hurt and upset she'd be if she knew what I was up to. What kind of friend does that make me?

And now she's talking about dyeing my hair back to my natural color?

The knife twists in my chest, making it hard to breathe. I pick at my fingernails, suddenly very interested in the floorboards. "Uhh...yeah. Actually, I have. I've been meaning to, but..."

"But you don't like being a brunette?"

"No, it's just, my Mom. She and I have the exact same hair color. It made my dad so angry when she died, having to look at me every day, reminding him of how similar we are. We *were,*" I say, correcting myself. "He'll be furious if I change it back."

"Wow." Carina stops braiding and peers down over my shoulder, looking at me incredulously. "Your father's five and a half thousand miles away, Elle. You're nearly eighteen. You can do whatever you want. And besides...why the fuck should you need to dye your hair just to please him? He sounds like a fucking prick. Sorry if that's rude, but I'm calling it how I see it. I've heard nothing good about the man."

This is where I should leap to Colonel Stillwater's defense. That's what any other person might do, if someone had called their father out on his actions. But honestly, I have nothing nice to tell her. How sad is that? Every bright and shiny memory from my childhood was because of my mother. With her lopsided, warm smile, and the silly voices she'd put on for me when we'd have tea parties with my stuffed horses, and the way she'd hug me so tight whenever she sent me to bed that I thought my lungs might pop... she was the only light in an otherwise very dark storm.

"Yeah, he's kind of a law unto himself," I tell her. "The man barely even answers to Uncle Sam. He's not used to people questioning his edicts. He sure as hell isn't used to people disobeying direct orders."

"He ordered you not to dye your hair?"

"In no uncertain terms."

"All right. That's it. I'm driving to the pharmacy at some point and I'm buying a box of hair dye. I'll leave it for you outside your door. If you have any objections, air them now or forever hold your pe—"

"Ohhh, hair dyeing party. Sounds like fun." Carina and I both look up at the same time. It takes a second to process the fact that Mercy Jacobi's hovering on the precipice of my bedroom, leaning against the doorjamb while she inspects her flawless French manicure. She looks so much like Wren that my stomach promptly ties itself into a double knot.

"What do you want, Merce?" Carina asks. She doesn't sound surprised that the girl's showed up here. Not that she sounds happy about it, either.

"Lovely to see you, too, Carrie. Of all the people here at Wolf Hall, I was excited to see *you* the most." The cold, calculating smile that spreads across her face is unconvincing. It sets my teeth on edge. "Remember how much time we all used to spend here together," she says, entering my room and casually looking around. She pretends to be interested in the little knick knacks I have dotted around the place, but I can tell she's bored by everything she touches. Nothing's expensive enough, or rare enough, or valuable enough to capture her attention. I don't know this for a fact, but it's not hard to imagine what kind of person Mercy is from the way she sneers down her nose at the little music box in her hand.

"This is Elodie's room now," Carina says. "Maybe you should wait for an invitation before you saunter in here like you own the fucking place."

Mercy holds a hand to her chest, her mouth pulling down into a phony looking mask of horror. "Shit, you're right." Her green eyes, not quite as stunning as Wren's, flit down to me where I'm sitting on the floor. "Elodie, right? Sorry for invading your girl time with our delightful Carina, here. It's just I was walking past and saw you guys in here, and it brought back so many fond memories of my time here before I left Wolf Hall. Me, you, Pres and Mara. Right Carrie?"

Carina's eyes darken. Her whole mood darkens. Her expression's all storm and restless sea. "Don't you have anything better to be doing right now? I heard they're planning another Riot House party. Why don't you go and mess with your brother or something? I'm sure you've concocted plenty of evil trials and tribulations for the residents of Wolf Hall while you've been away."

Mercy shrugs at me, pulling a face. "She never used to be this boring, y'know." Then, to Carina, "As you well know, Wren's still pissy at me for what happened with Mara. I haven't been invited to the party, so I won't be participating in the planning this time. I'll still go, though. Dash still has a sweet spot for me, even if Wren is acting like a little bitch. Does Dash still have a sweet spot for *you*, Carrie? I have a feeling that he does." She grins, an unpleasant slash across her pretty face.

Carina glares at the girl as she wanders over to the largest window and looks out over the maze. "I don't give a shit about Dash," Carina growls. "He can go to hell for all I care."

"He *would* be perfectly at home there," Mercy says thoughtfully. "I take it that means that *you* won't be coming to the party, then?"

"Of course not."

Mercy pivots, turning sharply from the window. "And you, pretty little Elodie? I hear my brother's quite taken with you. Will you be going to the party?"

Fuck. What the hell am I supposed to say here? Pax and Dash said they were planning a party when I went to Riot House, but I wasn't extended an invitation. Wren never mentioned it to me. I have absolutely no idea, now, if he'll be expect—

"Don't be stupid," Carina mutters. "Your brother's fucking damaged, Mercy. Like, mentally unhinged. Elodie's not dumb enough to go anywhere near him. She's not going to the party, either, now please will you just go already? We're trying to enjoy what's left of our Sunday, and you're ruining it with your snark."

Mercy stands still, her eyes lingering on me, full of amusement;

262 | CALLIE HART

a slow, slanted smile spreads across her face. She looks like she's got a secret. Or rather, she *knows* a secret, and she's savoring the weight of it on her tongue. If she and Dash are close, then maybe he told her I showed up at Riot House last night. Maybe he told her that I disappeared up to Wren's room and didn't come back down until three in the morning. From the way she arches her eyebrow at me, toying with the ends of her hair, she does know and she's enjoying the fact that I'm squirming like a worm on a hook right now.

Horror coils itself tight around my throat. I need to change the subject. Now. "Who's Mara?" I ask.

Mercy's surprise doesn't look real. She lays it on thick, though. "You don't know who Mara Bancroft is?"

"I wouldn't have asked if I did."

Mercy shoots Carina a curious look. "This used to be her room. Before she went missing. She and my brother were...very *close*."

Carina gets to her feet. "Mercy, please."

Mercy ignores her. "She was really beautiful wasn't she, Carrie? All this beautiful long black hair. These big ol' bright blue eyes. I was surprised when I found out Wren was interested in you, y'know. You're nothing like her at all."

She looks at me like I'm some third rate, discount version of this Mara Bancroft girl. Like she has no idea why her brother would even look twice at me. I'm still stunned from the other snippet of information she just dropped, though. "She went missing?"

"Mmm." Mercy toys with the ends of her hair. "Last June, right after the last party my brother hosted. It was all very suspicious. She was upset about something and left in the middle of a game of beer pong. Just walked into the woods and...poof. Vanished into thin air. The police suspected foul play. They searched for her for days didn't they, Carrie?"

"What are you hoping to accomplish right now?" Carina snaps. "This is all in the past. Mara's gone. We all vowed we'd move on."

Fuck. When I first arrived at Wolf Hall, Pres made a weird

comment about girls leaving the academy. Carina had shut her down. Told her to let me settle in here before dredging up all of that. I thought it was strange at the time, but then I completely forgot all about it. And now I'm learning that the girl who used to sleep in this room, my room, fucking *disappeared*?

"Mara loved this room," Mercy continues. "She had all kinds of hiding places for her little treasures." It's a weird thing to just blurt out. Carina tenses, hatred radiating off her like smoke.

"Enough already."

"This bay window, for example," Mercy says, running her hand across the white paint of the windowsill. "Mara used to sit up here and write in her journal every night. She'd scribble away for hours, committing her most personal, private thoughts to paper. And when she was done, she'd hide her journal away, putting it in the safest place she could think of." She runs her hand to the edge of the windowsill, reaching underneath it, and a loud snapping noise fills the room. Mercy takes hold of the painted wood…and just *lifts it up* in her hands, pulling it away from the wall.

What the…?

"Jesus Christ." Carina spits out a string of curse words under her breath. "You've gotta be *kidding* me. The cops searched this room high and low and they didn't find anything. You knew where she hid her journal, and you didn't say a word?"

"What, you think I should have just handed it over?" Mercy laughs—a cold, silvery, cruel sound that makes my pulse thump at my temples. "I would have thought you'd be glad I kept my mouth shut. Mara didn't hold back when she held that pen in her hand. I'm sure there were plenty of things she wrote about you that would have raised a few eyebrows, if her journal fell into the wrong hands."

I get up, anxiety pulling taut down my spine as I cross the room, toward the bay window. Carina grabs my hand, trying to pull me back. "Elle, really, it's not worth it. Don't buy into her bull-shit, okay?"

I shake myself free, not listening, needing to see.

I'm not the only one who's been keeping secrets. Turns out that I've been shut in the dark, all of the students and even the teachers at the academy keeping me on the other side of a locked door that they won't open. This is the first time I'm learning anything about this girl, and now I *need* to know more.

There's a space in the bay window, concealed beneath the windowsill—a fairly large hidey-hole that would almost be big enough for a person to crawl into if they were set on doing so. Inside: a black lacquered box with white cherry blossoms painted on the lid; a scrunched-up sweater; a pink and grey stripy folder; and a small, fat little leather-bound book with the initials M. B. stamped in gold foil into the front cover.

"Ohh, would you look at that. I just solved a mystery. Maybe I'll start up a P.I. firm once I've been released from this hellhole." Mercy's smug as hell as she drops the windowsill onto the floor at her feet with a loud clatter. "My my. Would you look at the time. Turns out I *do* have somewhere to be after all. If you girls will excuse me, I have a hot date in town. Enjoy flicking through the journal, Elle. I think you'll find it a riveting read."

Wren's sister saunters out of the room with a swing in her hips. She doesn't bother to close the door behind her, but Carina launches off the bed and races across the room, slamming it behind her. I don't think I've ever seen her move so quickly. "You don't need to read anything," she says. Wow. When she turns to face me, I barely recognize her. She's ashen, the color drained from her face, and there's panic carved into the lines of her features. She looks ten years older than she is, and desperately haunted.

I reach into Mara's hiding place, taking out the leather-bound book. It's cold and heavy in my hands, fatter than a Bible, its pages wrinkled and dogeared in places, most of them written on. "What's this about, Carina?" I have to ask. I hate that my words are so hard and clipped, but there's something clearly going on here that she doesn't want me to know about. She strides across the room, holding out her hand for the diary.

"Give it to me, Elle. Seriously. This is one mess that you don't want to get involved in. Can you...can you please just trust me? Haven't I been looking out for you since you got here?"

The journal feels like an unexploded bomb in my hand. If I crack it open, it's going to go off, and everything I know, everything I *think* I know about this place will go up in smoke. Is that what I want? For things to become even more complicated? My whole life has been one problematic situation after another, after another, after another. Things with Wren are so complicated, I don't even know *what* the fuck is going on there. But the mystery surrounding the previous occupant of my room seems sketchy. It feels as though it would be dangerous not knowing what happened to the girl, and who was involved with her disappearance. And, I'll admit it, Carina's over the top level of panic right now is freaking me out. It's making her look incredibly guilty—of what, I don't know—and I have no idea what I'm supposed to do right now.

"Please, Elodie. No good can come from reading that journal, I promise you. We should just hand it over to the cops and let them deal with it." Carina sets her jaw. She locks up, her shoulders tensing, her back so ramrod straight, she looks like she's about to salute a four-star general. "It's been close to a year. Mara's parents have been worried sick about their daughter this entire time. The police will know what to do with new evidence. Handing it over to them is the right thing to do."

"Do you know where she went, Carina? Is that why you don't want me to read this?"

She blinks, her eyelids fluttering rapidly. "No! If I knew where she was, believe me, I'd be telling anyone who'd listen. I'm just trying to keep you out of a situation that's really fucked up and could put you in danger. You can't be mad at me for that."

"Danger? Why would I be in *danger*?"

Her pupils almost double in size. I can see them dilate from four fucking feet away. "Urgh, Elle. Just give me the journal. I swear to God, you'll be happier for not knowing what's inside it."

What the fuck? Am I supposed to just hand it over? Hold it over my head and play keep away with it? Carina's a foot and a half taller than me, so that shit ain't gonna work. It'll cause so much contention between us if I don't give her what she wants. I'll lose my only real friend at Wolf Hall. And for what? Because I'm suspicious as fuck that something untoward happened here? Yes. That's a good reason to make a stand, but if the police are already dealing with the matter...

Reluctantly, I hold out the journal to her. I don't want to lose Carina. And this Mara girl might be a ghost, wandering these halls and lurking in the shadows of my bedroom at night, but maybe Carina's right. Maybe that situation has nothing to do with me, and I should leave it well alone.

Carina sags with relief when her hand closes around the journal and I let go. Guilt hides in her eyes, though. She feels bad that she's strong-armed me into doing this now that she's got her way. "Thank you, Elle. Really. I mean it. I'm grateful that you're trusting me. I know...I know how it must look..."

"You do?" I'm sharper than the point of a blade. *"Really?"*

She sighs, hugging the journal tightly to her chest, like I might make a grab for it and run out of the room. "Mara was really troubled, Elodie. She was so much fun, and it was hard not to love her, but she was allergic to the truth a lot of the time. Just didn't want to hear it. Occasionally, reality and the way she wanted things to be sometimes got a little blurred around the edges. I'm sure this journal's full of things she half-fantasized about. Daydreams that could do a lot of damage if the wrong person read them." She huffs, exasperation on her face. "Can we just forget about it and move on with the day please? I just want things to be normal again."

Her last statement seems so loaded now. I suspect that she's not just talking about the chilled out, relaxing afternoon we had planned for ourselves; I think she's talking about life at Wolf Hall in general, and the fact that nothing will ever be normal again here if people keep on bringing up Mara's mysterious vanishing act. I suck in a deep breath through my nose, trying to release the tension that's built up inside of me. "Okay. Fine. I won't bring it up again. But you need to answer one question first."

She chews on her lip, anxious, but nods. "What do you want to know?"

"Did Wren or any of the other Riot House boys have something to do with Mara's disappearance?"

She stiffens. Shakes her head. "No. I'd love to be able to pin something on them, but they were inside the house all night. The three of them. I saw them with my own eyes. Dashiell..." she winces. "Dashiell was with me. All of us were in the kitchen, playing drinking games. We were all so fucked, none of us left the house until the next morning. Wren passed out in front of the fireplace and slept there 'til dawn. Pax was making cocktails all night. Whatever happened to Mara...it had nothing to do with them."

I parse this inside my head, letting it take root. Wren wasn't involved in the girl's mysterious vanishing act. He's innocent of any possible crime that took place that night. "Okay. Well. Fine. I suppose that's an end to it, then."

Carina gives me a relieved smile. "Great. You're the best, Elle. Anyone ever told you that?"

"All the time." I smile tightly, but no matter how hard I force it, I know it doesn't reach my eyes. I watch as she puts the journal into the backpack full of beauty products she brought with her to my room, zipping the bag up tight once the book's hidden out of sight.

"I'm done with the braids," she says. "You want me to give you a manicure? I have a gel light. I can do a proper job."

I register the stiffness in her voice; she's trying hard to wipe away the memory of what just happened, but it's going to take more than a gel manicure to erase this awkwardness. If she was one of my friends back in Tel Aviv, I'd call her out on her shit immediately and demand to know what the fuck was going on. That kind of pushing isn't appropriate here, though. Best just to forget about the journal, and Mercy's obvious meddling. Best just to forget about Mara, and the dark cloud that I can now feel hanging over the academy.

I replace the piece of wood, forming the windowsill again, and I amp up the wattage on my smile, trying to make it look real this time. "Sure thing. But only if you promise not to paint my nails bright yellow."

IN THE DARK...

I am nameless.

Lost.

Forgotten.

The air feels like shards of glass, bristling inside my lungs.

My throat's raw from screaming.

When the straw appears through the hole this time, I have no option but to drink.

I'm prolonging this torture by gulping down the tepid, foul water that flows through the plastic and into my mouth, but I'm not as strong as I thought I was.

If I die, it'll be because I was trapped here, and no one thought to come looking.

But I'm too weak to give up yet.

25

WREN

"I DON'T GIVE A SHIT, fuck face. I bought a bowler hat and I need to wear it. End of story." Pax throws back the remains of his beer and tosses the bottle so that it spins in the air, spraying amber liquid from its mouth as it flies end over end toward the trash can. Dashiell visually reprimands him with a trademarked Lovett family frown of disapproval. Pax ignores the look, smirking like a bastard when the bottle finds its mark and clatters loudly into the receptacle on the other side of the kitchen.

"Alex has *hair* in A Clockwork Orange. You're gonna look nothing like him." Holding his own beer bottle to his lips, Dashiell drinks, his throat working. I sit on the stool by the breakfast bar, saying nothing, brooding, glowering at each of them in turn to make it perfectly clear how little I'm enjoying this.

"Oh, ye of little imagination. If I can get a bowler hat, you don't think I can find a fucking wig?"

"It's 'Oh ye of little *faith*,' you heathen. And all I'm saying is, costume parties are for kids. And Halloween. At no other time should people on the verge of adulthood voluntarily want to play dress up."

"Come on. Don't be a prick. Girls always wear the sluttiest

outfit they can find at a costume party. Aren't you jonesing for a little T & A? It must have been, what, five years since you got your dick sucked?"

"Funny." Dash grins sourly at him. "Wren, we're at odds here. You have the deciding vote, mate. What do you say? Should we have an adult party, where the attendees can wear their normal clothes like big boys and girls, or should we have an infantile fancy dress party?"

I glance up from the laptop screen in front of me, waiting for him to see just how annoyed I am by this whole thing. He just stands there, waiting patiently for me to offer him my opinion, though, and I know the fucker. He's not gonna leave it be until I've made some sort of decree. "I don't give a flying fuck about this party, boys. If it were up to me, we wouldn't even be having it. So wear a fucking bowler hat and a tutu," I tell Pax. "And you can wear a cravat and a three-piece fucking suit if you like. And I'll wear what I'm wearing right now, and I'll drink myself into oblivion until it's all over, and then we can all move on with our lives."

Pax's eyes narrow, and narrow, and then narrow some more. I can't even tell if they're still open when he says, "You're master of this hunt this time, Jacobi. I wouldn't go getting too shit faced if I were you."

God fucking damn it. I knew this was gonna happen. I fucking *knew* it. "I'm *not* master of the hunt. I was master last time. Which means one of you fuckers is up to bat."

In unison, Dashiell and Pax shake their heads. They disagree, bicker, fight and squabble about everything, but it looks like they're of one mind about this. So typical. "Things went badly last time, so Pax and I made an executive decision. You need to get back into the saddle. You're all over the place, and frankly we're tired of living with an imposter."

"An imposter. *Right.*"

"Yes." Dash drops a couple of dry roasted peanuts into his mouth. "You're currently not yourself, and we've decided we want the old you back. So, you get to be master, and we get to revel in whatever sick, fucked up party game you arrange for us to play, and everything goes back to normal. Sound good?"

No, this does not sound good. None of it does. As master of the hunt, I'll be expected to do certain things. I used to revel in those arcane delights, but things have changed now. There's Elodie to consider. I haven't been able to shake the image of her, naked and beautiful, straddling me, the sweet sound of her panting in my ear, since last night. I'll die an old man in my bed, all of my other memories eaten away by the ravages of time, but *that* memory will still be burning fiercely behind my eyelids when I go.

Elodie is *mine*, and I'm not fucking letting her go. And I can't be master of the hunt and keep Elodie. There's no way in hell.

"Do what you gotta do," Pax says, snapping open another beer. He flicks the cap across the living room. "But this is happening, Wren. You're gonna have to man up. Dash and I have never balked when you've thrown us a gig. We sure as shit didn't kick up a fuss when you bundled us onto that plane last weekend. And that was some fucked up shit."

He's right. I've put both of them in really compromising situations before, for the sheer hell of it, because it made me laugh and watching them squirm was ten different kinds of entertaining. And my most recent ask of them could have ended in disaster for all three of us if something had gone wrong. I can't back out of this. If I refuse to play ball with them, it'll cause a rift in the house like nothing else. I chug from my beer to stop myself from cursing the motherfuckers out.

"In the meantime," Dash says, eyeing me sternly. He looks like my fucking father. "Mercy's asked if she can move in here."

I spray IPA across the kitchen counter. "What the *fuck* did you just say?"

"No need to overreact. I told her it was up to you, and your word would be final on the matter. She said you were never gonna let her stay here, and I didn't give her any reason to believe she was wrong. At which point, she called me and Pax cunting little bitches for not standing up to you, and then put a scratch in the Charger."

"*I* haven't put a single scratch on that car," Pax growls darkly. "Not one. And I take terrible care of my things. You'll be pleased to know that your sister is now on my shit list."

I don't like that Mercy's been talking to these guys behind my back. She thinks she fucking walks on water, that girl. At least one of them is beginning to see things from my perspective, though. Dash...Dash, not so much. "Personally, I think she'd be a great addition to the house, but I know how little my opinion counts for these days. You're lucky you have a sister y'know, Jacobi. Some of us had to grow up all alone, in a big, drafty house—"

"Oh, cry me a river. I've seen that sprawling mansion you call a house and it's fucking beautiful. You were raised in the lap of luxury with a silver spoon sticking out of your mouth. Having a sister's like having an annoying case of hemorrhoids that won't fucking go away."

"Little young for hemorrhoids, aren't you?"

I roll my eyes.

"I agree with him," Pax mutters. "I fucking hate both of my sisters. And my brother. *They're* the cunting little bitches. The dynamic of the house would be fucked if a girl moved in here. Mercy's blossomed quite spectacularly since she left last year, she's the hottest little fuckhole at the academy, but she's also fucking insane. I don't have time to be installing eight new locks on my bedroom door, and she could *whoa*—WHOA! What the fuck are you doing? Take your hand off me, Jacobi, or I'll fucking snap it off."

I have him by the collar of his t-shirt. I'm ready to lay the fucker out. We've gone four months without any of us hitting each other, though, so I shake him hard enough to make his teeth rattle instead. "She is fucking insane. She's the bane of my fucking existence. But she's still my fucking sister. Say something like that again and I'll take a pair of pliers to your front teeth. Get it?"

Pax slaps me away, eyes furious, his cheeks turning red. Fuck, he wants to land a right hook on my jaw so fucking bad. He won't, though. He's still thinking about Corsica and *The Contessa.* "All right. All right. Point made," he seethes. "Jesus. You take everything so fucking personally."

"I'll drive over to DC and finger bang your mom then, shall I? See how personally you take that?"

"Enough. Enough. God, it's a miracle you guys haven't given me a nervous breakdown by now. Let's all cool our jets and gather our composure, shall we? Pax won't say anything weird about your sister anymore. Mercy isn't moving into the house. And you will be master of the hunt," he reaffirms. "Come hell or high water, you, Wren Jacobi, will have something truly devious and perfect planned for us the night of the party, I just know you will." He pauses, his expression hard and judging as he gives me a meaningful look. "You haven't let us down yet."

26

ELODIE

MONDAY MORNINGS WERE SO MUCH EASIER at Mary Magdalene's. The weekends were my own in Tel Aviv. My father's schedule meant he was always away from the house on Saturdays and Sundays, and I was free to do my own thing. Go shopping with Ayala and Levi. Go to the movies. Do my homework and putter around the house in peace. He was around more during the beginning of the week, so going to school was an actual blessing. It saved me from his ire, walking the halls of the international school. I stretched out every single class I had, making the time away from Colonel Stillwater count. I signed up for as many after-school activities as I could. Anything to avoid going home, when I knew he'd be there, waiting for me, his never-ending anger rolling off him in waves, just waiting for me to do something or say something that warranted an explosion of epic proportions.

At Wolf Hall, there's no escape from my studies. I'm only ever three floors away from a classroom, and that fact in itself makes the beginning of the academic week more depressing than it should be. I don't really get to leave, so it never feels as though I've had a break.

It's gloomy again, rain slashing at the windows as I make my way down the stairs, dreading this morning's English class. When I reach the hallway, there are students everywhere, chattering loudly and joking with one another as they make their way to their first lesson of the day. I should feel lighter than I do. I get to see Wren soon, but this isn't some sweet high school romance that I can let myself feel giddy over. It's a secret. Wren didn't tell me to keep what happened with him the other night quiet, but it's there all the same, an unspoken agreement between the two of us: it would be bad for both of us if anyone knew we'd torn each other's clothes off and fucked in his bedroom.

My heart shoots up into my throat as I see Dashiell enter through the academy's entrance, shaking his head like a wet dog, sending droplets of water flying from the ends of his dark blond hair. Pax appears after him, a broad smile spread across his face, laughing at the top of his lungs at some private joke.

And then there's Wren.

My breath stills in my chest.

He enters the school, dressed head to toe in black, the shoulders of his hoody darkened by the rain, the hood pulled up over his head, his eyes already searching, searching, searching...

He finds me, standing on the bottom step of the stairs, and the lights overhead dim. I step down, sliding along the edge of the hallway, my back against the wall, and the Riot House boys shove their way through the crowds, still caught up in whatever conversation they were having when they arrived. Two of them are, at least. Wren stills on the other side of the hall, coming to a stop opposite me. A tense moment passes where we stare at each other across the sea of bustling bodies, our line of sight clear, then obscured, clear, then obscured by the flow of students as they pass us by.

How is no one else reacting to this? How can they not feel the electricity in the air? How is everyone else so blind, and deaf and dumb to the pressure that's building around them as Wren Jacobi and I share this blisteringly surreal moment?

"Forgotten the way?"

I glance up and Carina's there, clutching her school bag to her chest, wearing a pristine white t-shirt and a tartan skirt that should be illegal, it's so short.

"Sorry?"

"What are you doing, just standing there? You look like you've seen a ghost," she says, laughing.

"Oh. Uh, nothing. Sorry."

"I thought you were gonna go save us a seat. Come on. If we don't hurry, someone else will grab our sofa."

I look up and Wren's gone.

Doctor Fitzpatrick's already at the front of his room when Carina and I enter. "Come on, girls. You know the punishment if you're late," he says, grinning.

"What's the punishment for being late?" I hiss.

Carina grabs my arm and pulls me toward the sofa. "You don't want to know."

Once we're sitting down, I grab my notepad out of my bag, twisting a pen over in my fingers nervously, surveying the room. I look at every other student in the class before I give in and allow my gaze to drift (as casually as I can manage) over to the battered leather sofa on the opposite side of the room.

Wren's right where he's supposed to be...but he's not sprawled out, lying on his back, staring angrily at the ceiling today. He's sitting up like a normal person, eyes locked on his hands, his hair falling into his face, a tiny frown pulling at his dark brows. Dashiell and Pax are sitting on the floor, underneath the window, but they're not sniping at one another today. They both seem to be covertly watching Wren, muttering to each other under their breath. Dash must feel me looking at him. His head whips up and he looks right at me.

Wait. No. Not at me. At Carina.

"Asshole," she grouses. "What kind of sick fuck do you need to be to lead someone on, take their fucking virginity, humiliate them in the worst way imaginable, and then stare at them every available opportunity you get afterward? Like, what is he even trying to accomplish, looking at me like that?"

He's not trying to accomplish anything. He's reliving something. Replaying it over in his head, savoring every second as he remembers stripping Carina out of her clothes and fucking her senseless. I know, because I know that look. That same dazed, distant expression has appeared on my face at least ten times since Saturday night.

I didn't text him.

He didn't text me.

What does that mean? Were we both waiting for the other person to reach out first? Have we both been stubborn and stupid, too caught up in our own pride to even communicate with each other? Or have I gotten this wrong? Is he just content, now that he's had me? Have I given him the one thing he wanted, and now I can expect never to speak to him again?

"I'd love to walk right over there and smack the evil prick. He probably doesn't think I'll do it. I used to kickbox, though. I could hit him hard enough to leave a bruise." Carina's oblivious to my spiraling panic. I don't want to be that girl—the girl who freaks out over a boy, questioning every move she makes and overanalyzing everything to the point of madness. I make the decision, right here and now: *I will not be that girl.*

"He's probably ruing the day he messed with you, Carina. Don't worry about it. He's looked away now."

"Class. I hate to have to do this to you. I'm sure you've all been dreading this moment all semester, but it's that time again..." Doctor Fitzpatrick laughs as a chorus of groans goes up around the room. I lean forward, squinting at the handsome teacher, trying to get a better look at him. Something's off. Something—

"Carina?"

"Mmm?"

"Does Doctor Fitzpatrick have a split lip? Fuck, it looks like he's wearing *makeup.*"

My friend leans and squints, too, chuckling softly. "Wow. Yep.

That's a corker of a bruise on his jaw. Who knew? I wouldn't have pegged Fitz as a brawler."

I would. I can see it on him somehow. A hidden, secret violence that likes to spill out from time to time. I realize I've missed his announcement while I was talking, and now I have no idea why the rest of the class is grousing very loudly, hurling balled up pieces of paper at the doctor. He holds up his hands, shielding himself from the harmless projectiles, laughing when most other teachers would be losing their shit. "Okay, okay. That's enough of that, thank you. It's not up to me. The curriculum mandates this kind of stuff. You have to complete team projects to learn how to work together. How else are you going to know what to do when you move on from this fine establishment and begin your illustrious careers as line cooks in fast-food restaurants, huh?"

A rowdy jeer goes up at this. Apparently, Doctor Fitzpatrick's lack of faith in us is more entertaining than troubling. "You know the drill," he says. "Now, are you gonna pair up like adults, in a calm, reasonable fashion, or am I gonna have to draw names out of a hat again?"

A furor breaks out, bodies flying across the room, friends searching for friends, people squabbling like chickens over who gets to be with who. I don't move. Obviously, Carina and I will be partners for whatever godawful project we're about to be assigned.

Only...

"I want Carina Mendoza, Fitz."

Carina sits up straight, her eyes rounding out. What the hell just happened? By the window, Dashiell Lovett's on his feet, and he's pointing at Carina wearing a very cool, very entitled look.

"I think Carina's already partnered up," Fitz says.

"What's the point in us working with our friends? That's hardly helpful. How are we supposed to learn anything if we're simply hanging out with the people we always hang out with?"

Fitz studies Dash for a moment, frowns, then claps his hands together. "You raise an excellent point, Dashiell. Change of plan. Everyone in this room must partner up with a person they don't like. I don't mind how you go about it, try to be sensitive of each other's feelings or whatever," he mutters, waving his hand at us as he stoops to grab his bag from the ground. "You've got two minutes. Figure it out."

Silence falls like a stifling blanket over the room.

Well, this is fucking awkward.

People begin to reluctantly reorganize themselves, shuffling between the furniture like unhappy zombies as people decide who they're now going to sit beside.

Again, I repeat, *so* fucking awkward.

"Come on. On your feet, Elodie. I need to sit next to my partner." Holy fuck, how did Dash get across here so quickly? He looks so proper in his shirt and tie. It looks like he shined his Italian leather shoes before he showed up this morning. Beside me, Carina's as stiff as a board. "You'll regret this," she snarls at him.

"Doubt it." He quirks an eyebrow at me, jerking his thumb over this shoulder. "Are you gonna make this super uncomfortable, or are you gonna go sit next to Wren like a good little girl? We all know how much you *hate* him."

I am going to fucking kill him. I give Carina an apologetic look, slowly getting to my feet. My heart's racing like a runaway train as I grab my bag and begin to make my way across Doctor Fitzpatrick's den. Wren's eyes are sharp yet calm as he watches me approach. I'm four short steps away from the leather couch when Mercy just appears, like she was conjured out of thin air from the fucking depths of hell, and throws herself down next to her brother.

"I'm still trying to figure out if you're detestable, Elodie, but I'm afraid I've got you beat here. Wren doesn't hate anyone as much as he hates me." She grabs his arm and loops her own through it, smiling so angelically that my fucking teeth itch.

Fury pours off Wren like smoke, but he doesn't get to object. There isn't time for that. Because the next thing I know, I look up to find Pax scowling down at me. "Congratulations, Frenchie. Looks like I get to be a pain in *your* neck, now."

27

WREN

"YOU'RE FUCKING DAMAGED. You know that, right?"

Most kids were fascinated by the fact that Mercy and I were twins. *How unusual,* their parents used to coo. *They look so similar, too. It isn't normally that obvious when you have a girl and a boy, but they're just like two peas in a pod.* Mercy's my female counterpart, which is highly disturbing most days, and really fucking annoying on every other. No one should have to look at another person and know, without a shadow of a doubt, what they'd look like if they were born the opposite sex. It's just wrong.

She flutters her eyelashes at me, resting her chin on my shoulder. "Don't worry, big brother. I resent having to work with you, too. But it's time we swept all of this hostility under the rug, don't you think? It's getting a little old. Our parents are beginning to suspect something terrible happened between us. We wouldn't want Father taking it upon himself to investigate now, would we? He just retired. Plenty of time on his hands now. He might be blind to what's right in front of him most of the time, but he's very good at solving puzzles when he puts his mind to it. I think I take after him in that way."

"Yes, we both know how great you are at sticking your nose in where it's not wanted, don't we." Not a question. A statement. A fact.

She preens like I've paid her a fucking compliment.

Fitz goes around the room, handing out assignment sheets, which means we're all doing different presentations. He visibly flinches when he stops in front of us, offering Mercy our assignment. She rips it out of his hand, baring her teeth in a smile so terrifying that the muscles in his throat work overtime as he hastily heads back to the front of the room.

"You shouldn't have hit him," she says to me. "He wasn't doing anything wrong."

I'm not listening to her, though. I'm too busy side-eying Pax, trying to silently threaten him into behaving. Elodie's back's to me, so I can't see the look on her face, but I know she must be hating this. Pax is a daunting prospect, even to those of us who claim to like him.

"So, big brother, care to tell me what's been going on since I've been away? Any new and interesting developments you'd like to share with me?"

"They stopped serving spaghetti on Wednesdays," I growl.

"Oh, wow. You've got all the good gossip. I should have come to you first instead of Damiana."

I give up glaring at Pax and glare at her instead. Not before I catch the sour, smug smile on Damiana's face, though. "That girl's poison." That's all I say because that's all I *can* say.

Mercy fans herself with our assignment. "Why'd you fuck her, then?"

"Jesus, Mercy. Don't you have a fucking play you're supposed to be performing in or something? In New York? Far, far away from here?"

"Michael tried to make me an understudy. I'm not an understudy, Wren. I'm the leading lady, or I'm nothing at all. Damiana said you dropped her like a hot coal the moment the new girl came along. That can't be true, though, surely. She's so..." she wrinkles her nose, "...*average*."

"Just stay away from Elodie, Mercy. Ten feet at all times."

"Or what?"

"Or I'll make your life a living hell. You're not the only one who's good at piecing together people's secrets."

"Oh ho ho, holy shit. I didn't think it was possible, but you...oh my god, you *like* her, don't you?"

She twists around to face me, hooking her leg underneath her like she's settling in for a good girl chat. "Wren Jacobi, I never thought I'd see the day. I assumed, after all these years of lashing out and breaking people, that there was something fundamentally broken inside *you*. It's a real shock to learn otherwise. Fuck!"

I snatch the paper out of her hand, scanning the information typed on it, pointedly ignoring the shit-eating grin she's wearing. "We need to write an essay on an unsung hero in literature and present it to the class. You can choose."

"Really?" For an actress, her attempt at fake surprise is pretty piss poor. "You're usually so protective over your literary heroes, unsung or otherwise."

God, this is gonna be such bullshit. I crack my knuckles with a vicious enthusiasm that shuts her up. For five whole seconds.

"Look, I think it's great that you like someone. I know you don't believe me, but I care about you, Wren. And if this mousy, strange little girl blows your hair back, then I say go for it."

This is a trick. A really lousy trick that I'm not stupid enough to fall for. I bare my teeth, dropping the paper into her lap. "Pick the subject for the assignment. Then stop fucking talking, Mercy, or so help me we'll have problems.

She picks Sydney Carton. Of all the characters in all the books, she picks Sydney Carton from 'A *Tale Of Two Cities*,' because she knows how much it'll irritate me. Sydney's my guy. He's a wretch, the very worst and the very best. I identify with him on so many levels that it's not even funny. If she were anyone else, I'd be surprised that she picked him out of thin air as the topic of our assignment, but since she is who she is, I'm entirely *un*surprised. We're twins, after all. Our fucked-up brains work so similarly that I despise her almost as much as I despise myself.

The moment the bell rings, signaling the end of class, I take out my phone and power it on. I tap out a message as I bolt out of the class.

Me: Lunchtime. Find me. I'll be hanging with the poets.

28

ELODIE

I'VE NEVER wished harm on anyone before.

That's actually a lie, I have wished harm on one person, but my father doesn't count. He's a vile piece of work, and he deserves every ill thought I've ever had about him. Aside from Colonel Still-water, I make a point to give people the benefit of the doubt. I like to try and be a fair person. A just person. But it's no fucking good —Pax Davis is a motherfucker of the highest order and I hope he falls off a very high cliff. I suppose it'd be okay if he survived the impact. A few weeks in traction, writhing in agony in a dingy hospital bed, though? Yeah, that sounds like suitable punishment for a prick like Pax.

Eight: that's how many times he called me a whore during the forty minutes we had to sit together and plan out how we were going to tackle our assignment. 'Read an independent book with a profound and moving story arc, and then present it to the class.' I'm honestly not sure Pax can read. He showed no interest in the sheet Doctor Fitzpatrick gave to us. But then again, he did spend the last ten minutes of class hammering away at his phone's screen, sending out text after text to god only knows who, so he must possess some rudimentary understanding of the English language.

When we parted, he snarled something guttural and harsh at me in a language that I think was German, then he politely told me that I was to read the book and write the presentation myself, then he flipped me off and bailed without another word.

I haven't been able to talk to Carina to find out how her ordeal with Dashiell went, but I'm guessing, from the look on her face as she hurried to her next class, that it went just about as well as one might expect. In other words, terribly.

She has a meeting with the school counselor over lunch, which is why I don't feel guilty that I'm not trying to hunt her down, as I make my way across the academy. When I jog up the steps to the library, my mind's racing a mile a minute.

It was hardly a friendly text. Then again, Wren's not one to waste words. I wasn't anticipating anything flowery or romantic from him. Honestly, I was surprised that he'd messaged at all.

I find him right where he said he'd be, in the Poetry section, amongst the likes of Rilke, Hugo, Keats and Wordsworth. With his head bowed over a book, his hair messy and all over the place, hanging in his face as it's perpetually wont to do, he's cast in silhouette by the light pouring in through the enormous windows behind him. I can make out his profile, though—the strong line of his jaw, the arrow-straight, uncompromising bridge of his nose, and his sinfully full mouth that works as he shapes out the words on the page in front of him.

He's not who he portrays himself to be. Not really. Yes, he's hard to reach sometimes, and he's colder than the glacial waters of Antarctica on occasion. But there's a deep, ponderous part of him that he doesn't show people, too. I get the feeling that he hasn't really shown that side of himself to me, either. It's slipped out, unbidden, entirely by accident. The difference is that he hasn't tried to stuff it back down into its cage with me. He's let that side of him rest there, out in the open, for me to make of it what I will.

His mouth works some more as he continues to read, but out loud now—

"We look before and after,
and pine for what is not.
Our sincerest laughter,
With some pain is fraught.
Our sweetest tales are those
that tell of saddest thought."

Ah. So he *was* aware of my presence. Great. I pull myself together, having a fierce talk with my heart, making sure it knows to behave, as I enter the stacks and go to him.

"More Bryon?" I ask.

He shakes his head. "Shelley. He was a fucker, too, y'know. Complete drunk. Womanizer. Left his wife and knocked up another woman."

"Mary Shelley. I read about that."

Wren closes the book softly, looking at me out of the corner of those green eyes. No other part of him moves. "Like all the best artists, he was pretty fucked up."

"That poem didn't sound fucked up. It sounded sad."

Wren smiles, slowly looking back down at the book. "It's called 'Skylark.' One of his most famous pieces."

"What's it about?"

"The past and the future. Fear of death. Phantoms and ignorance. It's about how even the sweetest love songs are tinged with sadness. And how a man can never be as free as a bird."

"Sounds beautiful."

"It is," he agrees. Sliding the book back onto the shelf, he turns and faces me, picking over me with an intense gaze that makes me break out in goosebumps. "What did he do?" he demands.

"What?"

"Pax. What did he do? I know he did *something.*"

"Oh. Uh...he was just his usual, charming self. It's all good. No harm, no foul."

"You don't know if there's been any harm yet. You won't know until you're lying on the floor in a pool of your own blood. That's how Pax works."

I smile at his utter seriousness. "Are you telling me he's going to try and eviscerate me? Because I'm not okay with that."

Wren reaches out and grabs me by the hand, quickly spinning around and pulling me after him. Just like our run-in in front of Madame Fournier before my very first French class, shock spirals up my arm at his touch, surprising the hell out of me, but it's different this time. He hasn't taken me roughly by the wrist. He's taken me by the hand. *And he's interlaced his fingers with mine.*

I'm too stunned to say anything as he pulls me away from the windows and the grim, grey day outside, rushing, rushing, rushing until he reaches the rear corner of the library. He stops in front of a plain innocuous wooden door that anyone in the world would overlook if they weren't standing right in front of it. Wren drops my hand and rifles in his pocket, pulling out a fat bunch of keys. His fingers flick deftly through a series of Yale keys and cruciform keys and skeleton keys until he finds the one he's looking for.

A moment later and the door is open, my hand is in Wren's again, and I'm following him inside. The door clicks shut behind us, and everything is stillness and perfect, velvet dark.

I can hear him breathing, soft and calm, and every cell in my body stands to attention. "Don't suppose there's a light in this place?" I ask. Whispering feels appropriate, given the weighty silence pressing against my eardrums.

"What's the matter? You afraid of standing in a room with me in the dark, Little E?" His voice is a rough caress, slightly teasing in tone. I can picture the upward tilt of his mouth, the sharp challenge in his eyes, and my toes curl in my shoes.

"Not at all. I'm fine. I'm perfectly happy standing here with you in the dark." And I am. There's something freeing about it. I'm not worried about the way he's looking at me, and I'm not afraid of the fact that I'm blushing. I can just *be*.

"In that case..." Wren's other hand touches my stomach, making me jump. "Easy, Little E," he coaxes. "Just trying to find your other hand."

I give it to him, swallowing thickly when he guides my palms up to rest on his chest, right over the firm wall of muscle that forms his pecs. I can feel his heart beating beneath the soft cotton of his hoody, and with my sight taken away from me, the steady *dum, dum, dum* beneath my fingertips is everything. It anchors me, rooting me in place until I feel grounded and...*safe?* Wow. That's a new one. How is it even possible that I'd feel safe with him?

Wren steps closer, the soles of his boots scuffing against what sounds like tile, and his warm breath disturbs my hair, skating across my cheek. "I figured this would be easier for you," he says softly. "For me, too."

"Easier how?"

"Because it's less difficult being honest without having to worry about someone's reactions, right? You can tell me the truth, and I can tell you the truth. It won't be as frightening as doing it in the light of day."

Oh. Damn. What the hell does he want to say to me? I close my eyes—an unnecessary action that serves no purpose other than making me feel better. "Okaaay. This sounds serious. Should I be worried?"

He chuckles. "Perhaps."

"Then rip off the Band-Aid, Jacobi. Let's get this show on the road."

More laughter. "So willing to walk into the fire. Definitely one of the things I enjoy most about you."

"One of the things? There are other things you like about me?" This talking in the dark thing is already working a treat. I would never have said that with the lights on. I'm not that playful, especially not with dangerous creatures who have the power to do severe and irreparable damage.

I go very still when I feel the feather-soft brush of Wren's mouth against my cheek. He hasn't shaved this morning; his stubble scrapes against my skin, and I shiver against the heady sensation, barely breathing around it. "Yes," he whispers. "Plenty of things. I'll make you a list."

Oh, fuck me running. This is going to get interesting. I was worried that he dragged me into this...whatever kind of room this is...to tell me that he wants nothing to do with me. I'm not worried about that anymore. He places his hands on my hips, sliding his palms around to the small of my back, drawing me closer, so that our bodies are in alignment, my hands still firmly planted on his chest.

"First, I want you to tell me the truth," he says. "Did Pax do anything to upset you? Did he threaten you?"

"He implied that I accepted payment in return for sex a couple of times, but apart from that, no."

Wren grunts unhappily. "I'll make sure he doesn't do that again."

"Don't worry. I've been accused of way worse. I have a thick skin."

"No, you don't. Your skin's like fucking silk." He groans, deep and low, running the bridge of his nose along the line of my jaw, breathing in deeply like he's trying to inhale my very essence. "You don't need to worry about Pax. I'll take care of him. The second thing I wanna know...is if you're ready yet?"

"Ready for what?"

"To lay your cards on the table. To tell me that you want me. All of me. All of the time. For there to be no more confusion about what this is."

My chest tightens as if there's a belt synching closed around it. "Straight to the point, huh?"

"I told you. I like things to be black and white. Clear cut. No room for misunderstanding. You said you preferred things that way, too."

"I do."

"Then tell me what you think this is."

"I—" Well, shit. This would be a lot less mortifying if he went first. He'll think I'm a coward if I don't give him an answer, though, I *will* be a coward, and I've spent too many years convincing myself that I'm strong to let myself down now. "I do want you. I want all of you for myself. And..." Lord Almighty, this one's going to make me feel like a stupid, naive little girl, but here goes nothing, "I want to be your girlfriend."

Silence.

Roaring, deafening silence.

I can feel the smugness radiating off him, though, very real and very present. After a beat, he presses his hands more firmly into my back, pulling me up against him so that I feel the hardness of him between our bodies; his dick is erect, and from the way it pulses against my stomach, it wants some attention. "Do you have any idea what being my girlfriend would be like, Little E?" he growls.

Uh...words. I need words. Where did I put my ability to form coherent sentences? The same place I put my ability to think coherent thoughts, by the looks of things. "You're probably...very possessive," I manage.

"You have no idea. And?"

"And you probably like to hoard all of the power in a relationship."

"I like being in control of any situation," he admits. "But I am willing to share on occasion."

"You probably like to fight?"

"Nothing wrong with healthy disagreement. Nothing wrong with calling someone on their shit if they're misbehaving, either."

"You'd probably want everything your way."

"I'm capable of compromise."

"Okay..."

"Keep going."

"That's all I can think of."

There's another faint brush of lips, against my own lips this time, the contact so gentle and teasing that I make a needy whimpering sound when he deprives me of his mouth. "Then let me fill in the rest," he rumbles. "I'm arrogant. I like to fuck. I'm intense as hell sometimes. It's all or nothing with me. That's just who I am. I don't do things in half measures. There are days that you'll hate me more than you'll love me. And you *will* love me, Elodie. It's already too late for that. I'll love you, and you'll love me, and there won't be any turning back for either of us. So let me ask you again. Do you have an idea of what it will be like now? And do you still want that, knowing that it might not always be perfect? That it might be hard sometimes?"

My tongue sticks to the roof of my mouth. I can't fucking speak. He's so raw, and fierce, and dominant in everything he says and does. The picture of the future with him that he's just painted is terrifying and bewildering and so fucking exciting that I know I should be less sure about the answer I want to give. But I am certain. Damn it all to hell, this is the stupidest thing I'll ever do in my life, but I say the words.

"Yes, Wren. I still want it."

His hands tighten into fists behind me, clawing at my shirt. Suddenly, he's pushing me backward, lifting me off my feet, and there's a wall at my back. He snarls like a hungry wolf, crushing his mouth down on mine, and my mind becomes a void. His tongue probes my mouth, sweeping and tangling with mine, and it's all I can do to remember to breathe. He's everywhere. The smell of him floods my head, all citrus and fresh sea air, and bright cedar. I'm so fucking dizzy on him, and I don't even register what I'm doing until he hisses into my ear.

"Careful, E. You're almost down to the bone."

Fuck. I've wrapped my arms around him, and I'm digging my fingernails into his back, through the thin material of his hoody. "Shit, sorry."

"Don't be. I like it. But if you're gonna mark me as your property, at least take my fucking clothes off first."

A wave of heat slams into me, burning in my chest, my stomach, and between my legs. I'm like an animal, possessed and wild as I scramble to take hold of his hoody. I have it off him in record time.

We undress each other in the dark, frantic and desperate, sharing breath and moaning each other's names as we kiss, and touch, and knead at each other's skin.

I don't know where I am, *literally*, and I do not care. All that matters are Wren's demanding hands on my body and the strained urgency in his voice as he gives me a command. "Down on your knees for me, Little E. I wanna find out how good that perfect mouth feels."

I may have had sex before, but this is something that I've never done. Still, I'm not one to shy away from new challenges. Especially ones I *want* to participate in. I drop down, kneeling for him, knowing I'm relinquishing control to him, but strangely unafraid. His hands wind into my hair as he gently cradles my head. Then the tip of his cock is pressing against my lips, parting them and pushing inside.

"Holy...shit!" Wren hisses. "Fuck, Elodie, that feels..." Whether he trails off because it feels too good or because I'm doing a terrible job, I have no fucking clue. I lave at the hardness he slides into my mouth, enjoying the silken, rigid texture of his erection, and Wren begins to shake. The videos I watched on Youtube last year— *'How to give your man good head,'* and *'Best blowjob tips,'* and *'How to make him come in thirty seconds flat,'* —seem to be paying off, though. He shudders as I apply a little more pressure with my mouth, tentatively sucking, and a slew of curse words spill out of him.

"Jesus. God...damn, Little E. That....that feels fucking *incredible.*"

Pleased doesn't even cover it. Wren Jacobi, the scourge of Wolf Hall Academy, the bane of countless women's existences, harbinger of misery and suffering, is at my mercy now. I have him. I thought I was signing over my control when I obeyed his breathless command, but that isn't even remotely true. I'm at the wheel right now. I'm steering this thing, and with a simple flick of my tongue I know I can bring him to *his* knees.

He's so fucking hard. Harder with every passing second. His hands tighten in my hair, holding onto me with a steel-like grip, but somehow I know that, if I want to pull the plug on this at any point, I still have the power to do that.

"Elodie. God, Elodie..." he pants. Not Little E this time. I haven't given his little nickname for me much thought, but I like the sound of my full name on his lips. He utters it like a sacred prayer, as if he's worshipping me as I worship him, and my head swims with the sound of it. I'm just finding my rhythm, figuring out how badly I can make him shake by utilizing my tongue in different ways, when he jerks back, pulling himself out of my mouth with a wet pop.

"Black hell, E. It's too much. Too good," he gasps. "Get on your back. I wanna fucking taste you again. That pretty little cunt of yours is all I've been able to think about."

I thank the universe, God, and everything holy that it's dark now. My heart surges like a piston as I lay back onto the cold, hard floor. Wren's fingers dig into my thighs, pushing them apart, and then he falls on me like a demon. He's had way more practice than me; he proved that quite eloquently the other night when he made me come with his mouth. I'm still unprepared for how good it feels when he sweeps over me with the flat of his tongue, though. I tense, my breath hissing out between my teeth as I attempt to relax into the intense sensation building up inside of me.

"Goddddddd," he groans. "You're so fucking sweet. I can't get enough." He buries his tongue into my pussy again, and he doesn't just use his tongue this time. He uses his entire face, the bridge of his nose, everything, rubbing himself into my slick flesh so hungrily that heat explodes across my face. I'm ashamed, wet, mortified, and so turned on that I can't wrap my head around what's happening. He moans, feasting on me like an animal, and I lock my legs around his head, pulling him down on me even harder.

A staggering, overwhelming need blossoms in the pit of my stomach when he slides his fingers inside me, slowly pumping them as he licks. It's so much at once, too much emotion and desire and feeling, that I realize tears are sliding from my eyes and over my temples. I'm gasping for air in wet, desperate gasps that only seem to urge him on; he fucks me with two fingers, stretching me, exploring, stroking a point deep inside me that I didn't even know existed, until I'm vibrating, shaking against the floor, my arms and legs tingling to the point of pain, and I feel like I'm gonna...

"Fuck. Hold on, Little E. I wanna feel you come all over my cock."

Wren pulls away, leaving me whimpering and so close to falling apart. I'm only left to suffer for a second, though. He settles between my legs, thrusting himself deep inside me in one swift, breathtaking movement, and my blood sings in my ears. It sounds like wind rushing past me as I stumble and fall, descending into a bottomless pit of madness.

"Wren! Oh, shit! I'm going to—I think I'm gonna—" Even now, with him on top of me, driving himself into me over and over again, biting down on my collar bone, lighting the inside of my head up with invisible fireworks, I can't bring myself to admit that I'm about to come out loud.

Wren feels it, though. He claims my mouth so savagely that I probably would have come from the kiss alone. "Good girl. Good girl," he whispers hoarsely. "Let it happen. Don't fucking fight it."

That's all I need to hear. I release the tight leash I've been holding over myself, and my very soul shatters apart, stealing the oxygen out of my lungs, and my fractured thoughts right out of my head.

"WREN!" I shout his name, I know I do, but there's no stopping it. I can't help it. He locks himself around me, holding me tightly in his arms as he grinds himself against me, his cock filling me to the hilt. I come, shaking and trembling, lights flashing in my eyes, and he snarls into the crook of my neck.

"Steady," he whispers. "Steady, steady, shhh, good girl. Hold on tight. I'm not done with you yet."

He slows for a beat. Long enough to rain soft kisses down on my temple and the top of my head, gathering my hair and sweeping it out of my face, stroking his fingers over my cheeks and my lips.

"Your fucking mouth, Elodie," he moans. "The things I wanna do to your *mouth*."

He slips his fingers past my lips, pressing down on my tongue, and a low and terrible rumble works its way out of him, reverberating in my ear. "One of these days. God, just you fucking wait..."

He picks up the pace again, his hips grinding against mine, one of his hands palming my breasts and rolling my nipple, pinching so hard that I let out a sharp cry. I cling onto him, addicted to the shifting and bunching of the muscles in his back as they tense under my hands. In this moment, he is a force of fucking nature, more powerful and frightening than the lightning and thunder that split the air apart the night I met him in the gazebo.

He's fierce and demanding, nipping at my mouth with his teeth.

His hands are rough, taking what they want from my body, bringing me closer and closer...

The smell of him, the heat of him, the weight of him, the very sound of him raging as he draws closer to his own climax...

I can't get enough of him.

There's nothing else for me to do but hold onto him tight and ride out the storm.

We come together, fingers tightening, teeth gouging, bodies tangled together, breath frantic, and it's the most amazing thing I've ever fucking experienced. The hectic flow of my blood begins to slow, my muscles easing one by one, relaxing as Wren sags on top of me, and we spend a second catching our breath. And then Wren does something unexpected.

He places his mouth on mine and kisses me with the utmost care. No tongue. No urgency. Just a gentle moment, where he kisses me, and the fucking world stands still.

I've had so many expectations of him in my head that this...I don't know what to do with *this*.

Because never in my wildest dreams did I ever think that Wren Jacobi could be gentle.

29

ELODIE

AT THE BEGINNING of any new life in any new place, time passes infinitely slowly. Every small detail of your surroundings is interesting, or annoying, or beautiful or puzzling, and requires your full attention. But after a while, there are fewer and fewer new things to notice and everything becomes familiar. The same thing that's happened at every other place I've ever lived happens at Wolf Hall, too. I know what to expect when I turn a corner. I know the shape of the trees outside my window, and even the shape of the trees in the distance at the far side of the academy's boundary line, where the forest begins and reaches toward the horizon. I know the unique smell of the beeswax wood polish Jana, the academy's seventy-year-old housekeeper, uses to hand polish the wood paneling every Wednesday. I know the hollow echo of voices that bounce around the high-ceiling hallways and classrooms whenever the bell rings. I know the honeyed quality of the light that pours in through the library windows, and I know the texture of the wooden desk beneath my fingertips in my French class.

Two weeks pass, and gradually Wolf Hall begins to feel like a home of sorts. And every opportunity we get, Wren and I meet in the library's conveniently sound-proofed microfiche room—turns out *that's* what was behind Wren's secret hidden door—or the attic, and even in my room once or twice, when I knew for sure that Carina wasn't going to barge in unannounced.

Wren's ever himself, but I learn more and more of him every day; unexpected doors open to me, revealing something about him, details no one else knows, that I hoard to myself, the information more precious than gold or rubies.

He hates the texture of peanut butter in his mouth.

Whenever he smells the ocean, he thinks about losing one of his front teeth when he was eight.

He thinks the word sesquipedalian is the best word in the English language, which is ironic because it means 'given to using long words,'—which he most certainly is.

He secretly loves dogs but won't admit to loving anything if he doesn't have to.

Birds intrigue him.

Sailing, swimming, and reading make him feel alive.

We talk for hours. I *know* him now, but in the same vein, it often feels like I've barely scratched the surface when it comes to *Things To Know About Wren.*

We trade secrets and kisses and breath, and we hide away from the world, making sure no one knows when we're together. I don't mind the sneaking around or the thrill that chases up my spine when we come close to being caught. It just seems normal.

The last weekend in February rolls around, and out of nowhere, the weather picks up. The grey skies clear, and the rain quits relentlessly lashing at the academy's walls, and the temperature even manages to lift the mercury a little, rising into the sixties. It's been so long since I've seen the sun that the change in the weather, temporary though it might be, raises my spirits and makes me so giddy that Carina asks me if I'm doing drugs.

"I'm not saying I'd judge you if you were. I just don't think I've ever seen you this...bouncy."

On the front lawn of the academy, I stop bouncing on the balls of my feet, poking my tongue out at her. "I just forgot how good vitamin D is. Don't you feel alive? Like you could take on the world?"

"I have to fly to New York this afternoon to get two fillings. No, I do not feel like I could take on the world," she says dryly. "I mean, my mother's so fucking weird. She knows there are perfectly good dentists close by, but no. I have to go see *her* dentist."

"Yeah. But Andre's going with you. And you're gonna go out for a romantic dinner, *and* he got you tickets to see Hamilton. Once the dentist part's out of the way, you're gonna have an amazing time in the city and you know it."

She harrumphs. "I hate the fucking dentist. I can't stand the smell or the sound of the drill. Dentists get away with all kinds of fucked up things, y'know. The amount of women who get sexually assaulted by dentists is—" she puffs out her cheeks. "The number's frighteningly high. If you ever need to be put out for a procedure, always make sure you have someone come in and sit with you. Otherwise, you'll never know who's been touching you."

"A cheery thought to start Saturday off right," I say, beaming at her. "It's gonna be fine. You'll be in and out, and then you can enjoy your time with Andre."

"Mmm." She smiles, but she doesn't seem too convinced. "What are you gonna do today? Sorry I'm bailing on you again."

"Oh, y'know. I'm gonna sink my teeth into this." I hold up the book in my hands. "Harcourt delivered my new laptop and a bunch of other stuff last night. I can catch up on my Netflix to-watch list if I want a distraction."

"Okay, well. Next weekend, we'll do something cool, I promise."

When Andre's black Ford F150 pulls up into the turning circle, she groans like he's about to cart her off to hell instead of on a romantic weekend away. I smile at the retreating truck until my cheeks hurt, waving until it's out of sight, and then I'm up and running, heading down the driveway toward my own weekend getaway.

* * *

The car's set back from the road, parked down a narrow gravel track that obscures it from sight. Black, sleek and shining, the '66 Mustang Fastback looks brand new, even though it's well over forty years old. Wren leans against the driver's door, head down, hair hiding his face. The faded grey t-shirt he's wearing pulls taut over his arms and across his back, his low-slung jeans hanging off his hips. His scruffy, worn boots are missing, replaced by a pair of black Chuck Taylor high tops. A slow smile spreads across his face when he hears my feet crunching on the gravel.

"I was beginning to think you were gonna bail on me," he says.

He still hasn't looked at me. He does this a lot—refraining from lifting his head and making eye contact with me until the very last second, until I'm standing right in front of him. He finally looks up at me from under those expressive, dark eyebrows, and my toes curl in my shoes. "How do you even know it's me?"

"You're five-foot-four, Little E," he says, smirking. "You have a *very* short stride."

"Rude."

"*True,*" he counters, hooking his fingers through the belt loops of my jeans, pulling me toward him. He brings his mouth down on mine, and the birds stop singing in the trees. The air stills. The sun burns a little brighter. When he releases me, he slides his hands up inside my shirt, drawing small circles over my skin with the tips of his fingers. "You're late," he rumbles. "I don't like to be kept waiting."

I give him a look. One that he smiles at, running his tongue over his bottom lip, wetting it. We trade these silent exchanges often now—my wordless chiding in return for his entertained, half-felt apologies. "You're not the boss of me," I remind him.

"Aren't I?"

He ducks down for another kiss, but I scoot back, out of reach. "Most definitely not."

Fire ignites in his eyes. "If I tell you to do something, don't you do it? If I ask you for something, don't I get it?" he muses.

"Only because I deign to do or give you what you want, Jacobi. There'll come a day when I won't feel so accommodating."

"Well, I guess I'll just have to live in fear of that day, then," he purrs, prowling after me. I shriek, running around the car, but it's no use. He was right, I'm five four, and my legs are much shorter than his. He catches me with ease, locking his arms around my waist and lifting me off the ground. "In the car with you," he growls into my ear. "We've got places to be."

He holds me against his side with one arm, freeing up a hand so that he can open the passenger door of the car and bundle me inside. I land with a soft *uffff* on the leather bench seat. He slams the door behind me before I can play at making a run for it. Two seconds later, he's sliding himself into the car beside me and turning the key in the ignition.

There's something pretty fucking spectacular about Wren behind the wheel of a car. I've never seen him drive before; Pax always runs the Riot House boys up to the academy whenever the weather's bad enough to warrant the short drive. Seeing him like this now, his actions sure and confident as he throws the Mustang into gear and hits the gas, turns me on in the weirdest way. The strangest things tend to turn me on now. The act of watching him fix his coffee, popping the lid off his to-go cup, licking the foam off of it before sprinkling the tiniest bit of sugar across the top of his latte and snapping the plastic back on the cup again. The way his eyes flit quickly and surely over the pages of a book when he's reading something he finds fascinating. The way he absent-mindedly pulls his lip through his teeth when he's thinking deeply. Fuck, the way he looks in his clothes, and the sight of his bare feet, and the way my whole being vibrates with satisfaction whenever I'm lucky enough to earn a burst of laughter out of him.

All of it makes me want to rip my clothes off and fuck him stupid.

"Did you bring the stuff?" he asks, giving me a quick sidelong look as he pulls out onto the road.

I pat the bag I brought with me, raising my eyebrows. "Yes.

Though why the hell you told me to bring a swimsuit, I do not know. The sun might be out, but there's no way you're getting me in a lake. The water's gonna be freezing."

The corner of his mouth lifts up. "Don't you worry that pretty little head of yours. I'm not gonna have you freeze to death, Elodie Stillwater."

We burn down the mountain in record time. He drives even faster than Carina, but I don't feel the same lurching in my stomach when he takes a corner. Wren handles his car like a pro, braking ahead of the turns and speeding out of them with so much control that I have to press my knees together to stop the heavy, hot ache between my thighs. God, I am such a fucking loser. In town, Wren takes a series of turns through residential streets, avoiding the main roads as he navigates us toward our destination.

"You're really not gonna tell me where we're going?" I ask.

He gives his head an exaggerated shake, biting back a smile. "Not on your life. We're nearly at our first port of call anyway."

Mere minutes later, we're pulling into the parking lot of a ramshackle-looking building that looks like a rundown western saloon. The name *'Cosgrove's'* is scrawled in peeling once-white, now-grey paint down the side of the heavily weathered lap-siding. Wren pulls up next to a rusting old Buick and kills the engine, looking at me with a weird expression on his face. Takes me a second to recognize it as nerves. I don't think I've *ever* seen him look nervous before.

"Uhh..." He trails off, still deciding what he's going to say.

"Uhh?"

"This place is mine," he says.

I jerk my thumb behind me, out of the Mustangs's rear window. "The bar?"

"Yeah. The bar."

"What do you mean, *it's yours?*"

"I bought it. Last year."

"How? You were a minor?

"I have a guy. Edward. He manages my affairs for me. Just signs off on the legal stuff I can't do. At least he *did*, but I'm eighteen now, so..."

I shake my head, blinking at him. "With what *money?*"

He laughs bitterly, scrubbing his hands through his hair and then down over his face. "*Urrrrrghhhh*. With some of my annual stipend." He doesn't sound happy when he says this. He seems frustrated and pretty fucking miserable, actually. "My grandparents were very wealthy people, Elodie. They gave Mercy and me an annual allowance to survive on. January first, every year without fail, an obscene amount of money's deposited in my checking account, and every year I do my best to burn through the lot before spring."

Holy hell. I figured, since his father's just as high up in the military as my own, that his family had money. I didn't think for a second that he has his own. "And do you manage it? Do you fritter away all of your money by April?" I ask.

He gives me a tight, sharp smile. "Never. I'd probably have to buy a small nation with a massive national debt to clear out my bank account at this point."

Fuck.

"I have houses in Europe and Australia. I've got more stocks and shares than you can imagine. And when investing my money became far too responsible, I just started wasting it. Ridiculous vacations. Boats. Drugs. Lots of drugs," he says. "And then I got bored of that, too, so I started buying failing businesses that would never make any money and sat back to watch the fireworks when my father found out. Cosgrove's had the added benefit of being a licensed bar, where I could come and get fucked up whenever I wanted to, so..."

"Right. Makes sense." I laugh a little nervously. I live so carefully, watching the balance on the American Express my father loads up for me. It's one of the ways that he likes to remind me that he owns me, and I've never been able to forget it. Fall out of his good graces, and that's it, I'm scraping by on next to nothing until he decides I've redeemed myself. Turns out, Wren's never had to worry about money. He leans forward, resting his chin in his hands, staring out of the windshield into the empty road on the other side of the lot.

"I'd give it all away," he says morosely. "Only my father would find out and send more. For the Jacobis, money's an infinite resource, springing from a well that will never run dry. Mercy loves it. And I hate it more than I can say. Ungrateful, right? There are so many people out there struggling to make ends meet, and I'm bitching that I have too much fucking money. God, I even make myself sick. Come on, let's go." He explodes from the car, jumping out so quickly that his door's slammed closed and he's already opening mine before I register that he's gone.

The inside of Cosgrove's is a confusion of mismatched paraphernalia. There are quirky, at-odds items everywhere, ranging from stuffed moose heads to Native American wall tapestries. From old black and white photographs of construction workers sitting on the ledges of half-built skyscrapers in the 1920s, to an English telephone box, sitting in the corner like it just inexplicably fell out of the fucking sky and landed there all by itself. The bar smells of stale beer and sawdust, but it's a reassuring smell, and even the sticky film that covers the chairs, the tabletops, the bar's worn counter, and pretty much everything else inside the building doesn't detract from its weird, otherworldly charm.

Wren stands in the center of the quiet bar with his hands in his pockets, looking around like he just doesn't know what to do with the place.

"There are customers," he observes. "We don't usually have those."

A short, squat man bullies his way through a set of swinging saloon doors that presumably lead out back, his expression darkening when he sees Wren. "No text," he grumbles, clattering behind the bar. "I thought we agreed you'd text before you showed up. Can't just go showing up out of the blue, spyin' on me," he grouses.

"I agreed to no such thing," Wren sighs wearily. "It's my bar. I can show up whenever I feel like it. And I'm not spying on you, Patterson. We want breakfast. That's all."

Patterson squints at him. "*We?*"

Wren tips his head in my direction, where I'm leaning against the bar. Patterson sees me and lets out a sigh of relief. "Well, at least you didn't bring those animals down here with you. That's a small mercy." He's talking about Dashiell and Pax, I'm sure. Walking down the length of the bar, the old man stops in front of me, looking me up and down. "Got all your own teeth?" he asks.

I try not to let out a surprised laugh. "Yes, sir."

"Then you ain't from town. You got more money than sense and think the world still owes you?"

I shake my head gravely. "No, sir."

"Then you probably ain't from that school, either. I don't know where he found you, pretty girl, but you look too nice for him. My advice? Get out now while you still can."

I don't even know what to say to that. I don't tell him that I *am* a student at Wolf Hall, though. I feel like he'll be less enamored with me if I correct his assumption. Wren stands behind me, growling under his breath. "She *is* too nice for me, but that's none of your damn business, old man."

We order a disgusting amount of food and eat it out back on a picnic bench, away from the prying eyes of the four customers in the bar. Once we're done, Wren ushers me back into the car and tells me we're leaving Mountain Lakes altogether. For the first time since I arrived at Wolf Hall, I leave the town, and I don't look back.

30

WREN

Pre-Elodie, my best behavior looked very different to this. I would have reamed Patterson out for his sass, and I would have probably kicked everyone out of the bar, too. There have been so many times since Elodie became my girlfriend that I've curbed my anger and not lashed out. It's gotten to the point that I'm even doing it when she's not around, plagued by a conscience that I've paid little heed to up until now. Behind every action, every thought, and every word lies the nagging question: what would Elodie think of me if she could see me now?

It's a burden, this shift in attitude. It doesn't come naturally; it requires constant work, and the new restrictions I've placed upon myself chafe like nothing else.

She didn't ask me to change.

She hasn't really asked anything of me, but this gnawing desire to make her happy, to make her proud of me, is ever constant. For her, I want to be better than my soiled, rotten soul has ever been before.

The drive is long enough to require music. I turn on the radio, and Elodie immediately changes the station from the grinding hardcore metal I usually opt for to something more mainstream and folky. I hate the hipster craze and all of the Americana crap that came along with it, but for the first time I don't feel like I'm going to smash my fist into the dashboard when I hear the strummed guitars and the pretentious lilting lyrics. She seems to like it, so I like it, too.

I try not to react when she starts singing, her voice sweet and bright, always a second offbeat or very slightly out of tune, but my insides are rioting. She doesn't care if she doesn't hit every single note. She sings for the sheer enjoyment of it, laughing at me giddily when she catches me looking at her out of the corner of my eye. She's everything good and light in this world and being in her presence is like emerging from a prison cell after so many long, dark years and finally feeling the sun on my face.

I'm so broken and corrupted that it's always felt like the rough, jagged-edged pieces of me would never fit back together again. I never even dared think such a thought. But somehow, over the past few weeks, Elodie's been putting me back together and she hasn't even been trying.

We arrive at the estate just after midday. We're two short hours from the academy, but we might as well be half a world away. The day feels full of possibility, bursting at the seams with potential. Elodie's brow furrows with confusion as I drive us through the high metal gates and down the long, sweeping driveway toward the imposing structure up ahead.

"Monmouth House?" she says quizzically. "That's what that plaque just said."

"Plaque?" I pretend I have no idea what she's talking about.

"Yes. The one that was mounted on that giant sign in front of the gates. Wren, what the hell are we doing here? Are we about to get arrested for trespassing? I can't get a criminal record. Colonel Stillwater will kill me."

She can be so melodramatic sometimes. I throw off the jolt of nerves that attacks me when I see the white G-Wagon parked in front of the house, giving myself a stern talking to.

Keep your fucking cool, man.

Since when have you ever been worried about what these fucks think anyway?

I am tense as hell, though. Denying it serves no point whatsoever. This is something very new for me, untrodden ground, and I have no fucking clue how any of this is gonna play out. I pull up alongside the G-Wagon, steeling myself for what's to come.

"Wren, seriously. This looks like private property. Shouldn't we —" She looks around, worry in her beautiful blue eyes. "Shouldn't we find a hotel or something? I don't think this place rents out rooms."

"Not by the hour, anyway," I say, smirking.

I twist the key in the ignition, cutting the engine. Right on cue, Calvin appears in the open front doorway, dressed impeccably as always in Armani. Elodie scoots down in her seat, doing her best to become invisible.

"Wren," she hisses.

I wind down the window, offering a curt smile to the tall, grey-haired man who approaches the car. "Master Wren!" His greetings have always been warm, his smile always genuine.

I lean my arm on the door, grinning at him. "Hey, Cal. What's up?"

I've known Calvin since I was five years old. He was there when my grandparents died. My mother's parents. He was the one who consoled me when I skinned my knees. He was the one who used to sneak me cookies after dinner when I was sent to bed without dessert for not finishing my meals.

A light goes on in his eyes when he notices Elodie sitting next to me in the passenger seat. "Ah! A guest? Do my eyes deceive me?"

"All right, all right. No need to lay it on so thick. I've brought a guest home with me. Calvin, this is Elodie. Elodie, this is Calvin. Don't make a fuss. Where are they?"

"Your father hasn't arrived yet. Mrs. Jacobi's with her book club in the library."

I cringe, reeling away from that title. Calvin's been an integral part of this family for a very long time, but at the end of the day he's still the hired help. He can't call my father's bitch of a wife Patricia so he uses the title that used to belong to my mother. And I fucking hate it. "Don't tell her I'm home, okay?"

He nods. "I'll put the car in the garage for you."

"Thanks, man." I turn to Elodie, about to ask her if she's got her bag, but the stunned look on her face stops me in my tracks.

"*Home?*" she hisses. "You brought me *home?*"

Oh god. She looks like she's about to have a heart attack. "It's not a big deal. It's just a building. With a lot of fancy rooms inside."

Her face blanches of all color. "Wren. You told me to bring a bikini and some fucking lingerie. You didn't tell me to bring nice, respectable clothes that would be suitable for *your parents.*"

Calvin gives me a look that says it all: you're in for it now. "Leave the keys. I'll give you guys some time to gather your stuff and head inside," he says, his smile stretching from ear to ear. "It's very nice to meet you, Miss Elodie."

"Likewise, Calvin," she replies in a very high-pitched voice.

I get out of the Mustang and walk around the other side, opening her door for her. "Get out of the car, Elodie."

She glares at me balefully, crossing her arms over her chest. "Are you insane? Have you lost your fucking mind?"

"Better not curse so much in front of my father. He's a republican. And a Christian."

She throws her head back, closing her eyes and pulling a face that looks worse than pained. "Wren! This is not—this isn't—"

"Romantic? It really isn't. But there are things here I wanted to show you," I tell her.

"I thought you always told the truth," she says accusingly.

I lift both eyebrows, shrugging. "When did I lie?"

"When you didn't tell me we'd be coming here!"

I laugh, even though I know it's going to annoy the shit out of her. "Come on, Little E. That wasn't a lie. That was an omission of the facts. Now please get out of the car before I have to come in there and get you."

She knows I'll do it. I put her in there, for crying out loud. I'll just as easily carry her out again, kicking and screaming if I have to. Sulking rather dramatically, she gets out of the car, shooting a look my way that would flay any other mere mortal alive. I'm used to her emotional squalls, though. They last all of five minutes and then they're over again. "This is really unfair," she groans. "You're supposed to give people warning, so they can mentally prepare for this kind of stuff. And I really didn't bring anything to wear."

"Nothing?"

"Not unless you think a couple of lace thongs and some high heels would be appropriate dinner attire?"

"You won't find me complaining." Jesus, my dick's getting hard just fucking thinking about it.

"Asshole!" she wails. "Help me! This is going to be a disaster!"

I can only keep the joking around for so long. Seeing her this worked up has something inside me pulling taut like a bowstring until I feel like I can't breathe around the wretchedness of it. I'm such a fucking joke. Once upon a time, I thought I wanted to hurt this girl. It's karma that it hurts *me* more than I can bear to see her in distress. I pin her against the side of the car, cupping her face in my hands, brushing her hair back behind her ears. "Calm, E. It's okay. I wouldn't throw you under the bus. I ordered a few items online for you and had them sent ahead. Everything you could need is already inside, waiting for you."

Her panic fades, turning rapidly into annoyance. She slaps my arm. "Cruel, Wren Jacobi! You should have led with that!"

"I'm sorry! I'm—Jesus, stop hitting me, I'm sorry!"

She eventually does stop hitting me, long enough for me to kiss her. She's so fucking small in my arms. She melts into me, grumbling half-heartedly as she kisses me back.

"Come on. Seriously. We need to get inside before my stepmother sees us. I'm really not kidding."

Elodie reads the genuine warning in my eyes and relents. "All right, then. Fine. Lead the way. I suppose other people have visited here and made it out alive, right?"

All I can do is laugh. She has no idea what she's in for.

* * *

Monmouth House was built in 1878 by a wealthy oil tycoon by the name of Adar Jacobi. He was the first and only Jewish man (as far as the State records of Texas will attest) to ever strike a significant reservoir and make his fortune. He married an English woman by the name of Eleanor Fairfax Monmouth and built the house in her honor, giving it her family name. When Elodie steps into the sprawling foyer for the first time, I see the place through her eyes and the entire thing feels far too pretentious for words.

The white marble with grey and gold veins snaking through it underfoot speaks of just how much money went into building this place. The high ceilings, dotted with elaborate, glimmering chandeliers that refract the sunshine pouring in through the arched fifteen-foot high windows at the top of the staircase, scattering rainbows all over the walls. Everywhere you look, there are austere, foreboding oils of my dark-haired ancestors scowling disapprovingly down at us with judgment in their eyes. Elodie takes in the lavish decor, the opulent rugs, and the sumptuous furnishings with a level of horrified awe that makes me wonder if this wasn't a huge mistake after all.

I am not *this*. I've been very careful to be something entirely removed from this disgusting show of wealth. I wear my clothes until they literally fall apart, and then I wear them some more just to be fucking difficult. I reject any and all suggestion of a haircut until I'm forced to take matters (and a pair of scissors) into my own hands, hacking at my hair with a practiced level of disorder that drives my father to drink.

Mercy, with her outrageously expensive clothes and her perfectly manicured *everything*, fits in here. Even those equipped with a feeble imagination can see that I really fucking don't. I feel so far removed from this place that entering through the door is like cracking open the pages of a book you read a long time ago. Everything's familiar, as though the stories scribbled out on the pages feel like they happened to you, but they're so distant, so remote that you know they aren't really your stories.

I didn't really fall down the steps there and almost bite clean through my lip when I was nine. That was some other kid. And there? I didn't stand over there, with my ear pressed to the heavy walnut door to the formal dining room, listening to my father fucking some young girl who just appeared out of the blue and stayed at the house for three weeks when I was twelve. It doesn't matter that I can't remember what her name was. Or that Patricia was three rooms over when my father was eating some girl's pussy on the grand twenty-person antique banquet table. Nope. None of it matters because that wasn't my life. That happened in another plane of existence, to another Wren, before Riot House, and Wolf Hall. Before Elodie.

I refrain from kicking my shoes off. Patricia will have a conniption when she sees me tramping through the house with outside footwear on my feet, which is the sole reason why I leave them on. Elodie isn't a shit like me. She slides out of her Doc Martens, and Mariposa appears, as if the very existence of a pair of unattended shoes in the entryway created a portal through time and space, dragging her here to attend to the matter before polite society should notice such vulgarity. I have total faith that long after she dies, my old nursemaid will spontaneously return from the afterlife to make sure that correct etiquette is observed at all times within the walls of Monmouth House.

"Master Wren," she says pointedly, eyeing my feet. Unlike Calvin, Mariposa's less happy to see me. She holds a grudge like no one else. She's still pissed about the slugs I put in her underwear drawer when I was seven. By the time she's gotten over that and worked her way through all the other shitty things I've done to her, she and I will have been dead three lifetimes over. "They just had the carpets steamed," she fumes. In her late seventies, she's so stooped and hunched over now that her line of sight is always locked onto people's feet; no wonder she's so good at keeping track of their footwear.

"And I'm sure they'll have them cleaned again next month, too. Even though it's completely unnecessary. Where's Pickaxe?"

Her mouth scrunches into a sour grimace. Her eyes are sharp as flint. "Dead."

"What do you mean, dead?"

"I mean dead. Found him bringin' up blood in the stables. Ate the poison set out for the rats back in January. Your father shot him. Put him out of his misery."

I look away, staring up at the sky out of the windows at the top of the stairs, trying to work my way around the tempest of emotion that's spinning around the inside of my head. Everything's moving so fast. My thoughts are so blurred; I can't make sense of what I've just learned.

A warm hand takes mine. "Pickaxe?" Elodie whispers in question.

"Doesn't matter," I say, swallowing down the hard knot in my throat. "Let's go."

"Master Wren, your shoes!"

"Get fucked, Mariposa."

"*Dios Mio.*" She crosses herself when I walk past like I'm the very devil himself. My movements are wooden and mechanical as I climb the stairs. Elodie follows after me silently, still holding onto my hand, refusing to let go. I walk down the hall, past Mercy's wing of the house, past the left-hand turn that leads to the library, my father's office, and the separate rooms where he and Patricia sleep. At the very end of the hall, I open the door, recessed out of sight in its own little alcove that leads up to what used to be the servants' quarters. This stairway is nothing like the one we just came up; it's narrow and tight, barely wide enough to fit a man's shoulders. It's also so dark that anyone who isn't as familiar with the uneven steps as I am must place their hand against the rough stucco to brace themselves to avoid tripping on the wobbly boards.

"Jesus, where are you taking me?" Elodie mutters. Her voice is soft, but it sounds harsh and loud, bouncing around the narrow space.

"Not much further," I tell her. "You'll see soon enough."

I turn the handle on the door at the top of the stairs. And it doesn't fucking open. "What the fuck?"

"What's wrong?"

I squeeze Elodie's hand, then let go of her. With both hands, I feel the weighty, cold metal of a padlock above the doorknob—a padlock that wasn't there before. "That motherfucker," I snarl.

"Wren, seriously. What's going on. I may not have mentioned this before, but I'm kinda claustrophobic."

Ahh, fuck. How have I been this stupid? I know this about her. She might not have shared the information with me, but it makes complete sense, given what I've read about her. This isn't the kind of place to be hanging around if you're afraid of tight spaces. Grimly, I tug on the lock to see how solid it is. And it's really fucking solid. "My old man," I say, sighing. "He's had Calvin put a lock on the door. And I don't have enough room to put my shoulder into it. We'll have to go back down so I can find a fucking screwdriver."

"Or..." Elodie trails off. Her breath sounds a little labored like it's hitching in her chest. "Or I could just pick the lock," she finishes.

Surprise creeps in, over the top of my anger. "You can do that? In the dark?"

"In the dark. Underwater. With my hands tied behind my back. How do you think I found my way into your bedroom when you took my phone?"

"I assumed you'd just come in through the back. We always leave the kitchen door unlocked."

"Shit." She laughs nervously. "That would have been nice to know back then, I guess. Here, can you...let me by?" She slides up the steps next to me, her tits brushing up against my chest, and my cock immediately stiffens. She smells like spring and sunshine and floral like the tiny little white flowers that grow all over the ancient, crumbling walls of my father's chateaux in France.

I want to kiss her so fucking badly. My body wants far more

than that but now is not the time. I press my back against the wall behind me, managing to give her just enough room to sidle by so that she's in front of me. I hear her fiddling with the lock—a light rattling, and then silence as she stoops over, her breath no longer labored; it evens out, into long, steady and even pulls at the air, as she focuses on her work. She's only been working over the thing for a couple of seconds when I hear the metallic snap and a loud clang as the padlock drops to the top step.

She opens the door and walks through it, into the light corridor ahead. Her cheeks flame when she turns and sees the expression on my face. "What? What's that look for?"

I'm reeling from the fact that she managed to get that lock to open. Fucking reeling. I know precisely why she learned that skill, and I know precisely why she would carry the tools required to pick a lock with her at all times. It's just still pretty fucking amazing. "You're just full of surprises, Little E," I tell her, winking playfully. She still hasn't told me anything about her past in Tel Aviv. I've been waiting patiently for her to open up about it, but I'm not gonna fucking push her.

"You can learn all kinds of things on YouTube," she says. "I watched a thousand videos, learning how to do that in as many situations as possible."

A cold, sickly feeling creeps up my back. I quickly brush it off, forcing a smile onto my face.

"Why would your father lock that door? Seems like a weird thing to do," she says, smoothly changing the subject. Scanning the hallway with the little porthole windows along its north-facing side, and the four doors leading off from it on the other side, she frowns deeply.

"This was my mother's place," I say. "She would come up here to paint and read. She used to sleep up here sometimes. I've claimed it as my space now, but my father doesn't like it. He says it upsets his new wife. It has nothing to do with Patty, though. He just hates that I'd rather spend my time up here with the ghost of my dead mother instead of suffering downstairs with the rest of them in the land of the living. He threatens to clear everything out of here and brick up the door sometimes."

"Why hasn't he?"

"Because he knows I'd burn the entire fucking house down if he did."

She just nods, accepting this as something I would do. A truth about me that makes sense. "Are we gonna get in trouble for coming up here, then? Is he gonna be angry?"

"He's always angry. Don't worry, though. He won't be angry with you. You're a guest. When you meet him, he'll be sweet and interested, and charming, and you'll wonder how I could possibly hate him so much. You'll take his side and think I'm completely unreasonable when I don't fall down and worship at the fucker's feet."

She blinks at me owlishly. She's so fucking beautiful that the sight of her feels like a punch to the gut. Again, she shakes her head. "No, I won't. I know all about sociopathic fathers, Wren. I've been dealing with one my entire life. I know the front they put on for the rest of the world. I'll always see through that charade, no matter how many other people it might fool. Come on." She smiles gently. "Why don't you show me around? Tell me about your mom. I want to know all about her."

* * *

The paintings are calmer than mine. The blues, blacks, greys, and whites are softer, so much subtler and more intentional than mine, too. Elodie paces the floorboards of my mother's studio, studying each canvas in turn, pulling back the dust cloths and letting the heavy sheets sigh to the floor. Her inquisitive eyes pick over the brushstrokes, her fingertips poised just above the surface of the oil paint, as if she's reaching inside the painting in her mind, stroking them over the subject matter with a reverence that makes my chest pull tight.

I'm far more comfortable painting my stormy landscapes. My

mother painted people. She loved capturing the emotion and the intelligence in someone's eyes, and she was damn good at it, too. "She was so talented," Elodie breathes. "Who's this?" She gestures to the painting in front of her, of the man with the staunch expression and the curious light in his eyes. My jaw's so clenched that it takes real effort to work my teeth apart.

"My father. A couple of years before she found out she was pregnant. Amazing how twenty years can change someone."

She steps closer, investigating the lines of the man my mother captured with her art. She was generous with him. Made him look less stern than he was, even then. I've never seen the softness she depicted in his face. There's a glimmer of love in the bastard's eyes that's been missing my entire life.

"She was far better than I'll ever be," I say.

Elodie shakes her head. "That's not true. You're just as good, Wren. Just different. You use the same colors that she used. The tone isn't the same, though."

I grunt at that. "Yeah. She was optimistic. I've never had that in me."

Elodie's eyes convey many things as she looks back at me over her shoulder. Sadness. Regret. Kindness. The smallest ounce of pity that makes me want to claw my way out of my skin. I suddenly don't want to be in here anymore. As if she can feel me withdrawing, Elodie steps away from the paintings, coming to me, taking my hands in hers.

"Show me where you sleep?" It's a small request, but I'm shot full of nerves by the prospect of showing her my room.

"Where I'm supposed to sleep, downstairs? Or the room I claimed up here?"

"Up here."

My heart skitters treacherously as I walk her down the hall and into my room. It's not much. The slope of the roof is steep and means I have to bow my head; there's only a small section of the space where I can stand up straight without risking a concussion. I smirk to myself when I realize that Elodie doesn't have that problem. She's so short that she can stand tall the whole time. She wanders around, inspecting the room from one end to the other: the bookshelf, with the well-thumbed copies of my favorite books; the small bed, bigger than a single but a far cry from the huge California king I have back at Riot House. The sweatshirt, slung over the back of the chair beneath the tiny window, that I forgot when I last came here; the old tennis shoes, and my grandfather's old, cracked compass on the window sill; the notepads, and the sketches pinned to the walls, and the candles, melted into puddles of wax on the dusty floorboards.

She pores over each little detail of the room, assessing and weighing each little thing like she's putting together the pieces of a puzzle that have been missing until now. I watch her silently, my chest aching, my hands burning with the need to touch her. I keep them to myself, though, leaning against the wall, savoring the unfamiliar, troublesome emotions that are digging their roots down deeper and deeper into me, wrapping their tendrils around my bones.

I always thought I'd find ultimate happiness within the pages of a book. I've been so convinced of that fact that I've devoted so much of my life to disappearing inside them, searching for that which has always eluded me. I should have known that I wouldn't find what I was looking for on ink and paper. Even the poets entrusted their foolish hearts into the hands of others. *Especially* the poets. That was both their salvation and their ultimate downfall; without knowing the joy of loving another human being, they would never have been able to write about the soaring joy that always made my heartbeat quicken. And they'd never have been able to capture true desolation and sorrow without enduring the kind of suffering that can only come from lost love.

As Elodie spins around, breathing deeply, taking everything in for a final time, I admit something that I've stubbornly refused to ever admit to myself before: *I am fucking scared.*

This girl has no idea the power she holds over me. She can't begin to imagine the lengths I will go to or the worlds I will burn down in my mission to make her happy.

"Not quite as impressive as my room at Riot House," I say, when she comes to face me.

She shrugs, smiling. "I like this room just as much. It's yours. I can tell you've spent a lot of time here. I can imagine a younger, less jaded version of you drawing on the bed, and sitting in the chair, reading Treasure Island."

I laugh gruffly, nodding as I look down at my feet. I did both of those things more times than I can count.

"What's your room like downstairs?" she asks.

"Sterile. Bleak. Empty."

She accepts this description without question. "I don't want to sleep down there, then. I want to sleep here. With all the memories of you, before I knew you. Would that be okay?"

Christ, doesn't she know that I will give her anything she fucking wants? I'll rip out my mangled, blackened heart for her and set it at her feet if it'll please her. "Yeah. We can manage that."

"Won't your father be scandalized if we sleep in the same bed?"

"Probably. But he can go fuck himself." I haven't even considered the fact that we'll be sharing the same bed. The thought of it makes my blood pound at my temples. Elodie, naked and spent, wrapped up in the bedsheets next to me. Surrendering herself to unconsciousness, laying in my arms, not knowing what kind of a man I truly am and all the awful, hideous things I've done. I don't deserve it. Fuck, I don't deserve any of this.

A loud slamming sound disrupts the peace outside, sharper and more jarring than a gunshot. Elodie jumps. I head over to the window, irritation digging its claws into my back when I see the black Range Rover that's pulled up in front of the house. Even four floors up, I can hear my father's aggravated bark as he enters the house.

"Where is he, then? Where the fuck is my son?"

31

ELODIE

DONALD JACOBI WAS a general in the army before he retired a month ago. But men like him never really retire. Not in any way that counts. He was a general when he hung up his uniform, and a general he will remain until the day he dies. His very presence seems to swallow up the room, as Wren leads me into an enormous high-ceilinged space that I suppose would have been used as a formal reception room back in the day. I see the back of him first. Standing with one hand braced against the mantle of a looming fireplace and the other planted firmly on his hip, he strikes an imposing figure. Wren stands a little straighter, his shoulders pulling back as he clears his throat, announcing our presence.

"It's only good manners to call ahead if you're planning on bringing guests to the house," General Jacobi drawls. He affects a lazy, playful tone, but there's a very real reprimand in his words. He pivots with a flourish, pushing away from the fireplace, and a pair of cold, assessing eyes land on me. His gaze feels like a knife-point being driven up, between my ribs.

Wren was right; he's nothing like the man in the painting in the attic. His face is a roadmap of lines and crevasses that tell a clear story—one of anger and unhappiness. The deep brackets around his mouth and at the corners of his eyes speak of bone-deep unhappiness.

"Introductions, please," he says tightly.

"This is Elodie Stillwater. We're at the academy together. Her father's stationed in Israel." Wren gives him this sparse rundown of me in as few words as possible. "Elodie, this is my father, General Donald Jacobi, retired."

I think Wren tacks retired on the end of his father's title just to piss him off. Looks like it works, too.

"Pleased to meet you, General Jacobi," I say.

He gives me a curt nod. "Sir will suffice. I'm pleased to make your acquaintance, too, young lady. Your father's reputation precedes him. I don't doubt that, with a father like him, you've had quite the proper upbringing. Your manners do him proud."

I couldn't give a shit about doing my father proud. The colonel is obsessed with making an impression with his betters, though, even if they're no longer an official service member. He'd have a fucking fit if it got back to him that I somehow disgraced myself (and ergo him) during my introduction to Wren's father.

"Israel's a prestigious posting. I've heard things are calm over there these days, but you never know when that might change."

I've never wished for conflict to break out anywhere. The innocent and the downtrodden always suffer. That doesn't mean that I haven't hoped that something would happen while my father was outside of the base, though. Some freak accident, or an isolated attack of some kind, that resulted in Colonel Stillwater's untimely demise. If I'm hell-bound for thinking such things, then that's a price I'm willing to pay. Stoke the fires and lay out the welcome mat, I say. So long as I no longer have to bow to my father's crippling authority while I'm alive, then there's no price I'd be unwilling to pay.

"Thank you, Sir. That's very kind of you to say."

"You've just joined the academy?"

"Yes, Sir."

"And you're enjoying it so far? You're enjoying spending time with my son?"

I blush furiously. There's something underhanded about the question—a distasteful insinuation that makes me feel like he's accusing me of something. "Uh, yes, Sir. The academy itself is beautiful, and the curriculum's challenging. Plus...yes, it helps to have friends there to spend time with during our downtime."

"Friends?" General Jacobi looks sharply at Wren. Wren stares right back at him, the muscles in his jaw popping.

"Not friends," he says. "We're together. She's my girlfriend."

The general gives a curt nod. "Ah. I see. So you're fucking."

Wren doesn't flinch. His eyes narrow ever so slightly, but only for a heartbeat; his facial features are under his complete control. "Yeah. We're fucking," he answers flatly.

It's one thing having someone's parents know that you're probably having sex, another thing entirely to have it laid bare like this. And in such blunt terms? I'm so stung that I feel like I've just been slapped. By Wren, or by his father, the shock of it feels the same.

General Jacobi sighs. "Nice to know you're behaving like a gentleman up there, Wren. That school's one of the most expensive academic institutes in the country. And you're sleeping around now? Sullying a family name that's been held in high esteem for many generations?" He shakes his head, disappointment radiating off him. "Honestly, I had hoped you'd conduct yourself a little better."

A cold, searing fire burns in Wren's eyes. "I'm not sleeping around. I'm sleeping with one person. I'd say I was doing a better job at preserving the Jacobi name than you are, Father. Given your past indiscretions."

Oh my god.

My shoulders hike up around my ears. I would never...*could* never speak to my father like that. It wouldn't matter who was near. He'd beat the back teeth straight out of my head. It doesn't even bear thinking about. General Jacobi snarls. He's seething. He nods, running his tongue over his teeth. "All right. Well, that's enough of that. Dinner won't be until seven. Why don't the two of you make yourself scarce until you hear the bell? Elodie, in amongst rubbing your body on that boy, why don't you see if you can't rub some of those manners off on him, too."

What...the actual...*fuck.*

He did *not* just say that.

Again, Wren doesn't show any sign of emotion. I'd be impressed if *I* weren't so fucking angry. I've never expected a knight in shining armor to ride in on a white steed to rescue me. But some flicker of annoyance on Wren's face would be nice right now.

He just blinks at his father. "For someone who puts so much stock in manners," he says. "You're the rudest motherfucker *I've* ever met."

General Jacobi laughs. Harsh. Unfriendly. "Oh, my darling boy. I'd respect you so much more if you had the stones to come and say that to my face."

Wren doesn't hesitate. He walks right up to his father, and oh god, I cannot watch hi—

WOAH!

Holy fuck!

Holyshitholyshitholyshit!

General Jacobi's ready for his son to spit angry words in his face. He's unprepared for the powerful right hook Wren lands on his jaw. I watch, horrified, as the old man staggers into the mantle-piece, throwing out a hand to try and catch himself as he topples backward. It's no good, though. He lands in a heap in the grate, his feet up in the air, in the most undignified display I've ever seen. His face goes bright purple.

"Out! Out of my house!" he sputters. His arms and legs are everywhere as he tries to get up again. It takes him three attempts to right himself, and when he does find his feet, it turns out that the seat of his expensive black pants is covered in ash. He tries to grab Wren by the scruff of his t-shirt, but Wren smacks his hand away, laughing coldly under his breath.

"Try it," he seethes. "Go ahead and fucking try it. See what happens next."

The general lowers his hand, but he's not done with Wren. Not by a long shot. "Stupid boy. You've finally gone and done it, then. Fucked yourself over beyond measure. No more prissy, posh school for you now. You're finished. You're heading straight for military sch—"

"What's the date?" Wren asks.

His father jerks back. "What?"

"What's the date? Today's date. Come on. You read the paper every day. You must know."

"Don't be obtuse. Of course I know today's date. It's the seventeenth of March."

Wren feigns surprise. "Oh. Cool. And what happened on the fourth of March, Father?"

"I don't know! Lots of things, I'm sure. The fourth of Mar—" He stops short. His face goes blank.

"Yeahhhh, that's right. Good ol' fourth of March. You forgot your children's birthday again, didn't you, Dad? Only this time, you forgot our *eighteenth* birthday. Which means..." Wren steps closer to his father, getting up in his face. He stabs a finger into General Jacobi's chest with every point he makes. "No more orders. No more commands. No more threats. No more hanging military school over my head, every chance you get. I'm an adult. I've come into my majority. And you're done talking to me like I'm some unpleasant thing you've found stuck to the bottom of your shoe."

General Jacobi glows with rage. "Fine. Then your tuition's finished. I won't pay for another thing, boy. That house you and your friends live in—"

"Is *mine*," Wren spits. "The deed's in my name. And I'll pay for my own damn tuition. I'll cover my own expenses. You can't touch a cent of my money, and you know it." He blows down his nose, hard, nostrils flaring. "Why don't you sit back down, old man. *You're fucking embarrassing yourself.*"

Spinning, he crosses the formal dining room, taking me by the hand and pulling me away.

I guess he *was* angry about that comment, after all.

32

ELODIE

WE ESCAPE Monmouth House with armloads of paintings and all of Wren's personal belongings from the attic. We check into the Hubert Estates County Inn, and Wren paces up and down like a lion, silent and furious. It takes four hours for him to calm down, by which point it's gone dark, and my jaw is aching from clenching it so hard.

At seven, Wren's phone starts ringing, and it won't fucking stop.

"My sister," Wren grits through his teeth. "She probably wants to scold me for hitting the fucker. She's always just tolerated his bullshit, like none of it fucking matters. But it does. It fucking does."

"I know. It matters." I'd say more, but there are so many fucked up things ping-ponging around in my head that I can barely think straight. My own memories are hitting hard. I feel like I'm trapped, walled in by panic.

It wasn't you. It wasn't you, Elodie. You're safe. You're okay here. He's a million miles away. He can't hurt you.

Wren has no idea how similar our upbringings have been. The only difference is that he's big enough now to stand up to his father. I'll never be able to confront Colonel Stillwater the way he did just now. And that makes me feel hopeless.

The room we've checked into is beautiful, but neither of us has stopped to take in our surroundings. We've both retreated into our own little worlds, and I think it's going to take a while for either of us to return to reality again.

Wren's phone shrieks again, his ringtone blaring out in the tense silence.

"I thought you never kept that thing switched on?" I say.

"You're right. I should just turn the fucking thing—" He cringes when he looks down at the screen. "Fuck. She's messaging now, too. Apparently, he's gotten Harcourt involved." He turns the phone off.

"Shouldn't you check in if the Dean wants to speak to you?"

"Better if they all have a beat to calm down. Everyone's heightened right now. I'm trying not to be, but—" He sits down on the edge of the bed next to me, lacing his fingers together, blindly staring down at his hands. "I'm sorry, Elodie. I told you he was gonna be polite and charming, and he really wasn't. I'm—I don't even know what to say. I could tell he was in a bad mood, but I didn't think he was gonna turn like that. I would never have taken you there if I thought for one second that he was going to be that shitty to you."

"It's fine, Wren. Seriously. A few crass words from your dad aren't enough to affect me these days. I mean, Pax calls me a whore on a daily basis. I don't mind."

"Yeah. Well." Wren's eyes harden. "I mind. I really fucking mind. Elodie," Wren whispers. He's looked up now, but he isn't looking at *me*. His focus is locked on the window opposite the bed, which overlooks the hotel's swimming pool. "Tell me what's wrong."

"Wrong?" I blow my cheeks out, pulling my shoulders up around my ears. "I mean, I just watched you put your father on his ass. That wasn't exactly a fun time."

"No. You're anxious. I've never seen you this jittery before. You're scared of something, and I'm hoping to god over here that it's not me. 'Cause if it's me..." He laughs unhappily. "I don't think I would cope with that very well."

"No! God, it's not you, I swear. It's just the whole thing. It reminded me of how things were with Colonel Stillwater back in Tel Aviv. Your father's a lot like mine. I guess...it brought back some difficult memories."

He nods, clenching his jaw. He's suddenly even angrier than he was a minute ago. "I wanna talk about something with you, Little E," Wren says. "I know now's not a good time, but I don't want to wait anymore. I thought I could keep my mouth shut until you came to me, but..." He shakes his head.

Oh god. No. *No, no, no.* This is bad. "Wren, I don't—"

"I did a bunch of research on you before you arrived," he says stiffly. "I checked your social media. Dug up your school reports. It's severely fucked up, I know, and now that everything's changed between us, I feel like a fucking predator just thinking about it."

"This...isn't news," I say. "You already told me that you looked into me. I got over that a long time ago. We don't need to—"

"Elodie. Stop."

"Can you stop staring out of the window? You're beginning to freak me the fuck out."

He bows his head, closing his eyes for a second. Only after a deep breath does he finally look up at me. "I didn't tell you that I was also sent some official documents from Tel Aviv. I put in a request with a friend who lives out in Israel, and he sent me an envelope. There was a police report inside it."

I go very, very still. "What police report?"

Reality fractures, shatters to tiny pieces when he takes a deep breath and speaks again. "The one that was filed the night they found your mother's body."

33

ELODIE

THREE YEARS AGO

The metal chair creaks underneath me, the loud, abrasive sound cutting through the tense silence of the small, windowless room like a knife. The man on the other side of the scratched, wobbly table gives me a tight smile that doesn't come close to reaching his eyes. He looks like he feels sorry for me but he doesn't quite know what to do to comfort me. He probably doesn't have kids. Probably unmarried, too. There's no wedding band on his left hand, which means he's probably one of those cops who's dedicated his life to his work. When all you do is focus on the bad shit people do to one another, it stunts your heart's ability to feel anything other than contempt and mistrust.

"Won't be long now," he says in a heavily accented voice. Someone must have told him that I only speak English. I nod, looking down at my hands, resting on top of the table; I was allowed to wash them after the photographs were taken and the forensic analysts had swabbed me, but I was so numb that I didn't do a good job. There's old blood, black now, still

shored up beneath my nails—dark crescents of gore that keep on reminding me of the surreal scene I came home to from school.

Seconds pass.

Minutes.

The clock on the wall tick, tick, ticks, its hands marking off the unbearable stretch of endless time that I sit here at this table in my stinking clothes, feeling the emotionless eyes of the detective crawl all over me. Eventually, the door opens and a beautiful woman wearing high waisted pants and a crisp white shirt whirls into the room, carrying a stack of paperwork. She smiles at me; she has one of those soft, warm smiles that instantly makes you feel at ease. Like she could be a friend. "Hello, Elodie. My name is Aimée. It is a pleasure to meet you. I am sorry it has to be under such painful circumstances." Not Amy, like the Americanized name. Aimée, like the French verb 'to love.' Her accent's wonderful. You can always tell when someone's new to the English language. They don't use contractions. 'It is' instead of 'it's.' 'I am' instead of 'I'm.' They aren't comfortable enough with the language to get lazy with it yet.

She sits down next to her colleague, and a waft of jasmine water hits the back of my nose. I begin to piece together this woman's life as she flicks through the papers she's brought along with her. She's French, obviously. Early thirties. She takes excellent care of herself, working out every day in private behind closed doors but never talking about it, as is the way of all classically French women. She drinks her coffee black, dipping her croissant into the piping hot liquid at her desk each morning. She loves children, but she's never found the time to have them. She'll make a good mother one day if only she can settle down long enough to find someone and fall in love. She loves to be outside. She loves to live by the sea, and craves—

"Elodie? Yes, there you are. Good girl. Come back," she says, her warm brown eyes full of emotion. "I know this is hard, but I need you to try and focus for a little while, okay?"

I jerk my head up and down.

"I was asking you if you could tell me what happened, please? The officer who found you at your house said you were not making any sense when he..."

She can't even say it. So I do it for her. My voice creaks and cracks as I push the words out of my mouth. "When he opened up the box."

"Yes, Elodie. When he opened up the box."

"I don't remember what I said to him," *I tell her.*

"Yes. That is understandable." *She's perfunctory. She manages to hide her horror well. That could be why they chose her to come in to speak to me. Aside from the fact that she's a woman, and she has kind eyes, and she shares my mother's nationality—points that they probably figured would help me open up to her.* "Do you think you could start at the beginning for me?"

Everything's so confused. My thoughts are all tangled together, like an unspooled ball of wool. I pull memories through my hands like I'm searching for the end of a string, but it just keeps going and going. "I don't —I can't really..."

"Okay. It is okay." *Aimée reaches across the table, touching her fingers to the back of my hand. The contact startles me so badly that I reel back, knocking over the glass of water they gave me. The spilled liquid spreads across the table, running off the edge of its surface, dripping down into my lap, but I don't move. I don't try to mop it up. I just sit there and let it happen.*

"Merde!" *Aimée hisses. She runs out of the room and comes back a moment later with a wad of paper towels. Between her and the silent guy sitting next to her, they clear up the mess quickly, drying off the table. Aimée gives me a bundle of napkins to pat my jeans dry, but I don't bother. I just hold onto them, my fingers rustling over the rough surface of the cheap paper. Round in circles. Round in circles.*

"Elodie? Are you listening?"

I snap my head up. Aimée's back in her seat again. God knows how long she's been sitting there. "I cannot suggest what happened to you based on what we know at this stage, but I can read back what you told the officer. Do you think that would be okay? And then you can tell us if there is anything else you remember, or if there is anything you want to change? And don't worry. There is no right or wrong here. If you remember something differently, that is okay. You are allowed to tell us, and you are not going to get into any trouble."

I blink to let her know that I've understood.

She cracks her neck, inhaling in and out a few times as though she's steeling herself before she starts reading. And then she begins.

"I came home at six. He was already there at the house. My father. He was supposed to be away on maneuvers, but he must have come back early. I realized he was drunk right away. At least, I thought he was drunk. He was acting weird, staggering around and walking into the furniture. He wouldn't talk to me. I called out for my mom, to tell her that there was something wrong with him, but she didn't answer, so I went looking for her.

"She likes to write letters to my grandmother in the back sunroom, so that's where I looked first. She was lying on the tiles there, covered in blood. She was on her stomach and her skirt was up around her waist. I didn't understand what had happened at first. But then I saw the blood on her underwear." Aimée pauses. Swallows. Continues. "There was a hole in the side of her head." Aimée looks up at me. "What kind of hole, Elodie? Like a bullet hole?"

Bile rises up the back of my throat. I'm apart from myself, outside my body, removed from this place and this situation. It's the only way I can give her the information she needs, but it means that I sound like a robot when I speak. "No. Bigger. About the size of a golf ball. And her skull was...it had caved in around the hole."

Aimée taps her fingernail against the table in a staccato beat. She stops when she notices me flinch. She goes back to my statement. "I screamed for Dad to get an ambulance, but I knew it was already too late. Her lips were blue. I checked for a pulse, though. I turned her over and put her on her back. I tried to give her CPR, but she was already dead."

I remember saying all of this. And the look on the officer's face, too. He looked shell-shocked by the things I was telling him. But I don't remember feeling this rising anguish, rushing toward me like the inevitable end of a Shakespearean tragedy, refusing to slow or change its course. I know what's coming, and there's no holding it back. I wish I could.

"That's when he came and grabbed me," Aimée reads from the state-ment. "He grabbed me from behind. He was so strong. I couldn't fight

him. And I didn't think he was going to do anything bad. Not at first. But then he carried me over to the steel lockbox where he keeps his uniforms and his equipment. He handcuffed my arms behind my back, and then he put me inside. I kicked and screamed, and I fought, but I couldn't get out. A long time passed. I thought I was going to die. He came back later, and he seemed normal again, but he wouldn't let me out. He wouldn't let me out of the box."

Aimée stares blankly at the report for a moment. "Is there anything else you want to add, Elodie? Anything else that you've remembered?"

"Yes." I have to say this now, while I am not myself. I couldn't tell the officer who found me. He was too young. Too frightened. He'd thrown up on his shoes. This little room feels safer, though, and Aimée doesn't look like she will puke. "Something happened. Something before...he put me in the box."

The detective narrows her eyes. "Yes?"

"He did to me what he did to my mom. He forced himself...into me. Between my legs. He held my head against the tiles, and he...he hurt me. I screamed. I tried to stop him, but...I could see my mom. Her eyes were still open, and she was looking right at me, and..."

That's it. That's all I have. I don't fall apart. I just run out of steam. I can't continue. Aimée looks at me, her lovely brown eyes boring into me, and a single tear wobbles on the end of her eyelashes. That single tear is more than I've shed for myself since I escaped from that lockbox. It seems wrong that she gets to be the first person to cry over how terrible this nightmare is. She knows it, too. She quickly bats the tear away, clamping down on her errant display of emotion. "We need to get you back to the hospital. I don't think they conducted a rape kit."

Shame sets me alight. I try to shrink in on myself, trying not to imagine the humiliation that is to come.

"Just a few more questions and we'll get you out of here. What day was that, Elodie?"

"Yesterday. Friday. It happened after I came home from school."

Aimée pales, the color leaching from her face as she glances down at the report in front of her. She doesn't appear to be looking at anything in particular. Her hand trembles and she quickly tucks it under the table, *out of sight. "Do you have any idea what day it is now, Elodie?" she asks in a quiet voice.*

Those endless hours in the dark, cramped into a ball, my joints screaming in agony, begging me to stretch out, with my nose pressed against those tiny holes. They felt like an eternity. A hell that spanned full lifetimes. I know how the mind plays tricks, though. Hours feel like days, that feel like years. I've been here at the station since three in the morning, which means it must have been around midnight when that officer cracked the lock off the box and released me. My brain balks at the idea of tackling the simplest of mathematics, but I force myself to count off the hours on my fingers. "It's Sunday," I tell her. "The early hours of Sunday morning."

"You think you were in the box for nine hours?" Aimée whispers.

I look from the female detective to the man sitting next to her, back and forth, back and forth, trying to work out the complex expressions they're wearing. "Yes?" The guy's face creases into a mask of horror. He clears his throat, but it sounds more like he's choking. He pushes away from the table, bolting for the door. "Jesus Christ. I can't...I'm sorry. I need to get some air."

The door makes a quiet shush *as it closes behind him.*

Aimée sits back in her chair, rubbing nervously at the base of her throat. "We cannot continue this interview without two detectives present, Elodie. I'm sorry. But...you should know...you were not inside the box for nine hours. Today is Tuesday, my love."

I frown at that. That doesn't make any sense. "Tuesday?"

She nods.

"I was...in the box for...five days?"

Aimée looks away, covering her mouth with her hand.

Five days.

Pissing and shitting on myself.

Gagging on the smell of my own filth and the reek of my mother rotting on the other side of the room.

That thin straw poking through the hole in the box, providing my only supply of water.

The tiny pinpricks of daylight, blazing against the back of my eyes, and then the darkness creeping in. *Rinse and repeat. Did it all happen that many times? Did that many days really blur into one another? How could I, could* anyone, *survive something like that without losing their minds?*

But then again, have I kept mine?

Aimée leaves the room and comes back again almost immediately carrying a jacket. She places it on my shoulders, wrapping me up in it. "Come on. I know this will be hard, but I'll be with you, okay? I won't leave your side, I promise."

We aren't even out of the building when the military cops show up. In full uniform and armed to the teeth, a man I don't know with three stripes on his arm stops Aimée in the hallway, thrusting a piece of paper at her.

"The girl needs to come with us," he clips out.

Aimée's horror-stricken. Her eyes wide, mouth hanging open, she shakes her head, tucking me into the side of her body. As if she can protect me from what's about to happen. "This girl has been sexually assaulted and tortured, Sergeant. She's not going anywhere with you. I'm taking her to the hospital."

The sergeant side steps in front of her, blocking her way out of the building. "I'm afraid that's not possible, Detective Berger. This young lady is a minor and an American Citizen. And she was witness to an accident that took place in a building owned by the U.S. government, which is technically U.S. soil. Israel Police has no jurisdiction here."

"Accident? Her mother was murdered! And that building wasn't on your base. It was on Israeli soil! It doesn't matter who owns it."

"Take it up with your chief. We have our own way of doing things, Berger, and we have our own police. We've investigated the scene and deemed Mrs. Stillwater's death an accident, as a result of an unfortunate fall. You understand, Colonel Stillwater's a very well-respected man. There's no way he would have laid a finger on his wife."

Aimée's mouth works. She can't seem to find the words she's looking for. "Your precious Colonel Stillwater raped his own daughter! What kind of man does that?"

"Not the kind that commands thousands in the U.S. military, Detective Berger. I'd be very careful if I were you. Repeating slanderous accusations like that can have dire consequences."

The sergeant's hand closes around the top of my arm. He pulls me out of Aimée's grip. She reaches for me, grabbing, but it's no good. I was already far beyond her reach before these guys even showed up. She just didn't know it yet.

I don't know what happens next. The world begins to shrink in on itself, darkening around the edges. The next thing I know, I'm falling forward, legs collapsing beneath me, and the ground is rushing up to meet me.

34

ELODIE

I saw that police report once. It was very detailed. Incensed by the way the army handled my mother's death, Detective Aimée Berger petitioned the Israeli government to try and pursue the criminal case in-country, but the whole thing turned into a political nightmare. Her hands were tied, and so she could do nothing but sit by and watch as the military swept the entire thing under the rug. My father was exonerated of any wrongdoing, I never received that rape kit, and my mother was buried without ceremony in the back of a Jewish cemetery, even though she was Catholic, in a country that had never felt like a home to her. I wasn't allowed to attend the funeral, and my father sure as hell didn't go.

I do my best not to remember any of this. Remembering only makes things more difficult. But Wren's sitting next to me, holding my gaze with steady green eyes, and he has questions. I resent that he's dredging this up. Most of all, I hate that this whole time, the guy I'm insanely attracted to has known this horrible, dirty, dark, evil secret about me that no one in the world should know.

"I thought the army police had that report destroyed," I say. "They made sure to have all record of it expunged from the Tel Aviv police force's database. I know that for sure."

Wren nods, picking at his fingernails; he attacks the very last chip of black nail polish that he's been wearing since the first night I met him, finally taking care of it once and for all. "They kept a copy on their own system," he says.

"I see."

"I can't believe they sent you back there to live with that piece of shit," he says.

"Well. I was fourteen. And they'd decided he did nothing wrong, so where else were they going to send me?"

"What about your grandparents? Your mom's parents? Couldn't they have taken you?"

This is so futile. What good is trying to retroactively figure out a better alternative now, three years after the fact? It's all long done and dusted. "My grandfather was already dead. My grandmother had Alzheimer's. She never really understood that my mom had died. I went back to live with my father and that was all there was to it."

"It's just so..." He flares his nostrils, his hands curling into fists. He looks like he wants to hit something really fucking hard. "Did he ever touch you again?" he growls.

"No! No, god. No. It was only that once. He never did it again. I think he was high on something when...the day that happened."

"I've had bad trips before, and I've never raped anyone, Little E. I've never fucking killed anyone. And even if that were the case, he would have come down the next morning. What possible reason could he have had for keeping you in that fucking box for five days?"

Going back into those memories means going back into that box, and I just...I can't fucking do that. Slowly, I get up and move to the window. The sun's shining brightly outside, and everything is so green. The spring-like day contrasts so starkly with the grey, oppressive cloud that's descended over me that none of what I see on the other side of the glass feels real. "I don't know. We never spoke about it after that day. I knew that I'd wind up dead if I brought it up, and my father seemed content to pretend like nothing had even happened, so I just did what I needed to survive. He started training me into the ground after that. Every single day, he put me through the most *brutal* training. I couldn't understand it at first. But then I began to see the self-loathing in his eyes. He wanted me to be able to protect myself. From him. I think *he* always worried that...that he might do it again."

I suck in a gasping breath, but it doesn't help. I still feel dizzy, like I'm going to throw up. "Escaping Tel Aviv, being sent here to New Hampshire? I pretended to myself like it was an inconvenience and I resented being dragged away from my friends, but honestly...it was the best thing that ever happened to me. It might not be the healthiest coping mechanism in the world, but I want to forget that time of my life. All of it. Every single last day. So, please...I don't want to talk about it anymore. I can't. It won't help, and—"

His arms wrap around me from behind. He holds me tightly, nestling his face into the crook of my neck. "Shhh. Shhh, it's okay. It's okay. I'm sorry. Shhh, please don't cry."

I hadn't even realized that I was crying, but I am—desperate sobs punctuated with hiccuping gasps that echo around the hotel room. I used to lock myself in the bathroom at school during my lunch break and cry like this from time to time. I couldn't do it at home. Since he didn't have my mother to beat black and blue anymore, Colonel Stillwater had felt justified in laying into me during our morning gym sessions. Crying would have earned me the hiding of a lifetime.

"I'm sorry. I'm so fucking sorry," Wren chants into my hair. "I'm sorry I brought it up. I hate that I've made you feel this way, I swear to fucking god."

"Then...why bring it up at all?" I pant.

Wren sighs heavily, the sound pure frustration. He turns me around so that I'm facing him, holding my face in his hands. He makes me meet his fierce gaze. "You've been through so fucking much, and you've done it all on your own. I wanted you to know that you aren't on your own now. And I want you to know that it's been taken care of. You don't need to worry about him anymore, Elodie. He's never going to be able to hurt you again."

"You don't know that. You can't say that. I still have months before I'm free of him, Wren. *You* might already be eighteen, but I have to wait until June."

He shakes his head. "Calm down, E. It's okay. I swear to you. It's been taken care of."

There's a *tone* to his voice. He says, *'It's been taken care of,'* but he's saying something else as well. He's saying that he's done something, he's somehow taken care of my father, and he won't be able to hurt me again. A knot of panic rises in my throat. "Oh my god. What did you do, Wren?" I ask carefully.

"You knew I was a monster when you met me, Elodie. I've changed so much about myself for you because I want to be good *for you.* But there *are* parts of me that won't be denied, E. That bastard was a dead man walking the moment I knew how you felt. Once I saw my own feelings reflected in your eyes, I couldn't allow him to get away with what he did."

I...don't even know what to say. What to think. None of this is making any sense. "How I felt?"

Wren's mouth quirks up a little. "Yes. You know what I'm talking about, don't you?" He places my hand on his chest, right over his heart, laying his hand on top of mine. "I'm in love with you. And it'll be my fucking undoing if I'm wrong, but I think you're in love with me, too, Little E. Have I been deluding myself this entire time?"

I'm in love with you.

It's been taken care of.

I'm in love with you.

It's been taken care of.

I look up into his face—the savage, beautiful kind of face that poets have written about for millennia—and the terrible fear that's been crouched in the back corner of my mind since I was fourteen just disappears. "No. You haven't," I whisper. "I do love you."

He exhales, his head dropping, his chin hitting his chest, and I can feel his relief. "Thank fucking god."

"Wren? Did you kill my father?"

He looks up at me from under those dark, dark eyebrows, and my breath catches in my throat. "No, Little E. I didn't kill him. But I hurt him. I hurt him *real* fucking bad."

35

WREN

MARIPOSA USED to tell Mercy and me stories when we were kids. She'd tuck us up in our beds and settle herself on a chair in the corner of the bedroom we shared, and then she'd begin, whispering in a sinister, creepy voice that used to make my skin prickle with fear. Her goal wasn't to fill our heads with fantastical fairy-tales that would infiltrate our dreams. Hell no. She wanted to put the fear of God into us, and the tales she told of hideous monsters and disfigured creatures were her way of trying to control us.

The little boys and girls who fell foul of awful fates in her stories were always Bad Children. They didn't listen to their elders. They misbehaved. They were disrespectful, never did as they were told, and they were punished severely for it.

Mariposa had hoped that her tales of woe would teach us poor motherless twins a lesson and we'd fall in line. Unfortunately, her horror stories only taught me *one* lesson: that the best way not to fear a monster was to become one.

I'll tell Elodie anything she wants to know. If she wants every single little detail of what befell Colonel Stillwater the weekend I dragged Dashiell and Pax on a plane, halfway across the world to help me take down that motherfucker, then I'll sit down with her and go through it step by step. I don't think she wants that right now, though. I think she needs to process the fact that she's free, and this secret she's been keeping no longer needs to gnaw away at her soul. She can walk out of the darkness, into the light, and so help me God I'll be ready and waiting there for her when she does.

For now, the only question she asks is this: "If this happened weeks ago, why haven't they said anything? Why haven't they told me that he was attacked?"

I tell her what I know, trying not to sugarcoat the facts. "The first few days after he was dropped off at the hospital, they didn't know who he was. He had no ID on him, and his face was, ahh, swollen beyond all recognition. Then the military police made the connection and moved him to an army medical facility. Your father was conscious there long enough to insist that he didn't want you told what had happened. After that, he was placed into a medically induced coma so he could heal. My contact says he can't access any further information without raising red flags, so that's all I can tell you."

She nods woodenly, taking all of this in.

After what I've done, I expect her to recoil from me, but she doesn't.

We stay at the hotel until Sunday night, and I get far too used to Elodie falling asleep in my arms. It's the most terrifying, heavenly experience I've ever endured. I'm so fascinated by the sound of her slow, steady breathing that I hardly manage to sleep myself.

The drive back to Wolf Hall is silent. It's not an uncomfortable silence, though. It's peaceable and content, and Elodie leans her head on my shoulder, watching the world fly by out of the window, rubbing her hand up and down the inside of my thigh.

She gets closer and closer to my crotch, her movements becoming slower and more teasing, and I eventually have to pull off at the side of the road to adjust my raging hard-on.

"You're fucking trouble," I growl, giving her a loaded sideways look. "How's a guy supposed to concentrate on the road when a girl's millimeters away from rubbing his dick?"

I expect nothing of her. I haven't touched her since we spoke about what happened to her back in Tel Aviv. Not sexually, anyway. I've kissed her, and I've held her, but other than that I've been waiting for her to make the first move. She makes it now, parked next to a stand of Elm trees, by placing her hand directly on top of my cock and giving it a squeeze so hard it borders on painful.

"Fuck knows how you're gonna concentrate when I have your dick in my mouth, then," she says. *"Drive."*

I laugh. "You want us both to die?"

She bites the tip of her tongue as she pops open the button on my jeans and slowly, suggestively pulls down the fly. "I've seen how you drive. We'll be just fine. Just keep your eyes on the road, Jacobi."

I've had plenty of road-head in my time, but it's different with Elodie. That sweet, perfect little mouth of hers is so hesitant and gentle that it fucking kills me when she wraps her lips around me. And I don't want to kill us before we've had a chance at a proper life together, whatever that might look like. She slips her hand down the front of my boxers, her fingers fastening around my shaft, and she frees my erection. Her eyes go wide when she looks down at the swollen, glistening tip of my cock. "I'm not going to have to tell you twice, am I?" she asks.

She's fucking sassing me now? I like that. Still, I take hold of her wrist and stop her from going any further. "I'll make you a deal. You let me eat your pussy on the hood of this car and I'll let you do whatever the fuck you want to me when we get back to the academy."

She looks at me like I'm mad. "On the hood of the car? This car? Right now? At the side of the road?"

She's never going to agree to this. "Yes."

"Where anyone could drive past and see?"

"Yes."

"And we could get arrested?"

"Correct."

"Okay, fine." She fixes defiant blue eyes on me, daring me to fucking do it. She doesn't think I will. Boy oh boy, does she still have a lot to learn about me; when I say I'm gonna do something, I damn well do it.

"Sweet. Pants off. I want your naked ass on top of that paint-work in the next three seconds, or I'm gonna make you wish you'd kept your hands to yourself, Stillwater."

She balks, but only for a split second. Out of the car she gets. I follow behind her, poised to chase her around the car if she misbe-haves, but she hops herself up onto the Mustang's hood and leans back on her elbows, giving me a tempting, teasing look that makes my balls throb. God, I want to fuck her so badly.

"You're just gonna stand there?" she asks, her mouth quirking into a suggestive smile.

I tuck my hands into my pockets, shifting to rest my weight on one hip. "I'm waiting for those pants to come off. Don't mind me, though. You make for a very pleasing sight up there." Can she hear the ache in my voice? How far have I let myself fall? How bad is it gonna hurt when this girl finally realizes what a piece of shit I am, and she tosses my ass aside? And why do I keep experiencing these moments of panic out of the fucking blue, like I'm only a hair's breadth away from catastrophe?

I know the answers to the last question, though I pretend not to. Easier to pretend than to face that truth. That, up until now, I haven't made for a very good, honorable, or kind human being, and this new skin I find myself wearing now feels like a pretty suit that I stole. It doesn't belong to me, and at some point someone's going to want it back. It fits me, though. And I like fucking wearing it. I'm not gonna take it off without a fight.

The bright sound of her laughter makes me want to laugh, too. "I'm sure you've had plenty of girls sprawled out across the hood of this car," she muses.

I bite my lip, quickly shaking my head.

"What? *No?*" She laughs again, the sound peeling high over the tops of the trees that flank the road. "I don't believe it. I'm the very first?"

I move closer so that my shins are butting up against the fender, and I place my hands on the tops of her thighs. "This may be surprising to you, but you've scored a number of my firsts, Little E. First girl I've ever taken home. First girl I've ever called my girlfriend. First girl I've ever *loved*." This last admission's a hard one. It catches in the back of my throat, not wanting to come out. I say it shyly, unable to look her in the eye.

She sits up, delicate fingers stroking over my cheek, gently turning my face so that I'm looking at her. "Then we're in the same boat," she whispers. "I've never loved a guy before, either."

I catch hold of her, pressing my lips against the inside of her wrist. "First is a good start," I rumble. "But I plan on being the *only* guy you love, Little E. Period. For the rest of time."

"So greedy," she says, teasing her fingers through my hair. Her cheeks are glowing, though. I haven't seen her look this quietly pleased before, and it turns my insides into fucking Jello.

"So, so greedy," I agree. "What kind of fool would I be if I ever risked letting you slip between my fingers? I'm yours. I'll be your weak and pathetic plaything. You can use and abuse me how you see fit. I'll still be here, asking for more. Speaking of which." I lean forward and kiss her. I'm still getting used to how I feel whenever I do this: brimming over, too full, breathless and dazed. She sighs into my mouth as I lay her back onto the hood again. Her pupils are blown, the black swallowing the blue, as I work at the button on her jeans, unfastening them and dragging them quickly down her legs.

"Second thoughts? Change of heart?" I ask.

She shakes her head. "Get on with it, Jacobi. Don't you know how rude it is to keep a girl waiting?"

I pull her panties to one side, exposing her pussy. "Ouch. And you know how much I *hate* being rude."

She gasps when I sweep my tongue over her. It doesn't take long to have her panting and writhing on top of the mustang. Her toes curl and uncurl reflexively as I tease the shit out of her, using light, purposeful flicks with the very tip of my tongue to drive her crazy. She shakes and shivers underneath me so beautifully that it's almost enough to make me weep.

"Wren! Wren, oh my god. Fuck you. *Fuck you!*"

She knows my game. I want to keep her here like this, made vulnerable, trapped in a highly compromising position and seesawing on the edge of coming for as long as I can get away with it. I might not be the cold, callous, cruel prince of Riot House anymore, but I can still be a bastard when I want to be. I dig my fingers into her hips and the delicious plumpness of her ass, crushed against the car, and I bide my time.

"God... Please.... Please... Please... Wren! Let me come!"

Where would be the fun in that? Her whole body convulses as I laugh. She bucks her hips up, trying to earn herself more pressure from my mouth, but I lean back just far enough to frustrate her. "Mmm. *Now* who's being greedy?" Goddamnit, she's delicious. I can't get enough. I run the flat of my tongue up in a broad, torturously slow sweep, and poor little Elodie whimpers like she's getting desperate.

Not long to go now, though. I can hear the distant rumble of an engine coming up the road. Using the tips of my fingers, I prime her, dipping inside her pussy, enjoying the way she fists my hair and pulls on it juuuuust a little too much. My dick feels like it's about to explode, but I can wait.

"Please, Wren," she begs. "God, please. I need you. I—I want you inside me so fucking bad."

Closer. Louder. Whoever's coming up the road's almost upon us.

I thrust my fingers inside her, sucking the slick, tight knot of her clit into my mouth, rolling it with my tongue, and she fucking *screams*. My mouth floods with the sweet taste of her. I fuck her with my fingers, driving them up at an angle, finding that trigger that will make her see stars, and that's when the Winnebago roars past us.

The horn blares. Someone leans out of the window and yells something unintelligible, but I hold fast. Elodie bucks, startled, trying to cover herself, but I pin her by her hips, growling out a warning. "Finish it," I command. "Fuck my hand, Elodie. *Fuck it.*"

I move fast, climbing her body. I press the heel of my palm between her legs, right up against her clit, rubbing her, and I pump my fingers harder still...

Elodie's eyes roll back into her head. "Oh my *god.*" Her hips work. I stare down and watch, completely fucking mesmerized, as my Little E grinds her pussy against my hand, her back arching off the hood of the car as she comes.

I have never been this turned on in my entire fucking life.

She reaches down between her legs and presses my fingers deeper inside her, driving my hand down onto her. "Fuck! Wren! Holy *shhhhhhhh*—" Her legs pull up toward her stomach. She rolls onto her side, pressing her forehead into my shoulder, shaking violently as she tries to survive the nuclear bomb that's just gone off inside her head.

"Oh...my...*god,*" she pants. "Oh my *god.*"

I dip down, nuzzling past her hair so I can kiss her neck. It's here that I allow myself a smug as fuck smile, but only because she can't see me. "Shhh. It's okay." She lets out a plaintive cry when I draw my fingers out of her. She falls onto her back, her cheeks adorably flushed, and blinks up at the patch of blue sky above us like she's still in a daze.

"Those people in that Winnebago definitely saw us," she says.

I lay on my back beside her, resting my hands on my chest. "Yeah. They definitely did."

Laughing, she covers her face with her hands. "How did that even happen? *I* was the one who was trying to be bad with *you.*"

Ahhh, Christ. This girl right here. I turn my head to the side, biting playfully on her earlobe. "You should know by now, Little E. You can try and be bad. But I can *always* be worse."

Once she's wriggled her cute ass back into her jeans, we get on the road. She complains bitterly that I won't let her go down on me, but I know I'll plough straight into a fucking tree if I let her anywhere near me. I have to swear that we'll spend the rest of the night naked in my room back at Riot House in order to appease her.

We laugh and joke as I gun the engine, eager to get back. Everything feels so light and fucking *free*. That is, until we're thirty minutes outside of Mountain Lakes and I catch Elodie crying out of the corner of my eye. Fat, desolate tears course one after the other down her cheeks, and my heart seizes in my chest.

"Jesus, E. What the fuck? What—what did—did I *do* something? What's wrong?" I will literally *kill* myself if I've fucking hurt her already.

"What you—did—to my—father," she stutters, fighting for each word.

Fuuuuuuuck.

Everything sinks.

It was a risk, I knew that. I was prepared to deal with the consequences if she hated me for what I did. But the fear that wraps around my windpipe, choking me as I try not to veer off the road feels like it'll be the end of me.

"You flew across—the world—" she gasps. "On your —*birthday*—"

"Elodie. Fuck."

"And you hurt—a very dangerous man—because he—hurt *me*."

"I'm *so* fucking sorry."

She takes my right hand off the wheel, lifts my arm, and scoots into my side, hiding her face into my chest as she cries even harder. "Don't be sorry. It's the—most *romantic* thing in the—entire fucking world."

36

ELODIE

One Week Later

The invite's black, flocked with a plush velvet design that feels like sin beneath my fingertips. The gold scrollwork etched into the thick card is gorgeous. I hold it up to the light, wondering when he slipped this under my door. Wren made no mention of inviting me to the party. There's chatter all over the academy about it, but for some reason it hasn't even come up between us.

The residents of Riot House cordially invite Miss Elodie Stillwater to their fancy dress party, this Friday at their humble home. 8 pm. Prizes for most creative costumes.

No R.S.V.P. required.

I hide the flocked card underneath a book on my desk when I hear Carina wailing my name down the hall. "Elodie Stillwater, let me in immediately!"

I open the door, and there are dark circles under her eyes, which look puffy like she's been crying. She marches into my room and slumps onto my bed, groaning as she throws herself back against my pillows.

"Hey. Whoa, what's going on?" I clamber up onto the bed beside her, stroking her hair back out of her face. She screws her eyes shut, whimpering.

"Andre. He—we're through. He dumped me."

"What the fuck? What happened?"

"I don't know. Everything seemed to be going so well, and then yesterday he bailed on dinner. And then this afternoon I get this weird, vague ass text, telling me that he can't hang out anymore because his workload just tripled at college. Hang out anymore! Like we were just screwing around. He told me he was in love with me a week ago, Elle. How can a person fall in love and out of love in such a short space of time? That's a motherfucking record."

"That's so weird. He didn't seem like that kind of guy."

"I know! He *isn't* that kind of guy. Which is how I know Dashiell had something to do with this. I know it, Elodie. It's so like him, to interfere and meddle in other people's affairs. He can't stand anyone else being happy."

"Have you confronted him? Asked him if he said anything?"

"No." She sniffs. "It wouldn't help. He'd just deny it, anyway. That *asshole*! And all I wanna do is binge Netflix and eat pizza, but I have so much work to catch up on," she moans. "I'm gonna have to pull an all-nighter if I want to get my English and my Science projects completed for tomorrow."

"You want me to come work with you? I'm really good at the whole moral support thing."

She drags a pillow over her face, moaning again. "Please don't take this the wrong way, but I'm not the type of girl who wants to be around other people when she's hurting. I'm about to descend into a shame spiral of epic proportions. It's better if there are no witnesses." It's surprising how well I can understand her with the pillow covering her mouth. "If you come and hang out in my room, all I'm gonna do is cry and rage, and that won't be a fun time for either of us. And I really *have* got to get this work done."

I take hold of the corner of the pillow, attempting to tug it down so I can see her face, but she slaps a hand down on top of it, pinning it in place. "I came to see if you have any spare high-lighters. And Post-Its. And Valium."

"Yes, on the stationery. No, on the prescription meds, I'm afraid."

She groans even louder. The pillow gets thrown across the room. "Why does no one in this school have any good drugs? Fuck recreational use. You'd think at least half of us were medicated for our very *real* anxiety disorders."

I can guarantee that someone at Riot House has the kind of chemical relief she's looking for. No way in hell am I suggesting she go knocking on their door, though. "It's gonna be okay, babe. Andre's a fucking fool if he doesn't want to be with you. And you're gonna ace these assignments. You're a bad bitch. No doubt about it."

She wrinkles her nose, teetering on the verge of tears again. "You're a good friend, Stillwater. Hand over the highlighters before I lose the will to live."

I give her what she needs, and she goes. I close my bedroom door, knowing that she was wrong on so many levels. Hating myself for it. I'm keeping so many secrets from her now that I feel like a goddamn monster. And short of telling her that I'm in love with Wren Jacobi, nothing's going to change that.

* * *

WREN: You awake?

ME: Just about. You?

WREN: Nope. I text in my sleep. It's a problem.

ME: Funny.

WREN: You get the invite?

ME: Yeah. It was under my door when I came back to my room. You didn't feel like waiting for me?

WREN: Pax left it for you. I told him not to.

I stare at the message, the words stark and painful. *I told him not to.* Wren's been tight-lipped about the whole party, and I figured I was over analyzing the situation. He doesn't want me at the party, though? After everything we've been through of late, that doesn't make any sense. Even if we had to steal kisses in dark rooms, where no one would find us, I still would have thought he'd *want* me there. Something withers and dies inside me.

ME: Wow. Well, that stings.

WREN: I don't even wanna go to this thing, E. Believe me, it's gonna be a nightmare. I didn't want you to come because these things get fucking messy.

ME: What do you mean, messy?

WREN: We play these stupid games. I'd love to say I'm innocent, but I'm not. I used to enjoy fucking with people just as much as Dash and Pax. Sometimes things would get a little out of hand. We've hazed people pretty hard in the past. That's what they're expecting from me this time, too.

ME: From you, specifically? Just don't participate?

Eventually, he replies.

WREN: It's not that simple. I owe Dash and Pax a lot. I wasn't alone in Tel Aviv, remember? I've put them through hell in the past, and they know so many of my secrets. Things I haven't told you yet. Maybe we should meet...

Now it's my turn to tap out and erase my responses. I'm suddenly anxious. What kind of secrets can he possibly be talking about? And how bad can they be? My mind goes from naught to sixty in three seconds flat.

ME: Are you supposed to hook up with girls at this thing? Is that why you don't want me there?

Nothing but dead air.

I clutch my phone to my chest, struggling to breathe around the sharp pain that's stabbing me in the ribcage. What the hell kind of party *is* this? Eventually, my phone chimes.

WREN: Can you just meet me in the gazebo in an hour? It'd be easier to explain this in person.

ME: Okay.

My heartbeat's hovering somewhere around the one-thirties. I can't believe...fuck, I can't believe after all of the time we've spent together, and Wren telling me that he's in love with me, and all the promises we made to each other in that stupid fucking country inn, he's pulling this shit on me now. Horrifyingly, it feels like I'm about to get broken up with or something, and I don't think I can take hearing that right now. I get up from the bed where I was watching TV on my laptop, and I begin pacing the floorboards, back and forth, back and forth, back and—

I stop in front of the window, peering out into the darkness. There's already a light on out there in the maze—just the faintest glimmer shining through the boughs of the live oaks, but it's there. I see it plain as day. Which means Wren's already at the gazebo. So why, then, did he tell me to wait an hour to meet him? Jesus fucking Christ, I'm probably blowing this way out of proportion, but I'm not waiting a goddamn hour to find out what's going on if I don't have to. So help me, I'm going down there and I'm finding out what the hell is going on.

* * *

Unlike the first time I ventured into the maze, tonight the air is calm and still. It's even warm enough that I've come outside without a jacket. It's much brighter, too. The sky's clear and the moon is almost full; it casts so much light down onto the grounds of the academy that I'm able to navigate a path through the high walls of the maze without losing my way at all. My ears roar from the silence as I approach the gazebo. I've planned a litany of abuse that I'm gonna hurl at Wren if I find him sitting in here with his nose in a book. I haven't let myself consider what course of action I'll take if I find him in here with another girl. I know he wouldn't do that. I know it like I know the sun will rise in the morning, and the world will keep spinning on its axis. This awful feeling that keeps churning around in my stomach won't give me any peace, though.

Why didn't he answer the question I asked him in that text message? If he's not planning on messing around with other girls at this party, then why wouldn't he just say so?

I'm five feet away from the gazebo when I'm finally close enough to see inside. And it's not Wren inside, after all.

It's Dashiell.

And Carina.

Fuck!

I duck down, and the taste of copper floods my mouth; I've bitten my damn tongue. My eyes water around the pain, but I don't make a sound. Crouching down in the bed of rose bushes outside of the window, they can't see me from inside...but now I'm *stuck* here. It's a miracle they didn't see me marching toward the building. Even if I squat down low and scurry back towards the entrance of the maze, there's a very real chance that they'll spy me. I am well and truly screwed.

Voices float out of an open window into the still night air.

"You don't have any right!" It's Carina's voice, and it sounds like...ahh, shit, it sounds like she's crying. Fuck, this is the last thing I need—to get busted eavesdropping on this conversation. At least it sounds like she's giving him hell for messing in her relationship with Andre.

"You're right. And I'm sorry," Dashiell murmurs. The acoustics inside the gazebo must be ridiculously good. His voice is low and deep, but I can hear him perfectly. I have *really* gotta get out of here. "I just don't want any of this coming back to hurt us down the line, okay?"

Hah. Dick. He's got a funny way of showing her he cares. If he didn't want anything coming back to hurt him down the line, he shouldn't have arranged for Carina to walk in on him while he was getting his dick sucked by another girl. That would have been a great start.

"The cops *need* to know," Carina says. "This...what you're asking me to do. It isn't fair, Dashiell. There have got to be consequences. He can't just..." She's crying now. Crying hard enough that she's choking on her emotion. "He can't just be allowed to get away with it again. What if...what if he hurts someone else? What if he hurts Elodie?"

Everything stops.

My heart.

My brain.

All cognitive thought.

What the hell did she just say?

"He's dangerous, Dash. You know he is. We can't allow someone else to suffer because of him. Not because we're too chicken shit to speak up, for fuck's sake."

"Look, you have no idea what you're talking about. How can you know she wasn't high when she wrote that? She was out of her mind ninety percent of the fucking time. Mercy saw to that. Just throw it into the fire and let's just wash our hands of this whole thing."

"But Elodie—"

"I know she's your friend, Carrie, but I don't know the girl. If you care about her so much, then make sure she stays the hell away from him. Shouldn't be too hard. He'll forget all about her soon enough, and then you won't have to concern yourself with her safety anymore."

"How can you be so cold? How can you be so detached from this?"

I hear Dashiell sigh. "The only person I care about is you, Carina. I think I've made that abundantly clear. If you don't wanna hear that, then that's your business. I get it. I fucked up. We can deal with that another time, though. *Now give it to me.*"

What the hell does he want from her? And what the actual fuck are they talking about? I risk a peek over the top of the rose bushes, but all I can see is the tops of their heads. Carina's crying grows louder. "Fine. Here, *Lord Lovett*. You always get your way, don't you?" I've never heard such bitter hurt in her voice. Not even earlier, when she told me that Andre had dumped her via text.

"I have no idea why you're protecting him like this," she says. "He's not your friend. You know that, right? He might act like it, but he just uses people to get what he wants."

"Maybe you're right," Dashiell agrees. "But high school's nearly over, Carrie. We'll all be going off to follow our own paths in life. I'll probably never see him again. Until then, I have to see him all the fucking time, and I'm not risking him opening his mouth and blabbing to everyone about what went down that fucking night."

"Oh my god, what are you going to—" Carina's startled gasp cuts short. She whimpers, and the sound is so heartbroken and mournful that I want to run in there and comfort her. I can't, though. This exchange between them is most definitely private. And I'm worried that it also might be somewhat illegal. I'm so confused, but Carina mentioned my name, and—

The door to the gazebo flies open.

Carina races out into the night and I see that her face is streaked with tears. She wraps her arms around herself like she's doing her damnedest to keep herself together.

Thank god, mercy of mercies, she's facing away from me and doesn't see me scooting back into the bushes like a fucking criminal.

"Carina, wait!" Dash emerges from the gazebo, slamming the door closed behind him. He goes to my friend, placing a hand on her shoulder, turning her to face him. "We've all made mistakes, okay. Big ones. I don't think we should have to keep on paying for them like this."

She sniffs, wiping her nose with the back of her hand. "Are you talking about what *he* did? Or what *you* did to *me*?"

For a moment, Dash doesn't say anything. I think he's going to let her walk away without an answer from him, but then he stumps up the courage, looking up at the sky, and he nods. "Yeah. I'm talking about what I did to you. I hate it, okay. I hate that I hurt you. I let things spiral out of control and I took a wrong turn. I've regretted it every single day since then. When are you going to forgive me?"

Carina.

Poor Carina.

She blinks at him, her profile painted in silver by the moonlight. "When are *you* going to learn that your position in life doesn't automatically entitle you to a do-over whenever you fuck up?" She looks like the saddest person in the world as she walks away from him. That is until Dashiell's shoulders slump and his head drops, a weary, dejected sigh working free from his lips. Then, he claims that title for himself.

He goes, too, disappearing into the opening of the maze, leaving me alone, my thighs burning from my awkward, contorted position in the bushes. It hurts like a motherfucker when I stand, straightening out my legs one at a time.

What the *fuck* did I just witness?

They might as well have been talking in code; there was so much I didn't understand. I did gather quite a bit of information, though, and troubling information at that.

Something bad happened. Something that Carina and Dashiell were involved in. And Carina is worried about it happening to me, too.

A cold, dead fist closes around my heart.

I go into the gazebo, pins and needles prickling all over my body. It takes all of a second to see the book sitting on top of the burning logs in the fireplace, flames licking over its tan leather-bound cover. I singe my fingers pulling it out.

It's only when the book flips over, landing with a flat clap onto the floor in front of me, that I realize what it is.

It's Mara Bancroft's journal.

37

MARA

June 5th.

Words can't describe this feeling. If someone held a gun to my head and forced me to explain what's going on inside me right now, I'd tell them that I'm happy. And scared. Really, really fucking scared. Mom called and told me I shouldn't be getting involved with boys right now. She wants me to focus on my work, keep my head down and concentrate on my grades. Hah! Yeah, right. What the fuck does she know about real life? She's so caught up in her own shit that she doesn't have a clue what it's like to be here, trapped in this place, with nowhere to go and no one to talk to. Poe understands. Poe knows exactly what I'm going through. He's been here far longer than I have. He's the only one who listens. If I didn't have him, I don't know what I'd do.

Carina thinks I'm crazy for getting involved with him. She thinks he's too broken to feel anything at all, but I've experienced things with him she can't even begin to imagine. The closeness. The way he makes me feel when he tells me that he loves me. He's not who people think he is.

There are times, though. Times when he looks at me like he wants to pull my soul right out of my body. Those are the times that make me panic. He'll be at the party, of course. We have to pretend like there's nothing between us. He'll drink and have fun with those stupid fucking Riot House boys, and I'll have to fake it. Make out like he didn't meet me this morning in our secret place and fuck me senseless. I know he's troubled. I know he's not a safe bet and nothing good can come from this thing between us. But it's so hard to remember that when he's inside me, kissing my neck, whispering my name.

If Carina knew how sweet and gentle he was with me, she wouldn't say the stuff she does about him. She'd be on my side. She's my friend. She's supposed to be on my side. That's the most infuriating thing about this. You're supposed to be able to tell your friends anything.

I just hope he doesn't hurt me. Sometimes, when I'm lying in his arms, I feel like he might do something crazy. His mood swings can be frightening.

June 8th.

Bad day. I caught Poe looking at Damiana. He says he's not interested in her. That he'd never touch her, no matter what. But I know the look I saw in his eyes. He looks at me like that all the time. She was flirting with him after class. Such a fucking whore. She'd do anything to fuck him. To take something that belongs to me. If things were different, I wouldn't have to worry about this shit. One day, we'll be able to be open about how we feel and no one will stand in our way. I just have to be patient. If the guys at Riot House find out about us, there'll be hell to pay.

June 9th.

I can't do this anymore. I want to go home, but Mom's so fucking delusional. She thinks I'm overreacting, and I just need to distance myself from the situation. But how can I do that when he's always there? In the halls? In my fucking classes? Always looking at me, watching me like I'm something he wants to eat.

He hurt me today. I accused him of messing around with Damiana and he pinned me against the wall. He put his hand around my throat and for a second, I could see it in his eyes. He wanted to snap my neck. For a second, he dug his fingers into my skin, and I saw the violence inside of him. It was scary.

June 10th

I don't want to go to this stupid party. I know something horrible's going to happen. I can feel it in my bones. I wore the sweater to class today. The one Poe gave to me last night after I left him at the gazebo, and he flipped out when he saw me in it. He made me take it back to my room and hide it. I have no idea what's up with him, but this whole thing's starting to worry me. I'm going to go to the party, and then I'm going to leave. Otherwise...I know this is stupid, I'm stupid, but I'm worried that Poe might kill me.

38

ELODIE

I SIT amongst the charred pages of Mara's journal with my soul bleeding out all over the floor. This can't be fucking happening. There are so many pieces of evidence in Mara's journal that have clean taken my breath away. I'm too scared to acknowledge most of them.

Poe?

A hidden relationship, kept secret from the members of Riot House?

Carina's abject hatred for Mara's lover?

The connection with Damiana?

All of it...

I swipe the hot, angry tears from my cheeks, trying to make sense of everything I've just read.

Edgar Allan Poe is Wren's favorite poet.

How many times has Wren told me we can't tell Dashiell and Pax that we're together?

Carina despises Wren.

And he *did* screw Damiana. Carina told me all about it. He fucked her a month before I showed up at Wolf Hall. Does it make sense that he'd been interested in her for a long time, only to get bored of her once he'd had her?

Mercy already implied that Wren and Mara Bancroft were seeing each other. But they were fucking? And she was petrified of him? Scared that he was going to murder her. And then she just went missing out of the blue? What the hell am I supposed to make of all of this?

How could I have talked myself into forgetting about the girl who used to sleep in my bedroom? What the fuck was I thinking? Too desperate to keep the only real friend I've made here, not wanting to rock the boat, I let Carina take the journal. I believed her when she said she was going to turn it over to the cops, but she didn't. She fucking kept it because she's hiding something.

Many of the pages in Mara's diary are so burned they're impossible to read. The fire destroyed much of the first half of the book, so I'll never know what she wrote there. The flames left her final entries intact, though, and they paint a damning picture.

I haven't heard the door to the gazebo open. I haven't heard him come inside. I go very, very still at the sound of his voice. *"Elodie."*

What a disastrous mess I must look, sitting on the floor in front of the fire, loose pages covered in loopy blue ink scattered all over the place, the ends of my fingers black with soot. Wren stands over me, dressed in a white t-shirt and a pair of ratty blue jeans. This is the first time I've ever seen him dressed in anything other than black, and the sight of him in those clothes causes something to stiffen in my chest. He's never what I expect him to be. He always does something or says something to surprise me. I am officially taken aback by him now; I mean, is he who I thought he was at all?

Two tiny lines form between his brows as he bends down and picks up one of the pieces of paper at his feet. "What are you doing, Elodie?" He sounds wary. Unsure. As well he should.

"Tell me about Mara." My voice doesn't sound like my own. Or maybe it's just that my ears feel muffled and everything seems so very far away. "You were seeing her, weren't you?"

A strange, flat look forms on his face. He reads the journal entry on the paper in his hand, slowly shaking his head from left to right. It doesn't look like he's happy about what's written there.

"What is this?" he asks, holding up the page.

"Her diary. She wasn't very consistent about writing in it every day, but she managed to get most of the important stuff down. Why don't you tell me about her?"

"What's to tell? She was a student here. She went missing. It was all over the news."

"I was in Tel Aviv when she disappeared. I wasn't paying much attention to small-town New Hampshire news reports back then. Fuck, I didn't even know this place existed then. You didn't answer my question, Wren. You were seeing her, weren't you?"

His odd expression deepens. "I told you there were girls, Elodie. Before you. I'm not proud of how many girls I dated last year. I didn't think you were gonna crucify me for it, though. I went out with Mara once, but it didn't amount to anything. I'm sorry, this—" He shakes his head. "This isn't what you think it is."

"This isn't what I think it is?" A scathing burst of laughter rips up and out of my throat. "This isn't what I think it is. Right. What is it then, Wren? Just some shit a dumb party girl made up about you?" I fist a handful of the loose pages that have fallen out of Mara's journal, screwing them up in my fist. "This is some pretty fucked up shit, Wren. It reads like you hurt her. It reads like you're the reason why she went missing. Are you gonna tell me that you had nothing to do with that?"

The calm facade he's been maintaining up until now slips. "Are you seriously *asking* me that? Jesus Christ, E. *You think I killed Mara?*"

"There are too many coincidences here, little things that all tie back to you. Only an insane person wouldn't put two and two together."

"Elodie." He sucks his bottom lip into his mouth, his green eyes —eyes that have been soft for me lately—turn to ice-cold flint. "You have no clue what you're talking about. None at all."

"Then enlighten me, because I'm terrified right now. I'm starting to freak out over here because there's a strong chance that I might have fallen in love with a murderer."

His jaw hardens. He's clenching so tightly that I see the tension of it all the way up in his temples. "You really think that? You really think I'd do that?"

I look down at all of Mara's journal entries, strewn around on the floor like forgotten pieces of the past, cries for help, and I don't know what to think anymore. "I don't...know."

In the split second it takes me to look back up at him, Wren turns his back, and he leaves. Panic whips around inside me like a cyclone as I hurry back to my room. My heart won't stop thundering away. Once I've closed the door and I'm sure I'm alone, I hurry over to the windowsill and I pull up the piece of wood that conceals Mara's secret hidey hole. The day Mercy unveiled this spot and I pulled Mara's journal out of it Carina didn't see the black box inside with the cherry blossoms painted on it. Or the bundled sweater. My hands shake like crazy as I reach down and take out both items, laying them down on the end of my bed.

I inspect the sweater first. It's a Wolf Hall Academy sweater, navy blue with gold lettering across the front. I've seen plenty of students wearing them in the halls. It's only when I look inside the sweater and see the two small letters inked into the label that my heart officially shatters.

W. J.

Wren Jacobi.

I'm frozen all the way down to my core when I open up the black lacquered box and I pull out a handful of black feathers.

ELODIE

I MAKE it through the next day somehow. I respond to Carina when she speaks to me, but all I see in the back of my mind is her standing with Dashiell outside the gazebo, holding her cardigan tight around her body, talking about whatever happened to Mara, and her worry that it might happen to me, too. She mopes and she complains about Andre, and I make all of the appropriate noises. I pretend as though I'm listening, and I stumble from one class to the next, wondering what the fuck I'm supposed to do now.

I'm destroyed.

I don't see Wren. I don't see any of the Riot House boys. All three of them are notably missing from Wolf Hall, though no one seems to notice their absence. They're preparing for the party tonight, I'm sure. Though why none of the faculty have made any sort of comment about their truancy is a goddamn mystery.

I'm in my French class, the last lesson of the day when Dean Harcourt comes to find me. She's wearing a look of grim determination on her face as she walks me down the hallway to her office. When she's situated behind her desk and I've sat myself down opposite her, she clears her throat and gives me the news I've been waiting to hear ever since Wren told me about his trip to Tel Aviv.

"Elodie, I'm afraid I have some bad news. It would seem that…" She doesn't know where to look. "Your father was involved in some kind of accident, Elodie. He was out at a bar in Tel Aviv, and three men jumped him. They assaulted him in an alley and beat him pretty severely. I know this must come as a shock to you, but it seems as though he was paralyzed during the attack."

I stare straight through her.

"Now, it was a shock to me too that this happened so long ago. Usually, we're immediately apprised if something happens to a student's family members, but for some reason the military decided not to inform us of this uh, *incident,* until this afternoon. It seems that your father's injuries were complicated due to a stroke he suffered two days after being admitted to the hospital. He's still alive, breathing on his own, but I'm afraid he's unresponsive to external stimuli. The doctors are working with him daily, but they're saying that he's entered some kind of fugue state. He's fully awake, but…this might be hard to hear, so I apologize, but…he seems to be trapped inside his own mind. Are you okay, Elodie? Do you understand what I'm telling you?"

I make eye contact, gripping the strap of my bag, wringing the material in my hands. "Yes, I hear you. I understand."

"It's only natural that you'd want to go and be with him, Elodie. I can see just how traumatized you are by this news. But he's currently being cared for at an army facility, and they've said that because you're a minor, there's no way you can go back to Tel Aviv by yourself. Your father signed guardianship over to us here at the school while you're studying with us, so I'm afraid you're going to have to stay here until Colonel Stillwater recovers well enough to leave the hospital. I know that's probably the last thing you want to hear, but I'm asking for your help with this. I sincerely hope you won't cause trouble because you can't—"

"It's okay. I understand. I'll abide by the rules. I'm not going to cause any trouble."

Harcourt looks relieved. She likely thought I was going to burn the whole fucking school down in my attempt to get to my poor, catatonic, paralyzed father. If only she knew the truth. "Well, thank you, Elodie. I don't know if you're religious at all, but I like to lean on Jesus during times like this. If you pray to him for your father's recovery, then who knows? Maybe he'll be his normal self again before you know it."

"I believe in science, Dean Harcourt. I'd rather know what the doctors are saying, please. Specifically, how soon he'll be back on his feet?"

The dean's mouth hangs slack, revealing front teeth smudged with her mulberry-colored lipstick. "I'm afraid...that is to say, the doctors think that it's unlikely your father will recover fully, Elodie. It's unlikely he'll ever walk again. And if he'll come out of this fugue state remains to be seen. That's why I mentioned prayer. It is a powerful healing tool, you see. I'm afraid that without it—"

She rambles on, but I've already stopped listening.

How many times did she say that she was afraid?

I'm afraid I have some bad news.

I'm afraid he's unresponsive...

I'm afraid you're going to have to stay here...

Such a weird term for her to use. She wasn't afraid. She was inconvenienced, and she was concerned, and she's eager to get this matter hashed out quickly to avoid it taking up any more of her time.

I, on the other hand, have been afraid for a very long time. This news changes all of that. It's looking like I won't have to be afraid of my father ever again. And that's all thanks to Wren. I've floated through the day, so numb and detached from my surroundings, that I haven't taken a beat to analyze whether I'm afraid of *him* now.

Worryingly...I don't think that I am.

ELODIE

WHEN I HEAD BACK to my room, my bedroom door's wide open. And there, sitting at the end of my bed, is Mercy Jacobi. She looks so out of place perched on top of my dusky pink comforter, but she seems to have made herself perfectly at home. She beams like a Cheshire cat when she sees me in the doorway.

"Before you start, I didn't touch anything," she says, holding out her hands in a placating gesture. "I just wanted to drop off your costume for tonight."

I scowl at her; it seems like the safest thing to do. "Costume? I don't have a costume."

"Wren bought one for you, silly." She jerks her head in the direction of a black and gold garment bag hanging from the back of my closet door. "I was at the house earlier, dropping off some booze and ice, and I saw my darling big brother punch a hole right through his bedroom wall with his bare hands. Seems he's quite upset. Wouldn't happen to know anything about that, would you?"

God, she *is* good at this—all of the pretending. I suspect that she knows all about me and Wren and yet she's still feigning ignorance. "I have no idea what's up with him. Who *ever* knows what's up with Wren. He's permanently pissed," I say.

Mercy's smile is faker than her perfect white teeth. "Ahh. Shame. Nothing makes me sadder than trouble in paradise. Fair enough, though. You both want to be broody and miserable, that's entirely up to you. I'll leave you to try on your costume in peace."

"I don't need the costume, Mercy. I'm not going to the party."

"Oh, no. You have to! Everyone's going. You want to be the only person on your entire floor, sitting in your room like a sad sack, while everyone else has an amazing time?"

"Carina isn't going," I say defiantly.

Mercy smirks as she gets up and waltzes out into the hallway. "Sure about that, Stillwater? Carina's all talk most of the time. I'd put good money on her attending this evening's festivities."

"I'm not in the mood, Mercy. Can you please take the garment bag out of my room? If Wren wanted me to have it, he would have given it to me himself."

"He's probably worried that if he gets within five feet of you, you'll freak out and accuse him of trying to murder you," she says, with a feline smirk on her face.

Fuck.

So, she does know about what happened at the gazebo. I highly doubt that Wren told her, but who the fuck knows? I've been wrong plenty of times before. Like, a ridiculous amount of times. Wren could have told Dashiell, who then told Mercy? What does it fucking matter how she knows? She just does.

"Invite said eight but I recommend coming at around nine or so," she says. "Helps to make an entrance when you're fighting with a guy like my brother. And holy shit, are you gonna make an entrance wearing *that* costume."

* * *

I'm on edge as I unzip the bag, letting it fall to the ground. My heightened state of anxiety triples when I see what's inside it. This isn't some drug store twenty-dollar costume. It isn't even the kind of expensive costume you have to order online. This is the kind of costume you have made from scratch, to a list of specifications that you send to a dressmaker weeks ahead of an event.

It's beautiful.

The bodice is frost-white and shimmering with Swarovski Crystals. There's boning sewn into the luxurious fabric, as well as laces around the back, which look daunting as hell. I've never in my life worn anything so convoluted.

The skirt is made of a diaphanous, silky type of fabric, layers and layers of it in blue and silver and white, so fine and stunning that I can't help but run my fingers over it.

This is the most gorgeous piece of clothing I've ever seen in my life. I recognize it for what it is immediately: it's a Tinkerbell costume. I mentioned to Wren when we were verbally sparring in the attic that I always wanted to be Tinkerbell when I was a kid, but we didn't always get what we wanted…and he remembered? It was such a flippant, off-the-cuff remark. I can't believe he stored the information and then ordered this.

It's too beautiful.

It's too much.

All of it is too fucking much.

I've pieced together a really suspicious-looking picture of Wren's life last year and it's so frightening and awful that I can't bear it. I'm still in love with him, and I can't make myself stop. A wickedly sharp knife plunges into my heart, grinding up against my ribs, stealing away my breath as I sink to my knees, clutching the beautiful fairy costume to my chest.

This isn't fair.

I knew falling in love with someone like Wren was dangerous, but fuck. I didn't expect I'd wind up sobbing into the most expensive item of clothing I've ever held in my hands, worrying that he might have *murdered* another girl. The girl who used to sleep in *my* bedroom. God, the symmetry of it all is just too fucking terrible to even think about.

I lie on my back on my bedroom floor, crying at first, but I eventually end up just staring at the light fitting above my head, trying to make the high-pitched buzzing in my head quiet. It doesn't go away, though. It drones on and on, until I feel like I'm going to go mad from the incessant sound.

And then I snap.

I have to know the fucking truth.

I *deserve* to know.

I don't care how stupid it makes me. I'm going to that fucking party, and I'm going to get to the bottom of this once and for all.

But there's something I have to do first.

Stiff from lying on the floor so long, my back complains as I sit up and open the bottom drawer of my vanity. There, tucked in between my folded shirts, is the small white box that Carina left propped against my door five days ago. I glare down at the beautiful raven-haired woman on the front of the box, wondering if I'll be able to fake a smile as big as hers when I walk through the front door of Riot House.

I highly fucking doubt it.

41

ELODIE

THE DRESS FITS LIKE A GLOVE. Even when someone has your specific measurements, it's rare to find a dress that fits this well. It took a lot of effort to get into and required Pres's help to lace up properly at the back, but once I have it all done up, even I have to admit that it looks amazing. *I* look amazing. Aside from the dress, it feels as though I'm looking at *myself* for the first time in three years when I stand in front of the mirror in my room and observe my reflection.

"I like it. I think I like it," Pres says, standing back, tapping her index finger against her jaw. She's wearing a Beetlejuice costume made out of black and white stripy pajamas, a lot of black eyeshadow, and an Albert Einstein wig. "It was just a shock at first. I'm just used to you as a blonde. Y'know, it's weird, but dark hair suits you better now that I'm seeing it."

I dyed my hair back to my natural color in my bedroom, only briefly ducking into the bathroom to rinse it clean when the timer on my cell phone dinged. Being a brunette again feels like coming home. I've reclaimed a small part of myself that was taken away from me. Like this, I am the person I was supposed to be all along and not the stranger that my father tried to create.

"Yeah. I think it suits me better, too." I turn away from the mirror, collecting my invite to the party from the bed.

"Wanna walk down with me?" Pres asks. "I was running late. I told the others to go on ahead without me."

"Sure."

So, Pres and I walk down the hill to the party together in the dark. The driving, pounding music flooding the forests around Riot House indicate that the celebrations are already well underway by the time we reach the turn-off that leads to Wren's house. There's no need to knock on the front door; it's already yawning open into the night like some great, toothless mouth, leading straight down into the pits of hell.

Inside, rainbows follow me from room to room, dancing all over the walls; the Swarovski crystals on the dress catch and reflect the light, scattering bursts of color in every direction as Pres pulls me through the crowded entryway. Every single student at Wolf Hall looks like they're here, dressed in all kinds of weird and wonderful costumes. I curse myself for being so short as I strain to see over the tops of people's heads. I quickly come to the realization that it just isn't going to happen, so I focus on making sure I don't get stepped on, as people jump around, dancing to the blaring music. I see Rashida sitting by the fire, talking to a guy I don't recognize. She frowns when she sees me, squinting, then she finally recognizes me and waves, pointing at her hair, giving me a thumbs up.

I've never been in the kitchen before. It's huge, of course, with a giant marble island in its center, overcrowded with bottles of liquor and bowls full of food. Not the chips and salsa kind of food you'd expect at most house parties. No, there are crab cakes and vol-au-vents, deviled eggs and fancy-looking pastries. Has to be Dashiell's handiwork; I know for a fact that Wren wouldn't have ordered that shit, and I don't think vol-au-vents are Pax's M.O. either.

"You want a drink? I'm gonna grab a beer," Pres shouts over her shoulder.

I give her a bland nod. A moment later, I have a bottle of Corona in my hand, the glass cold and slick with condensation, and I'm being dragged further into the melee. It isn't long before Pres clutches my hand, squealing. "There he is! Oh my god, I wish I'd worn something sexy. What the fuck is wrong with me?"

Across the room, Pax stands at the bottom of the stairs, laughing raucously at something a girl in a skintight black cat suit has just said. She's wearing little black ears, and has whiskers drawn onto her cheeks, her cute button nose painted black. "God damn it. Fucking Beetlejuice?" Pres moans, pulling at her black and white pajama pants. "Seriously. I am such a fucking idiot."

"You're better off steering clear of that one anyway," I mumble into my beer.

"God, don't you start," she gripes. "You're beginning to sound just like Carina. Oh hey, look! There she is! *Carina!*"

No fucking way. No *way* Pres has just spotted Carina. But when I look over to the far side of the room, my friend's standing by one of Wren's paintings, dressed in a purple tutu and a frilly bodice with a tiny little top hat balanced on her head. There are playing cards tucked into the ribbon on the hat, and bright green feathers.

"Wow. Her costume's fucking cool. She's the mad hatter. Come on, let's go say hey."

I tug my hand out of Pres's grip, taking a step back. "No, I—"

Too late.

Carina looks up and sees me, and her face turns the color of ash. Worse still, the guy she was talking to turns around, and low and behold...

It's Wren.

He isn't in costume. He's wearing his usual black uniform— black t-shirt and worn black jeans. Absolutely zero effort on his part to join in on the costume competition, then. His eyes widen when he sees me, standing next to Presley. He breaks away from the conversation he was having with Carina, entering the crowd, pushing his way toward me. Blind panic scrambles my brain. "Uh, excuse me. I need to find a restroom."

"Elodie, wait and I'll come with you!" Pres shouts after me. I'm not listening to her, though, and I'm sure as fuck not waiting. I feel like I'm stuck on a merry-go-round as I bully my way through the press of bodies. My heart won't stop slamming. It takes forever to find a bathroom on the first floor, but thankfully when I do there isn't a line. I dive inside and lock the door behind me, leaning up against the wood, trying to catch my breath.

Ten seconds later, there's a knock on the door. "Elodie. It's me. Let me in."

Of course he was going to find me. I had hoped it might take him longer than this, though. I need some time to think. I prepared a slew of questions I was going to ask him but I'm groping at thin air now. The only thing chasing through my head is disbelief. Carina came to the fucking party. She swore she wasn't going to, and yet there she was, dressed up to the nines, having what looked like a very friendly conversation with the guy currently rapping on the bathroom door.

"Go away, Wren."

"Not happening. Let me in. I need to talk to you."

"Just give me a minute!"

"Elodie, this is fucking stupid. Open the door."

"Go back to the party, Wren. I'll come and find you when I'm ready."

God, please just go away. Please just go away. Please just go away.

Silence, on the other side of the door. Blowing out a shaky breath, I step toward the mirror, studying my reflection in its surface. Who was I kidding, coming here? Thinking I could just waltz right up to him and demand answers? My heart just about shattered into a million pieces when I set eyes on him, for crying out loud, and now I'm—

The door to the restroom opens quickly, and Wren hurries inside, closing it behind him. I stare at him, mouth hanging open, unable to form words.

"I'm sorry I did that." He winces, rubbing his hand over the back of his neck. He sheepishly holds up a quarter in his other hand. "You don't need to be a master lockpicker to open up those locks. Just a coin."

"You shouldn't be in here," I hiss. "What if I'd been using the fucking toilet?"

"You came in here to hide from me, Little E. It was pretty obvious."

I want to hit him hard enough to make his teeth rattle. But the expression on his face is so tortured that I stop dead in my tracks. There are dark shadows beneath his eyes, his skin extra pale, his hair extra wild. He looks like he's about to come unhinged. "Elodie, I just want to talk to you. Can you stay calm for fifteen fucking minutes?"

"You had every opportunity to talk to me in the gazebo, Wren. You chose to walk away. Do you know how suspicious that looks?"

"Yeah, well, you'd just accused me of something pretty insane, and I didn't want to say anything that might..." He blows out a frustrated breath.

"*Implicate you?*" I finish for him.

"No! Jesus Christ, Elodie, come on. I did not have anything to do with Mara's disappearance. I didn't fucking touch her, okay?"

"Then how do you explain the diary? Everything she wrote in it pointed to you. And the sweater she had in her hiding place? She had handfuls of feathers in a box, too. Feathers exactly like the one you gave to me."

Wren grimaces, running his hands back through his hair. "What sweater?"

"The Wolf Hall sweater, with your initials on the label, Wren. God!"

He shakes his head. "I—I don't know how she had that. I owned one of those things for five seconds last year, and then it was gone. I didn't know what the fuck happened to it. And the feathers... fuck, I don't know what to tell you, Elodie. She knew I collected them. Maybe she was saving them for me. I swear I didn't leave her a single one, though, let alone handfuls of them. There's so much you don't know, okay? About Mara and what went on at the academy last year. I promise I'll tell you. I'll explain every single last sordid detail. But until we can sit down and talk about this properly, please, just…you have to believe me. I did not hurt her."

He looks so wretched. My stomach turns over, nausea rolling through me in a wave. "How the hell am I supposed to believe a single thing you say? How am I going to listen to this story you've been keeping from me and accept that it's the truth?"

A flat, distant look flashes over his handsome face. "Because I told you, Little E. No lies. Ever. I *swore* I'd never lie to you."

My throat constricts. I'm achingly miserable. I want to believe him. I want nothing more than to hear what he's saying and trust him. But—

"WREN JACOBI! Where the fuck are you!"

A roar goes up out in the living room—a riotous yell that could only have come from Pax. Other voices begin shouting and cheering, growing louder and louder on the other side of the door.

What the hell is going on?

Wren presses his fingers into his eyes, huffing. "For fuck's sake. I have to go, Elodie. If I don't get out there, they're gonna break down this door—"

"WREEEEEEEENNNNN! You've got three seconds, asshole! Show your ugly face!"

Those vivid green eyes meet mine, pleading and full of misery… "Just don't leave, Little E. Promise that you'll hear me out?"

Lord, what a fool I am. I waver, but only for a second. "Fine. I'll hear what you have to say. But the moment I think you're lying to me, that's it. I'm walking away."

He looks so relieved. It almost hurts me to see that kind of desperate expression on his face. He nods, grimacing deeply. "Good." Turning, he lets himself out of the bathroom and walks straight into the chaos on the other side of the door. It's madness out there, Wolf Hall students all jostling and shoving at one another, trying to get by one another. I can't figure out where they're all going until I slip out of the restroom and stand against the wall by the front door, watching as they all flock to the foot of the staircase.

Pax and Dashiell are already standing there on the steps. Wren climbs up to meet them, dragging his feet, wearing an expression so dark and stormy that he looks every inch a monster. Pax is dressed as Alex from A Clockwork Orange. Meanwhile, Dashiell's dressed much like Wren, as himself, in his regular clothes—an expensive black shirt and immaculate grey pants that look like they cost a fortune. Both Pax and Dash cheer, slapping Wren on the shoulder and back as he turns to face the crowd.

"Students of Wolf Hall! The moment you've all been waiting for has arrived!" Dash calls out.

Pax follows right after him. "Ladies and gentlemen, may we present to you, *the master of the hunt!*"

A deafening furor breaks out as everyone in the foyer loses their goddamn minds.

42

ELODIE

I DON'T CHEER. I stand stiff as a statue, watching the insanity around me with stunned detachment. Fifteen feet to my right, Carina emerges from the living room, biting on her fingernails. She doesn't seem as excited by what's going on at the stairs like everyone else. She's focused entirely on me.

"Elodie, can I speak to you outside for a moment?" she asks.

I look her up and down, recalling the way she'd sneered at Mercy when she'd told her that she wasn't coming to this party. She's lied to me more than once now, and I do not fucking like it. "*No.*"

"Elle, please—" She tries to take me by the hand, but I pull away.

Up on the stairs, Wren starts to speak. "You all know the deal. As master of the hunt, I call the shots tonight. And as always, we have a Riot House game that will either elevate your social standing for the rest of the academic year or leave you all in the gutter. Your fate rests entirely in your hands!" He sees me by the door and flinches. "Tonight's game has been crafted to root out the smartest amongst you. In the forest surrounding Riot House, there are a series of red flags like this one." He pulls a length of red material out of his back pocket, holding it up in the air. "There are a hundred of them hidden within a two-mile radius. Collect as many of them as you can and bring them back here to base. The person who manages to bring back the most flags wins a room in Riot House for the remainder of the school year, along with a fifty-thousand-dollar check with their name on it."

A surprised gasp goes up amongst the crowd. The most surprising thing is the look on Dashiell and Pax's faces. This was clearly *not* the prize they were expecting Wren to announce.

"The person who collects the fewest flags, however..."

A hush descends over the gathered flock of students.

"...will become a Riot House shit-kicker until graduation. You'll cook for us. You'll clean for us. You'll be the lowest of the low. The choice is yours. Live here, unchecked, unbound by pointless, stupid rules, or become our whipping boy. You don't have to play, but if you do...*there will be consequences.*"

"Well that's new," Carina breathes beside me. "Last year..." She trails off, looking uncomfortably down at her hands.

"Last year what, Carina? What was the game last year?"

She won't meet my eye. Not that I expected her to. Her cheeks color bright red. "Last year, everyone had to fuck as many people as they could before the end of the party. These things always involve sex. This is the first time..."

She doesn't get to finish her statement. I turn my back on her, disgusted by the implications of what she's already told me, sick to my stomach and not wanting to hear the rest of it.

"You have until three a.m.," Wren shouts over the renewed hubbub of noise. "Until then, happy hunting. And be warned. There will be *wolves* out tonight, hunting down *their* prey."

Pax's eyes flash murder. Dashiell's face is unreadable. I don't care about either of them, though. I only care about Wren, as he stoops down and picks something up from the step in front of him. The wolf's mask is hideous—a contorted, snarling beast's head that looks like something out of a nightmare. He slowly lowers it down over his face, and blood drips from the creature's exposed teeth.

Carina makes a strangled sound. "God. Looks like I was wrong."

"Wrong about what?"

She glares at Dashiell as he picks up a mask and places it over his head. "When a Riot House boy talks about hunting down prey, Elodie, they're most definitely talking about sex."

43

WREN

"JUST WHAT THE *fuck* do you think you're doing?"

My back hits the wall before I get a chance to respond. Pax is in my face, glowering with open rage. "You don't get to invite people to live here without clearing it with us. What the hell, Jacobi? Where the fuck is this person supposed to sleep?"

I laugh, because his anger just looks plain stupid on him with his bowler hat cocked at such a jaunty angle. "They can have my room for all I fucking care. I'll go sleep in the back room at Cosgroves'. No big deal."

"You are *not* moving out," Dashiell hisses from the other side of the room we use to play Call of Duty. I was dragged up here by the collar of my shirt the moment people started filing out of the house to begin the hunt. "What the hell's gotten into you, man? You're not the guy we started this thing with. Frankly, I don't recognize you anymore. If you hadn't thrown in that last clause with the wolf masks, there was gonna be fucking hell to pay."

God, he's so fucking predictable. A Riot House party isn't a proper party unless there's a whole fuck-load of anonymous sex. "I wasn't going to add that part." I shove Pax away. "But I knew you'd both feel cheated if you didn't get your dicks wet."

"We're *all* gonna get laid tonight, Jacobi," Pax spits. "You, included."

Laughter bubbles up the back of my throat again. "What, are you gonna *make* me fuck a conga line of girls? Seriously?"

Pax wheels on Dash, throwing his hands in the air. "God-damnit, you deal with him. I've had enough."

Dashiell doesn't say anything. He stands with his hands in his pockets, watching me quietly for a second. Then he says, "This is about Elodie, isn't it?"

I stare back at him defiantly. "Yes. Of course it's about Elodie. Who else would it be about?"

"You're in love with her."

"Yes."

"*God save us!*" Pax roars. "You are not in love with that girl, Wren. She's fucking nothing. She's just some little French who—"

Pain rockets up my arm, screaming in my shoulder joint. Pax hits the ground ass-first, sliding across the floorboards. In half a second flat, I'm on top of him, grabbing him by the throat, winding up to hit him again. I'm deadly calm. "Say it. Go on say it. Finish that fucking sentence."

Pax throws me off him, scooting out of my reach as he scrambles to his feet. "This has gone far enough. We agreed. No girlfriends. Ever. Is that what you think she is, Wren? Because you know neither of us are gonna stand for it."

I look to Dashiell, waiting for him to back up Pax's threat. He remains noticeably silent.

I am so fucking done with this. Riot House used to be a sanctuary for me, back when Dash, Pax and I became friends, but it's been nothing more than a prison these past few months. "Yeah. Elodie's my girlfriend. There. I fucking said it. And you two can either accept it with good grace and move the fuck on, or you can find yourselves rooms at the academy post haste. Act accordingly."

I go to leave, but Dashiell grabs me by the arm. "You think it's so easy to sever this friendship, Wren? It's not. There's a fucking army colonel in a coma on the other side of the world right now, because we agreed to do something that could get us all put away for the rest of our natural lives. If not executed in a fucking firing squad."

"Is that supposed to be some sort of threat, Lord Lovett? Because I've done plenty for you that would result in the same outcome and then some."

"And what about Mara?" Pax adds.

"I DON'T GIVE A SHIT ABOUT MARA!" My vision's blood-red. I swear to god, I'm gonna lose all self-control in a minute. I take a breath, reining in my fury. "Mara is not my problem. I didn't hurt her. I did nothing to her. She's long gone and there's nothing any of us can do about it. So stop bringing her up."

I'm out of the door and down the first flight of stairs when Pax calls after me. "You'd better hope that girl of yours doesn't go out into the forest tonight, Jacobi. You know the rules. If she does, she's fair fucking game!"

He's looking for a reaction. I don't give him one.

He won't fucking *touch* Elodie.

I jog down the stairs with my stupid wolf's mask hanging from my hand, dreading the kind of trouble the rest of this night may bring.

44

ELODIE

THE NIGHT AIR is cool and crisp. The trees rustle, whispering amongst themselves as I skirt along the edge of the forest, walking up the road back toward Wolf Hall. I lasted all of fifteen minutes at a Riot House party and now I need a shower. I feel dirty. I feel tricked and deceived, and I want my mother, but I can't have her because she's fucking dead.

"I can keep up with you, y'know," Carina mutters behind me. "Doesn't matter how fast you walk. I'm not going anywhere."

"I really wish you would."

"Elodie, come on, now. Please. You're not being very fair."

"FAIR?" I whip around, ready to take her head off. "You don't get to pull the 'you're not being very fair' card on me, Carina Mendoza. I thought you were my friend, and you've been hiding things and keeping secrets from me this entire time. You swore you were gonna take that journal to the cops. You didn't even tell me anything about Mara in the first place. You said you weren't gonna come here tonight. And, surprise surprise, what did you do?"

"You didn't tell me you were seeing Wren," she counters, her eyes hard as flint.

"Yeah. I know that was shitty, but I didn't feel like I *could* tell you. There was no reason for you to keep me in the dark about Mara, though, was there?"

A loud whoop echoes amongst the trees, the sound half animal, half human. Both of us stop, peering into the pitch darkness, and the hairs prickle across the back of my neck. "Why would anyone run out there into the forest with no fucking lights," I mutter. "It doesn't make any sense."

Carina sighs. "Cabin fever's a very real thing, Elle. You've only been at the academy for a couple of months but try living here for a few years. You start to go a little stir crazy. You don't get it. If you're a student at Wolf Hall, the guys from Riot House are a big deal. They set the tone for the entire year. If you're a guy, you wanna be them. If you're a girl, you wanna date them. That's the way it's always been. So when they pull stupid shit like this, everyone's always tripping over themselves to join in."

"Is that what happened the night Mara disappeared? She was trying to join in whatever dumb game they were playing?"

Carina nods. "Yes."

"So what? I'm supposed to just traipse right on in there and make a fool of myself like everyone else? Is that what they expect?"

"Pax and Dashiell, probably. Not Wren. I was talking to him before you showed up and he wanted you as far away from this thing as possible, Elle. It's good that you're going back to the academy, okay?"

Huh. Yeah, that's right. Wren didn't want me at the party. He wanted me as far away from this thing as humanly possible. Well, Wren's going to have to learn that he isn't always going to get what he wants with me. I set my jaw. "You know what, Carina? Maybe I will just join in this stupid game. That way there won't be any more secrets. I'll know if he sleeps with half the academy. I'll know exactly what went on, and no one will be able to hide anything from me anymore!"

"Elodie! What the hell are you doi—wait! Elle, you can't *see* anything!"

I've already stepped off the road, though. I'm already walking into the woods, towards the excited cries and shouts of the other members of Wolf Hall Academy. Far be it from me to let them have all of the fun.

Cursing loudly, Carina comes crashing through the undergrowth after me. "This is nuts. What's the point in any of this? Who cares what Wren does or doesn't do?"

"Me. I do. He made me fall in love with him and now *I* fucking care. It's the worst thing that's ever happened to me."

"Then just stop!" Carina cries, exasperated.

"Oh, yeah. Of course. Like you stopped loving Dashiell? It's that simple, isn't it? Just a flip of a switch? I saw how you looked at him outside the gazebo the other night."

She swears some more. "Okay, okay. Slow down a little, will you? Thank god I wore flats. How the hell do you even know where you're going?"

I point up at the clear night sky peeking through the tree branches overhead, refusing to give her the courtesy of actually looking at *her*. "I know how to read the stars. Good Ol' Colonel Stillwater taught me, amongst *soooooo* many other things. Who knew that one would come in handy. We're heading south-west. If I want to head back to the road, it'll be easy. Now either keep quiet or head back to Wolf Hall. Either way, I'm done talking."

* * *

We walk for an hour.

Carina screams at the top of her lungs every time a student comes tearing out of the dark clutching a wad of Wren's red flags in their hands. The entire thing reminds me of a haunted hayride Levi's parents took us to on Halloween two years ago, where actors covered in gore ran out of the night, brandishing prop chainsaws, trying to scare us. I'd screamed then, enjoying the spectacle of it all, but this isn't a spectacle. It's the stupidest shit I've ever heard of and I can't believe people are participating in it.

I guide us back to the perimeter of the house, scanning the trees for any sight of a wolf mask, but I don't see one. The beautiful Tinkerbelle dress Wren bought me gets caught on nearly every single tree branch I pass and I do nothing whatsoever to keep it from tearing.

Realizing that everyone's probably fled deep into the interior of the forest, I change direction and head back to the north, counting my steps to keep a rough gauge on how far we've come. Eventually, we come across a small clearing.

"For God's sake, can we break for a moment. My ankle's killing me." She rolled it about a mile ago, and she hasn't quit complaining about it since. I grunt, sinking down onto the flattest rock I can find, listening for signs that someone might be approaching, but the air is still and silent.

Carina sits down beside me. "Look. I'm sorry that I didn't tell you everything, okay. I love you, Elle. You *are* my friend. I care about you, and everything that happened with Mara was such a mess. I didn't want your experience of Wolf Hall to be as fucked up as ours, okay?"

"That's why you told me to stay away from Wren," I say numbly. "You didn't want him to do anything bad to me."

Her forehead creases, her brow marked with confusion. "No. I mean, I told you...Wren was at the house the night of the party. He really didn't leave. He and Mara were over before they even got started. She wouldn't accept it at first. She kept following him around like a lost little puppy dog. Then, out of nowhere, she just got over it one day. Like, out of the blue. She was acting really weird. Mercy said she'd found out she was seeing someone, but none of us could figure out who it could be. She came to the party and seemed perfectly happy. She didn't even speak to Wren. We were all having fun. And then...one minute she was there...the next she was gone."

I don't think she's lying to me. I really don't. I don't think Wren's lying to me now, either, which is the most confusing thing in the world to parse given all of the evidence that pointed to him.

I'm just…I'm so fucking tired of trying to figure this thing out. My head hurts, and I'm stuck in the middle of a forest, for fuck's sake, wearing a sparkly fairy costume, and nothing makes any goddamn sense!

Carina takes my hand, squeezing it tightly. "I really am sorry, Elodie. Please just believe that I kept you in the dark for a reason. I'll tell you everything I found out after that night, okay? Right now. No more secrets, I swear."

She looks so damn earnest. Her eyes shine brightly, a little glossy, like she might be on the verge of tears, and the anger that's been popping and flaring, putting out a wall of heat like a campfire, suddenly gutters out and dies, leaving me sad and cold. "Okay. Then start at the beginning. And don't leave a single detail out."

She smiles. Nods. "That particular party was weird. I knew something was up the moment I walked through the door. Everyone was more reserved than usual. I asked Mercy what was going on, and she told me that—"

A loud crack splinters the silence. Both of us lock up, tensing, as we wait for another sound. It comes a second later—a heavy crunch, followed by another, followed by another. And then a figure steps out of the trees into the clearing. It's a guy—shirtless— wearing low slung jeans, resting on his hips. His face is concealed by one of Wren's wolf masks.

"Go on, Carrie," a low voice rumbles from beneath the mask. "I wouldn't wanna interrupt story time."

45

WREN

I SEARCH the house from top to bottom.

She isn't anywhere to be found.

I drive up to the academy and bust open her bedroom door. She isn't there, either. But my Wolf Hall Academy sweater is. It's hanging off the back of the chair by the window, and the moment I set eyes on it, I remember the last time I wore it. It comes rushing back to me all at once like a slap to the face, and dread coils like a viper in the pit of my stomach. I wore it a week before the last Riot House party, because it was cold out and I was meeting someone in the gazebo.

I threw it on, not even thinking about it. Took it off while I was there. Left it there in my haste to escape afterwards. It was a bad night. A complicated night. It hadn't ended well, and I'd done everything I could to blot it from my mind afterwards.

Now the details of it come roaring back with all the subtly of a sledgehammer.

"I want you, Wren Jacobi. And I always get what I want."

I'd smiled. Laughed it off. Dismissed him, because that's what I was good at.

"Tough shit. You can't have me, old man."

And then he'd turned my world upside down.

Elodie's probably just playing the game. She's probably fine. But something sick and worrying niggles away at the back of my head, screaming at me to find her. She has no idea how much danger she's in if she's out there in those woods.

I have to find her. I have to find her before *he* does.

I take out my phone and power it on. I'm racing down the academy steps by the time I open up my texts and tap out a message.

Me: Where are you right now?

The reply comes moments later.

"Where do you think I am? I'm about to join in the fun."

46

ELODIE

"Pax, stop fucking around."

I get up, brushing down the dress, scowling at him. I don't have the energy to be dealing with this shit tonight. And yeah, I might have put him on his ass the last time he tried to sneak up on me in this forest, but he didn't know I was capable of defending myself then. He'll be ready for me this time, and that makes life so much harder. "I'm sorry if you're having a shitty night, but I just wanna find Wren and get the fuck out of here, okay?"

The wolf mask tips eerily to one side. Pax creeps closer. "Wren. Yes, Wren. We're all so desperate for Wren, aren't we?"

"Well, you know where the guy sleeps at night. You can settle whatever issues you have with him later back at the house. I think *my* issues with him are a little more pressing than yours."

I step to the right, trying to get around him, but Pax mirrors the movement, stepping to his left, blocking my path.

"Elodie?" Carina says.

"Pax. Get the fuck out of the way. Or do you want me to embarrass you in front of Carina?" I try to move to the left this time, but he's right there with me, stopping me in my tracks. I can hear him breathing thickly through the small air holes in the mask, and the sound is raspy and wet.

"Elodie," Carina repeats. "Elle...*I don't think that's Pax.*"

I frown, eyeing the guy. He sure as hell isn't Dashiell. The smattering of hair on his chest is dark. Dash's hair is far lighter. It isn't Wren, either. He doesn't even *have* hair on his chest. A bolt of something like panic chases up my spine.

I take a step backward.

"Who...?"

Suddenly Carina's at my side, threading her fingers through mine. "We kept your secret, okay," she hisses. "We kept our mouths shut. You swore you wouldn't do this again."

The guy in the wolf mask slowly shakes his head, tutting under his breath. "I hate breaking promises, Carrie, I really do. I thought I'd be over it by now, but..." He reaches up, tugging on the wolf's horrific snout, slowly drawing it back to unmask himself. "I just can't stop loving him. It's an obsession, I know. I thought I could handle him caring about someone new but it's impossible. I hate her just as much as I hated the other one." He turns sharp, hate-filled eyes on me, considering me with disgust. "He's *mine*, Elodie. The sooner you stupid little bitches get that into your thick skulls, the sooner you can all stop dying."

Doctor Fitzpatrick.

My brain can't stop stuttering over his name.

Doctor Fitzpatrick?

Always so friendly and caring in class. Always rambling on about the poets, giving Wren a hard time, telling him to sit up straight. Reading Wren's Victorian porn out to the class, trying to embarrass him. I'm so fucking confused, it feels like my brain is melting out of my ears. The spiteful twist to the doctor's features makes him look like a stranger. Someone I've never met before. "Awww. Poor Elodie. He didn't tell you, did he?" he sneers.

"Tell me what?"

"That he and I were together for a time. A short time, sure, but he just needed some time to see it. He and I, we're kindred souls.

We're supposed to fucking be together. But you know him. He's stubborn. Sometimes he won't admit something unless it's on his schedule. That's why he hasn't told you that he loves you yet, Elodie."

My mouth feels like it's filled with cotton wool. I can't seem to close it. I'm having the hardest time understanding what I'm hearing. "He has told me that he loves me," I whisper.

Doctor Fitzpatrick's eyes narrow to cruel slits. *"What?"*

I say it louder. "He *has* told me that he loves me. He *does* love me."

"Don't, Elle," Carina warns, digging her fingernails into the back of my hand.

Doctor Fitzpatrick shakes his head violently. He presses the heel of his hand against his forehead, screwing his eyes shut, which is when I see the massive bowie knife he's clutching in his hand. How the *fuck* did I not notice that before? The blade glints maddeningly in the moonlight that lances down through the canopy of the trees into the clearing.

Doctor Fitzpatrick's top lip pulls up, disgust radiating off him as he lurches toward us, pointing the tip of the knife at my face. Carina shrieks right next to my ear, but I...don't...blink...

"He didn't *say* that," he spits. "He'd never say that. He can't. Wren's not capable of loving a girl like *you*. He needs more than stupid, silly dresses and scruffy Doc Martin boots, and dumb debate questions. There's just no way."

There's no way the man standing in front of me is sane. He can't be. No one in their right mind would be aiming a knife that size in someone's face and ranting the way he's ranting if they had even the weakest grasp on reality. I should say something to placate him, but that's a dangerous game. Such a fine line to try and tightrope walk, and Doctor Fitzpatrick is a high-functioning madman. He has to be to have fooled the world for this long.

I realize something, as I'm about to speak, though. "Wait. That knife. I recognize that knife. That's the knife that I found sticking out of my bed!"

Fitz laughs, tossing his head back. "God, you're so fucking self important, aren't you? Oh my bed. My precious books. My things. Wah wah wah. Dean Harcourt left it in the drawer of her desk, so I took it back. I've had this knife a very long time, y'know. I didn't really feel like letting her keep it for good."

"Why the *hell* did you trash my room?"

The doctor growls, inching closer. "I didn't have a choice, did I? That room sat empty for months, but then you came along. I still hadn't found Mara's stupid journal or Wren's sweater. It was only a matter of time before you stumbled across them and started asking questions. So I tore everything apart. I looked high and low. I would have found them, too, but then you came back to your room. I could hear you on the phone complaining about your father in the stairwell, and I bolted."

"God, you are *so* fucked up," Carina mumbles.

I'm still processing all of this, but the muddled pieces of information that were making my head hurt all begin to snap together. "*You're* the one she wrote about in her journal. Not Wren. *You're* the one she was afraid of."

The English teacher grins, twisting the knife in his hand so that the light bounces off its serrated teeth. "I may have messed with her a little, I admit. She wasn't my type, but it was fun tricking her into thinking I wanted to be with her. I just wanted her to stay the hell away from Wren, but…" He shrugs, chuckling softly. "She was so fucking gullible. Not like you, eh, Elodie. No, you're smart. Pointless putting it all together now, though. It's far too late for that."

47

WREN

"Whoa! Where's your mask? I thought you were hot as hell as a wolf, Jacobi."

It's just my miserable luck that the first person I stumble across in the forest is Damiana. There are five reg flags tied around her wrist. Her slinky naughty nurse outfit looks like it's going to fall off her any second. It's a goddamn Christmas miracle she hasn't fallen down a ravine and snapped her neck in the white stilettos she's wearing. She rubs her hands over my chest, purring like a satisfied cat. "Never mind. I don't care about the mask. Doesn't matter. You still caught me. Now I'm yours for…" she purses her lips, "…however long you want me."

"Stop, Dami."

She lunges, trying to kiss me.

"Jesus, fucking *stop!* I'm looking for Elodie. Have you seen her?"

Her pleased look turns sour. "Fuck Elodie, Wren. How many times do you need to hear it? I a—"

I leave her in the dark, flying into the forest, my pulse racing so fast I'm shaking all over. She's got to be around here somewhere. Turns out a two-mile radius is a really fucking massive area of land, though, and I'm not having much luck finding anyone useful in the dark. I check my cell phone, hoping and praying to god that there'll be a message from Elodie, but I only have one bar of reception and—scratch that. I have zero bars of reception, and I doubt anyone else has any either.

What a fucking disaster.

This situation could not get any worse right now.

But then, typically, thirty seconds later they do.

I blaze right into Mercy. She's sitting on a fallen tree trunk, smoking a cigarette like it's totally normal for her to be out by herself in a forest in the middle of the fucking night. She's dressed in a red and white cheerleader uniform, her hair in pigtails, makeup smeared all down her face. I think she's supposed to be some sort of zombie. She doesn't even look surprised when she looks and sees me.

"S'up, big brother. Enjoying your little game?" She blows twin jets of smoke down her nose.

"Elodie's out here somewhere. I've gotta find her."

"Huh. *There's* a shocker."

"I don't have time to trade punches with you right now. Just tell me if you've seen her."

Her eyebrow curves. She takes another drag from her cigarette. "Why would I tell you, even if I had? You've been quite terrible to me recently, Wren."

I feel like fucking screaming. "You know perfectly well why I'm mad at you! This entire mess is your fucking fault!"

She twists to face me, anger in her eyes. "What the *hell* are you talking about? I did nothing wrong."

"You meddled in my shit, Mercy, just like you always do. You told Fitz that I was seeing Mara when I wasn't. You made out like we were serious and in a fucking relationship, when you *knew* he was out of his fucking mind. Mara went missing because you said that. You made *me* responsible for what happened to her!"

"I was just trying to help," she hisses, flicking her smoke into the undergrowth. She gets up and stalks toward me, jabbing at my chest with her finger. "And we don't know what happened to

Mara, okay. She's probably in Cabo, drinking trailer park margaritas and blowing frat boys on the beach. She was always the type to *'Gone Girl'* you morons."

"You tell yourself that if it helps ease your conscience, Merce. But Fitz would never have screwed with Mara if you hadn't told him I was with her. She was your friend. Whether you like it or not, you threw her under the bus."

For the first time in years, tears shine in Mercy's eyes. She's never shown one ounce of remorse for what she did. And, real though it looks, I'm not about to believe that this display of emotion is real now. Mercy's always turned on the waterworks to get what she wants. "You're right. She was my friend. And yeah, I said something that I shouldn't. But I was trying to help you extricate yourself from a situation that you should never have been dumb enough to get yourself into in the first place. Christ, Wren, you don't even *like* guys. What the fuck were you thinking?"

I shouldn't have avoided her for this long. We should have hashed this out months ago, but I've been too angry to even look at her. I still feel that way. "Look, I can't stand here arguing with you about my sexual orientation when Elodie's in danger. Fitz is out here, and I think he's looking for her. I have to find her first. If you're not gonna help, then this is where I leave you."

I charge off through the trees, heading to the north. My eyes are accustomed to the dark now. I'm surefooted and fast as I pick up the pace, my senses on high alert.

"Jesus, Wren! Wait!" Mercy calls behind me. I pause long enough to let her catch up. She's panting and out of breath when she jumps down from a rock, arriving at my side. "Since you've never given me an opportunity to redeem myself, I s'pose I'll help you find your silly little girlfriend."

"This won't make us even, Mercy. Not by a long shot."

She pouts, rolling her eyes at me the way she's always done since we were five. "Fine. Whatever, asshole. But you have to agree that it's a start. Now lead the way. I knew there was a reason why I wore tennis shoes tonight."

402 | CALLIE HART

The minutes tick by. Then an hour. By one in the morning, I've reached the conclusion that it's going to be fucking impossible to comb this entire area and find one girl. It's insanity. Even with Mercy shrieking Elodie's name at the top of her lungs, it's unlikely that we're just gonna stumble across her.

"She's not out here, Wren," Mercy says. "She's tiny, and she can't weigh a hundred pounds soaking wet. What business would she have participating in one of your dumb hunts anyway? I bet you a hundred bucks she's at that atrocious café, drinking milkshakes and gorging on fries with Carrie Mendoza."

"You don't know a thing about Elodie, so how about you keep your mouth shut, huh? I *know* she's out here. I just do. And even if she isn't, I'm still gonna crawl over every square inch of this forest to make damn sure. Fitz told me he was coming to *'join in the fun.'* If there's a chance that he might hurt her, then I'm gonna fucking stop him."

"Wow. You really are smitten. I've never seen you care this much about anything," she says softly. For once, it doesn't sound like she's mocking me. She sounds genuinely surprised.

"Yeah. Well. At some point, you've gotta care about something, Mercy, or else what's the fucking point?"

"The point in what?"

I look back at her. "In even being alive."

Her eyes round out, flicking past me, her focus shifting up ahead. She grabs my wrist, tugging me to one side, behind a tree. "Shhhh. I heard something."

"It was probably a squirrel, Merce. Come on, let's go." She hisses and sputters, slapping my back, trying to get me to stop, but I press on regardless. She follows, swearing with every step she takes. Fifteen seconds later, I hear something, too: a low, breathless moan.

"What the fuck?"

Mercy points over to the right, and I discover the source of the noise. Presley Adams is naked, pinned up against a tree, her tits bouncing up and down as a guy wearing a wolf mask fucks the living shit out of her. Naturally, it's Pax. Unfortunately, I've seen his bare ass enough times that it's easily recognizable, even without the Calvin Klein underwear.

"Gross," is all Mercy has to say on the matter. I know for a fact that she'd fuck Pax if given half a chance, so her comment must be aimed at Pres. I give them a wide berth, skirting around a huge boulder in order to avoid walking right past them.

We're almost at the boundary of the search area, bordering the academy grounds, when we find the cave. Set back into the rock at the foot of a large buttress that juts skyward above the trees' canopy, Mercy takes one look at the gaping black maw and shakes her head. "Uh uh. No way. Not happening. I'm not going in there."

"Fine. Then don't." I stand at the mouth of the cave, peering into the bottomless black. I can't see a fucking thing. "*ELODIE!!!*" My shout echoes back to me, repeating itself, growing quieter as it gets further and further away. Sounds like it goes back a long way. I wait, listening for a response that never comes.

"We're almost at the academy," Mercy says. "Why don't we just go and take a look there. She could already have gone back there."

I chew the inside of my cheek, considering it for a second. This niggling worry won't stop gnawing at me, though. The very idea of giving up the search and going back to the school fills me with such inexplicable dread that it's simply not an option. "Wait here, Merce. Holler if anyone comes."

"For god's sake, Wren. This is stupid! Let's just go back!"

I take a deep breath and I step inside.

48

ELODIE

THE THING ABOUT KRAV MAGA? The system was designed to train the Israeli Defense Forces how to disarm an attacker with a weapon. Specifically, a gun, or *a knife*. I could take Fitzpatrick's bowie knife from him in three short moves, but I'm biding my time. He's so sure that he has complete control over the situation that he's talking, spilling all his secrets like a villain in a goddamn Bond movie, and I want to learn as much as I can before I break his wrist and run.

Carina walks ahead of me, her hands tied behind her back. I'm restrained, too—the thin twine the English teacher used to bind us bites, cutting into my skin—though I'm not particularly worried about that just yet. I'm more concerned about where he's taking us. "Let's pick up the pace, ladies. We'll be here 'til dawn otherwise."

He sounds chipper. He hasn't forgotten what I told him earlier, though. He doesn't believe that Wren confessed his love to me, and now he's trying to convince *me* that I'm wrong. "He was lying to you, y'know. He took your file from Dean Harcourt's office. Stole your picture. He was planning on toying with you. Did you know that?"

"Yes, I knew that. He told me everything. I know *all* about his little obsession when we first met. Things changed, though. It became real. For both of us." Maybe I should sound a little less bored. A fraction more scared? Don't get me wrong; I'm absolutely shitting myself, but I'm also confident that I'll be able to wrestle over control of the situation when the time comes. And I want to push the doc's buttons a little. Nudge him over the other side of angry just far enough that he gets sloppy. Carina looks back at me, giving me a stern look that speaks volumes. *What the fuck are you doing, girl? Don't antagonize him. You're gonna get us both killed!*

"Eyes front, Carrie. Good girl. Wouldn't want you tripping and breaking your neck, would we?" Fitz commands.

"He told me that I was the first person he's ever loved. What we have is special," I say in an airy tone. "I never thought a guy like Wren would go for a girl like me. But the way he looks at me sometimes…" I sigh dreamily. "We're gonna live together when we go away to college. It's gonna be amazing. We'll—"

I go down hard. With my hands tied behind my back, I have no way of breaking the fall. The impact sends pain jangling through me from head to toe. Well, shit. Facedown in the dirt, I vaguely wonder if I've pushed a little too hard. Doctor Fitzpatrick looms over me, snarling in my ear. "Keep your slut mouth closed, Elodie. Unless you wanna wind up bleeding out in this dirt, right here and now."

49

WREN

THE MOMENT I turn the first corner, I see a light up ahead. My hope soars. Maybe she didn't hear me call out for some reason. Could be that Elodie's just up ahead, killing time before she goes back to Wolf Hall. I stumble, tripping over unseen rocks that litter the narrow path, barely catching myself against the rough, sharp walls as I hurry onward.

"Elodie?" I should have fucking told her everything when I had the chance. It was so stupid of me to keep this from her. She needed to know the truth, so she could be prepared for what she was getting herself into. I was a coward, though. I was weak. It took so long to earn her trust. I was so convinced that we could make it to graduation without Fitz finding out about us. What a fool I was. "*ELODIE!*" The shout carries even further this time, bouncing around the inside of the cave.

Before I can suck down another breath and call for her again, I come out into an open, high-ceilinged cavern. The light I saw just now comes from a series of electric lamps, strung up along one side of the wall. Water runs down the roughhewn rock, gathering in filthy puddles on the ground. And there, right in the middle of the cavern, is a stone plinth, rising up out of the dirt.

Not a plinth.

An altar.

That's what it seems to be, at least. I approach, my heart a clenched fist in my throat, and...*Oh my god.* A high-pitched buzzing sound floods my head. It's Mara. She's laid out on top of the altar, hands resting on top of her chest—nothing more than bone and matted, dull hair.

This is where she's been.

All of this time...

The cops searched these woods. They never found her. They've been looking for her back in Florida where her parents live, plastering her face all over the sides of milk cartons and noticeboards, but she was here all along, quietly rotting away to dust.

"Holy...fuck."

I reach out, my fingers hovering over the blackened skull—

"Oh my god!"

I pull my hand back, nearly jump out of my skin. Mercy stands in the opening of the cavern, staring at the body of the girl who used to be her friend. Shock distorts the planes of her face. Even in the dim lighting thrown off by the electric lamps, I can see how pale she is. "Jesus, you nearly gave me a heart attack!" I hiss.

She comes toward me on wobbly legs, reaching out, like the ground's shifting underneath her and she's fighting for balance. "I swear—" she whispers. "I swear I thought she was fine. I thought she'd just bailed. I guess she isn't blowing frat boys in Cabo, after all."

"No." The word comes out clipped and hard. Mercy has a lot to answer for here. I won't say it, because what would placing blame accomplish now? But Mara and I barely knew each other. We went out once, didn't even make out, and I decided she wasn't for me. Bastard that I was, she wasn't innocent enough for my tastes. She was just as tainted and troubled as I was at the time, and I couldn't even bother having a one-night stand with her. She'd pursued me at first, but then given up the chase. There'd been no bad blood between us. And then Mercy stuck her oar in and wound up getting Mara killed. Fitz wouldn't have touched her if my sister hadn't said what she did.

Mercy stands over Mara's corpse, the muscles in her throat working. I think she's beginning to understand now. It's finally hitting home. Tears course down her face as she surveys the bones from the skull, down over the ribcage, pelvis, femur, tibia and fibula. "I wouldn't have been chatting with him in the street if I really believed he was capable of this," she whispers. "I just…I thought it was a game. I thought it was funny, the way he wouldn't leave you be. I never thought—"

I wrap my arm around her shoulder, pulling her into my side. She's been the cause of so much of my guilt over the past year, because I *did* know. I knew Fitz was this crazy. I feared he'd done something like this, but I had no way of proving it until now. Mercy's hurting, though, and she's still my fucking blood. She will have to deal with this for a long time to come, but for now I'll comfort her, because that's what brothers are supposed to do.

"We need to call the police," she mumbles into my shirt.

"I know. We will. But first we need to find Elodie. I don't want her to end up on this slab next to Mara. Let's search the rest of the cave and—"

A loud *CRACK!* echoes down the passageway behind us—it sounds like a rock, skittering along the ground and hitting the wall. Mercy and I trade a stunned look. *"Hide,"* she hisses. But it's too late. There is nowhere to hide. The cavern is where the cave ends, and it's empty apart from the plinth.

So, I do what I should have done a long time ago.

I turn and wait to face down a monster.

50

ELODIE

CARINA LETS OUT A STRANGLED CRY. That's how I know something bad waits for us up ahead. The walls of the passageway close in, swearing they'll crush me to death, as Doctor Fiztpatrick pushes me from behind, shoving me through an opening in the cave. And my heart stops dead in my chest.

Wren.

His eyes widen when he sees me, full of terror, and then they go utterly blank. At my back, Doctor Fitzpatrick lets out a hollow, surprised bark of laughter. "Well, well, well. Look who it is! We were just talking about you, weren't we, girls? Mercy, too. Wow, we've got the whole gang."

Wren stares at me, his jade eyes working their way up from my feet, traveling over my body; I can tell that he's assessing me for injuries. I give him a quick shake of the head to let him know I'm okay. He steps forward, sliding his hands into his pockets. Such a normal, everyday *Wren* gesture. "What's going on, Wes? What are you doing?"

"I'd have thought that was obvious," the doctor replies. "We seem to have ourselves a reoccurring problem. These girls keep on crawling out of the woodwork, trying to come between us. I take care of one and another just pops up." He chuckles. "It's like whack-a-mole. Lucky for us, I was always good at whack-a-mole. Why don't you grab hold of Carina? Keep her quiet while I take care of Elodie."

A glimmer of disgust works its way onto Wren's face. "What fucking planet do you live on, old man? I'm not keeping anyone quiet. For fuck's sake, *untie their hands*. What's *wrong* with you?"

Doctor Fitzpatrick's head jerks back. There's a streak of dirt on his cheek. Down his left-hand side, too, where I gave him hell when he yanked me back up onto my feet. His bottom lip wobbles, the way a child's mouth works when they've just skinned their knee and they don't know if they should cry or not. "You don't need to talk to me like that. I'm trying, okay? I'm just trying to do what's best for us. How are we supposed to be together when you keep getting distracted by these *whores?*"

"You're not in your right mind," Wren whispers. "You need help."

"You're the only one who can help me now. Help me take care of these two and we'll let your sister go. She's family, right? You won't say anything, will you, Mercy? You understand why this needs to happen. You were the one who told me about Mara in the first place, right?"

He sounds so desperate. His demeanor now is so different from the show he puts on in his classroom; it barely makes sense that this is even the same person. I spin around, putting my back to the wall of the cavern while Doctor Fitzpatrick's distracted. Quickly contorting my hand, making it as narrow as possible, I twist my wrist from left to right, working the twine down over my hand a millimeter at a time.

Mercy's as white as a sheet. She looks from Wren to Doctor Fitzpatrick, her whole body shaking uncontrollably. "I—I didn't—know this would—happen."

I almost have my hand free.

"Why bother pretending, Mercy?" I spit. "You've hated me from the moment you came back to Wolf Hall. You've been a raging bitch since day one. Just go, for fuck's sake. Get out of here."

Mercy jumps. It's as though she's forgotten I'm even here. Wren frowns, but he quickly understands what I'm doing. "Yeah, Merce. You're family. Blood's thicker than water, no matter what. So just...go. Don't breathe a word of what you saw here tonight."

Fitz watches the exchange, eyes quick, shifting from one person to another. His presence was always so domineering and powerful in class. He was master of his space, and he oozed confidence. He's twitchy and weird here. I'm nervous just looking at him.

"Fine." Mercy swallows. "Whatever. Like I care anyway. I'll see you back at the house, Wren."

I pray to god Mercy's figured out that she needs to call the cops the moment she gets reception on her cellphone. She needs to be able to find her way back to the road first, though, and I honestly don't think she'll be capable. She shuffles around the perimeter of the cave, eyeing Fitz warily.

I ought to keep my mouth shut, but of course I don't. "Wait. Why not just let Carina go with her? Carina's got nothing to do with this. She doesn't care about Wren. I'm the only one you have a problem with."

Fitz flips over the bowie knife in his hand, grinning manically. He shakes his head, disappointment on his face. He cuts Mercy off, moving to block the exit of the cave. "You guys are terrible actors. Mercy, I expected better of you. You've had actual *training* in this. You embarrass yourself. Get back with your brother. Go on, go." Mercy flinches when he raises the knife, showing her the blade. She's back beside Wren in a flash, and I don't blame her either—the evil glint in Fitz's eyes is fucking demonic.

"It seems we've arrived at a bit of an impasse, wouldn't it, class? Wren, you're unwilling to admit your true feelings. Mercy, you can't be trusted, even though you should have your brother's best interests at heart. Carina, you're a victim of circumstance, and Elodie, well, Elodie just plain needs to die. So, where do we go from here?"

"There are four of us." Wren glances at me out of the corner of his eye. "And only one of you. The chances of you managing to hold us all off before we put *you* down are pretty slim." He shifts forward, holding out his hands in a calming gesture. Horror tugs at Fitz's features. "What are you talking about? I'd never kill *you*, Wren. I *love* you. It's just the girls that have to go."

Both of my hands are free. I drop the twine, readying myself.

A cruel and terrible smile plays over Fitz's face. "I'm not worried about three skinny little girls. And I don't think you're going to hurt me," he says. His attention's all for Wren. He's dazed, fanatical, fixated on him. It's sad, really, that he's this sick over him. And he *is* sick. The things he's done to try and win Wren... The things he's willing to do...

Fitz jolts sideways, rushing toward me. The ugly, brutal knife he drove into my bed is raised in his hands, prepared to strike. Fear electrifies me. Time slows. I'm ready for him. I wait until the last second—

"No!" Three different voices shout at the same time, the word ricocheting around the cave. Wren hurls himself forward, reaching to grab the man...but Carina's closer. I watch, feet frozen to the floor, as she throws herself at him, but her hands are still tied behind her back. She has no means of stopping him, other than to angle her shoulder and piledrive into his body.

I already know what's going to happen before it plays out.

Fitz will see her coming.

He does.

"CARINA, NO!"

He'll have time to turn.

He does.

He'll be waiting for her when she collides with him.

He is.

The knife will—

The knife—

I can do nothing but scream as Fitz spins the blade over and thrusts it upward, right into Carina's stomach.

51

WREN

CARINA, Carina,

Sweet little Carrie.

Mother hen of the fourth floor.

This is precisely why Harcourt designated her protector over all new female students. Because she's selfless, and she's brave, and she's willing to sacrifice herself to ensure the safety of others. I see it now.

The blade finds its mark, disappearing up to the guard, and a wet, rattling gasp flies out of Carina's mouth. A deranged laugh slips out of Fitz as he cradles Carina's head in his hands, catching her as she slides off the blade. He seems morbidly fascinated by her expression, as her eyelids flutter with surprise. I'm still moving toward them, covering ground. I get there in time to stop him just before he drives the knife into her stomach for a second time. Elodie's right there, too. She grabs Carina by the arms, dragging her out of the way as I bulldoze Fitz to the ground.

"GET OFF ME!" he roars.

He's older than me, not to mention bigger, but I'm stronger. A bright slash of pain sears up my arm. Blood spills over my skin, crimson and gushing, but I don't let go. I wrap my arm around his throat, my feet kicking in the dirt, fighting for purchase as I try to get behind the bastard. If I can only get him in a proper chokehold, I'll be able to cut off his air supply. He's fighting like the very devil himself, though, and he won't drop the fucking knife.

"Carina! Oh my god, Carina!" Elodie lifts her, yelling to Mercy. "Untie her hands! For fuck's sake, don't just stand there!"

"Accept—it—Wren!" Fitz snarls. "The job's—half—done!"

My hand is so slick with my own blood that I lose my grip on his wrist. Fitz seizes the opportunity and slashes back, over his head. The razor-sharp steel catches me on the crook of the neck, another lash of agony burning bright and hot, but still I don't let go. Fitz whimpers, flailing, stabbing backwards again and again. I scramble, twisting to avoid the point of the weapon.

"Let *GO!* It's not supposed—to go like—this!"

I don't give a fuck how it was supposed to go. I finally manage to get myself behind him. I tighten my hold around his throat, using my other arm as leverage to apply pressure. "Stab me all you like, Wes. I'm not letting go until you're down."

"You can't—let them—take me," he growls.

Another cut to my forearm. One to my thigh. Another to my side.

Fitz's movements begin to slow. The knife clatters to the floor. His fingers lock around my arm, trying to prize it loose, but there's no way in hell he'll succeed. I won't let him hurt anyone else. I'll bleed out here in the dirt, holding the fucker down until my very last breath, before I allow him to hurt one more person because of me.

"She's not breathing! *She's not breathing!*" Mercy's piercing cry fills my ears. The next thing I know, Elodie's standing over us and the knife is in her hands.

"Evil…sick…twisted…" she pants.

I expect that she'll gut him from stem to sternum, but she doesn't. She spins the weapon over, holding it by the guard, and brings the heavy metal handle crashing down on Fitz's head with a sickening *crack*.

52

ELODIE

THE MOTHERFUCKER'S OUT COLD.

I snatch up the twine that bound my hands, as well as the length Mercy just ripped from Carina's wrists, and I toss them to Wren. "Make sure he can't go anywhere before I end the bastard."

Even after my father killed my mother and trapped me inside that box for days, I never thought I'd have the courage to kill him. Without a shadow of a doubt, I *will* murder Wesley Fitzpatrick if he so much as stirs in the next few minutes, though.

Carina shivers, her hands shaking as she holds them against her stomach. Mercy thought she wasn't breathing, but she is. Her gasps for air are shallow and raspy, though, and it doesn't sound good. She hasn't said a word, just stares up at me, terrified, with the whites of her eyes showing as her blood flows sluggishly out of the nasty looking wound in her stomach.

"We have to get her back to the academy," I say.

"We—we shouldn't move her. We should get help," Mercy moans.

Wren shakes his head. "She won't make it. Here. I've got her."

Carina lets out a frightened, pained cry as Wren scoops her into his arms and lifts her from the cold cave floor. We're moving before I know what's happening. Fitz is still unconscious when we leave him, hog-tied and lying face down on the ground.

The forest presses down on us, dark and foreboding. Wren doesn't say a word. He orients himself, panting, and then takes off at a run with Carina in his arms, heading for the academy.

Even carrying Carina, his breath labored and short, he's much faster than Mercy and me. I don't feel the tree branches lashing at me. I feel no pain when I stumble and fall. I keep my eyes locked on Wren's back, and I keep on running.

I lose my shoes.

Relief hits me in a dizzying wave when we reach the road. The soles of my feet tear against the black top as I charge after Wren. He doesn't falter. Not for a second. We're still so far away from the academy, though. Too far. I think about the jagged knife wound in Carina's belly, and I begin to lose hope.

We're not going to make it. Wren won't. There just isn't time.

A car horn cuts through the night, startling me half to death. For a horrible second, I think it's Fitz, escaped from the cave somehow and burning toward us up the road, but then Pax's charger screams past us, gunning for Wren. The tires squeal as the car screeches to a halt, and I catch a flash of bright blond hair.

Mercy's fifty feet behind me, but I hear her shout. *"It's Dash!"*

I pause for her to catch up. "How did he know?"

She puffs, shrugging. "I texted him back in the cave. I didn't know if it went through. I—"

She trails off, fighting for oxygen. It doesn't really matter how Dash knew. He *showed up.* I've never been so grateful to see the bastard. I'm so exhausted, I can barely keep my feet underneath me when I reach the car. Dash has Carina in his arms and he's lying her on the back seat, cursing like a madman. His face is grey, his movements frantic.

"Get in the car, Wren!" he yells. "Right fucking now!"

Wren weaves, staggering into the side of the car. "I'm okay. Just take her. Don't wait for the ambulance. Go!"

I realize just how bad he looks when he drops down on one

knee. Oh my god. Holy shit, holy shit, he's covered in so much blood. There's a gaping wound on his shoulder, and his t-shirt is sliced clean through. His arms have been cut to shreds.

Dashiell slams the rear door closed, shaking his head. He grabs Wren roughly by the arm, dragging him upright. "Get in the fucking car this instant, Jacobi. You're on death's door."

"I'm—right—I'm—ffffine," he slurs. Then his eyes roll back into his head, and he passes out in Dashiell's arms.

I didn't see his injuries back at the cave. I was so focused on Carina, and now it looks like he's…it looks like he's gonna…

He ran.

He *ran* through that forest to save Carina, and the entire time *he* was bleeding out, too. I cover my mouth with my hands, stifling back a sob. This isn't fucking happening. It can't be.

Dash manhandles him into the front seat of the car and finally acknowledges our presence. "Are you two okay? Can you get back to the academy from here?"

I nod, even though I don't know if it's true. "Go, Dash. Run every red light. Just don't let them fucking die."

53

ELODIE

THE POLICE OFFICER murmurs into her radio, all business, as yet another cruiser tears up the driveway toward Wolf Hall Academy with its lights and sirens blaring. There are five patrol cars here now, though most of the cops who arrived with them are gone. They ran into the forest, heading south for the craggy knuckle of rock that can now be seen above the treetops in the early morning light, looking for the cave.

"And that's it? That's the whole story?" the officer asks, narrowing serious eyes at us, as she clips the radio back onto her belt. She introduced herself as Officer Haynes Hartung, but told us to call her Amy. "A *teacher* did this? Your *English teacher*? Because of a student?"

Mercy's in shock. She nods dumbly, staring at the steps in front of us. "Yeah. My brother. He carried Carina, but he—she—"

"I've just heard from one of the officers down at the hospital," Amy says. "Both the boy and the girl are in rough shape but they're stable. The girl would have died if she'd gotten there any later. Whatever your brother did, young lady, he saved her life."

Something inside me snaps in two. I haven't been able to breathe until now. Getting coherent words to form and come out of my mouth has been close to impossible, but hearing this news—both Wren and Carina are going to be okay—pushes me into hysteria.

I start crying, and I can't fucking stop.

Mercy puts her arm around me, and the two of us sob.

One by one, disheveled students in frightful looking costumes begin to appear on the road, walking back up to the academy. Dean Harcourt ushers them each inside, telling them to go and wait in the cafeteria for someone to come and talk to them.

At nine in the morning, a crew of police officers emerge from the forest with Doctor Fitzpatrick hanging limp like a rag-doll between them. I hear the words *'resisting arrest,'* and *'psych hold'* but I don't really process much after that. Around midday, a bunch of guys in white coveralls that look like HAZMAT suits load a blue body bag into the back of a coroner's van.

That's when the detective arrives and begins asking us questions that I'm too numb to answer. Mercy does most of the talking. She knows more than I do about Mara anyway.

After that, we're taken to the hospital to be checked out. Aside from a few cuts and scratches, as well as the soles of my feet being in a sorry state, there's nothing really wrong with me. I don't fight them on it, though.

I want to see Wren.

* * *

WREN

I felt bad when they loaded me onto the gurney and rushed me into the urgent care. I feel just fine now, though. Whatever drugs they've given me must have been potent as hell, because I feel like I'm floating on a cloud and my bones are made out of cotton candy. The police question me until I've answered the same set of questions fifteen times over. Someone comes to tell me that Carina's improving, which I'm man enough to say makes my eyes sting like crazy. I find out Fitz has been taken into custody shortly after that, and everything gets a little hazy.

I sleep like the *almost* dead.

At four, they bring me meds that make me a little more alert, and Elodie creeps into the room. She smiles a small smile, leaning her back against the wall on the far side of the room, picking at her fingernails.

"When I bought you that dress, I didn't think you were gonna treat it so badly." She's covered in blood. Carina's. Her own. Perhaps there's a bit of mine staining the fabric for good measure, too. The skirt's torn to shreds and half of the crystals that were sewn onto the bodice are missing now. Still, even covered in dirt and looking like she just fought in a war, she's beautiful. She smooths her hands down the front of the skirt, little good that it does.

"Yeah, well. I admit I didn't actually take very good care of it at the beginning of the night. And after things went to shit with Fitz, well…" She shrugs. "I'm sorry it got ruined."

I laugh down my nose, wincing when a snap of pain lances through my body. "It's okay. You don't need to apologize. You'll be pleased to know that there won't be any more Riot House parties for the foreseeable future. Dean Harcourt was here before. She said that we would all be expelled if we even thought about it."

"Can't really blame her," Elodie says.

"No, I don't suppose we can." I take a beat to look at Elodie, feeling…feeling for the first time like the future might not be so fucked up after all. "I didn't get to tell you that I liked your hair," I tell her.

"Really?" She ducks her head, touching her fingers to it. "I thought you liked the blonde."

"It doesn't really matter what color your hair is, Little E. I'll love you all the same, no matter what."

She sighs, pushing away from the wall. She makes it to the foot of the bed, which is where she stops, resting her hands on the metal frame. "I'm surprised that you can still say that. That you love me. I feel like shit for thinking you'd have done something to that girl. I just—everything got so confusing—"

I brace myself, sitting myself up a little straighter. The thick gauze they taped over the stitches at the base of my neck pull tight, but I grimace through the pain. "I'm not angry with you. Anyone would have thought the same thing. I left that sweater in the gazebo, the night I told Wes I wanted nothing more to do with him. He must have kept it and given it to Mara later. He's just as obsessed with poetry and Edgar Allen Poe. So long as you know now that I'm innocent—" A flash of panic makes me break out in a cold sweat. "You do know that I *am* innocent now, right?"

"Yes! Oh my god, yes! That's why I feel so terrible."

I hold my hand out to her. "Come here, then."

She's hesitant at first. As soon as she's within reach, I take her by the hand and I pull her closer so that she's sitting on the edge of the bed beside me. "If I'd just explained everything with Mara and Wes in the first place, then we wouldn't have ended up in this situation to begin with."

She cautiously studies my face; I can see her thinking about what she wants to say next. "Then why didn't you?"

"Because I was stupid. Because I thought everything would be fine, if we kept our mouths shut. I figured, as soon as graduation was over, we'd be free of the academy and free of Fitz, too. I didn't want to have to tell you that'd I'd gotten mixed up with Fitz, of all people."

"Why?" She gives me a teasing sidelong glance. "Because he's a guy?"

"Hah! No. Because he was a member of fucking faculty, and the whole student/teacher thing is just so fucking cliché. I like to pride myself on having *some* originality."

"So...you don't like guys?"

I can't read her expression very well, but...well, shit. It looks to me like she's feeling a little insecure. Shifting on my side, I—oh shit, nope, that's not gonna work. I lie back against the pillows, humming with exhaustion. "I've always been attracted to *people*, Little E. Their gender never really mattered. But that's all irrelevant now, anyway."

The bridge of her nose crinkles. She toys with my fingers, stroking her own over mine, frowning ever so slightly. "Why?"

"You know why. Because I've found *my* person now. In case you haven't realized it yet, you are endgame for me, Elodie Stillwater. And everyone else in the entire world can go and eat a dick."

EPILOGUE

WREN

Two weeks later

"Are you sure about this? You can always change your mind," Pax grumbles. He's been sitting in the car for the past twenty minutes, trying to talk me around. I'm not quite sure where all of this resistance is coming from, but I'm pretty sure he's allergic to change. Everything's been the same for years now. Just the three of us. And even though we're all still going to be living together and there are only a few months left until we all graduate, the idea of someone new, someone more permanent, entering our official orbit is bringing him out in hives.

From the backseat, I reach through the gap into the front of the car, giving his shoulder a halfhearted punch. "It's not the end of the world, man. Everything's cool. *You* need to be cool. You make having a girlfriend sound like a fate worse than death."

"It's alright for you. You get regular sex out of this arrange-ment. What do we get? Our spots on the sofa stolen? Weird clumps of hair in the shower? Frilly fucking underwear caught up in our laundry? Tampons in the medicine cabinet? Urgh."

"She's not moving in asshole. She'll stay the night on the weekends. I'll make sure she keeps her tampons to herself. And don't worry. No one would *dare* steal your spot on the sofa."

I feel like I'm counseling a traumatized child, whose father has just started dating someone new. Any second now, I half expect him to throw a tantrum and come out with the old, *"I'm not gonna call her Mom!"* line.

"Don't you have anything to say about this?" Pax glares at Dashiell in the passenger seat.

Dashiell sighs, but his frustration's all for show. "After much consideration, I've decided that Wren can do whatever the fuck makes him happy. Besides. Change is good. Maybe you should get yourself a girlfriend."

Pax recoils in horror. "Absolutely not! Why would I voluntarily incarcerate myself?"

I laugh. Dash laughs. The only person who isn't laughing is Pax. He's taking this upheaval to his daily routine very personally. "Alright. Whatever, pricks. I'm leaving." He gets out of the car and stalks toward the academy's entrance, his shoulders pulled up around his ears. With the clipped gait and aggressive arm swing he's got going on, even his walk looks pissed off.

"Don't worry. He'll come around," Dash says.

"He'd better, for your sake. He's gonna flip his shit when he realizes that *you've* got a girlfriend, too."

"Don't you breathe a fucking word," Dash says in a very serious tone. "We have to ease him into this one step at a time. He's already being difficult enough as it is. Living with Pax, mid existential crisis, would not be a fun time."

I'm inclined to agree.

We head inside the school, and I'm weirdly nervous. I've done the unthinkable and faced down my father. I've stood in preliminary court hearing and testified against a madman. Everything else in my life should be a cakewalk at this point, but publicly announcing to the world that I'm in love with someone and I want nothing more than to make her smile on a daily basis is a terrifying fucking prospect.

Spring break's right around the corner, so I only have to deal with the staring and the whispered comments for another couple of weeks, but even so…my palms are sweating like they've never sweat before.

The 'incident,' as the Wolf Hall faculty are calling it, is still a hot topic of conversation, and probably will be until the end of the school year. It's not every day that a teacher loses his goddamn mind and tries to murder a handful of students. It's not a common occurrence for a dead body to be discovered on academy grounds, either. Students chatter and gossip about the latest developments —Fitz's face plastered all over the internet, interviews from Mara's parents on CNN, reports that Fitz confessed to his crimes and hasn't denied a thing—as we head towards English. There was talk that the class would be relocated to another, regular classroom after everything that's gone down, but there was so much push-back from the students that Harcourt announced we could still study there, providing concentration levels or grades didn't suffer because of our surroundings. Personally, I don't give a shit where I take my classes now that Fitz is gone.

A hushed silence falls over the class when Dash and I enter the den. Damiana guns me down with a scathing stare. At some point, she's decided that she hates me, and I am A-okay with that. Pax is already sitting in his spot on the floor underneath the window. Dash rolls his eyes at me as he crosses the room, going to take up his regular place beside our friend.

I make it halfway toward the battered leather sofa underneath the bank of windows before I veer to the left, changing direction. My ribcage pinches tightly when I see her, sitting there on the floral couch beneath the print of Gustav Klimt's, 'The Kiss.'

Elodie Stillwater is the most breathtaking creature I've ever laid eyes on.

Her newly dark hair is pulled back into a purposefully messy bun, long, wavy tendrils hanging down on either side of her face. Her eyes are even more blue with the warm, early morning light washing over her face, highlighting the freckles that have started to spring up across the bridge of her nose.

She chews on the end of a ball point pen, her eyebrows slightly arched in amusement as she watches me walk toward her. The seat next to her is notably empty. It'll be another week or two before Carina's released from the hospital. She's been doing her school-work from her hospital bed. Dash has been taking it over there to her every evening, claiming that he's going to the 'gym.' Hah.

I stand in front of Elodie, pointing with my chin at the open spot next to her. "Shall I do the whole, *'this seat taken?'* thing, or do I get to maintain the illusion that I'm still cool?"

She pouts, considering this. "I suppose I'll save you from the cliché. But only because you look hot in that shirt."

I run my hand over my chest. "What this old thing?" I'm glowing like a fucking moron from the compliment, though. It's one thing knowing you look good—I do. Sorry—and another thing entirely when the girl you love most in the world tells you so. Horrified, I suspect that I might even be blushing. *Blushing*, for Christ's sake. Who the fuck *am* I?

I throw myself down onto the seat next to her, and I can feel the gaze of every other student in the room homing in on us. At the front of the class, Damiana makes a strangled, choking sound when I spin around, throwing my legs over the arm of the sofa, laying my head in Elodie's lap. Her mouth opens a fraction, a flash of surprise in her eyes, but she recovers herself quickly, toying with the ends of my hair, winding it around her fingers.

"If you're not careful, people might start to get the wrong idea about us, Jacobi," she jokes.

"Can't have that, can we?" I catch hold of her hand and gently kiss the inside of her wrist, enjoying the way her pupils double in size at the open, public display of affection. She's on the back foot. Likely, she thought I'd sit with her and keep my hands to myself, but I've gone way beyond that. The thing is, I didn't have anything to worry about. 'Cause this is nowhere as frightening as I thought it was going to be. Turns out I've been panicking over nothing; it's freeing as fuck to have everything out in the open, for everyone to see.

"Feeling pretty pleased with yourself?" Elodie asks, quirking an eyebrow at me.

"Yes." I nod. "Very."

"Oh, yeah? How quickly are you gonna fly across the room if I try kissing you *on the mouth?*" She gives me a look that's half dare, half mockery.

"My ass will remain firmly in this seat, no matter where you decide you wanna kiss me." I look suggestively down at my dick, unable to resist the opportunity to tease her. Good God, I'm never going to get used to this. She's so fucking beautiful. So fucking perfect. So fucking mine. Her cheeks color bright pink, and I have to fight the urge to drag her out of the classroom and up to her room, so I can fuck her brains out.

She's feeling brave, though. She tries to duck down to kiss me, but it's impossible in our current position. I help her out by popping up onto my elbow, meeting her halfway. The kiss isn't overtly sexual. I keep the tongue to a minimum. We're not animals. At least Elodie's not, and I don't want to embarrass her. It's a smoldering kiss—a slow burn, packed with emotion, a heat kindling between us that I'll most definitely have to address later. I cup her face, stroking my fingers down the back of her neck, making her shiver, and an exasperated shout goes up on the other side of the room.

"Oh, for fuck's sake! *Seriously?*" None other than Pax, naturally. Something hits the back of my head—balled up paper by the feel of it—but I don't pull away. I don't do that until a *hail* of paper begins raining down on us, hurled and thrown by the rest of the other students, too.

Elodie laughs against my mouth. "Okay, you've proven your point. You're fearless. I think they want us to stop now."

I give her bottom lip a quick tug between my teeth before I let her go. "Lucky, Little E. Saved by your fellow classmates."

"He—*oh*. Hello, class. Young man, if you wouldn't mind putting down that poor girl, I'll pretend that I didn't see any of that." At the front of the room, a woman in her early thirties hovers by the new chalkboard that's been freshly installed in between the book cases. I twist around in my seat, slouching down into the sofa next to Elodie, earnestly pretending to study the ceiling. However, just like everyone else in the room, I study the interloper, scoping her out. She's pretty. Sweet-looking, like she bakes on the weekend and feeds the birds outside her kitchen window. I catch Dashiell elbowing Pax in the ribs—a dig hard enough to knock the air right out of him—but Pax doesn't even seem to notice. He's staring at this new person like he's just unveiled the face of God and he cannot look away.

The woman smiles, clears her throat, and takes us all in.

"Class, my name is Jarvis Reid. You can call me Jarvis. As you've probably surmised, I'm your new English teacher. I've just moved to Mountain Lakes from New York and I'm still figuring out where everything is at the academy, so please bear with me while I get the lay of the land. If one of you would like to catch me up on what you've been studying, that would be a good start."

Pax hops to his feet. He smiles the kind of smile that's destroyed the hearts of countless supermodels from Rome to London and back again. "Hi Jarvis. I'd be happy to lend a helping hand."

Elodie and I trade a look that says it all.

Christ.

Here we go again.

Author's Note: Thank you so much for reading Riot House! I hope you enjoyed Elodie and Wren's story.

If you'd like to find out what went down when the Riot House Boys flew to Tel Aviv, turn the page!

54

BONUS CONTENT - TEL AVIV

Tel Aviv

Happy Birthday

The sky over Tel Aviv is an oil slick. The vista looks like something I would paint on a bad day—clouds dark and ominous, the color of weathered steel, gather along on the horizon, promising all kinds of chaos. The sun hasn't risen yet, but its approach is evidenced by the nasty purple-red hue that hovers over the sprawling city like a bruise.

Somewhere over the Atlantic, Pax realized that there won't be any strippers, and now his mood is even more ominous than the weather. He leans an elbow against the door frame of the taxi, ferociously chewing on his thumb nail. "You realize I have to go to Jerusalem. My mother will kill me if she knows I came here and didn't visit the holy city."

"How would she even know?" Dash is sitting in the front next to the driver, observing the buildings that fly past the window with a level of detachment that comes from having traveled the world eight times over already. I'm sure nothing looks *new* to him anymore. "You haven't been on speaking terms with Meredith in two years. I doubt she has an alert set up to notify her when you leave the country."

Pax stills, his thumb nail trapped between his front teeth. His eyes are like liquid mercury as he drills holes into the back of Dash's head. "Where the fuck do you get off, calling her Meredith?"

"That's her name, isn't it?"

"It doesn't matter if it's her name or not. You can't talk about her like that."

"Like what?"

"Like you know her."

Dash looks back over his shoulder, smiling his angelic *boy-can-do-no-wrong* smile. "I *do* know her. I've met her at least eight times. Fascinating woman. She's always been very nice to me."

An outsider would hear Dashiell's words and think them cordial. Polite, even. It's the accent. Dash can sound perfectly civil because of that damned English accent. The edge to his tone means that he's suggesting that Pax's mom was *very* nice to him, though. Nicer than she should have been. And Pax can hear that tone just as well as I can. His ears pull back like a dog's.

I lean forward, knuckling Dash in the spine hard enough that he yelps. "We're not doing that. Not today. We're all jetlagged as fuck and in need of a bed. Fighting in a taxi isn't gonna do any of us any favors."

"Speak for yourself. I feel fine." Dashiell presses the pad of his index finger against the window. "Look at that. They have Seven-Eleven here. Weird."

"I can't be in Israel and *not* go to Jerusalem," Pax growls. "She *will* find out. She'll know. And what the hell am I supposed to tell her? Sorry, Ma, I couldn't visit the birthplace of our lord and savior because we were too busy killing a man?"

The taxi driver, who's spoken broken, sporadic English since we got in the car, descends into a fit of coughing, grasping at the steering wheel as if he's having trouble maintaining control of the vehicle.

I give Pax a look sharp enough to puncture a lung. "We're not *killing* anyone. We're here for a light maiming and that's all."

"I don't see why we even came to do that." Dash takes out his cell phone and begins to flip through the messages that started to filter through to his phone the moment we left the airport. "This has nothing to do with us. It also has nothing to do with *you*, which makes the whole thing even more perplexing. I thought you hated that girl."

"Hating people is for children. I don't hate anyone."

"Apart from Mercy," Pax mutters. "And your father. And Fitz. And *me* sometimes."

I grin at him, all fucking teeth. "Only when you leave your shit all over my room or borrow books without asking."

"We live together. It's not like you won't know where they are," he gripes.

"Okay. I'll rephrase. When you borrow books without asking, don't return them to me, and when I do get them back, they're dogeared and covered in hot sauce, *you fucking philistine.*"

He just grunts at that. Can't deny his crimes. They've been too frequent and heinous for anything other than a complete admission of guilt. He changes the subject instead. "So. This guy did something bad to the girl you're *not* interested in. And you've dragged us across the world to come and hurt the motherfucker, because you *don't* care about Elodie, and you couldn't give a shit if she lives or dies. Can we just go over this again so I can get it straight in my head? This all seems very drastic, un-Wren-like behavior from where I'm sitting."

I gouge my fingernails into the stitching of the pleather seat beneath me, my *feelings* roiling away like a swarm of angry wasps. I didn't even think I was capable of anything so obvious and clichéd as feelings, and yet there they are, making my life a living hell.

"You didn't read the file," I say tightly. "You didn't read what he did to her."

"I understand that the guy might be a piece of work, Jacobi," Dash says. "But you're no fucking saint. You were planning on breaking the girl's heart up until a few days ago. And—no, no, no, don't even. If you try and pretend like that's still the plan, I will unfriend you on Facebook and never speak to you again."

I swallow down the objection I was just about to make, staring glumly out of the window. "I don't have Facebook."

"Semantics. You *were* planning on causing this girl grief. Now, you've done a complete one-eighty and designated yourself her knight in shining armor. This is an act of chivalry."

"It's an act of *insanity*," Pax grumbles.

I don't want to lie to them. I also don't want to admit the fact that they're right, either. I take the file out of my bag in the footwell, silently handing it to Pax. He rolls his eyes—clearly doesn't want to read it—but he opens it up and begins to scan the page. A frown creases his forehead. I watch him as he reads, and then goes back to the beginning, his eyes moving more slowly as he takes it all in for a second time. "Jesus Christ," he hisses.

Dash holds his hand out, waiting for Pax to give it to him. I'm too hot. My clothes are itchy as fuck. I'm so uncomfortable, sharing this part of Elodie's history with them, that I almost snatch the file away from Dash and call the whole thing off. This was a very reckless decision on my part. I have put these guys in an untenable position that would make most people flip their fucking shit. Am I so bewitched by this girl that I've thrown them in harm's way without really thinking it through? Maybe it would be better if—

"Holy...fucking...*shit*," Dash whispers. "This is...I don't even..."

"I know."

"All right. Fine," Pax grinds out. "I see where you're coming from."

I catch sight of Dash's face in the rearview mirror and he looks like he's about to throw up. "Yeah. Fine. I get it now."

"So, we hurt the guy," Pax says, nodding. "He fucking deserves it. Fair enough. But this…this doesn't mean I'm gonna be *nice* to her when we get back, Jacobi."

I laugh, even though my throat feels raw and cut to ribbons. "I'd never dream of suggesting such a thing."

The taxi driver hits the gas, burning through traffic. I get the feeling that he wants to drop us at our destination as quickly as possible and then pretend he never laid eyes on us. I let my head fall back against the seat, breathing a sigh of quiet relief. I hate sharing secrets that even I have no business knowing, but it had to be done. I knew they wouldn't question the logic behind this terrible task once they'd seen the evidence before them in print. We Riot House boys might be assholes to the extreme…but even *we* won't stand by and allow this kind of evil to go unpunished.

****

Twenty-Four Hours Later

The Longhorn Saloon is one of many American bars in Tel Aviv. It just so happens to be the closest one to the home address that I stole out of Elodie's student file at the academy. It's also the closest American bar to Colonel Stillwater's base. I've done my research. We don't just pick the spot on the off chance the bastard will be there. I hired someone to hack Elodie's father's financial accounts. Aside from noticing that his bank balance is in the high six figure range, it quickly became apparent that he spends at least eighty to a hundred dollars every couple of days at The Longhorn Saloon, and he's always closing out his tabs well after midnight. So, the fucker doesn't just drink here; he's a regular.

Pax scored us all fake IDs a *long* time ago. Getting into the bar isn't a problem. No one even asks to see the damn things, anyway.

It's only after our first beer that we realize the legal drinking age in Israel is eighteen and the bar staff really don't give a shit. The place is packed with Americans. Half of them are tourists, the other half jar heads. They're rowdy and boisterous, the staff are too harried to worry about the three of us.

We order a beer a piece and claim a corner booth—the best vantage point to clock people as they come in and out of the bar. Dashiell pretends to pore over a *'Lonely Planet Pocket Jerusalem and Tel Aviv'* guidebook. Meanwhile, Pax does absolutely nothing to reinforce the idea that we might be tourists by openly glaring at everyone who walks through the door.

"If you don't quit that, we're gonna get lynched," Dash tells him. "I do *hate* getting lynched in bars with you. Plus, we're supposed to be doing the lynching this time."

"I can't help it." Pax wrinkles his nose. "Smells weird in here."

"Smells like peanuts and stale booze." I knock back a mouthful of beer. "If you blow our cover before we've even seen Stillwater, I'm gonna be royally pissed, man. Just chill, for fuck's sake."

Pax holds up the *New York Times* he picked up by the front door, shielding his face with it. The move doesn't help our cover, but it does hide his scowl. "This guy's a Colonel," he grumbles. "Why the fuck would he drink in a bar with marines? Your father would never have hung out in a place like this."

"My father likes being surrounded by his equals. I get the feeling Colonel Stillwater likes having his subordinates around, even when he's off the clock. Probably the only form of respect a man like him can get."

An hour passes. We order another round of beers. I try not to fidget, but it's not as easy as it sounds. I've made my peace with what I came here to do, but this whole thing is still really fucking stupid. If we get caught…

I erase the thought from my mind as soon as it rears its ugly head.

I can't afford to even *think* about the consequences, should this all go sideways.

Another hour slips away. A fight breaks out on the other side of the bar by the pool table. Pax grins like he wants to join in, but a pointed look from Dash has him slumping back in his seat.

At ten, a group of girls enter the bar—from the Maple Leaf patches on their bags and their quirky vowel pronunciation, they're Canadian. A lanky blonde wearing a tank top that exposes her tanned stomach takes one look at us and I know we're in trouble.

"Pax. Do not engage," Dashiell says. "Now's not the time."

It's too late, though. He's up and out of his seat before either of us can grab him.

"Mother*fucker*." I slam my beer bottle down, ready to go after him, but Dash kicks me under the table.

"Let him go. It'd look weird if none of us were sniffing around the prospect of getting our dicks sucked. If anything develops, we'll grab him."

I don't like this. Pax heads straight for the blonde, smiling charmingly in a way that makes me want to slap him upside the head, but I can't do anything about it. He came here because I asked. He's doing this because I asked. He's made it perfectly clear that he thinks I'm making a mistake getting involved with Elodie, but that didn't matter when it came down to it. He's here because he's a good friend. I can't begrudge him a little flirtation.

The Canadian girls waste no time. The four of them gather around Pax like he's the second coming of the Messiah, and the guy disappears, dragged down to the other end of the bar.

"I wonder if Elodie told Carina," Dash muses, studying his fingernails. "Y'know. About the box. And…well, all of it."

He won't say the word *rape*, but that's what he's referring to.

I swallow down bile, wondering how a man could do such a thing to his own child. "I doubt it."

"They seem close, don't they? Elodie and Carina?"

"They're friends, yeah."

Dashiell pouts, twisting his empty beer bottle around on the table in front of him. "Elodie probably knows if Carina's seeing someone. That's probably something they talk about. Y'know. Because they're girls. That's what girls do."

"Jesus, man. And you call *me* out for liking a girl?" I raise my eyebrows at him. "What the fuck's wrong with *you*? If you liked her so much, why'd you mess with her like that?"

He's suddenly very engrossed in the *Lonely Planet* guide. "Whoa. They have a preserved acropolis in Jaffa. Looks like a fun time."

"Pathetic."

He shoots me a scathing look and tosses the guide back onto the table. "Let's just say we're both pathetic and leave it at that, huh?"

"Hey, *fuckos*!"

I look up. Pax is waving at us, a loose, drunken smile plastered across his face. He's not drunk. His tolerance for alcohol is legendary, and he only had three beers. He can't have fit in more than a couple of shots with the girls in the time that he's been gone. "Assholes! Get over here! You gotta meet my new friend. He's a fuckin' *Army colonel*."

Fire courses up my spine, my senses all triggering at once. He's found Stillwater on the other side of the bar? "You've gotta be kidding me," I hiss.

"Should have known. Pax is a trouble magnet. We should have let him loose two hours ago." Dash grimly drains the dregs of his beer and gets up from the booth. I follow after him, my heart pounding like a sledgehammer as I weave my way through the crowd. It stops dead altogether when I see Pax with his arm thrown around the shoulders of a man I recognize immediately.

The man's a tank. His shoulders are broad, his neck is nonexistent. It's as though his head just goes straight into his barrel of a chest. His hair is light but buzzed close to his scalp, much like the other Army personnel inside the bar. Jason Stillwater is a bruiser and a tyrant. I see that when he locks eyes with me—eyes that are the same color blue as Elodie's, but there is nothing kind, or sweet, or gentle about them. A violent, cruel light dances within them that has me setting my jaw and baying for the man's blood. I would have hated him on sight, even if I *hadn't* known what he did to Elodie, but I *do* know. He's a giant compared to his daughter; all I can see is his hulking frame pinning her to the ground, forcing her legs apart, pushing himself inside her—

Get a grip, Jacobi. No time for that.

Dash sways a little. He claps a hand on my shoulder, seemingly for balance—we'll both need to play into Pax's drunken ruse now —but I know the contact is also a reassurance. A *'don't worry, man. We got your back.'*

Pax's eyes are glassy and unfocused when we pitch up next to him. God knows how he accomplishes that. "Listen. This guy's been out here for—" *fake hiccup* "—nearly six years! He's a higher-up in the Army. Tell 'em where else you've lived, man. Go on, tell 'em!" Our friend nudges Elodie's father, bumping him with his shoulder, and Colonel Stillwater clenches his jaw. Beer sloshes over the side of his pint glass, spilling a pool of beer onto the lacquered bar top. I can practically see the steam billowing out of his ears, but Stillwater reins in his temper. He's a fan of hero worship. Why cause a scene if someone's planning on deifying you to his friends? Stillwater's the kind of guy who'd happily suspend his rage in exchange for a glowing compliment.

There's a moment where he's organizing what he's going to say, his lips parted, his eyes full of self-importance, and I breathe in that second. I haven't heard his voice yet. The voice that haunts Elodie's nightmares. Just like her, I won't be able to unhear it.

And then the bubble bursts.

"England. Germany. All over the Middle East, of course. Honduras. But the most interesting places, I can't tell you about. Most of my work's top secret. The kind of stuff that'd make little boys like you piss your pants and go running home to Mommy." He laughs into his pint glass, so goddamn pleased with himself. "God. I really wish I *could* talk about some of that shit. It'd blow your minds to Timbuktu and back again, believe me."

Oh, I believe you, Jason. I'm sure you have tales so horrific that they'd turn my stomach until the end of days. How many human rights atroci-

ties have you committed? How many international laws have you broken? How many men have you murdered, and women have you raped, because the uniform on your back gave you the power to do so?

I shiver as I contemplate the number.

Jason circles a finger in the air at the bartender, wordlessly ordering a round of drinks for us all. An anger so hot and acidic rises up the back of my throat, burning as it climbs. I'd rather die of thirst than drink anything this man buys for me, but I have an act to maintain here. It's imperative that he doesn't grow suspicious; he'll be out of here in a shot if I do anything to raise the alarm.

I laugh and holler with Pax and Dash as the bartender puts our beers down in front of us, making sure that my grin makes it to my eyes as I *cheers* my glass to Jason's.

"That's so fucking awesome, dude," Dashiell drawls. Gone is his English accent. In its place: a perfect, easy American accent, clean enough that he could be from California, but with the tiniest hint of a clipped vowel sound that could hint at southern roots. It's flawless, this transition that he undergoes when the situation demands it. No one would guess he wasn't an American, born and raised. Maintaining his regular accent in a place like this would be a bad idea. It marks him as different. Noticeable. Memorable. And the last thing any of us needs to be right now is memorable. "My grandfather was in the Navy. I thought about joining up—"

Jason's face twists with open disgust. "Fucking Navy pussies. You got a vagina, kid?"

Dashiell lowers his beer, a picture of chastised youth. "No, sir?"

"Then why the fuck you wanna join the Navy for? Are you a man?"

"Yes, sir." More firmly this time.

"Then stop being a little bitch and join the Army. That's what *men* do. An' if you ain't a man yet, don't worry yourself. The Army'll *make* you one in short order."

"What's the pay like?" Pax leans an elbow on the bar next to Jason, drunkenly slipping a little, almost falling face first into the guy's lap. When this is all over, I'll be having words with him about his performance. There's being persuasive, and then there's being a little on the nose. He's going to blow this entire thing if he carries on like this.

"What's the pay like? What does it fucking matter?" Jason snarls. "If you love your country, and you want to protect its people, and defend the American way of life, you'd do the work for free, ya little punk." He laughs, though, letting us know that he's joking. "But since you ask, the pay is about what you'd expect. It's garbage. You'll have to save three month's wages just so you can afford a hooker for the night. But there are other benefits. Tax breaks and shit. Plus, the longer you're in, the more you make, naturally. I got myself a neat little nest egg these days."

"So, you're, like, some big swinging dick, then?" Pax asks. The girls that brought him over here have grown bored and are filtering away, slowly making their way to a booth that's just opened up. That's for the best. The less time they spend with us, the more our faces will fade from memory once their shots start to kick in. Pax gives Elodie's father a sly look, one eye screwed shut. "Are you the highest-ranking officer in this room?"

"Hah! Boy, I'm the highest-ranking officer in a two-hundred-mile radius. Nothing happens in Tel Aviv without me knowing about it. Screw the Israeli police. I'm the fucking king of this city. I can do whatever I want. Say whatever I want." His alcohol-soaked gaze follows a pretty waitress as she hurries over to a table, her arms full of food. "Take what I want…"

Motherfucking sick, evil, piece of…

"What's wrong with *you*, anyway, pretty boy? Cat got your tongue? You haven't said a word since you came over here."

Pretty boy? He's gonna wish he'd never called me that. I flash him a dumb, inebriated smile that seems to appease him. "Sorry, dude. I just…I'm not feeling…I'm—" I hold a hand against my stomach, puffing out my cheeks.

"Uh oh. He's been chugging scotch since we got here," Dashiell explains. "Is it safe to stand on the street out front? I reckon he needs a little fresh air."

"Safe? Of course it's safe."

"Okay. Cool. We'd just heard that tourists can get jumped around here is all. We'd be screwed if we lost our money and our passpo—"

"Christ sake. Bunch of pussies." Jason sets his beer down. The legs of his bar stool screech as he pushes the chair back and gets to his feet. "I'll come with you. Just long enough to finish a smoke. If he's still green around the gills after that, you'll have to figure it out on your own."

Ahhh, good ol' predictable Jason. Such a big man. No one would dare fuck with *him*. Of course he was going to offer to play bodyguard. He likes how being in charge makes him feel. Dashiell's father is exactly the same, which is how he knew that little ploy would work, I'm sure. Pretend we're completely inept, useless, spoiled teenagers who need their hands held, even to step outside for a minute? Jason Stillwater couldn't resist.

Dash and Pax lead the way, drunkenly carousing with one another as they head for the exit. I follow, weaving from side to side, colliding with a chair or two for effect, and all the while I feel Jason's presence close behind me. It takes a monumental effort not to turn around and smash a beer bottle over his head. Jagged, broken glass, biting through flesh, scraping against bone. I imagine it. The feeling's so real that my palms begin to burn...

Outside, the warm night air slips over my skin like silk. Opposite the bar, a row of fast food joints and takeaway spots are all lit up, spilling the smell of delicious grilled meats, herbs and spices from their open doorways. My stomach growls, which is a little wrong, given what's about to happen.

Elodie's father pulls a pack of smokes from the back pocket of his jeans, tapping a cigarette out of the torn opening at the top. I watch him as he lights up, head bowed over the flame, imagining the damage and destruction he's wrought with those meaty, clumsy hands of his.

"Can I bum one of those?" I ask.

He squints at me, shaking his head. "Shit. You kids never have your own damn cigarettes." Still, he gives me the pack. I take a smoke, pinch it between my teeth, and give them back to him.

He squints even harder at me. "I know you're drunk, kid, but typically you *are* supposed to light the thing."

"Oh. I'm saving it for after," I tell him.

"After what?"

"Whoa!" Pax grabs Dashiell by the arm, hitting him repeatedly. "You just see that girl? Fuck, she was hot. Like, a fucking eight."

I'm instantly forgotten about. Like a shark that's scented blood, Jason's head whips around. "Where?"

Dashiell groans morosely, letting his head hang back on his shoulders. If this situation wasn't what it is, this whole play-acting thing of his would be entertaining. He's always so uptight, his back so uncompromisingly straight, everything about him so overly controlled. This loosey-goosey American version of him is fucking fascinating. "She went down that alleyway. And she wasn't an eight, dude. She was an *eleven*."

"Brunette?" Jason asks.

Before I know what I'm doing, I'm jumping in on the charade. "Nope. Blonde. Small. Petite. Big, beautiful blue eyes. She looked like a little china doll, man."

Jason bares his teeth in a telling, horrific way. A mixture of anger and lust war against one another on his face. His reaction tells me everything I need to know. He's already thinking about this innocent blonde-haired, blue-eyed girl. Thinking about fucking her. Thinking about hurting her. He doesn't realize that I've just described his own fucking daughter to him, and that any shadow of doubt or remorse I might have had over this violent course of action I'm about to embark upon is now well and truly dead in the water.

Sick. Mother. Fucker.

Jason's gaze bounces from me, to Dash and settles on Pax. "You *all* saw her apart from me? Well, that doesn't seem fair, does it, boys? Which way did she go?"

Pax points down an alleyway on the other side of the street, the slack, drunk smile falling from his features. "Down there."

"That's a dead end. Probably ducked down there to take a piss. Drunk chicks are always doing that around here."

We already know the alleyway is a dead end. We scoped all of the side streets close to the bar before we even stepped foot inside The Longhorn Saloon. We settled on that particular alleyway because there were no security cameras. Plus, it's narrow and dark enough that passersby on the main drag will never notice a disturbance down there and risk coming to find out what was going on.

Jason chews the inside of his cheek, assessing the mouth of the alleyway. He comes to his decision—the decision I knew he was going to make—very quickly. "Come on, boys. If the dirty bitch wants to piss in public, she needs to be prepared for the consequences. Let's go scare her a little."

"Sure that's a good idea?" Dash nervously rubs at the back of his neck.

One last chance.

One brief opportunity to redeem himself.

Jason waves him off. "Like I said. She needs to learn a lesson. If she's gonna drop her drawers in public, she can't get upset if a group of guys wind up seeing her pussy. Serves her right."

Perfect, Jason. Thanks for doubling down and reinforcing the fact that you are a disgusting, vile, wicked piece of shit who does not deserve to draw breath.

He sets off across the road, pulling on his cigarette and sending a voluminous cloud of smoke up into the night sky as he urges us to follow along behind him. "Quick. We'll miss it," he hisses.

I trade a look with my friends, each of us now stone cold sober as we jog across the street, following Jason into the alleyway. Neither Dash nor Pax flinch as we give each other a stiff nod.

This is what we came here for. We flew thousands of miles to take care of this problem, and now the time is upon us. Jason's almost at the very end of the alleyway when he turns around, a deep frown creasing his brow. "You guys must be drunk as fuck. There's no girl down he—"

The whole thing's beautiful: the wind up; my elbow coming back; my hand forming a fist and then flying forward. I've punched plenty of people in my life, and I'll punch plenty more, but this right hook will forever be emblazoned in my mind as *the* punch.

When my knuckles make contact with the bastard's face, pain screams up my arm like a lightning bolt, settling into my shoulder. His head jerks back, jaw exposed, and then he's toppling backward like a felled tree, hitting the ground with a bone-jarring crack.

"Ooooof. Was that your *head?*" Pax laughs, lazily propping himself up against the crumbling brick wall. "You just got your bell rung, son."

"Jesus. His skull probably split open like a watermelon." Dashiell's English accent is back with a vengeance.

Sprawled out on the floor of the filthy alleyway, Colonel Jason Stillwater stirs, groaning in pain. I think I actually knocked the fucker out. Must have, because he collects himself out of nowhere, as if returning to his body. He's all arms and legs as he tries to get back on his feet. Following three failed attempts, he manages it, though he's so wobbly he looks like he might go down again at any moment.

His eyes flash with fury. "What the fuck, kid? Are you...?" He spits blood, his face turning purple when he holds his hand to his mouth and it comes away red. "Are you fucking *insane?* I'm a goddamn colonel in the United States Army. You...you can't just fucking *hit* me."

I robotically slide off my leather jacket, holding it out to Dash, who takes it from me, folding it neatly over his arm for safekeeping. "But I just did," I tell him. "You don't want me to hit you, Colonel Stillwater? You're gonna have to stop me, you sick fuck."

He frowns, incredulity plastered all over his ugly face; it's impossible that such a beautiful girl could have come from such a repellant man's DNA. Elodie's mother must have been breath-taking and had very strong genes.

"I don't know what the fuck you think you're doing, boy, but you are in way over your head right now." From his tone, Jason thinks I'm mentally compromised in some way. Obviously, he can't grasp how anyone in their right minds would dare lay a finger on a man as important as himself. "No helping you now. You've committed a serious felony. Damaging the government of the United States' property? Bad, kid. That's very bad. There's gonna be consequences. No two ways about it. But...turn yourself over now. I'll go easy on you. I'll make sure they know you were drunk. Tryin' to act the big man an' shit. You'll probably get off with some community service."

God, this feels way better than I thought it would. The man who raped and killed his wife, and then raped and beat his daughter is actually *scared*. He's a brute of a guy, with muscles on top of muscles, but they're all for show. The motherfucker's been taking steroids for years by the look of him. He has no real stamina. He won't move quickly. He's a lumbering, heavy, clumsy giant, who's about to get his ass handed to him and he knows it.

I crack my knuckles, running my tongue over my teeth. "Not happening, Jason. Not in this lifetime." With quick, methodical movements, I roll the sleeves of my shirt up, cuffing the material at my elbows—a doctor, ready to perform an unpleasant but necessary task. "We've got time for a chat, though. Just a brief one, before we get down to business."

I take a step toward him, and Jason balks. He lunges to my left, trying to slip past me, but Pax is suddenly there, blocking his escape route. Stupid fucker actually tries to dart the other way, to the left, which is where he runs straight into Dash. The three of us proceed as one, walking toward him, which leaves Jason no choice but to back the fuck up.

"You're dead men. God, can't you see how fucking nuts this is? You can't just assault a high-ranking member of the military, boys. It ain't gonna work out well for you."

"See, on paper, there are a lot of things a person shouldn't be able to get away with." I glance up at the moon, visible in the snapshot of sky overhead, framed between the two buildings on either side of the alleyway. "For instance, a man shouldn't be able to murder someone, no matter his status, rank or position. Nor should he be allowed to violate his own daughter and trap her in a box for days on end, either. Those are definitely two things that no one should be able to get away with."

Stone-cold horror pools in Jason's eyes. I can smell it on him—the disgusting reek of animal fear. He had no clue why we were doing this a moment ago, but now he does. It's a pleasure to watch the realization dawning on him as he fumbles, hands going to his pockets.

"Uh uh uh." Pax goes for the fucker, grabbing him, forcing his right hand behind his back. "We don't like cell phones," he spits in the guy's face. "Be nice if we kept this friendly little conversation between the four of us, if that's alright with you." He shoves his hand into Jason's pocket, fishing his phone out and dropping it to the floor. Jason wrenches himself free, dropping to grab the device, but Pax has already kicked it, sending it skittering across the alleyway toward me.

I wonder what kind of poison is stored on the phone of a man like Jason Stillwater. I could bring it back to the States with me. Have it cracked. I bet there's some really dark, messed up shit on there that could have Jason thrown behind bars for the rest of his natural life. I don't plan on letting the law deal with this fucker, though. He's right, he's too powerful for that. The military will step in and have him cleared of any wrongdoing in the blink of an eye, just like they did after he shot his wife and hurt Elodie. No, whatever sinister evil is saved on Jason's phone is irrelevant. I'll make him pay for what he's done and then some. I'll make him bleed enough to cover whatever sins he's hiding on the iPhone at my feet and then some. Casually, I place my boot down on the screen and I transfer my weight, smiling slightly as the glass cracks beneath my heel.

"Listen, whatever she's told you is a lie, y'know. Elodie. This is about my daughter, isn't it?" Jason casts a glance back over his shoulder, his ruddy face paling when he realizes that he's almost out of alleyway. Behind him, a ten-foot-high brick wall stands between him and his freedom. "She...she's just like her mother," he stammers. "Always lying. Always manipulating everyone around her. She...she wouldn't know the truth if it leapt up and bit her on the ass. Whatever she's told you— wait!"

I grin, looking up at him from under drawn brows, and he knows it's too late. Bargaining won't get him anywhere. There's no lie he can tell that will save him now. I throw myself on him and my adrenalin-soaked rage takes over.

He'll never hurt her again.

He'll never threaten her again.

Once I'm done with him, he'll never utter the name Elodie Stillwater again. He'll be lucky if he even fucking *remembers* it.

After the first few hits, Jason seems to recall that I'm just a seventeen-year-old guy and starts swinging his own fists. But I don't mind the pain. The bright sting of freshly opened knuckles, and the dull thumping in my jaw, and the breathless agony in my ribs is all worth it. Just like Jason said a minute ago, there are consequences to a man's actions; I'm perfectly willing to pay this price if it means this sick psychopath gets what he deserves.

When I begin to flag, scrambling to pin the monster down, Dash and Pax both jump in, playing their part in this symphony of pain.

Soon, Jason Stillwater is nothing more than a raw lump of meat, lying in a pool of his own blood in the moonlight.

"Shhhit! Come on, man, it's over," Pax hisses, pulling me away from the body. I can't look away, though. Can't make my legs obey the simplest of commands. A bark of manic laughter bursts out of my mouth, bouncing off the alley walls.

"*Wren?* Jesus Christ, he's fucking losing it," Dash says, somewhere behind me. "Quick. Get him up. Get him moving."

"What are you doing?" Pax snarls.

"Getting the bastard's wallet. We play our cards right and this looks like a robbery—"

Dash keeps talking, but I don't hear him. Pax grabs me by the arm and drags me to my feet, but I feel none of it.

All I can see is the bloody, swollen face of the man who hurt her.

And all I can feel is an overwhelming joy in the knowledge that he will *never* do it again.

As the boys drag me away from Jason Stillwater's mangled, lifeless body, I spark up the cigarette the sick fucker gave to me.

The burn of the smoke in my lungs tastes like goddamn victory.

ALSO BY CALLIE HART

WANT TO KNOW MORE ABOUT ZETH, SLOANE ROMERA AND DETECTIVE LOWELL? The Blood & Roses Series is out now and available to read for FREE on KINDLE UNLIMITED!

FREE TO READ ON KINDLE UNLIMITED!

DARK, SEXY, AND TWISTED! A BAD BOY WHO WILL CLAIM BOTH YOUR HEART AND YOUR SOUL.
Read the entire Blood & Roses Series
FREE on Kindle Unlimited!

WANT TO DISAPPEAR INTO THE DARK, SEDUCTIVE WORLD OF AN EX-PRIEST TURNED HITMAN?
Read the Dirty Nasty Freaks Series
FREE on Kindle Unlimited!

FOLLOW ME ON INSTAGRAM!

The best way to keep up to date with all of my upcoming releases and some other VERY exciting secret projects I'm currently working on is to follow me on Instagram! Instagram is fast becoming my favorite way to communicate with the outside world, and I'd love to hear from you over there. I do answer my direct messages (though it might take me some time) plus I frequently post pics of my mini Dachshund, Cooper, so it's basically a win/win.

You can find me right here!

Alternatively, you can find me via me handle @calliehartauthor within the app.

I look forward to hanging out with you!

DEVIANT DIVAS

If you'd like to discuss my books (or any books, for that matter!), share pictures and quotes of your favorite characters, play games, and enter giveaways, then I would love to have you over in my private group on Facebook!

We're called the Deviant Divas, and we would love to have you come join in the fun!

ACKNOWLEDGMENTS

I just had to write a quick note to say a massive thank you to a few people.

Gemma Sherlock and Kylie Sharp, you are fucking legends. You keep me on track, despite how embarrassingly disorganized I am, and I love you both to bits.

Again, another thank you to Kylie, Imogen Wells, Sophie Ruthven, Crystal Solis and Deborah Daken, THANK YOU from the bottom of my heart for beta-reading this monster of a book on such short notice. It means the world to me, and I'm so grateful to you for your help.

Lastly, thank you so, so much to you guys for reading this book! You have no idea how important you guys are to us authors, and I am so thankful to have you in my corner. I really hope you enjoyed Elodie and Wren's story!

Printed in Great Britain
by Amazon